creeping Beautiful

new york times bestselling author

ja huss

ISBN: 978-1-950232-27-7

Edited by RJ Locksley
Cover Design by JA Huss

about the Book

McKAY

I wasn't the one who broke her but I played my part. She came to us when she was ten. I raised her. I loved her. I taught her how to survive in a world of evil men. But it wasn't enough.

ADAM

I wasn't the one who saved her but I did my best. She needed me as much as I needed her. Bought and paid for on the auction block. But not for the reasons you think. She was my weapon.

DONOVAN

I wasn't the one who lied to her but I hid her truth. She was broken before I got there. Wild and angry. Defiant and bratty. But she trusted me most. She loved me best. So I set her free.

Indie Anna Accorsi is a woman lost in her past.

A pretty little nightmare.
A gorgeous piece of misery.
A mess of lovely darkness.
She is creeping beautiful.
And now we want her back.

INDIE

If I had to choose between them, I would die. There is just no way I could only choose one.

I need them all.

I don't even care if that's selfish. I want them all.

And if I thought I could have Nathan St. James, then I would. I would have him too. I would keep all four of them because they are each different, and unique, and give me something I can't get from anyone else.

Every single way they fill me up has been written in this journal. So if it's not clear by now, there is nothing left to be said. There are simply no words to describe my need.

But I am afraid that you will see this and you won't understand. And I don't care if you are Nathan, or McKay, or Adam, or Donovan. I need you to understand.

How many other ways are there to describe Nathan St. James? He is my boy next door. He is my best friend. He is the firefly-catcher, and the treehouse-builder, and the swamp-charmer.

Oh, I know what Adam would say. "He was running around on you back in high school." Yes, Adam. He told me all about what he did. He told me that you caught him. He told me what you said to him. And I get it. If Nathan loved me best, he would be more careful with my heart. He'd be like McKay.

McKay is so very, very careful with me. McKay is my soul. He is my trainer. He is the dinner-maker, and the hair-washer, and the nightmare-chaser.

But McKay will never admit he has always loved me. That I am his first, and only, one true love.

So I have Donovan. Donovan is careful too. He is my mind-reader. My note-taker. He is the light in the dark, he is the filler of holes, he is the voice in my head that keeps me calm during my stormy nights of insanity.

But he's part-time. We all know it. He will never take me

with him to LA and I wouldn't want to go. This is my home. Right here. This is where I belong.

And that's where Adam comes in. Adam. My owner. My knight. My protector. He is my partner in crime. The fixer of mistakes, the leader of us all, the untouchable one.

He is like a mean old dog who will bite anyone who gets too close.

Everyone but me.

He lets me get close.

But will he share?

Will any of them share?

Only if I make them.

So this is how I made them…

PART ONE
ignorance is bliss

Everyone has secrets.

They can be big or small.

Mean a lot or very little.

They can change lives, they can destroy bonds, they can break hearts.

But a secret always comes with a reason.

Everyone has been told a lie at least once.

That lie can be bad or good.

It can spare your feelings or crush them to dust.

It can hold you prisoner or set you free.

But a lie is just a secret in the shadows.

Everyone has been discarded by someone at one point.

That rejection can kill your spirit or lift it up high.

It can set you down a path of revenge or redemption.

But secrets, and lies, and rejection are almost never about *you.*

So before you go lookin' for those secrets. Before you go uncoverin' those lies. Before you let that rejection seep into your heart and wound your soul—ask yourself this:

Do you really need to know the truth?

Because that truth doesn't come with a return policy.

You cannot unknow things once they are known.

You can't unsee things once they are seen.

So be very, very sure that you need those answers.

Because it will change everything.

Ignorance is bliss, my friend.
Pure. Bliss.

CHAPTER ONE

PRESENT DAY

Indie Anna Accorsi blows into a life the way a hurricane spins across the Gulf of Mexico on a late summer night. She is both terrifying and sensational. The kind of girl you can't walk away from even though you know damn well she is out to destroy you.

She is hard rain that stings your skin, and overflowing rivers that carry things away, and there's always a debris field left behind. Little smudges of dirt and detritus that remind you she was *there*.

She was fucking *there*, ya know?

But she is someone else too. She was small once. And OK, maybe she was never exactly *sweet*. But she had her moments of balance and peace. I call those moments the 'eye of Indie'. Like 'eye of the storm?' Wild winds raging all around her. Fuckin' shit flying everywhere. Houses blowing by, air-raid sirens blaring, and she is standing in the middle of it all with her eyes closed and her chin tipped up. *Calm*.

And you never quite know if she's just immune to the chaos or if she's controlling it like some force of nature.

I don't care what she's done or will do in the future. It doesn't matter how many years pass or how many other ways I know her, in my mind she is *this* girl. The Eye of Indie. The one I first met when she was ten.

This afternoon she is swirling dark skies pouring out tears. Drenched through to her skin, cornered, wide-eyed, filled with fear, and with no way out.

She needs something.

Not specifically me, just *one* of us. And I'm easy to find.

Indie's long straight hair always looks dark even though it's blonde. Her face is too pale even though she tans brown in the sunshine. And her eyes remind me of angry thunderheads backlit by wild blue lightning.

That's a storm right there if ever there was one.

But she always comes with flowers too. There is always another, hidden side to this girl.

There's no telling how that flower will present—a small bud tucked behind her ear, an embroidered patch on her old, ripped jeans, or a new tattoo on her wrist.

I have seen her with all three in times past but this afternoon it's just a graphic design on a t-shirt partially visible through the opening in her jacket.

But let me be clear. Because it would be a mistake to assume her obsession with botanicals and her Bohemian name accurately describe the monster inside her head.

Indie Anna Accorsi is fragile like footsteps on thin ice. She is soft like the skin of a poisonous snake. And she is quiet like a panther watching you from a tree.

You do not take your eyes off her.

Today Indie is faded, ripped jeans and tough-girl brown boots. Black leather jacket with a maroon-checked flannel underneath, and a vintage band t-shirt peeking through the haphazard button job.

Guns N' Roses. I recognize it—used to be black, now faded to gray. White skull flanked on either side by red roses. She stole it from me when she was eleven—and immediately I start wondering how much thought she put into this little impromptu visit.

Indie Anna Accorsi is not spontaneous. She is a well-thought-out plan.

She wears a faded pink velvet choker around her neck. Also, something I recognize. And she's turned the cuffs of her flannel into fingerless gloves. Small holes at the wrists with thumbs poking through.

She is not the Eye of Indie right now.

And I did that to her.

I made her—I *shaped her* into this wicked paper-doll of a girl.

This isn't bragging.

It makes me sad to see her. It makes my heart hurt in a way I can't explain. It fills me with regrets.

But it wasn't *just* me.

I wasn't the one who broke her, but I definitely played my part.

When I open the door, it's raining so hard there's a waterfall rolling off the awning covering my stoop. The loudness that comes with the storm is like a background soundtrack to a very sad movie.

Indie's leaning against the old wooden fence on the far side of my gravel driveway smoking a cigarette. How she even keeps that thing lit in this downpour, I'll never understand. It's like she's got a shield around her hand and the rain never touches it.

She didn't knock so I have no idea how long she was standing outside looking through the front window of my shop. From the state of her drenched clothes it was a long time. And right now everything about her is cold and wet.

Something about her is always cold and wet.

"Indie," I say. But my whispered greeting is way too soft to make it past the pounding of the storm around us.

Lightning strikes off in the distance. Right above her head like she's the goddess of storms. And then, seconds later, the low rumble of thunder formally announces her arrival.

I extend my hand, beckoning her with two fingers and calling to her the way someone might call to a fearful stray dog. "Come here," I say. "Come inside. You're wet."

She takes a long drag on her cigarette, drops it in the gravel, and then crushes it with the tip of her soaked brown boot.

"I need something." She calls this from across the driveway.

"Come inside. I'm not talking to you like this."

She never takes her eyes off me, but her left hand dips down to her flannel and she pulls it up. Just a little. Just enough to show me the gun tucked inside the waistband of her jeans.

"Understood," I call back. "Now come inside."

She looks to her right, down the length of my long, lonely driveway, then pushes off the wall and walks through the downpour like it's a calm summer day and not a violent, late-winter evening.

My hand is still extended when she approaches but she doesn't take it. Just pushes past me, her leather jacket dragging against my t-shirt, transferring some of her wetness to me as she enters.

I turn with her, close the door, and stand there. Just watching her as she places a hand on the surface of my small shop table and starts kicking at the heel of one boot to get it off her foot. She does it again with the other one and then she's barefoot.

No socks. Never wears socks.

"Don't start with me about socks." She reads my mind as she shrugs the jacket off, water dripping everywhere on my concrete floor, and drapes it over the back of a metal folding chair. Then she lets out a long breath of air. "I wouldn't ask. You know I wouldn't ask. But I need you, McKay."

"Of course." I whisper this, afraid she will run if I talk too loud or get too aggressive with her. "Whatever it is, I'm here. You know that."

She smirks at me, crooked smile revealing the perfectly straight teeth I paid for when she was fourteen. "I guess I do." She says this as she peels off her flannel and then tosses it onto the table.

She doesn't remove the gun from the waistband of her jeans.

I have a lot of questions for this girl. Starting with, *Where the fuck have you been for the last four years?*

I don't say it out loud. But I don't need to. She can read my mind.

"Where haven't I been? I've been everywhere. Every-fucking-where. But this isn't a social call."

Immediately my mind is spinning with possibilities. Why is she here? What has she done now? How hard will it be to clean up this mess? And… will this nightmare ever end?

"He's done it again. I'm so fucking pissed off right now, I could *murder* someone."

"Who?"

"Who do you think? Who is the bane of my existence? Why is he always so uptight and controlling, McKay? Why isn't he more like you? Huh? I mean… does he like being the asshole? Does he get off on making me angry? Why? Why does he do this?"

I was holding my breath during all that. So I let it out. "What did he do this time?"

She presses her lips together, frowns through it. And her eyes get glassy and bright as she takes a deep breath. "He took him."

Holy fucking shit. "Who?"

"Adam."

"No, who did he *take,* Indie?"

"Nathan. Who fucking else? I can't find him anywhere."

"Nathan?"

"My *husband*." She snarls these words out like she can't believe I'm playing this game with her. But I'm not playing at anything. After four years I'm just genuinely sick hearing that name come out of her mouth. "Ringing any bells here? You're such a fucking piece of work, you know that, McKay? And if you're just going to defend Adam, I'll go back the way I came and you can pretend you never saw me."

She bends down, reaching for one of her boots like she's going to put it back on, but I put my hand on her arm and give it a squeeze.

She looks up at me, then straightens. Tight-lipped and sad.

"No. I'm not defending him. I'm just confused, Indie. I'm trying to understand what you're saying."

"What I'm saying is this. I'm sick of this shit, OK? I'm fucking sick of it. He has no right to tell me what to do anymore. None."

"I… I don't understand, Indie. Have you… *talked* to Adam?"

Her face screws up for a moment. Like she's thinking about this. Then she lets out a long sigh. "No. But I don't need to talk to him to know what he's up to."

"… OK." I play it cool. "I get it." Even though I don't. If there's one thing I've come to terms with over the past four years it's that I don't understand one goddamned thing about what we were doing with this girl all those years.

I don't understand any of it. I don't understand why Donovan was brought in, I don't understand why I was brought in, and I don't understand how we all fit into the big picture.

And there's always a big picture. There's always an ulterior motive when it comes to the Company. Even if the Company is gone, the remnants are still there. The objectives still linger. We all played a part in that too. And if there's one thing I've learned over the past fourteen years it's this: Letting go of your purpose is not as easy as it sounds.

But Indie is in no state to hear the truth right now.

Funny. For as long as I've known her, she's never been in a state to hear the truth.

"I'll help you. Whatever you need, Indie. I'm here. And I'll help you."

She nods her head, swallowing hard. "Good."

She sighs that word out in a low, soft whisper. And I think to myself… she *can* be soft. When she's like this, she can be fragile like a snowflake. And soft like the wings of a butterfly. And quiet like whispers in a church.

She's not *really* made of sharp corners and hard edges.

She's a girl. And she's real underneath it all. She's still in there after all the things we made her do and were done to her. She has to be in there. I have to believe that.

"Do you know where he is? Have you talked to him recently?"

"No. We don't really talk anymore." Indie looks disappointed for a moment. And I can't stand to see her like that. "But I'm sure I can find him."

Adam has been my best friend for as long as I can remember. We went into this whole Indie project a team. And if we were on speaking terms, we'd still be a team. Still be on *her* team, at least. But she's been missing for four years and I need to know what's rolling around in that messed-up mind of hers before I start thinking about getting in touch with Adam again. Because it's not Adam she should be blaming.

"I tried calling. I must have an old number. He's not picking up. Goes straight to voicemail. He went to Daphne, Alabama. Did you hear about that? Did he tell you about Nick Tate?"

I shake my head, a sinking, sick feeling rolling around in my stomach. "No. He hasn't mentioned Nick Tate to me. Not in years. I don't think he was there meeting Nick, Indie."

"Well. Then he probably has a girl there. Did you know he had a girlfriend?"

"Adam?" I say this too loud and too surprised. "No, Indie. Adam doesn't do girlfriends."

I want to say more. I want to say things like… *Adam does you. Adam does us. We do him. He doesn't do girlfriends.*

Indie just huffs at my answer. "When's the last time you talked to Donovan? Where is everyone? Why aren't we working?"

I run my fingers though my hair, take a deep breath. "You, Indie. You're the reason we're not working."

"You didn't answer my question. Where's Donovan?"

"At home. I guess. I don't know."

"He moved." She says this like she's tired. "He moved out. I went to Donovan's first and some old lady answered the door. Said he didn't live there. Said she'd never heard of him."

I spend two whole seconds wondering if that old lady is still alive.

"Where the fuck did he go?"

"You went to Donovan before you came here?"

"Don't get jealous on me, McKay. I can't deal with that shit right now. Where *is* he?"

"You want me to call him?"

"Duh. Tell him to get here. I need to talk to both of you. I did everything you wanted when I was a kid and now it's your turn to do things for me, you understand? I want Adam. He needs to pay for this. For everything. I get it." She laughs a little. "I do. He's always been jealous of Nathan. But he's gone too far this time."

"Hold on." I put up a hand to stop her. "How the fuck exactly did Adam get a hold of Nathan?"

"How do you think? Why are you taking his side?"

"Indie." I don't laugh. Because this truly isn't funny. But she's being ridiculous.

"Don't you dare, McKay." She points a finger in my face. "Don't you fucking *dare*."

I put up both hands in surrender. "I'm not. I'm not, OK? I'm just trying to figure out what's going on, that's all."

She wraps her arms around her wet t-shirt and hugs herself.

"You need some dry clothes. And a bath. You wanna take a bubble bath?"

She pouts when I say this and suddenly, she looks ten again. Like the girl she was the day Adam brought her home. Small and thin. Young and defiant back then. Feral. Wild. Already dangerous.

But she wasn't angry. She didn't come to us angry. If I had to pick an emotion for Indie that first day I'd call her unaffected. Distant. Maybe even… *cold*. Not cold like snow. Cold like serial killers who have no conscious.

But when did that ever stop me from loving her?

We all have a little serial killer inside us, don't we?

"Come on." I take her hand and pull her through the shop. "And mind the floor, OK? There are all kinds of sharp metal shards lying around. If you cut your foot—"

"I know. I won't be able to run."

This fucking girl. "No. If you cut your foot, you'll have to go get a tetanus shot, you fool. I know for sure you're due for one."

"I'm not gonna step on anything. And you don't know me that well. I could've gotten a booster."

I peek at her over my shoulder as I reach the stairs. "Did you?"

"No. But that's not the point. I could've. OK? You don't know shit about me anymore."

She's wrong. I know Indie Anna Accorsi better than anyone on this planet. I made her. I shaped her. I turned her into this… whatever she is now. I understand what's lurking inside her mind far better than she ever did.

But there's no point in arguing with her when she's like this, so I don't say anything. Just lead her up to my second-floor apartment and hold the door open so she can go inside.

I follow her in, shut the door, and lean against it.

Here we go again.

Indie wanders around my apartment picking up small things and looking at them with an innocent child-like wonder.

A wrench from my small dinette table. And while I wouldn't normally see anything particularly special about this wrench, today, from a distance of ten feet away, I see what she sees.

The oil stains. The marks on the open end. Evidence that this tool has been used. The slight discoloration of the steel on the handle that earned me a ten-percent discount when I bought the set from the salesman.

She sets it down and moves on to a pen. Just a regular, cheap ballpoint pen to anyone else. But Indie studies the chew marks on the cap end. The crack in the plastic along the barrel.

She sets it down and looks at me. "It's been a while." Her tone is small and soft, all trace of the badass girl she was downstairs gone now.

I nod. "About four years, I'd guess."

She hugs herself and smiles. "Did you miss me?"

"What do you think?" I ask it to be sarcastic but also to hear what she has to say about that. Because you can't ever *really* know what's going on inside that head.

She shrugs and turns. Picks up a candle. Smells it. Looks over her shoulder at me. "Who gave you this?"

"Misha. A while ago." But I feel the need to add qualifiers to that answer. "For my birthday. Thirty-fourth. You missed it."

She nods, puts the candle down and wanders over to the couch where she takes a seat and picks up a ring of keys.

I study them with her, then answer her unasked questions as she holds up a fob. "New truck. Bought it last year. New, like *actually* new. Nice too."

She holds up another key. Not a fob.

"You know that one."

"Motorcycle," she affirms, dropping it to pick up the next key. "House," she says. "Yours," she adds. And for the last one she says, "House. Adam's."

She slips Adam's key off the ring and slides it into her pocket.

"That all you need, then? That why you came?"

"No." She leans back into the cushions. "I'm cold, so…" She shrugs. "I'll take a bath with you."

"Uh, no. Not *with me*, Indie. You know better."

She squints her eyes at me. "*Do* I know better? Who taught me better, McKay? You? Adam? Donovan?"

"Well." I cross my arms, still blocking the door. If she wanted to leave there's really nothing I could do to stop her. But it doesn't hurt to send all the right messages. "I'd go with Donovan, I guess. If I had to choose."

She holds my gaze for a moment and then agrees with a nod. Maybe a smile too. But I can't see it. She drops her head and her long, wet hair falls forward to cover her face.

"I'd have gotten you something better than a candle." She lifts her head up so I can see a sliver of one stormy, blue eye peeking out from behind her hair. "For your birthday, I mean."

"Yeah… well. You weren't here and Misha was."

"Misha's *dead* now."

"I know." I sigh as I rub both hands down my face. "I'm aware."

"She deserved to die."

"You want me to run you a bath, then?"

"Everyone's dead now, huh?"

"Indie." I say this sternly. "We're not getting into this."

"Into what?"

"You know what."

"I'm just saying. Just making an observation, that's all. Everyone is dead now."

"We're not dead. You're not dead, I'm not dead. Adam's not dead. Donovan's not dead…" I stop because she's right. Plenty of people *are* dead. But I don't want her thinking too hard about that. Not when she's in this frame of mind. "Who cares about dead people anyway? We're still here."

She inhales deeply and sinks a little further back into the couch cushions. Pulls her legs up to her chest and wraps her arms around her wet jeans. Hugs herself.

She told me once that Donovan taught her that. He told her to hug herself when she was alone and afraid because hugs cure everything.

"We are still very much here, aren't we?"

"Bubbles?"

She nods. "Sure. Why not?"

"You gonna be here when I come back?"

"Do you *want* me to be here?"

I nod. "Please don't go."

She smiles at me. And when Indie smiles… fuck. I don't even know how to describe the feelings that run through my body when she smiles. It's relief, and happiness, and a sense that everything is actually going to be OK. Like this shit will work itself out and we'll all be normal again.

But it's a lie.

That smile is a lie and those feelings are lies too.

Because we were never normal.

There is nothing normal about the feelings I have for this girl. Woman, really. She's a woman now. But she didn't start out that way. No one starts out that way. There has to have been a time in her past when she was just… what? Just a child? An innocent child?

I want to believe it. I really do.

But it's not true.

This girl was *bred*. She was *made*. She was a *plan*.

I know there's a contradiction in there somewhere. Maybe it's not even that hard to find if I cared to push the curtain aside and take a good look at my life, and my actions, and myself.

And all the ways I contributed to the plan called Indie going off the rails.

But this isn't the time for self-reflection.

She's home.

After everything that happened that day, she came back. And she came back to *me*.

Not Donovan. Not Adam. *Me*.

I walk to the bathroom and flick the light on. Stand there, still and silent. Listening for the tell-tale sound of a front door closing quietly behind her as she makes her escape.

But that sound doesn't come. I know she could sneak out without me hearing, she's that good at her job. But I also know that if she is leaving, she'd want me to know it so she'd make enough noise so I'd hear.

She made some mistakes early on, but in the grand scheme of things Indie's job performance was impeccable. She is the meaning of the word professional.

Not professional like she says all the right things and always follows instructions. She's almost never that kind of professional. I'm talking about that feeling you get when you know someone can take care of shit. Can get the job *done*.

Relief. That's the feeling you get when you send Indie Anna Accorsi in to do a job. Relief that she will come out the other end and you can tick this particular task off your checklist.

But she never saw herself the way we saw her. I guess all truly talented people are guilty of that particular divergence. Geniuses are all insane, aren't they?

I start the water, adjust the temperature, then pick up the bottle of cheap strawberry shampoo and squirt some under the roaring faucet.

If she leaves now, I'd never know. I could go check, but then she'd know I was checking. So instead I sit on the toilet lid, lean forward, and hold my head in my hands as I start falling into the past…

I met Adam Boucher when I was nine years old. I don't *think* Adam was a part of what his father was doing that day they showed up at my family's compound in Alaska. I don't think he knew the real reason Mr. Boucher bought me and took me home with them.

I certainly didn't.

I still don't know all the specifics. All I know is that one day I was living at home with my family and the next I was living in New Orleans with the Bouchers.

The day we got home—my new home—Adam's father took me into his office and sat me down in a chair that was monumentally too big for me and started spelling things out.

Adam would be leaving soon.

I would be staying behind.

We didn't have much time to put this whole thing together.

Adam had a job and I had a job. This was the way of the world we lived in.

I just kept nodding my head. *Yes. Yes. Yes. Whatever you say.* It's not like I had a choice. My decision had been made. He had already explained some things to me back in Alaska. He had already spelled out my choices in no uncertain terms before we left.

So there was nothing else to be said on my part. Just… *yes, yes, yes.*

But Adam didn't go away. Something happened. His father changed his mind? He got kicked out of the program? I'm not sure.

All I know is that Mr. Boucher's grand plan for Adam and I was upended. Never happened.

And everything was pretty normal after that—if you don't count the martial arts training, the trips to the private shooting range, and the way Mr. Boucher, and about two hundred other Company higher-ups, died that night in Santa Barbara all those years ago.

Everything was pretty damn normal until Adam went down to that island in the Caribbean and came home with Indie Anna Accorsi.

I wondered about that a little bit back when it happened.

But I never quite wondered *enough.*

"Knock, knock."

I glance up and find Indie leaning against the doorway peeling her wet jeans down her legs. She kicks them aside and then sighs. "So, really. How have you been, McKay?"

"I'm OK. I can't complain."

"Still building things with your hands?"

"I do a job here and there."

She lifts her t-shirt up over her head and lets it fall to the floor. I know I shouldn't look but I look anyway. Her bra isn't sexy. There's no lace. No flower pattern. It's just black cotton. Same as her underwear. More practical than anything else.

I distract myself with thoughts about her gun. Where did she put it? It doesn't really matter. The only thing that matters is that it's not still tucked away in her jeans. And that means she's not here to kill me.

I stand up and push past her. Go out into the hallway and walk into the kitchen to try to collect myself.

"I had a job too," she calls from the bathroom. She shuts off the water in the tub and gets in, hissing at the heat.

"What kind of job?" My heart is pounding. I place my hand over it as I wait for her answer.

"I was a dog walker."

I smile, then huff out a small laugh. "When was this?"

"Oh…" She hisses again. Then I think she goes under. But a few seconds later there's that sound people make when they resurface and then some sputtering. "Like… last year, I think."

"Last year? What have you been doing since then?"

She sighs in the other room. Says nothing. So I go back down the hallway and now it's my turn to lean against the doorjamb. I fold my arms and wait her out.

She's sitting in the tub the same way she was sitting on the couch. Knees pulled up. Hugging herself. Bubbles up to her shoulders. Staring straight ahead at the subway tiles on the wall. Her hair is wet and slicked back over her head and her teeth are chattering a little.

"I'm not really sure, McKay." She wipes her hand over her eyes to get the water out and then looks at me.

"That's OK." I say it softly to soothe her. "It's fine. You don't need to remember. You're here and so… so you're here and it's fine." I'm talking in circles because that's what this feels like. One. Endless. Circle.

She frowns and nods. "That is why I'm here. I need you to help me. Adam, you know. He took him and…"

"I'll handle it," I interrupt her. Because whatever is going through her head about Nathan St. James right now, it's got nothing to do with Adam.

Or reality, for that matter.

She nods again, still frowning. "Will you wash my hair for me?"

This is something she talked me into doing a lot when she was small. Until Donovan told me to stop. I liked it though. I like taking care of her. I don't know if it helps her, but it helps me. And I like it. So I did it back then and I'm gonna do it now too.

"Sure." I walk into the bathroom and sit down on the toilet lid. I swing my legs to the side, just like I used to, and squirt some of the cheap strawberry shampoo onto the top of her head.

She sucks in a deep breath and lets it out. Then glances up at me with a smile.

I smile back and start working the shampoo into her hair, my fingers gently massaging her scalp just the way she likes it.

She slides her body sideways so she's leaning against the side of the tub, making it easier for me to reach her. And she's still so fucking small she can do this without effort. Just tuck her legs up to her chest and fold herself into a little bundle of girl.

But she relaxes. I can see it in the way her shoulders drop. The way her head drops too. She rests her chin on her knees and even though I can't see her face, I know her eyes are closed.

"I'm going to keep you," I whisper.

She nods. Doesn't reply.

"And we're gonna figure this out, OK?"

She nods again. Then her hand comes up and wipes her eye. She digs her palm into it. Rubs it. I know she's crying. Indie isn't the kind of girl who cries so I pretend it's not happening.

I'm good at pretending too. We're all experts in pretending now.

I take a good long time to wash her hair. I like doing it as much as she likes me to do it. And it's been years since we've had a moment like this. But eventually I have to admit I'm done. "Close your eyes," I tell her, then reach for the cup sitting next to the sink.

Usually I'd use a small bowl for this part but I don't want to leave her like this. I don't *think* she'd get up and walk out, but why take chances, so I use the cup.

She tips her head back and holds one hand over her eyes as I pour water down the back of her head. Over, and over, and over. Until there are no more suds.

Indie tsks her tongue. "You don't have conditioner, do you?"

"No. But I'll pick some up tomorrow, if you want."

"My hair will be a rat's nest."

I smile at that. Because that's what Adam used to say when she didn't want to brush her hair. *Fuckin' rat's nest, Indie. Go brush it out!*

But it hurt to brush it out because it *was* a rat's nest, so she always balked. She was a wild, feral little girl. Most evenings she'd come home for dinner covered in leaves. Twigs hanging from her hair. Mud on her cheeks and scratches all over her arms and legs. Usually a frog or two in her pockets. She kept a frog in her jewelry box for three days once. Before Adam found it and made her take it back to the swamp.

I called her Swamp Thing because that's where we lived. Adam's old… whatever you call it. Not really a plantation because our land was surrounded on two sides by the twisting bend of the marshy Old Pearl River and there was no hope of growing anything profitable out there. Nothing but acres and acres of cypress trees, and duckweed, and spider lilies. But our house was an old mansion that reminded you, every moment of the day, that you were in Louisiana.

Sometimes I just called her Thing, for short. And when she got older it was Miss Thang or Little Thang. With a little extra Southern drawl at the end because she liked the idea of being from the South, even though she wasn't.

"I'll comb it out for you." I say this both in the past and in the here and now. "You want me to do that now? Or after you get out?"

"Now." Her chin is still propped up on her knees and I have a feeling her eyes are open now. Literally. Not metaphorically.

She always picks 'now'. Never wants to get out of the tub until I make her.

I wish we had gotten her earlier. Before she was ten. I'd like to have known her from the beginning. I like her all the ways she is, but I still find myself wishing for those first ten years of her life that I missed.

A lot happened in those ten years and I just… wish I was there. Not that I could've changed anything. I don't wield that kind of power. But at least I would know things. At least I'd know what really happened to her before Adam took her away from all that.

Our relationship is weird. I get that. Donovan has told me so many times in so many ways that nothing about us is normal and there's no way to make it right. And I never needed him to tell me that. I knew it. We all knew what we were doing with her—*to* her—it was *always* wrong. So I really do get it. And once Donovan finds out she's here with me he'll be knocking on my door so fast my head will spin.

But I just don't fucking care anymore.

You can't help who you love and I love this girl more than life itself. I will do anything to make her happy. Anything. Even go along with this new plan she's cooking up for Adam.

Because I hate that I helped shape her into this broken little *thang* and there's a part of me that wants to take it all back.

But here's the real truth.

And I'm not sure I'd admit it to anyone but myself, but…

There's an even bigger part of me that wants to *do it all again.*

CHAPTER TWO

adam

FOURTEEN YEARS AGO

Les Fleurs Island isn't a place to vacation. There are no long stretches of white-sand beach. There are no thatched-roof huts along the shoreline. There are no six-star accommodations.

All of that is located thirty miles south east on L'Île de Beauté.

No. Les Fleurs is a six-hundred-acre tip of an oceanic mountain covered in jungle and ferns. It has only one purpose.

Well, two, I guess. If you count the zoo.

It holds a collection of exotic animals. Big cats, small cats, snakes, giant tortoises, wild goats, gators… that's about all I've seen so far but I hear on the north side there's a small herd of zebra and mustangs, two elephants, and a few giraffes.

I've also heard there's a bunkhouse for the employees, but I've never personally seen it.

There is quite a nice marina though. And, of course, the reception area where I am now. It's really more of a pavilion draped in long gauzy curtains that billow and blow in the ocean wind. The roof is metal, the floor is concrete, and there are about a hundred folding metal chairs facing the auctioneer's block.

Definitely not six-star accommodations, but we won't be here long, so no point in dressing it up too much.

Along the perimeter there are two bar stations and about twenty waiters carry trays of champagne flutes back and forth. There are no women here. Just men. All ages. Some young, like me, some old enough to be my great-grandfather—if I had one of those—and every age in between.

We are all here for the auction. Only twenty-seven girls are up for sale tonight but most of the men under this pavilion aren't here to buy. Just watch.

The whole thing is an act. A show. A production. An annual event.

These girls won't be paraded onto a stage and made to turn in circles like a nice piece of horseflesh. Oh, they will be well groomed, and pretty, and mostly clean. They will start that way, at least. They will wear white, like virgins. Though it's highly unlikely they're still virgins.

But they will be scared. They will be surrounded by animals that want to eat them. They will probably be crying. Some might even be hysterical.

They will beg.

To be set free, or to be bought, or sometimes to be killed.

And we, the men who hold their futures in their hands, we will be taken into the jungle, inside the zoo where the animals roam freely in large enclosures, and we will meet each girl through the bars of a cage.

Because they are pets.

We are here to buy pets.

What the other men will do with their girls when they leave, I have no idea. I don't want an idea. I only know what I'll do with mine.

"Adam Boucher?"

I turn at the sound of my full name and find Gerald Couture already heading towards me with two outstretched hands. He's a tall, thin man wearing a perfectly tailored light gray suit and a broad smile that shows off straight, white teeth. His hair is silver, styled, and even though he's got to be almost eighty years old, he doesn't look a day over fifty.

I extend a hand, almost on autopilot, and he takes it in both of his, giving it a squeeze. "I thought that was you." He nods, then says it again. "I thought that was you. Well." He pauses again to smile at me and take a breath. "I wasn't expecting you this year. Also, I never had the chance to say… I'm just very sorry about your father." He frowns to prove his sympathy.

"And your son," I say back. "It was… a terrible tragedy."

Gerald presses his lips into a forced smile. Nods. Probably pictures the estate in Santa Barbara where everything went wrong. Where my father and his—what to call that guy? His friend? Co-worker? Employee? Protégé? Let's just call him Gerald's son for now—walked into a mansion for a wedding and never walked back out.

I wonder if Gerald knows the truth?

Probably not. He wouldn't be smiling at me if he did.

"I wasn't going to come, but…" I shrug. "Trust fund matured a couple years ago. I have a lot of money at the moment and not much purpose in life. So…" I wave my free hand at the room like this explains everything. "I'm gonna do this for a while, I guess."

"Excellent." Gerald is still smiling. "Excellent." He pumps my captive hand up and down in both of his. "Your father would be proud. He always saw this as your future."

Did he? Did he really? Because… why then? Why did he buy Core McKay for me when I was eleven if he always saw this as my future?

That's what I want to say, but don't. Even though I'm fairly certain Gerald would probably have an answer for me, and that answer might even be the truth.

But I can't think about the past right now. I need to keep my eyes set firmly on the future.

"Yeah." I pull my hand out of Gerald's grip and swipe two flat fingers across my brow. It's fucking hot tonight. Still almost ninety degrees and even though I'm only wearing dark slacks and a white button-down—not entirely buttoned—and even with the ocean breeze, all I can think about is getting back on the boat and taking off these clothes. Maybe going for a swim before I head back to Nassau and catch the jet back to Louisiana. "Sure," I blatantly add. "I'm sure he did."

"Well." Gerald takes in a deep breath. "What is the budget tonight? And what are your plans with her? Perhaps I can give you some tips?"

I exhale, having second thoughts about this now that it's all becoming very real. "There's no budget. Just… whatever it takes. And I'm looking for a partner."

Gerald raises one eyebrow. "Which kind?"

"You know. Military shit."

He nods. Then frowns. "I see. Hmm. Well, I'm not sure *that* was your father's plan."

"No. It wasn't. But he's gone now so all the fucks I gave about his plans went with him."

Gerald purses his lips. Doesn't smile. He and my father were tight. A team once, much like the one I'm putting together now. He trusted my father enough to let his son join my father's team after Gerald retired. And in this business, that's no small thing. "It's not as easy as you think, Adam. I know that the idea of taking one home as a breeder doesn't sit well with a lot of men your age. But trust me. It's easier."

I wonder how that word 'breeder' can just roll off his tongue like that. And also, what in the name God gave Gerald the impression that I ever thought anything was easy in this life? But I nod. "Maybe. But I'm twenty-three years old, I have more money than God, and I'm fuckin' bored. So… the hell with it. I'm not ready to settle down."

"It's not what you think. The jobs. They're not what you think. Trust me on this. I've been there and I was a lot like you when I came here and bought my first girl. It was exciting and we were good at it. But six months later the only people still alive were your father and me. I was devastated."

He frowns and looks somber about his devastation.

"I'm sure you were. But you did it again, and again, and again. You bought more girls, you got more teams, and life went on, didn't it?"

"We paid a price."

I shrug. "That's what money's for."

"It wasn't the money, son. It was..." But he stops. "Your father wasn't happy until he settled. Until he bought the last girl—"

"My *mother,* you mean?"

"—and had you. That's when his life really began."

Such bullshit. He knows it, I know it, but neither of us says it.

"Well, I'm not there yet. If I live to see thirty, maybe I'll take another look at my choices."

Gerald forces a smile. "OK." Then he looks around and back at me. "But let me help you choose tonight. I know all of the girls very well. This is an exceptional crop. I'll tell you what. I'll take you around in my private truck. Your father would want you to have the best one. I'll make sure you get the best one."

"Sure. Sounds good."

"Great." Gerald beams. "Let me go talk to some of the others and then we'll take off early so we're not rushed."

I nod and he walks off to talk up all the other buyers here tonight. I grab a champagne flute off a tray going past at eye height and down it in one gulp.

I said I'd never do this. I told my father over and over again, hundreds of times, that I'd never do this. And he would yell. God, he would yell at me. "Don't you realize," he would say. "Don't you understand how hard I worked to get you out of that program?"

I did. I mean, I think I did. Can one ever really understand the sacrifices a parent makes for a child? But I know I turned out different than the others who were training with me. I knew that much, at least. Just stand me up next to Nick Tate and compare us side by side. Even if you have no idea who we are and what we were meant to do, you can tell the difference between us. Immediately.

I'm no Nick Tate.

And I do appreciate all the ways my father worked hard, and made deals, and manipulated people to make sure that distinction was recognizable.

But here I am anyway. Going right back in.

My life might not end up the way he planned, but it all evens out in the wash. What's the difference, really? Between a man who takes a child home for breeding and one who takes her home for killing?

A sick feeling in my stomach makes me regret the alcohol, and I set the flute down on another passing tray, then wander across the pavilion to the far edge that overlooks the water.

The Company superyacht is docked offshore. Lit up brightly for the party that comes later, after all the sales are final.

I will have to go over there to sign all the paperwork. But I won't stay long. My own yacht is just a little further out. Dark now. No crew, just me. But I like it like that. I like being alone.

So why am I buying a girl? Why am I putting together this team?

I don't really know.

The only thing I do know is that I have a lot of fuckin' money. I have no family to speak of. And I'm bored.

I would kill myself and get it over with, but it feels… wasteful. I should at least make an attempt at living. I have all the makings of a perfect life. I should try.

There's no way I'll make it to thirty. There's no way I'll settle down into the life my father wanted for me and raise good Company kids.

But that's not entirely true, is it?

That is still very much a possibility, so I need to do everything in my power to make sure it never happens. I need to live fast, and hard, and die young. I need to spend as much money as I can, complete as many missions as possible, and then… go out with a bang.

That's my plan.

Go out with a bang.

Maybe, if I'm lucky, I'll get hit right in the chest.

Thirty minutes later Gerald and I are passing through the first gate in his personal safari truck, a vintage Land Cruiser with thick, steel bars surrounding us just in case any of the big cats get hungry. The driver is an older man wearing the standard black and white uniform suit. His tie is so snug up against his neck it makes me want to suck in all the air he must surely be lacking from such a cinch.

Gerald and I sit in the back seat, which has been elevated so we can get a good look around. There's a bucket of ice between us, two bottles of champagne sticking out, and a special drink holder for champagne flutes.

While Gerald did start out just like I am now, he gave up the dangerous life for this cushy job running Les Fleurs a long time ago. So I imagine that he's taken hundreds of people around in this truck on nights like this over the years.

Does he enjoy this job? I can't imagine getting any kind of joy out of his job. But he's smiling. Not complaining. I guess there are worse jobs. Wild animals aside, this island is one of the safer work stations within the Company.

But I know what they really do here. I know who Gerald's family is. My father left a lot of documents behind for me. Or, maybe not *for* me. Just… to me. If there's any kind of meaningful distinction between those two objectives, I'm fairly certain it was the latter.

"Twenty-seven?" I ask. "That's how many are for sale tonight?"

"Yes. Twenty-seven perfect Company specimens. All of them have been bred for the cages." I'm looking at him when he says this. It's dark out here. Very fuckin' dark out here. But there's enough light from the dashboard up front to see him frown.

"What?"

"Twenty-six, actually. The last one… well. She's…" He shakes his head.

"She's what?"

"Very young, for one. And very wild. But her house mother is done. She wants her sold now. Or killed. Or probably both." Gerald chuckles. "But don't worry. I will not waste your time with her." He points up ahead. "Here we go. This is number one. Fifteen years old, blonde hair, blue eyes, very nice-looking girl, if this old man can say such things. She's been trained in music and art. A beautiful specimen for breeding. Her bloodlines are impeccable. Her father… well, as you know, the genetics are well-guarded secrets. So I can't divulge specifics. But believe me when I tell you, she is the best of the best tonight."

Up ahead there is a spotlight shining down on a large steel cage. We pull up to it, stop, and the driver turns off the Land Cruiser. A tiger is on top of the cage, precariously prowling the length of the flat bars that make up the roof, tail swishing as it turns, stops, and then a low, throaty growl fills the nighttime silence. Makes the air even heavier with heat and danger. When he inhales it sounds a little like wheezing. Almost… soothing. But the exhale is something altogether different.

A threat.

"This is Anastasia." Gerald makes a twirling hand motion in the air between us like he's adding a flourish to the end of her pretentious name.

Anastasia is crying. Hard. Sobbing, really. There are metal cuffs around her wrists and her arms have been hoisted up above her head by a chain that attaches to the roof of the cage.

She's wearing a thin, white, cotton dress that hangs down the length of her torso and barely covers her white panties. It's a shapeless dress. We're not meant to see their curves tonight. We're meant to use our imaginations. Indulge in the fantasy.

Blood is dripping down her bare arms and staining the shoulder straps of her dress. A moment later I see why. The tiger drops to the roof and slips his huge, meaty paw between two bars, snagging the top of her hand with a three-inch claw.

Anastasia screams, twisting in place, desperate to get away from that claw.

She's not successful and the tiger snags her again.

"She's loud right now." Gerald shouts this over the roar of the tiger. But he's still calm. "Trust me, though. She's very well behaved under normal circumstances. She would make an excellent concubine."

"I'm not looking for a concubine."

"Right." Gerald sighs, but wisely decides to keep his disapproval for why I'm here tonight to himself.

"Can she fight?"

Gerald gives me a tight-lipped smile. "Onward, Philip. Not this one."

Anastasia begs us not to leave but her wails are drowned out by the roar of the tiger and the starting of the Land Cruiser's engine.

We do leave her there, our vehicle slowly meandering down the gravel road that twists and turns through the jungle until we get to a massive double gate. Thick beams of vertical steel wall one enclosure off from another. We have to drive up, press a code in the security system, then drive through. Stop, as the gate behind us closed, then wait as security cameras scan the lock for animals, and then drive through the second gate once some unknown signal indicates we are clear to move forward.

Think Jurassic Park. That's what that gate looks like.

The next girl is pretty much the same. Blonde and blue-eyed. White dress. Screaming. Maybe a little louder than the last one. But she is surrounded by gorillas. One has a hold of her long, yellow hair and is yanking her head towards the bars of the cage.

"Jesus Christ, Gerald. When did you get gorillas?"

"These old things?" I can just barely make out his chuckling words over the screaming girl. "Some shipping intercept late last year." He is practically yelling over the ruckus. "Smugglers. They're only temporary. We have seven internationally famous zoos coming for a bidding war next week. But while they're here, might as well make the most of them."

"Hmm." I say this just as the girl breaks free of the gorilla's grip—losing a handful of hair in the process.

"Her name is Dalia." Gerald is still raising his voice to be heard. "Any interest?"

"Does she fight?"

"Onward, Philip. Mr. Boucher will be putting us through our paces tonight."

Philip didn't even bother turning the engine off for this one so he just starts rolling forward. But in that same instant a gorilla attacks us, flinging his massive four-hundred-pound body against the bars surrounding the back of the truck. We rock to the side and for a moment I hold my breath and wonder if we will be tipped over.

"Fuck!" Another gorilla attacks, his face right up against the bars where I'm sitting, his arms reaching in to grab at my shirt. He yanks it tight until the fabric is almost choking me around my neck.

Then he opens his mouth, baring long, inhuman canines, and vocalizes some mixture of a scream and a roar.

Gerald leans an outstretched arm past me and an airhorn blares in my ears.

The gorilla drops off, temporarily stunned, my ears ringing as Philip drives forward with some speed.

I glance over my shoulder, expecting them to trail after us and attack again, but they turn back to the girl in the cage.

"Fuck!" I say again.

"It's all very exciting, isn't it?"

"I guess." Then I take one last look over my shoulder as I adjust my shirt, pulling it away from my neck. "Why do you do this? What's the point? I mean, can't you just sell them on a stage somewhere?"

Gerald huffs. "Like a racehorse? Like something ordinary? These girls are not ordinary, Adam. *We* are not ordinary. We want everyone to know what they're getting when they come to a sale like this."

"Animals?"

"Some of them. But these girls deserve this much drama. They are worth it."

"I'm not sure the one who just lost a chunk of her hair would agree with you."

"She will look back on this night with awe. One day her life will be predictable and boring and she will remember the night she was chosen and paid for. She will remember the way her heart beat fast. She will remember the pain of getting her hair ripped out by a massive, full-grown silverback gorilla. She will remember her fear and she will *long* for it."

I find that hard to believe, but I don't say so.

"Really, it just makes the men feel good."

Which is just… sick. But I've said enough tonight. My disapproval has been communicated and logged. No need to make a scene. My position in the Company is high and absolute, but only to a point.

If they ever figured out how that whole Santa Barbara incident came to be… well. I would no longer have this position and influence and that kind of defeats the point, doesn't it?

So I shut up about the girls.

"They see one." Gerald is still on topic though. "Connect with her. Feel sorry for her. Want to alleviate her fear and save her. It's a special moment for both parties."

I look through the bars of the truck and bite my tongue.

We drive through the next lock, then cross a bridge and enter a swamp. The first cage holds a girl—younger than the other two, and perched precariously at the top of the cage. Her bare feet are planted on two shallow ledges on either side of the cage walls so that her legs are spread open.

When I look down I see why.

Gators. Lots of them. And a slot in the bottom of her cage that allows some—the smaller ones—to slither inside the cage with her.

This girl is not screaming. She's panting. Mad, ragged, breaths that come very near to being hyperventilation.

Philip shines a spotlight on her cage to give me a better look. There are at least five gators inside the cage with her. Some of them are leaping up with snapping jaws.

The girl's legs are spread so wide because her feet need to prop her up on each of the small ledges. And for a moment I wonder just how long she can last up there. What would happen if she fell? Would someone come get her? Would some hidden attendant jump out and fight off the gators?

Maybe. But honestly, I just don't think it works that way.

Her face is bright red and sweaty, her white dress dirty.

She glances at us. But just quickly, just for a moment. And then her eyes go back to the gators.

"This is Maria. Twelve years old. Very pretty, very sweet girl. She's a pleaser. Just look how she concentrates on her situation. So focused. So intent on staying alive. You'd really like her, I think."

"Can she fight?"

"She can learn. She's young enough. And she's a virgin. We have the certification to prove it. Only one of two, this time around. Of course, that means her price is higher than most of the others. Two point five million for this one."

"Pass," I say. Not because I don't have the money, and not because I'm not enticed at the idea of a virgin. But because Maria doesn't look intent on staying alive. She looks like she's considering her options right about now. Like maybe she should just let the gators eat her and put her out of her misery. And while I would like a girl who's not afraid of dying, the last thing I need is one who will give up in the middle of something terrible and take the rest of us down with her.

I'd bet money right now that Maria snaps before she turns fifteen. She either kills her owner—and that's more common than Gerald or anyone else out at this island would ever admit to—or hatches plot after plot to escape, or kills herself if all else fails.

Yeah. Maria is no survivor. She's a quitter if ever there was one.

We go through the motions after that. Gerald tries to interest me in each of the remaining twenty-four girls. But none of them are what I'm looking for. And I'm sick of this little tour. I'm fuckin' hot, I'm fuckin' disgusted—with myself for being here, and with everyone else because they're probably enjoying it—and I'm fuckin' tired. All I want is to go back to my yacht, take off all my clothes, and dive into the tepid waters of the Caribbean for a midnight swim.

Hours later, when Gerald finally gives up on me, he says, "OK, let's head back, Philip."

"Wait. I thought you said there were two virgins? You only showed me one. Unless you forgot to mention it?"

"No. I didn't forget. But the last one, Adam. She's… not very high quality. Not what you're looking for."

"Maybe you don't really understand what I'm looking for? Because none of those other girls you showed me even came close."

He pauses. Sighs. "Very well." He leans forward in his seat. "Philip, take us into the garden enclosure."

"Garden," I mumble under my breath. "Sounds… promising."

Gerald huffs out a laugh. "The Garden of Evil is the enclosure's full name. *Snakes.*"

"Nice touch." I lean back in my seat and look through the bars at the thick vegetation all around us. "What kind of snakes? Not rattlers, right? Tell me you don't actually let them get *bit?*"

"Rattlers?" Gerald chuckles. "No. Anacondas."

I lean forward in my seat once again. "All right then. That's kind of badass."

Gerald shoots me a look.

"Do not judge *me*, old man. You have twenty-seven girls out here in the jungle screaming for their lives as wild animals try to *eat* them."

"We take every precaution. It's not a sport, Adam. It's a well-researched matching exercise."

"Whatever. Just show me the snake girl and then we can go back for the auction."

It takes almost fifteen minutes to make our way to the other side of the island where the garden is. And the name fits. The moment we drive through the lock I feel like we enter another world. The air is even more humid and heavy than the rest of the island. The whole place smells like a bog. The trees alongside the road cover it in a canopy of dark, menacing branches and leaves.

I like it.

It reminds me of the marshy woods back home. It makes me think of all those days I spent as a kid out there in a small boat, fishing on the river and catching little gators, and generally being a wild heathen.

But I am not prepared for what I see when we pull up to the cage and Philip turns the Land Cruiser's engine off.

Maybe there's more than one snake in this swamp but it doesn't even matter. The one I see is the only one necessary.

It has to be more than thirty feet long. Has to be. The thickest part of its long, almost greenish, body looks wide enough to eat me whole if it was hungry enough. And when

Gerald shines the spotlight on it, a deceptively small head arcs towards us and stares with unblinking eyes that are as dark as pits. The forked tongue slips out, then back in, then out again. Like two baby snakes. And even though I'm not a hundred percent sure the hissing sound I hear isn't just insects, I'm fairly sure it's the snake.

A chill runs up my spine.

Not because of the snake, but because of the girl.

The cage she's in is a skinny rectangle standing on end. Or, more accurately, hanging from a large support beam. I would not fit inside it. Only a child like her would. And just barely, at that. She's standing upright, arms at her side, head forward. The bars of the cage press against her shoulders. Trapped in this position until someone buys her.

Or… that snake crushes the cage and her with it.

Because that's what it's in the middle of doing.

The entire body is wrapped around the bars of the upright cage, squeezing it with every bit of power it possesses. I lose a few seconds watching the serpentine muscles contract underneath the skin and then blink out of it when I hear the cage creak.

"What the fuck?"

"She won't last long." Gerald says that loud enough that I know the girl heard him. Though, he doesn't have to speak loudly. Even with the hissing that may or may not be insects, this enclosure is very quiet.

She doesn't move. No screams from this girl. No begging. Not even a squeak of panic when the snake contracts again, desperately trying to break the bars of the cage and reach the meal inside.

The air here is thick and musty. Like dirt on the ground after a hard rain. And I swear to God, I think there's a bit of drizzle in here. Like this garden is separate from the rest of the world. A little walled-off piece of paradise.

If you're a snake, that is.

Its skin is shiny and smooth, a little bit of green mixed in with the black and brown. It looks slick and slippery and a little bit soft, if you were to touch it. Just a glint of light here and there along the edge of the scales on the bend of its body ruins the imagery.

And the girl. She is a haunting figure. Shadows from the Land Cruiser's headlights climb up her body at weird angles. Her blonde hair is straight and some of it is caught between the snake's body and the bars of the cage, because it's being pulled taut and tugging on her scalp.

Her dress is longer than the ones I've seen the other girls wearing tonight. But the space is so tight, it's riding up her legs. Like she was squirming at some point and that was what she got for her trouble.

But her face is… angelic. Calm. Pale. No frown. No smile. Her lips are a flat line and nothing more. Like she finds herself inside cages trying to be eaten by snakes every now and then and this is no particular big deal.

She stares at me and a chill runs up my spine.

The whole thing is repulsive and evil, but creepingly beautiful at the same time.

"We've been withholding food for over six months."

For a moment I think he's talking about the child, but then I realize he's referring to the snake.

"She has probably eaten some rodents and even a few of the smaller males, but there are no other large animals in the enclosure so she is very hungry tonight."

Again, Gerald says this loud enough for the girl to hear.

She does not even blink.

"Can she fight?"

"Doubtful. She's not smart, or talented, or even pleasant, if I'm being honest."

"I can fight." The small girl spits her words out, venom in her voice. "I'd kill you both with my bare hands if I wasn't in this cage."

"Not a great way to attract a buyer, Indie Anna."

I let the little girl mesmerize me for a moment. I get lost in her future and potential. Then repeat her name back at Gerald. "Indiana? That's what you call her? Sounds pretty trailer trash if you ask me."

"Fuck you."

"That's quite enough, Indie. Remember your manners. Rich men don't buy little girls with dirty mouths."

"He's not a man. He's an animal like this snake."

The bars of the cage creak again and this time I can actually see them collapse a little. The girl hisses when the hard steel presses tight against her shoulders.

"How will you even get her out of there?" I ask, because the head of the snake is positioned right over the top of the cage like maybe it's considering swallowing the whole thing. Metal and all.

"She's not getting out. Let's go, Philip. We've seen enough."

Philip starts the engine and we begin to roll forward. I wait for the girl to call out. To beg us to come back.

But she doesn't.

The last thing I hear is another dramatic creak of the cage as the monster snake takes another go at collapsing the bars.

And that's that.

That is my first look at Indie Anna Accorsi.

I see Donovan mingling with other men in the pavilion just before the auction starts. I have known him his whole life. At least, I know who he is and I know how he's connected to me, and we have met maybe a handful of times in the past before our fathers died.

Here's the most important thing I know about Donovan: I understand who and what he is. I appreciate how we are the same, even though we're different.

Donovan Couture is Gerald Couture's grandson. Donovan's father and my father had a team together back in the day. They came to these auctions a lot for girls, and like me, they were not looking for concubines.

At least… not at first.

Gerald can talk all the shit he wants about my desire to be part of the Company black ops, but he took the same path. Most people in the Company don't get choices like us. You're given an assignment, and God help you if you don't follow instructions.

But our families—mine and Donovan's and about a dozen others—they go back to the very beginning of the Company. You can trace our pedigrees back nearly three hundred years. We are called the Founders, but more commonly referred to as the Untouchables.

Because we *do* get a choice and Untouchables is a very dramatic name.

We are into drama.

Anyway, the point is—Donovan is here. He's a skinny, fifteen-year-old kid wearing a ten-thousand-dollar suit and a fifty-thousand-dollar watch, clean-shaven, dark hair slicked back like he's a mafia boss.

I don't laugh because he catches my eye just as I recognize him, but I want to.

He holds up a crystal glass with a couple fingers of whiskey in the bottom in a 'cheers' gesture.

I hold up my champagne flute and cheers him back.

He must decide this is an invitation to join me, because he crosses the room. "Adam Boucher. As I live and breathe. I heard you were coming this year. How'd the tour go? See anyone you like?"

I shake his hand, because he's offering, then nod. "Yeah. I have one on the list."

"Just one?" Donovan raises an eyebrow. "Let me guess… snake girl."

"Yeah." I chuckle. "She is creepy as fuck."

"So why? Why buy her?"

"Because honestly"—I lean in and whisper—"I don't want anyone else to have her. The thought of that girl out there, not on my side? Nah. I won't be able to sleep at night."

Donovan laughs. "I totally get it." Then he goes serious. "But I know her. Fairly well. She's been on the island for about six months now. Her house mother threw her out and… this is pretty much her last chance."

I cringe, reconsidering my choice.

"But don't worry. I told her about you."

"About me?" I point to my chest. "What the hell could you have told her about me?"

"Just that she could do worse. And you're young. And obviously not looking to…" He juts his chin up. "You know."

"She's *ten*."

"Yeah, well. They like them young."

I close my eyes and shake my head.

"So, listen." Donovan touches my arm. "I heard some rumors about you."

I open my eyes again. "What kind of rumors?"

Donovan's crooked-smile response makes my heart skip. But only once. "From who?"

He shrugs. "I have feelers out there." Then he leans into me again. "But you need to be careful with her."

"Who?" I ask, because I have to. I'm not gonna admit anything to this kid. Not about me, not about him, not about his father, or my father, or the things I've heard. And I'm sure as fuck not going to admit I had anything to do with Santa Barbara or Sasha Cherlin. But that's what he's getting at.

Donovan smiles. And even though he's only fifteen, I have to give credit when it's due. He's fucking smooth like that whiskey in his glass. "Just… lie low, man. Don't do it again.

And don't ever talk to her again, either. She is the whole reason snake girl is in a world of shit."

"What do you mean?"

"The Zero Project is a failure. You know that, right? Indie—that's her name, by the way. She's one of the last. There's maybe half a dozen younger than her. Mostly babies, but the older ones didn't pan out like we'd hoped so they're just shutting the whole thing down."

"So she's a waste of my time and money? Is that what you're saying?"

"No. I'm not saying that." He looks away, takes a sip of his drink, then side-eyes me. "But you gotta train her, Adam. Right from the start."

"I have Core McKay waiting for me back home. He's taking care of that."

"McKay, huh?" Donovan considers this. "He's not a *bad* choice."

"You know him?"

"Not well. But I've read his file. Patient. That's always a plus when dealing with kids like Indie. But he's... young, ya know? You might consider someone with more experience under his belt."

"He's older than you."

"He is. But he doesn't have my connections."

"He's only a year younger than me."

"Or your connections either, for that matter."

"So what are you saying, Donovan? I should buy her? Or not?"

"Buy her. One hundred percent. I kinda promised her I'd make sure she went somewhere good. Just... be careful. Her kind... they're... fragile."

I sigh and run my fingers through my hair, wanting this whole trip to be over. I've been renovating the family home since my trust fund matured two years ago and it's finally fucking ready. All I want to do is go back there and settle in to... something. Something normal, and predictable, and easy.

And snake girl is starting to sound… well… *not* easy.

"Did you hear that I'm off to medical school?"

I pull back from my thoughts. "Yeah? Good for you."

"Duke. Not too far from your stomping grounds."

"I guess. Not really a day trip though."

"I'm not driving, Adam." He laughs. "Private jet."

"Sucking down all the old money now, are ya, Donovan?"

"My trust matured when I finished undergrad." He holds up his glass. "Here's to early graduation."

"Nerd." But I laugh. "It's smart though. If I had your brain, I'd have done the same thing."

"The reason I bring it up isn't to brag. It's to make you an offer."

"What kind of offer?"

He leans in. "A mutually beneficial one."

I pause here. Because maybe I don't know Donovan all that well. I wouldn't even really call us friends. But I know his *type*. I know his *bloodlines*. The Couture family is involved in some deep-ops shit. For sure, all of the Untouchable families are in the deep-ops shit. But this goes further than that.

They are the shadows behind the secrets. The reason behind the lies.

My father was a cleaner and that certainly qualifies as deep-ops. The Coutures were cleaners too. At times. But they were assassins, and zookeepers—obviously—and heads-of-state in several powerful governments. They have been breeders too. It's like that family has its baby toes in all the little Company pools.

So when a Couture sidles up to you hinting at a mutually beneficial deal, you never really know what that means.

"OK." I look Donovan in the eyes. "You gonna explain that?"

"I have to… perform. Ya know? For the powers that be. And they want another addition to the PSYOPS project."

The PSYOPS project is all about mind control and fucking with people's heads. That's how you raise up a psycho assassin like James Fenici and make him kill people for you for the better part of fifteen years before he loses his shit and goes off the rails. "Hmm. That surprises me after what happened in Santa Barbara."

"I know. Me too. I'm not really into it, to be honest. I want things, Adam. In LA. Plastic surgery, specifically. I want a house on Mulholland Drive, and an office in Beverly Hills, and a weekend home in Malibu."

I almost find this funny. And I'd tell him that to his face if I thought it would help me. But letting secret-keepers in on the fact that you know their secrets? That's not wise or productive. So I say, "Well, go buy that shit, then. You have enough money."

"Doesn't work like that. Not with me. The next step in my trust fund states I need an MD/PhD, and I have to *practice*."

"Sucks to be you, I guess."

"But here's my idea. You let me do a case study on little Indie to impress the higher-ups in the Company and I'll keep her on the straight and narrow."

"How's that gonna work?"

"Therapy sessions."

I think about that for a moment and shake away a chill clawing its way up my spine. "What do I get?"

"You get a well-behaved little psychopath who will do everything you tell her to."

"I thought you liked this kid?"

"I do." He says it a little too loud and a few men nearby turn to look at us. Donovan and I both hold our drinks up to cheers them. "But nothing's for free, right? I give her you. A good home—heard about the reno, by the way. Sounds fantastic. And she gives me her mind."

So that's his angle. He wants to practice PSYOPS techniques on her. For a minute there I thought good old Donovan here had an altruistic side. "I'll think about it."

"What's there to think about? You need her to work, I need a research paper, she needs a friend."

"I don't even know if I'm gonna buy her now. You've done a pretty good job convincing me she's a bad idea."

"Well… think on it then. I'll be here. Watching." Then he fuckin' winks at me, points to his head and says, "I see everything, Adam Boucher. I know more than you think."

He walks off, already calling out someone else's name, and leaves me to ponder what he sees.

Or rather… what he's *seen.*

I think he knows.

I think he knows my secrets the way I know his. And even though his father died with mine when that shit show in Santa Barbara went down five years ago, he still wants to be on my team.

I buy her.

There's no way I'm leaving this island without buying her.

She sets me back almost three million dollars because there are other men who want her. Men not here on the island, but who bid with proxies, and who have decided my filthy-mouthed snake bait should go home with them instead.

I consider walking away. I almost do, twice. But then I imagine that creepy little girl being out there on someone else's team and I raise my auction paddle again.

And again.

And again.

And again.

Donovan is at the party on the Company superyacht afterward. Still yucking it up with everyone, still smiling, and still creeping me out.

No one trusts the PSYOPS docs. No one. Their mission in the Company is to fuck with the heads of kids, turn them into little killers, and keep them sane until they burn out and need to be cleaned up by teams like… well, like the one I'm trying to put together, actually.

But his little I-want-to-be-a-Beverly-Hills-plastic-surgeon plan isn't fooling me for several reasons.

One. He's not gonna get a chance to put that plan into motion. Not the way things are now. Because plastic surgery was never his path in life and he knows it. Which means he's either lying about his so-called dream or… he wants to take the whole thing down just to make it happen.

We have that in common. My path wasn't the one spelled out for me either.

But he'll be *in* PSYOPS, regardless.

Best-case scenario—he's only in that line of work for several years. Then we take care of business, the Company collapses, and he's free.

Worst case—the Company is business as usual, he stays there forever, and I'm stuck with him and the properly PSYOPS-ed little snake girl for life.

And I just don't like that idea.

Aside from the fact that I just bought a kid in a slave auction, I also just bought a long life of… not easy. Not normal. A long life of looking over my shoulder at this girl.

Because I don't care how well behaved they look on the outside—the Company assassins on the inside are *damaged.*

And this girl is no ordinary Company assassin. She's a Zero. Like James Fenici. Like Nick Tate. Like Sasha Cherlin.

Like I *almost* was.

There is no way to fix the fucked-up inside this girl's head. Not once the work has started. All you can do is manage it. And I know she's only ten, but she's been through some kind of training. Probably failed out of it and that's why she's here before her time.

I know this because I was destined for that Zero program too. And even though I can play a good game and make people think it's all shipshape up there in my head… it's not.

It's all very hazy. Very messy. It's chaos, if I'm being completely honest. And while I have no problem lying to other people—it's not the lies we tell each other that kill us in the end. It's the lies we tell ourselves.

So I try not to lie to myself if I can help it.

I know what I am. My head is nothing but a swirling storm of unfinished training and business.

I didn't finish college. There were *issues* with me and the other kids in school. I didn't grow up like they did. Oh, I have the same money. Same privilege. The best connections and I'm smarter than most. Not as smart as Donovan, but not many people—even specially bred ones like me—achieve that level of genius.

I was being trained by PSYOPS before my father pulled me out of the program at age ten and even though they never finished me, it was enough to keep the chaos inside me alive.

Still, I manage. I haven't had a slip up in years now. So there's hope, at least. A small, sliver of hope that Indie can be as normal as I am.

I almost laugh out loud when I realize I just referred to myself as normal.

No one involved in making me who I am would ever call me normal.

But at least I will *get* her. I will *understand* her. And if Donovan can unfuck her head a little, and McKay can teach her what she needs to know to get the jobs done without stealing her soul—then maybe this will turn out OK?

A little while later I'm handed a tri-fold… menu? It looks a little bit like a multiple-choice test.

How would you like your girl dressed tonight?

A. Long, fantasy gown with flowing skirts.

B. Pastel-colored lingerie.

C. Black and/or red lingerie.

D. Please do not dress my girl.

I'm left wondering if option D means 'leave her naked.' Or 'don't put any of this sick shit on her, she's *ten*, for fuck's sake.'

I err on the side of caution and go looking for Donovan. I find him off in a corner texting on his phone, but he puts it away when he sees me approaching. "Mr. Boucher. Have you made up your mind?"

I hold the menu out for him. "I don't want her dressed in any of this."

"No?"

"No. She's fucking *ten*. I want her in shorts and a too-big t-shirt. Sneakers on her feet. I want her to look like my little sister. I need to take her *home*, Donovan. We're leaving as soon as the papers are signed. I want to be back in New Orleans no later than tomorrow afternoon."

"I can arrange that for you. No problem. But have you thought about my offer?"

I have been thinking about his offer. Because I will need him—or at least someone like him—if I want to keep this kid in line. Donovan Couture is the only PSYOPS agent available at the moment so I tell him, "I'm gonna say yes, but it comes with conditions."

Donovan looks eager and happy. And I have to say, even though he comes off as just another fifteen-year-old nerd, this dude creeps me out almost as much as my little snake girl. “Name them.”

“You stay away. You’re not on the team.”

“I will require a paycheck.”

I wave a hand in the air. “That’s fine. But you only come around when I call you. Got it?”

“I can work with that. As long as the visits are regular. She needs consistent guidance.”

“Maybe every three months.”

“That’s reasonable.”

“And you only stay one weekend.”

“Fine. Anything else?”

I draw in a deep breath, then tug at the tight knot of my tie at my neck. “You record everything you say to her. And you leave those recordings with me.”

“I, of course, can keep a copy for myself?”

I shrug out some reluctant acceptance.

“Then we have a deal.” Donovan offers me his hand.

And for the second time tonight I shake it.

CHAPTER THREE

Indie

Nathan St. James was the boy next door.

I didn't understand what this meant when we met. So I didn't know it was a thing until many years after we had become our own thing when I picked up a romance book at a garage sale about a young girl who falls in love with the boy next door.

I think I read that thing cover to cover dozens of times since then.

Adam threw the old copy out, or maybe it got lost sometime in my early teens. But I never forgot the title and every time I wandered into a used book store, or I was browsing a bookseller at the flea market, I would look for it.

I've had three or four different copies over the years. The cover changed once. I bought it with the new cover because it was only forty-five cents. But I didn't like it as much. Just didn't do anything for me the way the original did. Because the original people on the cover kinda looked like me and Nate.

She had long blonde hair, like me. And blue eyes, like me.

And he had sun-kissed skin and dark blond hair, like Nate. And brown eyes that weren't really brown, but almost the color of an almond shell in the shade. And I thought that was some kind of sign. Because I have never *ever* seen another boy with almond-shell-colored eyes like Nate had. He said they came from his great-grandfather's werewolf blood. Ha ha.

But I didn't care where they came from, I just loved them so much.

Nathan St. James was my boy next door. He was my first friend, he was my first kiss, and later, when we were older, he was my first love too.

Nate and I met about three days after I had moved in with Adam and McKay on Old Home Island when I was ten years old. It wasn't really an island because when I think of islands I think of oceans. I come from an ocean island so I know what islands are.

We didn't live on the ocean, we lived on the Old Pearl River in lower Louisiana. But it felt like an island because the river wound around two sides of Adam's property and there was a small duck lake on another side. So Nate and I just called it an island anyway.

He lived on the other side of the duck lake, which was on the west side of my island. I could see his house from my bedroom window. It was a brick house the color of the rusty mud in the Old Pearl River when the water level was low. And his bedroom was in the attic. His window was small but when I used my night vision scope, I could see him walk past the window from time to time.

I lived in the smallest room on the second floor of Adam's old family home. It had old-time wood paneling painted white—McKay did that for me. It had an old claw-foot bathtub in the corner and a small sink, but no toilet.

Even though I laughed at that tub the first time I walked through the door, I loved it. And I took a bubble bath nearly every night once I settled in.

My bed frame was made of old iron that used to be painted white, but the paint had been chipping for decades before I showed up. The sheets were the softest white cotton I had ever felt in my life, and there was a blue quilt as a bed cover. An old, soft quilt that many people had used to keep warm in the past.

There were little pillows on the bed, propped up in front of the real pillows. They were also quilted and handmade. All of them had large flowers pieced together with geometric shapes of varied fabric on the front. And on the back, there was a checkerboard of all these same fabric patterns.

The floor was old bare wood. But it had been polished and sealed before I got there so there was no chance of splinters. And there was a big, round coiled-rope rug on the side of the bed that matched the blue and white color scheme of the room. Half of it was hidden underneath the bed, so when I swung my legs out of the bed in the morning there was a perfect half-moon of blue below my feet that made me think of the sea.

My room faced the trees, but beyond the trees was the duck lake and that's how I could see Nathan St. James from my bedroom.

The house was old and white, but it had been recently remodeled so everything was fresh and clean when I arrived. Adam said it was a Victorian house because it had a turret in the front, just over the porch, which was just an atrium in the foyer inside and not even a real turret.

But it kinda looked like a small castle, if you didn't pay too much attention to the white-wood siding.

There was a gate at the end of the driveway with a weathered brass plaque on the front of it that read Boucher House, but no one called it that. We just called it Old Home. Or Adam's Old Home. Or sometimes just Home. And you couldn't hardly read that sign, anyway. It was covered in creeping vines. So you couldn't fault anyone for not calling it the Boucher House. They couldn't really see the letters.

In the early years it was hard to see Nate's bedroom window from my window because of all those old trees with creeping vines. But one summer, when we were eleven, we cleared a path through the trees with a chainsaw and then, and forever more, we had a direct line of sight to each other.

Adam was furious with us that day we came at the trees with a chainsaw. And really, it was McKay who actually did most of the work. But it was our idea and we started the project, so we took credit for it.

As long as we used a night vision scope we could see each other when we stood in front of our windows. I gave Nate one of my old scopes for his fourteenth birthday because I wanted him to look at me too, and up until that time it was just me looking at him, mostly.

A year later we had cell phones. And then we would talk on the phone and I would look through the scope and watch him through the window as he talked to me.

He knew I was doing it. I'm not a liar. Adam thought I was but McKay always said that one day my honesty would get me killed. I didn't care what Adam thought. And Nate didn't care that I was watching him, anyway. We were best friends and didn't have secrets like that.

Nate and I met because I was a runaway. Less than two hours after Adam brought me to the island I had decided that I would not live in Adam Boucher's Old Home, that I would live in his woods.

I mostly did this on principle, but also because it pissed Adam off and drove him crazy.

I really liked to drive Adam crazy back then. I feel like that was my only hobby during those first months I lived with him and McKay. Before Donovan talked me into "behaving myself".

But those few weeks in the woods were fun for me. I caught Nate fishing in the river on day three. He was in a little motor boat and he had already caught many fish by the time I wandered onto the sandy shore. He made a fire on the beach that afternoon and cooked up those fish. So I didn't starve while I was living in the woods. I think I might've gained weight, that's how well I ate.

Nate said he knew who I was. He had been watching when Adam brought me home in the rain. He likes to hunt for gators when it rains like that, so that's what he was doin'. And he heard me screaming as Adam dragged me into the house and locked me in the small upstairs room that would become mine.

But Nate didn't know my name so I told him that my given name was Indie Anna Accorsi, but everyone just called me Indie.

When Adam found out he said I was "a stupid little witch" for giving my real name out to a stranger and didn't I know any better? And what the fuck did they teach me anyway? Before he bought me in the auction? And then he said, "I should've let that snake eat you."

And I replied, and I remember this clearly, "That snake was not gonna eat me, Mr. Boucher. I was about to carve it up and roast it for dinner myself before you came along and ruined my plans."

And then McKay laughed and told me to go take a bath because I smelled like old mud on a hot day.

Which was just fine with me because the mud kept the mosquitoes away. But McKay offered up bubbles that smelled like bubble gum, and up until that very moment I had never had a bubble bath, so I got clean for him.

But the minute I saw Nate in that boat I knew we'd be best friends. And we were. We got into all kinds of trouble after that. I liked him because he was not afraid of the lake and the river and almost everyone else was.

Adam told me that. When he realized I had ripped a hole in my window screen and shimmied on down the side of the house towards my life in the woods that first afternoon, he spent two whole days yelling at me from the front porch.

He waved his fist and screamed threats at me. And McKay just sat in a rocking chair and drank bottles of beer and watched him.

McKay's feathers are hard to ruffle.

Adam's threats were many. He yelled out that there were gators in the water and leeches that would suck my blood. He told me there were cottonmouths too. I didn't know what a cottonmouth was, but Nate told me they were snakes.

I'm not afraid of snakes.

I will walk through a garden so thick with snakes I'd be tripping over them and it would not bother me one bit. I will stare down the mouth of any damn snake and tell them what's what.

But Nate did say they *would* kill me if I let them get too close. So from then on, when the cottonmouths came slithering by on the top of the water, I would give them space and they would stay clear of me too, and we had this kind of understanding.

The gators were another story altogether. Gators were not as smart as snakes. I know this from experience. I would not call them brave, but they were not the type to give one their space. So I had to stay clear of them without getting any reciprocal consideration.

I never did see a leech on my skin trying to suck my blood after swimming in the water. So I don't really have an opinion on leeches.

I had a good life on Old Home Island. I really did. I don't think I completely understood that until recently.

At first, I liked Donovan the best. Donovan is only five years older than me. He's some kind of genius. When we met, when I was ten and he was fifteen, he was already done with college and getting ready to start medical school to become some kind of psychiatric doctor.

He was not going to be a typical therapist, he told me. I'm not really sure what a typical therapist is because I have never talked to anyone about what's inside my head, just Donovan. But he was a Company kid, like me. And if there's one thing I know about being a Company kid, it's that our lives are never typical.

But Donovan was patient. And he talked in a low, calm voice. And he liked to ask me questions and something about him made me want to answer.

If Adam asked me a question back then, I would *never* answer. I didn't like to answer Adam's questions. And if

McKay asked me a question I would sometimes answer. If it was a question about something I was interested in.

But it didn't matter what kind of question Donovan asked me. I always wanted to talk to him. And he was a good listener too. He taped most of our conversations. And when he wasn't taping them, he was writing notes. Donovan said he did that so he would remember everything I ever told him.

It made me feel good when he taped our conversations. Like someone cared.

I'm not sure Donovan really *did* care about me. If I had to choose just one of them to call caring, I would choose McKay. Because he was the one who soothed me after jobs went bad, and taught me how to fight and shoot, and made sure I ate all my vegetables. He even bought me braces when I was fourteen so my teeth would be pretty.

And, in the later years, when I had to leave Old Home and go to the boarding schools for a job, he would be the one to come visit me on parents' day. Even though he was not my father, and I made sure everyone *knew* that he was not my father.

The girls at the schools would ask me, "Is he your brother?" And they did this because McKay was very handsome and charming. Maybe not as charming as Donovan, but he was definitely more of a looker than a brain.

Adam was not very charming. But he wasn't the kind of mean that scared me. He yelled a lot, but he didn't hit me. And, of the three of them, even though Donovan was the one who asked all the right questions and McKay was the one who paid the most attention, Adam was the one who protected me. And sometimes he even saved me.

One time, when I was in San Francisco and the job went bad, this guy had me by the hair with a knife to my throat. And Adam came in. Just kicked in the damn door and cut that man's throat with his own knife. And then he said, to the dead man on the floor of that apartment, "Don't you *ever* touch her again." Even though he was dead and there was no chance of that happening, Adam said it anyway.

It wasn't the only time he had to do that. When I was first starting to work the jobs I messed up a lot and Adam was always there. Saving me. He always came in the nick of time to save my ass.

So. I don't hate him.

And he never did tell me I was a fuck-up. Ever. Even though I was. He just said, "Indie, you'll learn. It's fine." And that was the end of it.

So they were all three different. But alike in a lot of ways too.

They all liked to drink after a job. Donovan wasn't always there in the beginning. He was away at medical school. But he came at least once a month for our talks. And Adam was always going places. This place and that place. And when he came home he'd have a job for us to do. So McKay was the one I spent the most time with on the day to day.

And they were all young. Much older than me, but I was *very* young. They were just regular young. Adam was the oldest and he was twenty-three when he bought me at the auction. McKay is only one year younger than Adam and they had been friends since they were boys. Like the way Nate and I were friends. And Donovan—well, he was practically my own age by the time I was fifteen and everything fell apart.

I didn't know everything was falling apart when it happened but I think they did. At least Adam did. He knew that what happened to the Company was bad. Even though the Company was also bad, having no Company was worse than bad, at least for us. Because then we had no protection. And if we were smart—this was what McKay kept saying after everything went down—if we were smart, we'd have stopped what we were doing and found a new way forward. I should've gone to school for real and not just to kill some senator's daughter in her sleep and make it look like an overdose or a suicide.

But we didn't. Adam decided to keep us going. Donovan found us new jobs. And we were our own team.

That was our downfall.

People like us… there's always someone watching you. They are all insiders, otherwise how would they know where to look? But to be fair, Adam was always watching them too. So why he didn't immediately understand that the other Company leftovers were looking at us, well. That was just a flat-out mistake.

And by the time Adam realized that we were being watched, it was probably too late.

I think that's why I blame him most. He should've seen it coming. He should've prepared us for what came after the Company fell.

He should've known there were lingering secrets and he should've taken care of them before they festered and boiled.

But he didn't. So that's why I blame him most.

I blame McKay too. Because once things got past a certain point, he looked at me differently. And I hated him for that.

Donovan just wasn't around. All that time he was in medical school he was getting two specialty degrees, not just one. So he left to be a fucking plastic surgeon in LA after things started falling apart.

I guess I could blame him for leaving me. But I don't. Because he just wasn't there.

Adam was there.

McKay was there.

And Nate was there.

And then, one day… none of them were there.

But someone else *was.*

CHAPTER FOUR

MIND CONTROL IN CHILDREN: A CASE STUDY OF COMPANY ASSASSINS

INTERVIEW WITH INDIE, AGE 10.2

SESSION #1

DONOVAN: OK, Indie. Tell me what we're doing.

INDIE: You already know what we're doing.

Tell me again. This is what we call permission. You know what that means, right?

I'm telling you that something is… OK.

Exactly. So tell me what we're doing so I can get it on this recording and if anyone objects to this in the future, it's very clear that you gave me permission to do this.

Fine. I give you permission to record me. But I'm not gonna talk to you.

Why not?

Because it's *my* head, that's why. And what's inside of it is none of your business.

I get that. I totally understand that. You're a private person.

Yes. I am.

That's fine. But you know *why* you're here, right? You know how you got here to Old Home. You know why Adam brought you here. And you know why McKay is here. Right?

They explained it to me.

Now I want you to explain it back to me. OK? Just so we're all on the same page.

Why do I have to answer *your* questions? How come you don't have to answer *my* questions?

Well… you haven't asked me any questions, Indie Anna.

Don't call me that. I hate it. Adam said it's a trailer trash name. And I don't know what that means, but it doesn't sound nice.

It's a state, you crazy girl. It's got nothing to do with trailer trash.

Well… what is trailer trash, exactly? Like… old newspapers and stuff?

No. It's… not important. And don't use that saying anymore. I don't like it.

It's mean, then. Isn't it?

It's mean. Yeah. But Indiana is a place. It's a state here in the US. Up north near the lakes. But if you don't want me to call you Indie Anna, then I won't. I'll call you Indie, like everyone else.

No… it's fine. You can call me that. But no one else can.

I feel special.

You should. I don't make exceptions for most people.

I'm truly honored. Now tell me why—

No. You have to answer *my* questions first. Then *maybe* I will answer yours.

OK. Ask me anything.

Why did you let them buy me?

You know why. You weren't mine. But I think the question you're really asking is… why did I let them *take* you?

Yes. You told me we were friends back on the island. And then… poof. They took me and you stayed behind.

I'm going away to medical school. I told you that back on the island. I can't be here with you all the time. But I told you I would keep track of you and here I am. And… I would like to add that I'm the one who got Adam to buy you. I did that so you'd be taken care of.

How did you get him to buy me?

I talked to him before the auction started.

Is that old guy your grandfather?

Mm-hm. He is. I spent a lot of time on that island growing up.

But they never put you in a cage and sold you.

No. My grandfather is too important. I'm… special. Like Adam.

What's that mean?

Let's stick to one question at a time, OK? That will keep things on track.

Because you have to leave. You're in a hurry. Adam called you here to talk sense into me and make me behave.

That's… not actually true, Indie. McKay called me. And he's just worried about you. We all want you to be successful and that means you have to listen to Adam and McKay because one day you'll be doing things that are dangerous and if you don't do as you're told, bad things will happen.

Bad things? Like… I'll be put in a cage again?

No. That's never gonna happen again. That's all over now. You're Adam's.

No one asked me if I wanted to be Adam's. Maybe I want to be McKay's?

McKay didn't pay for you. Adam did.

So?

McKay works for Adam. And now you work for Adam.

Do you work for Adam too?

No.

Then why are you here?

I just told… never mind. Do you want to know how I got Adam to buy you and why I did it or not?

I do.

OK. Then I'll tell you. But don't interrupt me again.

Bossy.

I was in the pavilion—*don't* interrupt me.

I was just gonna ask where that was. That's all. I need to picture it in my head.

It's… the place where the auction was. On the top of the hill on the island. Maybe you saw it when they brought you in by boat?

Oh. Yeah. OK. I did see it. Go on.

Girl. You tire me out.

Are you gonna talk? Or just whine like a baby?

We were in the pavilion. Adam came back first from the tour and—

Yeah, he was the first to come see me.

Indie Anna.

Sorry. I'll zip it.

OK. So… as I was saying. Adam came back first because my grandfather took him out on the tour in his personal truck. And by that time the place was all set up for the auction. There were a ton of people there waiting for everyone to come back and get things started. All men, of course. Everyone was drinking and there was a little string quartet in the corner playing soothing music.

Adam was there off to the side. By himself. Adam is like me. He's a little bit older, but we're cut from the same cloth. Both of our fathers died doing a job five years ago.

Don't you dare interrupt me. I'm not talking about that tonight. I only mention it because I'm making a point that we're the new generation of Company kids and… I've noticed that all the other kids my age, and Adam's age, we're not as committed as the generation that came before us. We like the money and the privilege, but the price is high. We understand this and the world has changed so we're not as comfortable with it as… say… our parents were.

We're looking to make changes and I had heard that Adam was involved with something regarding this change a few years earlier. And to me, that meant that he was not there to buy you for the wrong reasons.

OK. Wait. I have to interrupt. What reasons? Like… what are the bad ones and what are the good ones?

Maybe I should clarify. All the reasons you buy someone are wrong, Indie. All of them. So Adam is not some kind of saint. He's just as guilty as anyone. Including me. But… what he did… if he really did that… I mean… I respect the guy for that shit.

What shit?

We're not gonna talk about that today, either. Maybe, when you get older, I'll tell you everything. But not today. And don't make that face at me. You're ten years old.

But when? When will I be old enough?

After you finish your first job I'll come back and—

No. No, no. Wait. You're not coming back until then? Donovan—

I didn't mean it that way. I'll be back once a month. Adam and I agreed on three months at first, but it's clear you need more consistent guidance. So once a month.

For how long?

How long will I stay? Or—

How long will you keep coming?

For as long as you want.

You promise?

Indie Anna. I'm trying to tell you things right now. Do you want to know them or—

I do. Just… I need you to keep coming back forever. Like… that's not even a joke. For. Ever. Donovan. I mean it. Once a month *forever.*

Fine. I promise I will. Anyway… of all the men there that day at the auction Adam was the only one I knew who would take care of you. He wasn't interested in you the way the others might be. And don't ask me to explain that, because I won't. Ever. It makes me fucking sick just thinking about it. So I made sure he saw you the way I saw you.

You're smiling. Why are you smiling?

Because you see me.

I see you. And I'm trying to help you. Because while this situation with Adam and McKay is better, it's not… the best. It's just… you're different, Indie. You're not like other people. None of us are. We don't fit in anywhere but in the world of the Company. Adam was… he's just a lot like you. More than you understand right now. I know he looks like he's in charge, and as far as you're concerned, he is. But he's not. His mind is… OK. I'm getting too far off track here. What I really want to say is this. They're going to make you do things. Dangerous things. And you have to follow Adam and McKay's directions and rules because they really do know what they're doing. I'm coming here to talk to you because I like you, but I'm also

coming here to talk to you because Adam is paying me now.

I thought you said he wasn't your boss?

He's… he's not. Not really. He's just paying me to help you. That's all. Because he knows we were friends back on the island and I took a liking to you.

I like you too.

Thanks. So that brings me back to my question. Did you get enough information from me? Or do you need more before I can ask it?

Go ahead. It's your turn, I guess.

OK. Tell me why you're here with Adam and McKay.

You just explained it.

Indie Anna.

Fine. I'm here to be their… I don't really know if there's a word for it.

Explain it. Then if there is no word, we'll make one up.

I'm here to… clean things up.

Go on.

Kill people who get in the way.

Not yet, though. Your first job is to…?

Learn how to do that.

Correct. You're in training right now. But one day you will be sent to clean things up. Adam will get orders from the Company and he will have to take care of people. Problem people. Dangerous people. Now listen, not all of those jobs will require your help. Adam and McKay will do some of them. All of them, until you're ready. But one day… one day they will ask you to take care of things only you can do. And you must follow orders. Exactly as they are given to you.

Just… kill people?

Maybe. Maybe not. It depends on what needs to be cleaned up.

Are all of the girls from the auction going to be cleaners like me?

No. None of them will be like you. They're… doing other things.

…

OK.

You promise?

I promise. As long as you don't miss a visit. Not even one, Donovan. I'm serious. I will go live in the woods again if—

You stay out of those woods. There are dangerous things in there.

There are dangerous things in this house too, Donovan.

Point. But…

No. I love the woods. And Nate is in the woods.

That kid… he's not one of us, Indie. You don't want him involved in this shit. Trust me. It won't end well.

But he's my only friend.

I'm your friend. McKay is your friend. Even Adam is your friend. He might not seem like it now, but he's on your side. We're all on your side. And we want you to get through this.

I don't think Adam is my friend. I make him yell.

Yeah, but… he's doing it out of concern. He sees you as a little sister.

Ha. He does not.

Trust me. He does. After he bought you, we had to go out to the yacht for paperwork and shit. There was a private party out there too. And the new owners get to choose what their girls will be dressed like when you leave. And Adam put you in shorts and a t-shirt for a reason.

I don't understand. What does that have to do with anything?

One day you'll get it. But for now, just… trust me.

Are we done now?

Sure. We're done.

SESSION #1 NOTES

Indie Anna Accorsi presents as a bright ten-year-old girl with very little concern for the reality of her situation. She comes off as desensitized and distant. Almost unable to connect herself with what is really happening to her.

In a way, this is helpful. She has learned to cope with her life in a way that makes her both likeable and reasonable. Contrary to what Adam believes, she *is* reasonable. Her decision to take off into the woods upon arrival at Old Home was a way of asserting control over a situation in which she felt powerless.

Noting her preoccupation with my 'abandonment' back on the island during our first session, her actions after coming to Old Home are logical and expected.

When I examined her bedroom, I found the screen had been ripped open. She felt trapped up in the bedroom. Probably due to the fact that Adam locked her in.

And when I observed the roofline outside her window, as well as the old tree bumping up next to the edge, her escape was inevitable and obvious. Also preventable, had Adam seen the tree and roof for what they were.

An invitation to escape.

The tree was convenient, possibly fortuitous, and—depending on her view of fate and destiny, if she has one—maybe even a *sign* that this opportunity was given to her as a gift.

A way out was presented and she took it.

I think her improvisation skills, in combination with a sense of self-preservation, will be an asset in the future once she is working.

However, as a friend, and not her pseudo-doctor, I am very concerned about her mental state.

All Company kids learn to cope early and most of the time this does not turn out well once they reach their late teens.

The most famous case being James Fenici who, while on his first job, was captured by a Central American drug lord and tortured until his unauthorized rescue years later. He survived, but it had dire consequences on his psyche and he was certified insane by Company PSYOPS just a few months later.

Normally, that would be the end of it. James Fenici should've been put down. But he, like myself and Adam, is an Untouchable. To his credit, he successfully completed more than a decade on the job after that, but was involved in the death of almost three hundred Company members during an incident in Santa Barbara, California, five years ago.

His current status and whereabouts are unknown. As is his state of mind.

It is my desire to help Indie Anna Accorsi navigate her way through her working life and I will keep my promise to visit her monthly for as long as I can.

SESSION #1 NOTES – PRIVATE

The main purpose of this study is to internally assess the ongoing viability of the Company Zero Program. The

Company's official statement is that it's a failure. But not all the graduates had to be put down.

Nick Tate is still working, James Fenici hasn't gone completely insane yet, and Sasha Cherlin is living a normal life as a Colorado teenager.

The secondary purpose of this study is to get closer to McKay and Adam and assess the outcome of their premature withdrawal from the Negative Program.

McKay presents a completely sane, under-control, almost thoughtful twenty-two-year-old male with one exception: He is bound to Adam in ways I don't quite understand.

Is this loyalty?

Guilt?

Shame?

Or mind control?

I don't have enough information on that yet.

After Indie's regular session I made my first hypnosis attempt. On a scale of one to ten I would rate this session a five. She went under without drugs, but it wasn't deep. Indie's previous PSYOPS operator's notes indicate that she was unwilling to submit to training of any kind. They used many different techniques on her with little success.

I can't say for certain that Indie hasn't been put under before, but my limited educated guess is that if she has been, it was probably not productive.

Either that or they wiped her.

In this first session my only goal was to assess her reaction. I asked her very basic questions. Name. Age. Date of birth. She answered them all without fuss. But when I asked about Carter she showed no signs of distress to indicate he had been involved in her training.

Which is frustrating and disappointing.

Maybe I was wrong?

Maybe this whole thing is a waste of time?

CHAPTER FIVE

mckay

PRESENT DAY

Indie is always with me. Even when she's not.

She is my world.

And if taking it all back means she never came home to us here in Louisiana, then I don't take it back. Not even a little bit.

It's selfish, but I don't care.

She is mine. I raised her. I took care of her. I taught her how to survive.

And maybe it wasn't enough, but it kept her alive this long.

So I did something right.

"Are you ready to get out?"

I get a long, soft sigh as a response.

"I'll get you some clothes."

I get up and walk out of the bathroom and into the small bedroom before I sigh as well. We've been here before. So many times. And every single time I say to myself, *I can't do it again. I just… can't do it again.*

And each time I do it. And we come through it.

Because that's the only thing we can do.

Get past it. Move on.

But this time feels different.

She pulls the bathtub plug and the sound of water rushing down the drain fills the small apartment. "Did you call Donovan?"

"No. Not yet."

"Are you going to?"

"Sure." I open a drawer and pull out a pair of sweats and t-shirt that says 'Babette's on the Bayou'—a tavern that has, somehow, become my local haunt.

When I turn around Indie is standing in the doorway wrapped up in a towel. And I swear to God, I lose my breath.

She was a pretty child but as a woman she is beautiful. She just doesn't know it.

"Are those for me?" She points to the clothes in my hand.

"Yeah." I throw them to her and she catches both with one hand. "I'll let you get dressed." Then I push past her and go back to the living room.

"Call Donovan. I need to talk with him."

"I will. But I can't promise anything. He doesn't really answer my calls these days."

"He's too busy being a fancy plastic surgeon in LA?"

"I guess. But I'll give it a try." I grab my phone off the small dinette table and flip through my contacts to find his name, then press send.

It rings. And rings. And rings…

"This is Dr. Couture. I'm not on call at the moment, so if this is a medical emergency please call nine one one or find your way to the nearest emergency room. If this is personal, please leave a message."

"Donovan… uh." I turn away from the bedroom and lower my voice. "I need you to call me. Indie is here and she needs to talk with you." I hesitate. I have a lot more to say to this guy, but… probably not the best time to get into all *that.* So I just end the call.

"He didn't pick up?"

I spin around and see Indie standing in the hallway. Leaning against the wall like she was listening.

She's already dressed. The clothes are far too big for her. But she absently ties a knot in the extra length of the t-shirt and cinches it tight until her belly is showing above the folded-over waistband of the pants. The elastic around the ankles has been slipped up to her knees and the overall effect of all these alterations is one of familiarity.

Indie, age sixteen. Happy, seemingly well-adjusted teenager. God. I wish I could go back in time and do it all again.

"No. But he'll call back. Don't worry. Are you hungry?"

She sighs again. This time loudly. "Sure."

"Go sit down. I'll warm up some pizza for you."

"You don't have to feed me like a kid, McKay. I'm not your responsibility anymore."

"You're always gonna be my responsibility, Indie."

She goes into the kitchen, opens the fridge, and helps herself to a Ziploc bag of leftover pizza. Doesn't heat it up, or even bother to get a plate. Just takes the whole baggie over to the couch and flops down. Two seconds later she's shoving cold pizza in her mouth and smiling at me.

She thrusts the baggie in my direction. "Want some?"

"Nah." I walk over to the chair opposite her and sink into it. Rest my elbow on the arm and prop my head up with my hand as I watch her eat. "I went out to eat earlier."

"I know." She chews. "I saw you." Then she tugs at her t-shirt and says, "You ate here. Burger, well done. And fried pickles on the side. That shit will kill you, ya know. Is Babette your special friend?"

I can't tell if she's joking, or jealous, or angry. "Did you *see* Babette?"

"I didn't get anyone's names, if that's what you're asking." And when she says this her acquired Southern accent is more pronounced.

"She's like eighty-seven years old."

"So you're not into her?" She says this around a mouthful of pizza, trying to hide her smile.

Joking then.

"No. I'm not."

"Good to know. God, I'm so hungry. When was the last time I ate?"

"How long have you been watching me?"

"Why? Does it make you nervous?"

"No," I lie. "Just asking."

"Hmmm." She chews. "About ten days?"

Ten. Fucking. Days. She's been stalking me for ten days and I never saw a thing.

"I'm damn good at my job." Her words echo my thoughts.

"I know. You learned from the best, right?"

"Past your prime now, old man."

"Don't underestimate me, Indie."

"I'm joking. God. Why are you looking at me like that?"

"Like what?"

"Like you think I'm hiding a shank in my sweatpants."

"Where did you put the gun?"

"Somewhere safe. Don't worry. Why? You got kids or something?"

"Do *you* think I have kids?"

She stuffs more pizza in her mouth as her answer.

My phone rings on the table and I'm way too happy to hear that sound, because I jump up and cross the room before it gets to the end of the Ramones ringtone. I tab accept and say, "Hey. Thanks for calling me back."

"Put it on speaker," Indie calls from the couch. "I want to hear everything."

I turn away from her, ignoring her request. "I need you, Donovan. *Now*. How soon can you get here?"

"Hi, Donovan!"

"He says hi," I tell Indie back. Even though Donovan hasn't said a fucking word yet. Not even hello. A few beats of silence on the other end of the phone. "Donovan? You there?"

"I'm here."

"I need you."

"I... I can't get away right now."

"You're not on call. Your fucking message said so. I. Need. You. *Now.*"

"It's a four-hour flight. And it's already pretty late to make it there tonight."

"Three and a half. And take your fucking jet."

"Three and three quarters," Indie calls out. She does not miss anything, does she? And why this surprises me, I don't know. Because I'm the one who trained her to be that way.

"She sounds fine."

"She's *not* fine. She's pissed off at Adam because she thinks he—"

"He took Nate! He has him, Donovan. I know it. And I'm sick of this shit! It ends now. He can't get away with this again. Do you hear me?"

"I'm on my way." The call drops.

I turn back to Indie. "He's on his way."

"Good."

"You knew he was in LA."

"What?"

"Earlier you said you went to his house. His old house. But you knew he was in LA. So you went to some old house in LA?"

"Oh." She thinks about this for a moment. "I guess I did. I… must've forgotten."

I don't push her any further. There's no point. Donovan is on his way.

"Are you tired?" I study the look on her face. It's one of confusion. She's thinking about my comment. "Do you wanna sleep, Indie? Donovan won't be here for a while."

"Will you sleep with me?"

I shake my head but don't state the rejection outright.

"Why not?"

"Just… it's not appropriate. We've been over this a million times."

She gets up from the couch and walks towards me with a sly smirk on her face. I back up instinctively, but bump into the table. And there's no easy way to get away from her without it looking obvious. So I stay there and wait until she's right in front of me, her head tilted up to mine, her fingers playing with the fabric of my t-shirt until she's got it bunched up in her fists just under my arms.

"Do I make you nervous?"

I nod. "Yeah." Then I take both her hands and remove her grip from my shirt. "And you know why. So knock it off."

She smiles at me, then turns and walks back to the couch to grab another piece of pizza. "Your excuses don't hold water anymore, McKay."

"They're not excuses."

"You don't love me, then?"

"You know I love you."

"Just… not like that."

"Indie…" I close my eyes and rub my hand over them.

"What? You've been selling me this same line of bullshit since I was seventeen."

"Because you were *seventeen.* And I was…"

"You're not my father. And you're not my brother, either."

"It's just not right."

"Who cares? If we love each other."

That's not even what I mean. But I can't explain that to her. At least… not until Donovan gets here.

I got over the age difference between us a long time ago. And I do love her. I would like nothing more than to take her to bed and hold her all fucking night long.

Just… not when she's like this.

It's not right.

And the whole thing between us—all of us. It's very fucking complicated. Adam wants one thing, I want another, and Donovan? Well, I have no clue what that guy wants. But somehow I doubt it's anything like what Adam wants, and that's the only part of this that matters.

"Do you want me to go?"

"No. Don't be silly. I don't want you to go."

"Why, though? Why do you want me here? If you're not going to let me touch you."

"Because… I missed you. I'm glad you're here. I really am. But I think you should talk to Donovan before we…"

"We fuck?"

"No." And then I just have to laugh. God. Why is this girl so hard?

"Before we what? Tell me what you're thinking."

"Before we… reconnect. You know? It's been four years. I thought you were dead. I have spent the last four fucking years wondering where you were, what you were doing, and if you needed help. And you know what?"

"What?"

"I'm pissed at you. Like… a lot. Super. Fucking. Angry with you. You just walk out? Never come back? What the actual *fuck*, Indie?"

She pulls her knees up to her chest. Gives herself another hug.

And now I regret my outburst. Because she didn't really do that. Not consciously. So it's not her fault. And even though I did think she was dead, and I have been beating myself up for four fucking years because I didn't realize how close she was to the edge, I was not, nor have I ever been, *angry* with her.

In my mind there is nothing about India Anna Accorsi I would change.

And that's a problem.

I should want all the things about her to be different.

And I don't.

I love her just the way she is.

And that's… wrong.

"I'm sorry."

God. I hate this. I fuckin' hate it. "You don't need to say sorry, OK? Everything is fine."

Or it will be. When Donovan gets here.

"So where's Adam? You really don't talk to him?"

"I do. Every once in a while."

"He doesn't live at Old Home anymore."

I picture our old house on the river and a stab of regret and sadness fills me up. "You went out there?" I try to imagine her back in that house. Or even just walking around the grounds. What was she thinking?

"I did. But it was all locked up and I didn't feel like breaking in. When was the last time you went out there?"

I haven't been out to the old house since… well, since shit went sideways and Indie took off. But this is definitely an off-limits subject with Donovan still at least four or five hours away.

Because everything went wrong that day. Everything. And when it was all said and done, I came here to my shop and I don't think I left for a month.

I don't even think I ate for a week. And then, when I did, I just called for delivery.

I played that day over and over in my head for years. That's not even an exaggeration, either. I was broken after that. Never the same.

And yeah, Indie was too. We all were.

But I just felt like… like I *failed her.* And I get it. There was no way to prepare her for a day like that, but I could've handled it better.

I was the one who fucked up that day. Not Adam. Not Donovan. Not even Indie. None of it was her fault. We were supposed to protect her. Keep her safe. And she was not safe that day.

"I miss it though."

I look over at Indie, sitting there on the couch, hugging herself. "Me too."

"My favorite room was the atrium. Didn't you just love the atrium, McKay?"

I smile at her. "I did. Especially when you had birds in there."

We both laugh.

"God, that drove Adam crazy, didn't it?"

I nod at her.

"It wasn't my fault. They just flew in the door."

"Right." I laugh again.

"Seriously. I'm not like some bird whisperer."

"Indie. Come on. You're trying to tell me that a great blue heron just flew in the front door?"

"Maybe not that one. But he liked the pond."

He liked the pond. God, I love her.

"If Adam didn't want wetland birds inside his stupid house, he shouldn't have a stupid pond in his foyer atrium."

"I'm pretty sure they call that a *water feature.* Rich people like that kind of shit indoors."

She snort-laughs. "Same thing. Anyway. You loved the birds too."

I just look at her. I love it when she smiles. And it's been so long. I mean, I have pictured this day in my mind for four years and it never happened like this. I thought there would be tears. Lots of crying. From all of us. But mostly her.

I didn't picture her smiling and laughing. Not after everything that happened that day.

But that's the gift of trauma-induced amnesia, right?

All those bad things just get wiped clean and you're left with nothing but the good ones.

All the days that ended just fine.

The house and the birds.

The marsh and the river.

The boy next door.

That's all she remembers now.

And there's a part of me that wants to keep her like this.

Innocent, and happy, and unaware of what really happened on her twentieth birthday.

But I really do love her. I love her way too much. I want her way too much. And if we ever have a real chance at becoming what we always knew we were meant to be… then she needs to know.

She *has* to remember.

And then she will leave us again.

I will lose her.

She will run away and this time she might not ever come back.

She gets up from the couch, crosses the room, and stands in front of me. I look up at her and wait.

"Can I sit with you, McKay?"

I know what the right answer is. The same answer it's always been—except for that one time on her twentieth birthday.

But I say, "Sure," anyway.

Because I don't want to lose her again. Not tonight. Not tomorrow. Not ever.

She settles in my lap, one arm around my neck, her legs sideways over my thighs, her head tucked under my chin. And when I wrap my arms around her, I know there's no going back. Once I cross this line for real, all this pretending is over.

I just don't care anymore.

I want her.

My hand slips down to her thigh and I begin rubbing it.

Indie turns her cheek and a chill runs through my whole body when her lips touch my neck.

I sigh.

"You were always my favorite, you know that, McKay?"

"Lies," I whisper back. "You always loved Donovan more."

"That's not true. It was always you. But you were so… so… *focused*."

"Focused?" I smile.

"Yeah. On doing the right thing."

I lean back a little and push her away. "What the hell are you talking about? The right thing? I can't think of a single fucking time in my entire life when I did the right thing."

"You did the right thing with me all the time. That's why we're not together."

I'm not sure if she's joking right now or this is just her unreliable memory talking. "Indie. Come on. I taught you how to kill people. In no way, shape, or form did I ever do the right thing with you."

"You didn't want to fuck me."

"Stop that. Just… stop that."

"It's true. You drove me to Nathan St. James. He was all I had."

"That's funny. He was all you wanted. He was your number one. Not me."

"When I was little." She snuggles up against me again. "But not later. It was always you. And you just… never wanted me."

I want to tell her everything. That she is everything to me. I want to make all these years fit together inside her head and make sense for once. I want to force her to open up and understand all the reasons why I did the things I've done.

"And when I left you never even looked for me. I could've used you, ya know."

"Literally? Used me?"

"Not just literally. All the ways. But yes. There were so many times that I needed you, McKay. And you weren't there."

"That's because I was *here*. And you knew I was here. And you didn't come back to me."

She relaxes against my chest and breathes for a few moments. "I needed you to come back to *me*."

"I wasn't the one who left."

She sits up in my lap. "Really?" Her eyes are locked with mine. But then she frowns and a stab of panic washes through my body. I don't want her to remember. I don't want her to know any of the shit she's forgotten.

I reach up and grab her hair. Pull her face to mine. And I kiss this creeping beautiful girl the way she should be kissed.

I kiss her the way a man kisses a woman he's spent several lifetimes dreaming about.

I kiss her the way a woman made of messy, lovely darkness needs to be kissed on a stormy night.

I kiss her like a man who accepts all the pieces of gorgeous misery locked inside her heart.

I kiss away all her pretty little nightmares until there is nothing left but emptiness.

And then I just… fill her up again.

She moans into my mouth. Her tongue searching for things she'll never be able to find. Her soft lips lingering on mine like this connection is the last thing she'll ever feel before she dies.

"Take me into your bedroom, McKay. Before you change your mind."

I wrap my arms around her and stand up. Her legs immediately grip my waist and I slip my hands under her ass and hold her as I walk down the hall and into the dark bedroom.

I don't flip on the lights. We need the darkness tonight. We might need the darkness every night after this too.

I lie her down on the bed and paw at the waistline of her sweats, jerking them down her legs. And when the back of my hand touches the soft, young skin of her thigh my cock swells inside my jeans.

I toss her sweats aside and she reaches for me. But I step out of her reach and just bend her knees—slowly hiking them up to her chest as I lower myself to the floor and press my mouth against her pussy. Wet, and warm, and waiting for me.

All these years. Waiting for me.

My hands reach around her legs. I tug her forward to the edge of the bed and then my thumbs begin caressing small circles over her hipbones.

She arches her back and moans, her fingers digging into my hair, clutching at it like she's falling and I'm the only thing that can save her.

I wish that were true. I want to be the one who saves her.

But I can't change that. Only she can. I lick her. Flick my tongue against her clit until she lets go of my hair, slips her fingers up my short sleeves, and begins clawing at my shoulders with her fingernails.

I shove her shirt up her stomach, reaching for her tight, round breasts, then roll her nipples between my thumb and forefinger.

She moans. "I want you inside me, McKay. Now, *please*."

And my heart hurts for her.

For all the bad things coming, even though they've already happened.

For all the tears she will cry, even though she sobbed herself dry years ago.

For all the memories that will be ruined, even though they haven't even been made yet, and never will now.

I pull away from her, unbuttoning and unzipping my jeans as I stand. I kick my jeans off, push her up towards the top of the bed, and then ease my body between her open legs. The top of my cock pushes against her opening as I brace myself on the mattress with open palms and lean down to kiss her mouth again.

I want to give her all the breath she will need to get through the pain. And when I enter her, she gasps into my mouth, giving it back.

"Take it," I tell her. "Take all of it and all of me, Indie. It's yours. I'm yours."

It's a slow fuck. And nothing about this time is anything like the last time.

There is no rush. There is no urgency. There is no one else. Watching, or waiting, or second-guessing what we're doing.

It's just us.

And everything about that feels wrong.

But we don't care.

Because nothing about this has ever been right.

CHAPTER SIX

Indie

I have gone through two journals now and I have a feeling that I will go through dozens more before I'm done. Donovan always said it was a good idea to journal. He says getting things down on paper helps you see things clearly.

Sometimes I think seeing clearly is overrated. Most of the time, really. Show me a person who prefers sharp clarity over a soft hazy fog and I'll show you one cold, mean bitch.

That's how they are.

I know. I was one of them once upon a time.

Back when I first came to Old Home I was all about seeing things clearly. *Face the facts, Indie. The truth shall set you free.*

But there's another saying that many people forget about.

Ignorance is bliss.

Like Adam and Eve before they ate that stupid fruit.

Or was it just Eve who ate that apple? I can't really remember. Never was much of a biblical girl. And even though Adam dragged me to church every fuckin' Sunday, I didn't pay attention. I just counted things. Ladies' hats. Stained-glass windows. The number of birds in those windows. Not sure why there's always a damn bird up in that glass, but the church we went to near Old Home had seventeen birds up there. I always thought that was a little excessive.

They were all doves too. Which are kinda boring, if you ask me. Doves. What do doves do but fly through the air and remind you of Jesus?

They don't scare people like snakes do. And who wants to think about Jesus when you're killing people?

They should put a big, black raven up in those windows. Now that's a bird that demands attention.

Not sure it matters who ate that apple though. That's my point. It's all just good and evil in the end and you just take your pick and live with it.

That's why I'm not afraid of snakes.

They come bearing gifts, don't they? Apples. Adams. It's all one and the same.

Adam was always big on telling truths, though. God, how that used to drive me crazy.

"Indie," he'd say. And he always said my name like it was a curse word. "Indie. You tell lies like a bee gathers honey." By which he meant, like it was my job.

I wasn't a liar though. That's the part he never understood. I was just a storyteller. And who doesn't like a good story?

Everyone does. I don't care who you are. If you tell a good one nobody is gonna complain about your story being lies. That's the whole point of stories. It's fake. That way you can make your story say anything you want and no one ever gets hurt.

All the stories are fake. Even the true ones.

That's a lesson I learned early.

But I should clarify this right here, right now. Nathan St. James was neither a storyteller nor a liar.

He saw facts. But you know why this was OK with me? Two reasons, really. One. His real-life truth was better than anyone's fake story.

Even mine. Even my true one.

And I think I already made it clear that I can tell a fuckin' story.

Two. Nathan St. James also peppered his real-life true facts with the prettiest words you ever heard.

For instance. Nate would say, "Indie, you see that tree over there with the green velvet trunk? That velvet only grows on the north side of the tree because that star up there in the sky is a ball of fiery heat and velvet doesn't like heat. So that's how you know where north is."

And I would look and look for green velvet and a star in the blue sky of daylight and only see moss and the stupid old sun. And of course, I knew that he was talking about the tree with the moss and the fuckin' sun in the sky, but that word 'velvet' and the way he saw past the surface of the sun and peeked inside it… it just changed everything about the way I saw moss on a tree from then on.

He was like that with all the things in the woods. He's the one who told me that his little brick house was the color of the mud in the Pearl River when the water was low.

I didn't make that up on my own. It was all Nate.

In Nate's mind's eye the world was pretty pictures made up of soft, hazy words.

Who needs clarity when you can have Nathan St. James's outlook on life?

After I went home—rather, after Donovan came and called me home from the woods those first weeks I was living at Old Home—Nathan and I got tight. We even did the whole blood brothers thing, even though I was not his brother, nor was I a boy. It's just what you call it and I am not easily offended by labels like that. But we did that blood brother thing. I always carried a knife and so did Nate. But his was a folding knife handy for things like cutting fishing line and peeling apples. And mine was a hunting knife handy for things like huntin'. Animals. People. Whatever.

But we used my knife for our little ritual. One slice across our palms. It hurt too, because at this point in time McKay had already showed me how to keep that knife sharp. In fact, we actually had to get stitched up that same afternoon because it might've went just a little too deep.

Adam was furious about that because he had to go over to Nate's house and explain to his grandfather why McKay had to stitch up Nate's palm and it was now covered in white bandages.

I heard Adam yelling about that in the nighttime. He was telling McKay, "It's your job! It's your job!" Meaning it was McKay's job to keep me in line and 'in line' did specifically *not mean* letting me carve up the neighbor boy with a knife I had used to kill someone two weekends ago.

Of course, I was not in the same room when this yelling took place. I was upstairs sitting on the top step, spying on them. But if I had been in the same room, I would've said that I wanted to do this ritual two years ago, before I was killing people with that knife. But Nate was too chicken. So… sometimes things just shake out that way and it's nobody's fault.

Nate was grounded for two months after that. Not from going outside or anything. Just me. His grandfather said I was a bad influence. And what kind of little girl lives with two grown men who are not her brothers, or fathers, or uncles and doesn't even go to school?

Me.

That was the answer. Just me.

But Nate and I were a special thing. And he did live just across the duck lake. And there were no other neighbors. There was a nature preserve on the other side of the river and their little brick house used to be some kind of carriage house on Adam's family land. Which there was plenty of. And so the nearest neighbors were almost a mile away.

Who else was Nate gonna play with if not me?

So. Two months. We took our punishment and then when it was over, and our hands were all sealed up with new skin and matching fancy white scars, we got back to the business of being best friends.

Nate did not know what I did on the side.

He probably guessed, though. I mean, we were always shooting guns off in the woods. McKay had set up a shootin' range in this gulley down on the north side of the property. And he took me out there almost every day. And Nate would mostly watch. His grandfather threw a fit about our shooting habits. But sometimes McKay would let Nate shoot too. He wasn't as good at it as I was, but that's because he grew up with a proper grandfather who didn't let him shoot nothing, not even cans, until he was twelve. Then when he was twelve his grandfather used to take him turkey hunting.

So after that happened McKay said he could shoot on our range. And Nate got to watch me shoot. And he could tell right away that my shootin' skills were something special.

That was all McKay. He made me sharp like that.

But I tell you what Nathan St. James was very good at—besides fishing. He could out-fish me any day of the week.

He was very good at the martial arts McKay and I did.

I started learning that the day after my runaway trip into the woods when I first arrived. And Nate saw that happening too. Because by the time I decided to not be a runaway anymore, Nate and I were already well into our friendship.

And McKay was tired of pulling his punches. So he said I should learn with Nate. And that's what we did.

Nate kicked my ass in martial arts nearly every day. I was good, don't get me wrong. But it's like Nate saw into my soul when we were sparring. He knew what I was gonna do before I did it. Every time.

Back then McKay didn't mind Nathan so much. Nate had grown a little so he was a few inches taller than me by then. So McKay had to teach me how to take down people bigger than me. Which was everyone. And I had just started doing jobs—real jobs—the year before when I was thirteen.

I had started the jobs when I was twelve, but they weren't real dangerous jobs. Just thieving, mostly.

But anyway. Nate was just good at martial arts. I loved that about him.

On the subject of school and Nate's grandfather's opinion on the matter… that's a sore one with me. Because I *did* go to school, I just didn't go anywhere but the back room of Old Home for my lessons.

At least, not until I was fifteen. Then I did go away to school. Just a semester though, because I had to kill a senator's daughter. Then I had to stay all fuckin' semester to make it look all natural. Then I went home at Christmas and never went back to that school.

I did that a couple more times over the years when certain things needed to be cleaned up for whatever reason.

So I did actually go to some very fine schools. And I could speak three languages because Adam was in charge of languages and he knew five. We would go months of just speaking Spanish. I even had to speak Spanish with Nathan during immersion training with Adam. But Nate didn't care. He just pretended to understand me and made up whole conversations in his fake Spanish.

And we would laugh about it.

He was so funny.

We would just laugh, and laugh, and laugh.

One day we were watching a movie at Old Home. And it was called *Forrest Gump*. And I swear, it's like those movie people were spying on me and Nate. And I, of course, was Jenny. And he was Forrest. Even though Nate didn't have leg braces. He was a runner. And when Forrest got up and ran Nate cheered. Every time. Every. Single. Time. He just cheered for him.

So we were peas and carrots like that. I even looked like her. I even played outside in a white dress like her. But Adam got mad because every time I came home, I was muddy and he said, "I'm not gonna buy you white dresses anymore if you're just gonna wallow in the mud like a wild hog."

So I stopped wearing the white dresses in the woods and only wore them to church after that.

After that first time we watched the movie I started talkin' like Jenny because I wanted to be her. Not big her. Little her. Even though I didn't want God to make me a bird and fly far, far away.

I loved my life on Old Home Island.

I loved McKay, and I loved Adam, and I loved Donovan when he was there.

But I loved Nate the most.

And he loved me. So much.

But I'm not gonna write about that.

Not yet.

All that love stuff came later. After we were grown and we understood each other better. After I told him what I really did. And why I really lived with Adam and McKay. And who Donovan was and why Nate wasn't allowed to come around when Donovan was there.

And then he told me things too.

Surprising things. Secret things.

That's when I fell in Love.

Before that it was just lower-case love. Not capital-L love.

What were Adam, and McKay, and Donovan doing during all this?

Adam was gone a lot. He would leave for meetings with the Company people. They would tell him what needed to be done. Then he would come home and we'd talk about it. And he'd tell me his plan, and I would give notes on his plan. Then, sometimes, I would come up with an alternative plan. But not always. Adam was pretty good at planning. Then we would rehearse the job. Over, and over, and over.

This was McKay's doing. He wanted everything to be set up perfect. So we would do a lot on the computer. We would do a virtual walk through the neighborhood with Google Streetview. And often times McKay would go to the job site and take pictures of the target and get other details. Then he would come back and we'd go through it again.

It was like this a lot in the beginning. Adam said, "I didn't pay three million dollars just to get you killed before you can even drive a damn car." Which was his way of saying, *I love you, Indie. And I don't want you to die. And even though I really did pay three million dollars for you, I really just want to make sure you come home with me when the job is done because Donovan and McKay will not be happy if I get you killed.*

So we did a lot of that. But even when Adam was not meeting with the Company he was in New Orleans with his sometimes-girlfriend, Misha. I met Misha. She was around long before I was. Though I would not say they were steady. Not the way Nate and I were steady, for instance.

At least *Adam* was not steady. He was with other girls all the time. Not girlfriends. Like Misha *kind of* was. But just… girls. No-name girls. Short-term girls. And he always lied to them. He never told them his real name. And he said I was his sister and we were visiting such-and-such place for such-and-such reason.

But Misha thought they were steady. I'm pretty sure.

McKay's trips were short and he did not do girls. Not ever. At least, I never ever saw him with a girl.

But what he did in his personal time was not something he ever shared with me. And he didn't leave the house much. Not nearly as much as Adam did. He was almost always home with me. Tucking me in bed. Harping on me to brush my teeth and eat my vegetables. Taking me to the orthodontist. Teaching me math and science and shooting and martial arts.

And he would run a bath for me in my bedroom bathtub every night. With bubbles. He bought cheap bubbles by the gallon at the dollar store. The kind that only last a few minutes and then start to fizzle out. But he said those bubbles didn't make me feel dirty when I got out the way the expensive ones did. And he was kinda right about that.

Donovan, of course, was almost never around. He came every single month for the first year. But after that it was just whenever Adam called him in. Which meant that Donovan was around a lot more instead of a lot less.

Not because I was being bad either.

Adam just had a rule that after every job I had to have a session with Donovan before I could go play with Nate again.

It didn't make sense at first. But later it did.

Because I would come home from the jobs and feel… funky. McKay would say, "You're in a funk, Indie. And you have to talk yourself out of it."

So that's when Donovan came. And he would talk me out of it.

But sometimes…sometimes even when he left that funk was still there. So I would go outside—because I would have the all-clear from all three of them—and I would find Nate, and he would take one look at me and take my hand, and lead me into the woods. To this little grass meadow. And in the summer, he would make me flower crowns. In the winter he would make me twig crowns. And he would tell his stories.

"Indie, do you see that bird up there on that branch? That's a violet eggplant-headfluff whistler."

I'm making that part up. But he would know what the bird was and he would change its hard, factual name into something hazy and soft. He would change my whole life into something hazy and soft.

He would take me out of this world and into his story.

He would empty me out. Just… spill me out all over the place.

And then he would fill me back up.

CHAPTER SEVEN

adam

THIRTEEN YEARS AGO

Indie was dressed the way I asked and she came with a little pink roller suitcase. Plus a sweater and a journal. She was waiting for me down by the dock, just standing there in the moonlight looking like a little girl should look.

Donovan came with me when we left so he could talk to her. I gave them their privacy, so I don't know what was said, I just watched them from afar. But when he was done, he came up to me and made a big deal about the journal.

"Don't take it away. She needs to write."

"Why?"

"It helps her." He turned me around so she couldn't read our lips while we talked. "You know what she is, right?"

"I know."

"She's not like the others. She's like you, Adam."

"I get it."

"I hope you do. Because I like her. A lot. I'm invested in her and I want her to make it."

"Define 'make it.'" I laughed. Because she was what she was. Her future involved lots of danger, and pain, and stress. Even if we did manage to break this whole shit show up into a million pieces, what did he think she was gonna do when that happened? *If* that happened?

Go to college? Get married to someone normal? Have a couple kids?

Her future was my present. Literally. *Look at me, Indie. Good and hard, little girl. This is as good as it gets. There is no version of your life that includes the words normal, or easy, or predictable, or safe.*

Donovan's face got serious. He was fifteen so it wasn't serious the way McKay's face might look serious. But I could tell he was not fucking around. "I want her to live."

"Everyone dies, Donovan. We're born waiting to die. That's just a part of life."

"OK. Let me be specific then. I want her to grow old."

"That's a nice thought."

"Make sure it happens."

"Whatever," I said. Then I walked away from him. Because I paid three million dollars for the girl. She was mine now. Not his.

He called out after us. "I'll see you soon, Indie."

Then we left.

The trip home was pretty uneventful. There was a yacht, there was a plane, there was car. Then we were driving through the gates of Old Home and McKay was waiting on the porch for us.

Indie did not say one fucking word to me. She wrote in her journal a few times. She sat still. She slept and ate when I told her to. She was actually pretty obedient.

But once we got home all that changed.

I won't lie and say it was easy. She is just not an easy girl. But after we got used to each other—and I did have to call Donovan to sort her out that first month—she settled in.

At least she started talking to us.

Now, one year later, I realize that it was Nathan St. James who really kept her in line. Donovan comes once a month to read her journal and talk with her. She doesn't let McKay and me read it, but I don't need to read it. I get the recordings of her talks with Donovan and he discusses the journal pages with her. So I know what's in there.

Nothing special, really. It's mostly all about Nate.

Which is fine. He's a kid. She's a kid. I don't mind that relationship. But I do worry about them now that she's getting older. Because I see where this is going.

Even though Nate goes to public school in the nearby town, he never brings any friends home. At least not that I've seen. And I've told Indie many times that if he does, she cannot play with him on those days. So maybe she warned him about this and that's why that kid has no other friends.

Or… maybe he just loves her the way she loves him?

That's the part I worry about.

This boy will be the first one to kiss her. He will be the one she falls in love with. He might break her heart, she might break his, but it's clearly one of those love stories you read about in books.

And I don't know how I feel about that.

No, that's a lie. I know exactly how I feel about that.

She's mine. That's how I feel. That girl is mine. He can be her friend, but that's it. That's all he can be. So today I'm gonna have a talk with that kid.

It's Sunday, so everyone around here goes to church. It's just something people do. I'm not particularly religious, but I was raised the same way and I'd like to think that church gave me another perspective on the jobs I have to do and the life I have to live.

I know Nate goes to church with his grandfather and Indie goes with me. But I also know that Nate's grandfather is sick so he's staying home today.

I'm staying home too. And Indie is going to church with McKay.

I make sure Indie knows I'm staying home because I have a meeting. Which isn't a lie. I do. It's just with the boy next door instead of some Company fucks.

I watch McKay's black truck disappear down the driveway and then push through the screen door, let it slam shut behind me, and set off into the woods towards the St. James place.

It's just a little brick carriage house that used to belong to my great-grandfather. Nate's great-grandfather worked for my family back in the day and was gifted the house and a few acres around it when he retired. But there's a well-worn path that leads from here to there, and I'm traveling down it when I spy Nate out in his backyard splitting wood.

He's taller now than he was last summer when I first took notice of him. And his ax-swing has form, splitting that wood easily. He's got the ax above his head when he sees me and brings it down hard on the upended log, cracking it neatly in half.

He pounds the ax head into the dirt near his feet, wipes his brow with the back of his free hand, and leans casually on the ax handle. "What can I do for you, Mr. Boucher?"

His accent is decidedly Southern. Like mine started to be when I was his age, but which was quickly trained out of me by my father. But it has creeped back in the years since he passed.

"You can call me Adam," I say, walking up to him.

"No, sir. My grandfather would not like that too much."

I shrug with my hands. "Where is he?" Meaning his grandfather. "Indie said he was sick. I hope he's OK."

"He's fine. Just… resting today."

Which is kind of a lie. I know the old man was diagnosed with emphysema a few years back and it's hard to miss the truck that delivers oxygen tanks twice a month.

Still, it's a polite lie. So maybe it doesn't count.

"Is that why you're here?"

"No." I say it bluntly. "I'm here to talk about Indie."

"OK. What should we talk about?"

"We should talk about…" I hesitate. Because he's *twelve.* And Indie will throw a fit if she finds out I'm having this conversation with Nate. "She's a girl."

"Yes, sir."

"But she's not an ordinary girl."

"Yes, sir. I know that."

"And you should not make any plans with her."

Nate makes a look of confusion at this statement. "What kind of plans?"

"Future plans. Girlfriend plans."

Nate laughs. "No, sir. She's just my best friend. Not my girl."

"I know that, Nate. And that's because you're both still very young. But in a year or two you will feel differently. And I'd just like to head that off at the pass, if I can. Because even though Indie is a girl, she's not girlfriend material."

I get another confused look from Nathan St. James so I decide to just spell it out. "Do not kiss my…" I pause, trying to come up with a term that adequately explains what Indie is to me. "Do not kiss my Indie. Do not hold her hand. Do not fall in love with her. Do not plan a future with her. She is not that kind of girl."

Nate just stares at me, face blank, stance relaxed. Then he says, "Can I fish with her?"

"Yes."

"How about swim?"

"If you're wearing clothes."

He laughs and looks away. "Of course we wear clothes."

"You can do all the things you two do. Just keep it… innocent." It's a bad word choice. Something a man would understand but not a boy. "Does that make sense, Nate?"

"I think so."

"Good." I suck in a deep breath. Let it out. Decide I'm done here and turn back to the path through the woods. But then I stop and look over my shoulder. "Don't tell her I was here."

"Yes, sir."

And then I walk home, thinking it was a dumb idea to have that talk with Nate. Because love doesn't have rules and these two passed the point of no return the moment they met last summer.

They will love each other no matter what I say or do to dissuade them.

And, I'm sorry to say, that's very bad news for Nathan St. James.

When Indie and McKay get back from church she changes her clothes and disappears into the woods and I take McKay aside for a quick chat. "Start her real training tomorrow."

He gives me a thoughtful look. "You sure?"

"I'm sure. I want her on the job in six months."

"I dunno." McKay rubs a hand over his clean-shaven jaw as he considers this. "Six months? Why?"

"Because I'm tired of working alone and that's the whole reason I bought her."

Then I turn my back to him and go inside to my office, close the door, and get back to the business at hand.

Core McKay and I grew up together. He's from Alaska, not Louisiana. His father was an arms dealer for the Company up there and normally that would mean that one day he would take his father's place. Keep the family business going.

But McKay had two older brothers so his future wasn't written in stone. My father and I were up in Alaska when I was ten and McKay was nine to coordinate with another Untouchable Company man about a job that was coming up in the Ukraine.

And I took to McKay. He was as tall as me, even though I was older. And we kinda resembled each other with the light hair, and the light eyes, and the build of our lean bodies back then. So my father bought him for me and he came home with us.

Not to Old Home. Back then this mansion was nothing but an old mess and while we did spend summers there before McKay came, afterward we lived in New Orleans in a big old house in the French Quarter. I didn't go to school, I had private tutors. This was common among the Untouchable families. So when McKay came to live with us I suddenly had a best friend and a classmate, when every day prior to that one, I had been alone.

This is how I know that Nate and Indie will be bonded forever.

She is who she is. Lonely, and sad, and tough, and eager for a friend.

Just like me.

And Nate, though not Company the way McKay was, is just like him.

Desperate for more.

And even though Nathan St. James is only twelve years old, and even though he doesn't know it yet, living next door to Indie Anna Accorsi will be the highlight of his life.

People don't walk away from that.

Just ask McKay.

And this bond is something special.

Just ask me.

I love McKay. I would die for McKay.

If McKay walks away, I go with him.

My father bought McKay for me back when he was nine for one reason only. To *be* me. To take my place. We were never going to be friends.

At least… that was my understanding.

But even the best laid plans have bumps.

Once it was clear that McKay would be staying with me, my father and I sat down for a very serious conversation about what that meant.

"He is yours now, Adam," my father said. "Forever. In every way. And if there is a thing in this world that threatens to break you apart, you need to eliminate that thing. He is the only person in this whole wide world that you owe loyalty to. His loyalty was bought so yours must be given freely."

I guess it makes sense. I get the feeling that McKay was holding a few secrets for my father. I get the feeling that my father was trying to protect his own ass, as well as mine.

But I never had that kind of conversation with Indie when I bought her. I guess I didn't think this pledge of loyalty needed to be stated outright the way my father did.

There might've been a natural tendency for McKay and I to cultivate an adversarial attitude towards one another. It would've been natural, given the circumstances.

But Indie and I never did have that kind of relationship.

Of course she has my loyalty. I'm on her side. Always.

But is she on mine?

And how does McKay fit in?

There's no rulebook that spells all this out.

For now, I guess it's fine. We're all on the same side.

But if McKay owes me, and I owe him, and Indie owes me, and I owe her—then what happens when we're not on the same side anymore?

"Indie Anna!" McKay is yelling from the bottom of the stairs. He shoots me an apologetic look. "Sorry. I told her to be ready. She said she was."

"She's a storyteller, McKay. When are you gonna understand that?"

He points his finger at me. "Do not yell at her. I'm telling you, she'll be fine as long as you keep your cool. But if you yell at her, she'll shut down and stop listening. So no matter what happens, you tell her it's all fine."

"What if it's not fine?"

"You lie to her, Adam. Jesus Christ. You're the best liar I know. I'm sure you'll come up with something."

"I can hear you, ya know."

McKay and I look up and find Indie at the top of the stairs.

"I'm not a kid, for fuck's sake."

"You are a damn kid," I growl at her. "And don't you cuss in front of me. Now get your ass down here and put your shit in the truck."

Indie opens her mouth to talk back, but McKay beats her to it. "Do as you're told, Indie. We're not playing. It's time to work."

She walks down the stairs dragging her pink roller-case behind her so that it bumps with a loud thud on each and every step. She simultaneously glares at me and pouts at McKay. Which is a hard thing to pull off, but Indie never was afraid of doing something hard.

I roll my eyes at McKay, then walk to the door and give them a minute for any last words.

Just as I'm pushing through the screen I hear McKay whisper to her. "Be good. And do as you're told. And if Adam yells at you, you have to ignore it. He's just…"

But that's all I hear because I'm outside now, hopping down the porch steps.

I get in the truck and start the engine. It takes Indie a couple more minutes before she joins me. McKay puts her small suitcase in the back cab, then buckles her in to her seatbelt in the front next me.

He gives me a little two-finger salute. "See ya on the other side."

Then he closes Indie's door, taps the side of the truck with his hand two times, and we pull away.

Indie and I don't do much alone. I mean, without McKay. I'm the one who takes her to church. McKay doesn't really care for church. So we drive into town for that alone. But other than that we're not usually alone and at first the silence is uncomfortable.

I don't know how to talk to her. I didn't have sisters growing up. Just McKay. And I don't really talk to the girls I'm with. Not even Misha. We just screw around and she cooks for me sometimes, but the whole reason I like Misha is because she keeps to herself. The sex is the only thing between us and she's happy with that.

"You wanna play a game?"

I look over at Indie when she says this. We're on a road trip because we're only going to Pensacola for this job. It's an easy one because it's Indie's first time out. All she has to do is what she's been told. If everything goes well, we'll be home tomorrow before lunch. Donovan is flying in tomorrow afternoon for her debrief, and by tomorrow evening she'll be back playing in the woods with Nate.

"What kind of game?" I ask her.

"Driving games. Nate told me all about them."

"Did you tell him what we're doing?"

"No. I told him you were taking me to see our aunt."

I chuckle. This girl can lie like nobody's business.

"I wouldn't tell him secrets like that, Adam. Do you wanna play a game or not?"

"Sure. Why not?"

"OK. This is how you do it…"

And she takes her time to explain the rules of the Slug Bug game. Which I have played before with McKay, of course. But there aren't enough Bugs on the road these days to have any fun at it. So we change the rules to include motorcycles when thirty minutes into the trip not a single punch has been slugged.

She laughs a lot and punches me hard when she spots a Bug or a motorcycle before me and I realize… I *like* her.

I would not call her a bad kid and I have always respected her, but *like* her?

Indie Anna Accorsi is not an easy girl to like.

But her smile is nice. She doesn't smile for me the way she smiles for Donovan, or even McKay when he hands out praise. But that's OK too. Because this smile is all mine.

PRESENT DAY

But by the time that job was over I realized something else too.

I loved her.

I guess that's what happens when you get used to something and then someone tries to take it away from you.

Because our trip home from Pensacola was two days later than planned and Indie Anna didn't smile a single second of that ride.

She didn't cry, either. But I could tell she wanted to.

And I did exactly what McKay told me to do if things went sideways. I did not yell. Not once. I just said, "It's fine, Indie.

It's gonna be fine," in the most soothing voice I could manage as I watched the Company doctor restrain her to the bed and fix her up.

And the game we played on the drive home was a new one called Let's Pretend *That* Didn't Happen.

Knowing what I do now, I probably wouldn't have played that game with her.

I probably would've done a lot of things differently if I had known how good she'd get at pretending shit didn't happen.

But hindsight can kiss my ass. You can't change the past.

Indie Anna Accorsi is a beautiful little mess. She is a lovely little bundle of blonde hair and blue-eyed darkness. And even though I should have all kinds of regrets about how she came to be mine and how we came to be hers, I would absolutely do it all again.

Knowing her now, I wouldn't change a thing.

Because if all those terrible things hadn't happened, she would belong to *him* right now. She would be living in that little brick house with Nathan St. James.

She would be whole, and normal, and maybe even happier.

And my heart would be shattered into tiny shards. Millions of bitty pieces.

So yeah.

I'm a selfish piece of shit.

But I want what I want.

That's the only way I can explain it.

Maybe she didn't become mine the day of the auction, but the day that asshole triggered her without my permission, she did.

She *is.*

CHAPTER EIGHT

MIND CONTROL IN CHILDREN: A CASE STUDY OF COMPANY ASSASSINS

INTERVIEW WITH INDIE, AGE 11.10

SESSION #19

INDIE: Well?

DONOVAN: Well, what?

Aren't you going to talk?

This is your chance to talk, Indie.

I know that, but you're in charge and you've been sitting there for seventy-six seconds saying nothing.

Seventy-six?

I counted.

I'm waiting for you. Adam said you stopped talking again. I didn't want to rush you. But… first. Are you OK? Do they… hurt?

I guess I'm OK. I'm still alive. And I'm not sure if they hurt. I guess when I move, they do. It stings. And I can feel the stitches pulling. But I know why we're here.

This time is no different than all the other times.

It is. Because I did the job. And it wasn't a job, Donovan. Did he tell you that?

What do you mean?

Or maybe that's not the best way to explain it. It was… it was an *inside* job.

Inside what?

The Company. He took me to a meeting with another team leader and then he told me I had to steal something from his hotel room while he kept him busy.

I'm confused. Was this the job you prepared for?

No.

So he…

Yes. And he didn't tell me that there were *two* men, not just one. And the other guy was already there when I entered the room.

Then what happened?

Then… then we fought. But he pushed me down on the ground face first and cut me. And then… then I passed out, I guess. I don't know.

…

Say something.

Sorry. I'm just thinking. How did you get away?

I *didn't* get away. Adam came. I guess. I don't know. I woke up in some creepy garage tied to a bed.

OK. Hold on. Go back. Because Adam didn't tell me any of this. He said you got hurt, but… so… can you try a little harder to remember exactly what happened in that hotel room? What did the man say when he caught you?

…

Indie?

I'm thinking.

…

Start from the beginning. When you entered the room. What do you remember?

It was dark in the room. It was bigger than I had pictured in my head. It was a suite with a bedroom and a dining area and a bar. So when I went in I hid in a corner so my eyes could adjust. I waited two minutes and then I could see in the shadows. No one was there. I was supposed to check the bedroom first.

Who told you that?

Adam did. He said look in the bedroom first. But I decided to check the bar first.

Why?

I dunno. I just wanted to check that whole room first and none of the tables had drawers so the only place to look was behind the bar on the far side of the room.

It was a real bar? Like a big bar? Not a minibar?

No. It was a bar with shelves and stuff behind it. But no alcohol on the shelves. Just glassware. But when I went around the bar to look there was a man crouched down.

What did he look like?

I don't know. I can't remember his face. But I saw him and then the next thing I knew I was holding a knife and I tried to cut him, but I couldn't.

Hold on. Did Adam give you a knife?

No. It wasn't my knife. It was a small knife from the bar, I think.

Like a paring knife?

Yeah. Maybe.

And then what happened?

I don't know. I was bleeding. Suddenly there was blood everywhere. All over me. And I was getting dizzy. Then I woke in that garage tied to the bed.

You don't remember anything else? Did the man say anything to you?

I don't know. I can't remember.

OK, Indie. That's all for now. We're done talking about it.

But… what happened?

I'm going to talk to Adam when we're done here and find out what he saw.

Will you tell me what he saw?

I don't know yet. If I think it will help you, I will tell you. But it probably won't be helpful and then it's just better you don't know. It's better that you move on. Try to forget about it. Your wrists will heal. You'll be fine.

But what if they come back for me? What if they come here, Donovan?

They won't. But I promise, Adam will take care of them if he hasn't already. Now… aren't you curious about what I've been up to?

Yes. Do you have a girlfriend yet?

Kind of.

Is she in school with you?

Yeah. We're in the same program. We just study together because she's like ten years older than me.

Oh, that sucks. I feel sorry for you. It must be hard to be so much younger than everyone.

Well, I guess you would know. You and I are the same in that regard. Is it hard living here with Adam and McKay? Do you wish you were older? Or they were younger?

No. Because I have Nate. And I know he's worried about me. I told him I would be back two days ago and that I would see him as soon as you left.

Just tell him I was late. And your trip took longer than you thought. But you have to wear long sleeves. You can't let him see your wrists. He will ask a lot of questions and maybe even tell someone because he's worried about you. But trust me, Indie. Telling people about this is not the answer. You are safe here with Adam and McKay. No one can hurt you when you're with them.

I know that. I won't tell him.

Good. Then unless you have more questions for me, we're done and you can go outside.

Really?

Yup. I have to leave tonight because I have class tomorrow and I can't miss another day. But I'll be back on the weekend.

Why so soon?

I just want to make sure you're OK. We're all worried about you.

You don't have to worry about me, Donovan. I'm fine.

I know you are. Now go. I'm sure Nate is dying to see you. But don't forget to change into long sleeves… And Indie?

Yes?

Next time Adam tells you to check the bedroom first, you need to check the bedroom first.

Transcript note: The recorder was left running for my conversation with Adam. And the next thirty seconds were just non-verbal sounds.

DONOVAN: Close the door.

ADAM: What did she say?

What the fuck were you *doing*?

Listen, you know I can't tell you everything. And if you don't know that all kids like her—kids like me—have an initiation, well. Then you're just stupid. They don't just turn us loose and say, "Have a good life!" I'm still under orders, Donovan. This was her initiation and as far as I can tell, she fuckin' failed with flying colors. And that guy triggered her.

What?

Yeah. So your fucking grandfather has some explaining to do. I was not told that she had been… worked over so thoroughly before I bought her. He triggered her and she slit her own wrists.

You're sure.

Yeah, I'm fuckin' sure. I saw the whole thing on the goddamned security footage. I was watching from the control room in the basement. She went behind the bar where he was hiding and the minute she saw him he said, "Deactivate." And her whole body locked up. What the fuck? And what kind of trigger word is that? Do you have any idea how many times in her life someone will say the word "deactivate?" It's like… it's like they put no thought into her at all.

I didn't know. I swear to God, I didn't know.

Well, someone knew. Because someone did this to her!

What happened to the men?

I fucking killed them! What else could I do? That asshole told her to slit her wrists! They set me up. They set her up!

And the Company?

Uh… pissed off doesn't even cover it. They are livid. Fucking livid with me. But I bought her, Donovan. She's mine. They do not get to come in and take her mind from me. You understand that?

I hear you. And I did not know.

Well, I'm about to go down to that island and cut your grandfather's throat for this.

He didn't do it. He's got nothing to do with that program.

I don't give a fuck. Do the words "full disclosure" mean anything to you? He knew. He had to know. She was there with him for six months. He had a file on her and if the Company is keeping that kind of information hidden from a guy like him… well, who the fuck is running this show? He's on the goddamned board! And the fact that they thought they could just come in and fuck up my girl? I want to kill every single one of them.

Just calm down.

No. I will not calm down. She slit her own wrists, Donovan.

But she lived. So she passed.

She passed because I killed them.

Maybe that's what they wanted? You *are* the clean-up guy.

They have no idea how badly they fucked up with me.

Were they targeting you? Do you think they know anything?

I don't fuckin' know. But we need to, excuse the pun, deactivate this shit inside her head. Now. You're not going back to Duke. You're gonna spend the next…fuckin' however long fixing her.

I can't quit school, Adam. I have a job to do too. I'll be up to my neck in clinicals starting next month. And so much for my research paper. I can't publish this. Not even internally.

You did not just say that.

I mean… of course I'll be back to fix her. But I can only come between classes, Adam. I can't disrupt my schedule. They don't even know what I'm doing here with you. And now is not the time to go off plan. We're very close. I've got a lead on Sasha Cherlin. And if we can get to her, then—

Fuck that girl! I don't want to work with her again. She's the antithesis of how I want Indie to turn out. And you're the one who told me to stay away from her. Remember that? Back on the island. You said…

I know what I said. But she got out and she's still alive.

She got out because of me!

Fun fact.

What?

I met another guy named Adam in the business.

Who?

Some FBI agent. Company black ops. He's on the inside. And his brother is how I tracked down Sasha. Her name's Aston now, by the way. I think this might be helpful in the future.

I don't want to see Sasha ever again. You understand me? Nick Tate is out there killing kids. Did you know that?

I've heard.

Well, then you know that Indie is on his shortlist. And if he finds out she has a trigger word—

I highly doubt he knows that. Or anything about Indie. She's been here for almost two years now. If he knew where she was, he'd have taken her out already, trust me. I know that guy pretty well. At least I used to, before that shit show out in Santa Barbara. Just… try to calm down. Have McKay put up extra security cameras. Get some dogs, maybe. I'll be back on Friday night, but I have to leave Sunday. I'd like to talk to McKay before I go though. Can you call him in?

Are you dismissing me?

No. Of course not. I just have to go and I need to make sure McKay understands how we're going to proceed. He's in charge of her training. Unless something has changed and—

Fuck you, Donovan.

(Transcript note: Several minutes go by on the recording while McKay and Adam argue in the other room.)

MCKAY: What?

Donovan: Close the door. Good God, don't you people believe in privacy?

Just tell me what you have to say. I need to go hunt down Indie and her little boyfriend and make sure he's not asking too many questions.

…

What? Why are you looking at me that way?

Are you… ***jealous*** **of him?**

Fuck you. You have two seconds to spit out what you need to say or I walk out.

OK. So she has a trigger word—

I just heard.

—and we need to fix that. I'll be back as often as I can come, but in the meantime, you need to keep her very busy.

Because you're the expert on this.

I'm all you've got, McKay. So shut up and listen. I've been studying this shit for as long as I can remember. I know more about it than anyone you know. Keep her busy. Plan some jobs for her to do. And by plan I mean fake, OK? Set them up. Set her up to succeed. Send her into… I don't know. New Orleans, probably. And make her complete simple tasks. Get her confidence back and help forget this… incident.

How long is this gonna take?

Years. Probably two or three? Hard to tell. Not many people have gotten out of the program. Only four total case studies over the past fifty years. But one of them went on to live a long, almost normal life.

Well, that makes me feel better. Not.

Well, it should. At least we have some hope. She's young. No one's used her much yet. We can undo it. It'll just take time.

You better be right about this.

SESSION #19 NOTES

Indie Anna is smart, capable, and is living as close to a normal life as she could've hoped for. Despite McKay's agitation with the boy next door, he will play a critical role in Indie's healing. The news that she has a trigger word is an unfortunate development. But I am confident that I can lead her through this deactivation period and get her back on task.

SESSION #19 NOTES - PRIVATE

I feel like I'm getting further and further away from my goal when I started this project. I have put Indie under hypnosis eight times since our first session and each time she becomes more compliant. But none of my questions, or her answers to them, led to any actionable information. If this job in Pensacola didn't just go sideways, I might be tempted to concede that all my suspicions were unfounded.

But she was triggered. And her command was to kill herself. So someone had to *program* her. And that someone *has* to be Carter. Nick Tate didn't do it. That's the only thing I'm sure of. Nick was already in the thick of his Zero Program exit strategy by the time Indie came to the island. He wouldn't have started her just to end her.

Carter. It *has* to be Carter.

I have to believe that. Because right now Indie Anna Accorsi is the only connection I have to him.

I know he was real.

My father told me over and over again that he was just a dream, but I know he was real.

I'm *not* crazy.

I *know* he was real.

CHAPTER NINE

mckay

PRESENT DAY

In bed, we sleep.

Well, she sleeps. I think so, anyway. I can hear her soft, deep breathing. And I recognize it like a fingerprint. There could be a whole room filled with sleeping people and I could find Indie in the dark by her breath alone.

She is flat on her stomach, head turned away from me, cheek pressed into the pillow. I lie on my back, hands behind my head, eyes on the ceiling.

I don't want this to end but Donovan will be here soon. Maybe an hour. Maybe two. And then this pause will be over.

The ceiling has no answers for me. Just more questions. How did she get here? Where has she been? Who was she with?

But I stare at it anyway because if I look at her—if I allow myself to look at her—then I'll want to touch her. And this can't last. We both know this can't last.

I might belong to her but she doesn't belong to me. Not me alone, anyway. Adam and Donovan own equal parts of her heart. Even if she does blame Adam for her current situation, she will never be able to detach herself from him. No matter how much she'd like to.

Just like I can't.

There's a part of me that still wonders what my life would've been like if I had not come to live with the Bouchers. I still wonder if what Mr. Boucher told me was the truth.

But there's no time to think about my past or my problems with it. Because Indie is back. I have spent the past four years wishing for this day. Hoping she was still alive and she'd come back to us.

And here she is and I can't even look at her.

Finally, I can't take it anymore and I turn my head. Stare at the long curve of her spine. Notice the lights and darks that play along the muscles of her back in the moonlight.

I turn onto my side just enough to reach over and trace a long, soft line down her back. And suddenly there is this overwhelming urge to wrap my arms around her. To pull her into my chest and hug her tight. So tight she melds into me. Becomes a part of me. And our hearts merge.

That's where she belongs. Inside my heart.

I press my head into the pillow and sigh.

"Why are you sighing?"

"Sorry. I didn't mean to wake you."

She doesn't turn or even move. Just lies still. I want to keep her like this. Forever. Just crawl on top of her and cover her with my body. Keep her for myself. My captive.

"What do you think is gonna happen now, McKay?"

I can't answer that. And my heart beats fast, then faster. Because I'm afraid she'll turn and look at me. And she'll see what's behind my eyes. The fear. The longing. The false apologies. The secrets I'm hiding from her. From everyone. "I don't know," I finally answer. "We'll go home, I guess. What else can we do but go home?"

And then she does turn and I suddenly want to cry. A hard rock forms in my throat and just grows bigger and bigger until I'm very sure that I will die.

My eyes become wet and sad.

I'm so fucking sad.

Her hands are tucked under her cheek and her blue eyes are wide open. There is no sadness there though. Because she doesn't even know that she *should* be sad.

She reaches out with one hand and places it on my cheek. "Don't worry. It's gonna be OK."

I place my hand over hers and nod. Then I pull her close to me and she scoots in until her breasts are pressing against my chest and both hands grab on to my hair.

"What's wrong with you?"

"Nothing," I lie. "I'm fine. How are you?"

"Better."

This makes me smile. "I've missed you, ya know. I've been worried about you. I want to know everything."

She frowns and pouts her lips. Just a little. "You really don't."

"Do you remember now?"

"Where I've been? Or what I've done?"

My heart skips a beat or seven. "Aside from the dog walking?"

"I don't really remember. I just… I just have a very bad feeling about it."

I take her hand off my head and hold it. Kiss the back of her knuckles. "We'll figure it out."

"Maybe I don't want to know? I mean"—she looks up into my eyes, searching for something—"if I'm supposed to know, then why do I keep forgetting?"

"You know why. You don't forget everything. You found your way here. Two weeks ago," I add. Louder. Sterner. "Why the fuck didn't you come to me when you got into town?"

"I don't know. I don't remember getting here. One day I was just watching you get drinks at the bar."

"From the inside?"

"Yup. I was there. I kept thinking, *He'll feel me*. Ya know? I thought you should be able to feel me watching you. But you didn't. So I just… stayed in the shadows."

She's right. I should've known. But it's been four years since she left. And maybe, that first year, I would've. But then… time just kept moving forward and things started to fade. I didn't exactly forget about her or the past fourteen years of my life. I just… let it slip away. Into the dark background. Into the shadows.

And that's where she was. Right there in the darkest corners of my memories. Close, but unseen.

"I'm sorry. I should've felt you. But you're here now and you're not leaving again."

"You don't know that. I don't even know that."

"I'm not gonna let you, Indie. It's not safe."

"Safe. What the hell is safe, anyway? There's no such thing. And besides"—she pauses to smile, like this is a joke—"I'm still here. And I'm all yours. At the moment. Don't waste it, McKay. We might not ever get this chance again."

I know what she means. It's not a threat. She's not saying she's gonna disappear again, though she might. She means Donovan will be here soon and then she will stop being mine and become ours. And eventually, Adam will be here too. Or we'll be there. Back at Old Home and all together. And that's it as far as McKay and Indie go.

Because like it or not, she is *his*.

Indie reaches down with her hand and finds my cock. "One more time?" She squeezes it until I feel the blood rushing towards the tip.

If I thought I could get away with it, I'd pick her up, take her down to my truck, drive away, and never look back.

But I know better.

"Sure," I say, leaning in to kiss her.

It starts soft. Gentle, feathery kisses with no tongue. Because I just want to be soft with her. But I can't control it. The urges inside me take over. I want to claim her and possess her. I want to take her away from here. Take her away from Donovan and Adam and hold her next to me forever.

We weren't like this before. We weren't a couple. We weren't a foursome, either. Except for that one time, that's not how it was. But if she stays… now that she's older… I don't understand how any of this will ever work.

"Maybe we shouldn't?"

"Stop it, McKay. You want this more than I do."

"Donovan—"

"He's not here yet. Just relax." She pushes herself on top of me, spreading her legs open and pushing both hands down on my chest as she moves her hips and rubs her pussy against my now fully-hard cock.

But I don't want to relax. I grab her hips, flip her over, knee her legs back open, and then slide between them. My chest presses down on hers so hard as I hike her arms up above her head, grab both wrists in one hand, and then squeeze them, she gasps for breath.

"Ow. That hurts. I can't breathe!"

"It's supposed to hurt," I growl back. "I'm fucking sick of this shit, Indie."

"What shit?"

And she's laughing. Like this is still just some fantastic joke. Like her disappearing for four years after what went down at Old Home was nothing. Meant *nothing.*

I want to slap her. Hard. Right in the fucking face and scream, *Wake the fuck up!*

But I'm too angry. And too sad. And I don't like to yell. Not at her. Not anyone, really.

"Fuck me, McKay," she whispers. "Do it hard. Make me scream. Make me cry."

I want to make her cry. Because she didn't cry that day. She did everything *but* cry that day.

I keep a hold of her wrists, but my other hand creeps up to her throat. Almost like it's not a part of me. Like it's on a mission of its own making. My palm lies flat against the soft cartilage of her neck and I can feel her pulse beating under my thumb. Thumping. Hard. Then harder. My thumb presses down and she gasps, blinking.

It's so easy to suffocate someone. So easy to cut off the blood flow to the brain and make them pass out.

I ease up and she sucks in a deep breath. Her eyes are closed now and I know what this feels like. I know she is seeing twinkling stars against a black background. That her head is swirling with the threat of unconsciousness.

"Yeah. Like that," she croaks.

But she doesn't get to tell me how to do this. She doesn't get to make any decisions at all. Not after what she did.

I don't think I fully understood it until right now. I was there. I saw every bit of it. I watched it all in real time. And I never fully comprehended what actually happened.

And it wasn't even about that day.

It was about all the days that came before it. All the days that led up to that one moment when the sweet, secret world we were living in came crashing down all around us and she… *disappeared.*

I kiss her again. Hard, this time. I punish her with my mouth as I hike one knee up to her chest and slip my cock inside her.

She gasps, not laughing now. She struggles underneath me, wriggling her wrists in my still-firm grip as I press them into the headboard of the bed like she wants me to let go.

But I won't let go. I won't.

I thrust my cock deep inside and she cries out.

Yes.

Yes. That's what I want. I want her to cry. I want to *make her sob.*

One of her hands slips out of my grip and her fingernails dig into the thick, hard muscle of my shoulder. I lean into her ear and whisper, "I like it."

She turns her head and bites me on the arm. And I wince at the pain. She pulls her mouth off my skin and then… gently… she kisses the mark she left.

I go still for a moment, breathing hard as she pants underneath me.

"What are you doing?"

"I'm sorry."

"Don't be sorry, goddammit! I need this! I need you to fuck me, McKay. Hard. Right now. Don't go easy. You said you would never go easy on me and then you did. You always did. You always pulled that punch and second-guessed yourself. And that's why I'm the way I am. You did that! You did that when you tried to make me soft! When will you ever learn that I'm not—"

I thrust inside her again. She squeals, her body inching up towards the headboard and her legs kicking underneath me.

But she asked for it. "Is this how you want it then? From now on, Indie? Hard and rough?"

"Yes. Yes. That's how I want it. That's how I *need* it."

I fuck her. But the anger inside me does what it always does when Indie is around. It fades. And then there's nothing left.

There's just nothing left.

I roll off her and resume my position staring at the ceiling.

"What are you doing?"

"Just fuckin' forget it. I can't. I can't do this. You just walk out for four fucking years and then come back and expect… what?" I look at her. "That we'll be the same? We're not the same, Indie. We're never gonna be the same ever again."

"I came back. That's the important part."

"That's not the important part. Because when you left…" I sigh and hide my eyes in the crook of my elbow.

She climbs on top of me, flat and still. Her cheek rests on my chest and when her hand grips my wrist and tries to pry my arm away from my face her touch is gentle. And I'm not used to that. I'm not used to her anymore.

I push her off me and turn my back to her. And that's something I never thought I'd do.

"Why are you acting like this?"

I just shake my head, still hiding my eyes. "I don't think I can do this anymore."

"What do you mean? McKay. Look at me. What does that mean?"

It means… I don't know what it means.

I hurt? I'm sad? I'm fucking lost? I want her? I hate her? I need her?

What the fuck does it mean?

There's a banging downstairs in the shop and I sit up and swing my legs over the side of the bed. "Donovan's here." I stand up, find my jeans on the floor and I'm already pulling them up my legs when I say, "Get dressed. Now."

Then I exit the bedroom and close the door behind me just as the front door of my apartment opens and Donovan walks through wearing a motherfucking tuxedo.

I huff out a disgusted laugh. "Oh, I get it. You were busy tonight. What? You had a party to go to, Donovan? You had guests over? Some fucking Hollywood awards ceremony happening tonight that I don't know about?"

He stops in the middle of the living room and just looks at me. His eyes track right to the bite mark on my arm and he shoots me his own version of a disgusted laugh right back. "I see you two didn't waste any time catching up."

"Fuck you." I head to the kitchen, take a bottle of Jack down from the top of the fridge, and pour myself three healthy fingers in a water glass.

I down the whole thing and then Indie appears in the bedroom door.

Her eyes meet mine first. They are cold and hard. Just the way I like them. But when they track to Donovan they go soft and she smiles.

Donovan opens his arms wide, beckoning her towards him with a huge smile. "Come on. Bring it in."

She walks forward like she's on a string and he's pulling her towards him.

But of course, she's not.

She just loves him best.

Always has.

I pour that Jack down my throat, straight from the bottle, my eyes locked on their embrace.

Back when she was little I didn't care so much. It wasn't like this. It wasn't anything like this. She was just a little girl and I was just there to prepare her for the world.

Donovan and Adam… they were the ones who protected her. Not me.

"That's enough." Donovan is walking towards me now, reaching for the bottle. He swipes it away and throws it into the sink. It clatters around the cheap metal and the dark amber liquid spills out and runs down the drain. "I was counting on you driving, you asshole. I've been up for thirty-six hours and it's a two-hour goddamned drive home."

I drag the back of my hand across the sticky, bitter alcohol on my lips and glare at him.

"What? Did I interrupt something?"

I don't answer him. Just look at Indie. Glare at her.

Why am I so mad? I don't know. I'm just fucking angry. At her. At Donovan. At Adam.

At myself.

I walk into the bedroom, pull a clean t-shirt from a hanger in my closet, and slip it over my head. Then grab some socks from a drawer and sit down on the mattress and pull them on. Head cocked towards the open door, listening as they whisper to each other in the living room.

I know what he's saying. *Did he do anything to you? Was he inappropriate?*

Old questions. Familiar questions.

They started right after Indie turned sixteen and things were getting serious with Nate.

I knew that was inevitable. And I wasn't jealous. Not the way Adam was. I wanted her to have a good life. I did. I wanted her to have all the things I never had. I took care of her for that reason. Not because Adam told me to. Not even because

I had to or she wouldn't live to see eighteen, let alone twenty-four.

But she did live. And I still feel like a fucking failure.

Donovan appears in the doorway. "You all right?"

"I'm fine." I reach for a boot and pull it on my foot, then the other one. Stand and adjust my cock in my jeans.

Donovan looks down at my hand as I do this, then back up at me, furious. "Asshole." He turns away and goes into the living room.

Whatever Indie was whispering to him out there, it wasn't about my inappropriate behavior. But Donovan has never needed to be told things to know things. And what just happened with Indie and me was just… inevitable. Just like that first hug she gave him was.

I walk to the door, then stop and lean against the wall for a moment. Run my fingers through my hair as they leave the apartment and start going down the stairs.

Indie is only wearing the sweats and t-shirt I gave her earlier, but when I get down into the shop, she's struggling with her still-wet brown boots, her leather jacket already on.

She stands up straight and looks at me. "I'm ready. Let's go home."

I close my eyes. Take a moment to think about yesterday. Before she came back. Before Donovan got here.

And wonder, much the way I did that very first day she came home with us fourteen years ago, if anything will ever be the same again.

Donovan drives.

Stupid prissy fucker.

My truck, too. Since he came in a 'car', which means he had a driver, whom he did not ask to stay and take him back to Old Home. So. My truck.

Indie sits in the back and I take shotgun. I probably managed to down six or seven shots in those thirty seconds I was holding that Jack bottle. And I did have sex. So I'm sleepy as I look out the window and watch the landscape go by.

There was very little traffic getting out of New Orleans and once we get on the Lake Pontchartrain Causeway, there's a long boring stretch until we get up north and finally head west towards the Old Pearl River.

Every now and then I glance over my shoulder to look at Indie, who is sitting behind Donovan for just this reason.

She wants me to look at her. And every time I do, I catch her staring at me.

I don't know what the fuck came over me back at my apartment. I should've just… pushed her away. Kept her at a distance. Because now she fills up my head and I can't make sense of things.

It's nothing but a swirling mess. And I wish I could say it was regret. I would fucking love to feel some regret when it comes to Indie.

But I don't.

And it's not.

It's just… conflict. And apprehension about what comes next with Adam.

"So how's…" Indie stops mid-sentence.

"How's what?" Donovan glances at her in the rearview.

"I was gonna say school." She laughs. "But obviously you're not in school anymore. I knew that. How's work?"

"I just finished my second residency, actually. And it's all… fine."

"Just fine?"

"Great. It's great. I can't complain."

"Did you ever get that Malibu house?"

I glance over at Donovan and find him smiling. "Nah. That dream faded a while back now, Indie. I'm… considering my options at this point."

"What options?" I'm still staring out the window when I ask.

"I've been meaning to talk to you about this, actually."

I turn my head to look at him. He keeps his eyes on the road. Fucking hands at two and ten o'clock like he takes his goddamned driving seriously. "Talk to me about what?"

He side-eyes me. "Later, McKay. It's not a good time."

Indie is quiet in the back, but I know she's listening intently. When neither Donovan or I say anything else, she pulls herself together and asks another question. "Are you married, Donovan?"

"Married? No, Indie. I'm not married."

I glance back at Indie again. She's looking out the window this time. Studying the Louisiana darkness all around us like there's anything to see out there.

We're all quiet after that, our pathetic attempt at small talk a complete failure. And then before we know it, we're driving down the long, empty lane that leads to Old Home.

The gate is open when we pull up to it and each one of us sucks in a long breath and lets it out, afraid of what we'll find at the end of this journey that started out long, but now seems way too short.

Donovan gives the truck some gas and we slowly ease our way down the long, winding driveway until we see the front porch of the white semi-Victorian mansion come into view.

Half of it is lit up with moonlight, the other side dark.

Perfect analogy, if you ask me. That's been my experience in life since the beginning.

You can't ever see everything at once.

It's gotten to a point now that I don't even expect it.

Old Home is in better shape than I thought it would be. There are hedges that line the driveway along the main portion of the house. And the gardens have been kept up. I can't see much in the dark, and it's winter, so there's not much to see anyway. But the short hedges trimming the edges of the geometrically-shaped beds all appear sharp in the moonlight, like people are trimming them regularly.

There are two massive pecan trees that flank either side of the porch and their boughs grow together across the front walkway, making a canopy that only adds to the charm of this old home.

"Is Adam even here?" I ask, looking around for his truck. Not that I know what he drives these days. We've talked a few times, but I literally have not seen him since the day of Indie's twentieth birthday.

Right over there. I track to the spot where I last saw him getting into his truck.

And then he was gone.

Donovan was inside taking care of Indie and I was… I glance over at the pavilion, which looks empty and unkept. I was… *dealing* with Nathan.

Donovan cuts the engine. "He said he would be." Then he opens his door and that all-too-familiar open-door alarm ding silences the chorus of crickets for a moment. But they recover and then it hits me.

We're here.

After four long years we're actually here.

We all get out of my truck and walk up to the porch. Stand at the bottom and look up at the house.

I lived here. With Indie and Adam. For ten years, we lived here. And even though I've spent the better part of four years away from this place—trying to *forget* this place—the moment my eyes find the front door, the past slams into to me like a wall of sticky heat on an August afternoon.

I'm back there.

Back in that moment when Indie got out of another truck—Adam's truck. Dressed up in jean shorts and t-shirt. Long, blonde hair tied up in a crooked ponytail.

I knew it.

From the moment I first saw her, I knew we'd end up here. Staring up at an empty house, thinking back on empty years, wondering where it all went wrong.

But we all know the answer to that question.

Here.

This is where it all went wrong.

PART TWO
trippin' on snakes

Finding that truth is messy. That's about the only way to define the in-between time when fantasy and reality are still fighting for control.

It's a long, winding road of 'this is', and 'that isn't', and 'we are', and 'we aren't'. And sometimes you get a little lost along the way. Or you stumble off the path, sidetracked.

You're still inside the walls. Still safe for now. But the gate is unlocked or the there's a crack in the stone where small, slithering things can get in and out.

But this is when you really need to take a good hard look at those snakes under your feet and ask yourself that question again.

Do you *really* need to know the truth?

CHAPTER TEN

Donovan came home a lot after that first job. I could tell everyone was concerned about something, but they wouldn't tell me what that something was.

Me, I presumed.

It was always me.

Everything around Old Home seemed to revolve around me.

We didn't do another job for several months. But Adam hemmed and hawed about the Company being on his ass and started taking me into New Orleans for practice jobs.

I wasn't supposed to know they were practice jobs, but I did. It was so obvious. They were easy things. Steal this thing. Attack this person, but do not kill him.

That was the dead giveaway. It was always McKay I was attacking. He always had a ski mask on, but come on. Did they take me for a four-year-old? I could pick McKay out of a crowd of a thousand people just by his walk.

But then, right after I turned thirteen and Donovan's visits had become fewer and fewer over the past months—I guess I was making progress?—Adam called all of us in for a meeting.

His office had been rearranged for this. That was my first clue that serious things were about to happen. He had a giant mahogany desk in that office, but on this day, he did not sit behind it. He had his desk chair, the two chairs that typically lived in front of it, and another chair from the dining room all arranged in a circular pattern in the center of the room.

He sat in his chair, Donovan and McKay sat in the other two office chairs, and I took the dining room chair. It was summer again, but all of us were wearing jeans and t-shirts.

McKay's were faded to light, light blue and his t-shirt was white and sleeveless. Adam's were some regular blue color and he had on a black tank top that showed off his muscles. He had been working out hard since the first job went wrong, and his upper arms were thick like cannons. And Donovan was wearing dark, dark jeans with a white button-down, long-sleeved shirt—sleeves rolled up—that made me uncomfortably sweaty just looking at him.

McKay was leaning forward with his head bowed and elbows on his knees. His hands were gripping his thick, light hair and he was staring straight ahead. So still. Like he dared not move or everything might fall apart around him.

Donovan was kicked back in his chair, one ankle propped up on one knee, shoulders open, head tilted back a little, slight smile on his face.

Adam had the only chair with armrests. And he gripped those tightly, I remember. His back was straight and his face serious as he looked us all over.

His eyes landed on mine.

I smiled. Trying to play things off like Donovan was.

"OK," Adam finally said in his gruff voice. "It's time. I know that first job did not go well, Indie. But Donovan is positive that he has fixed the problem and is confident you can get started again. So this weekend we're going to San Francisco and then we're taking a little side trip over to Colorado to watch someone."

I nodded at him out of habit, but inside I was stuck on the words 'fixed the problem,' wondering what that meant and how Donovan fit into the picture. And when I snapped back to attention, Adam had already moved on to McKay's part in this next job. Which was the San Francisco one I wrote about earlier where Adam had to come save my ass again. Only this time I made it out OK.

Anyway. That was when the real jobs began. Company jobs, like that San Francisco one, but also private things, like that surveillance stuff in Colorado.

This was also when I first learned about Sasha Cherlin. She was a Company kid like me. And when I say like me, I mean almost exactly like me. She grew up with men too, and was trained to kill people, and knew lots of secrets. She was also the one who fractured the Company several years earlier with Adam's help.

Donovan told me that part. But I was not to tell Adam that I knew these things. It was just between us.

Donovan told me a lot of things after our sessions when the tape was not recording. I don't remember all of them, just some of them. He told me weird things in those after sessions. Things about himself, mostly. Which I enjoyed. I was always interested in Donovan's life.

But this one time I'm thinking about he was talking about Sasha Cherlin.

I never actually met this Sasha girl. Adam said that was too dangerous. She had a lot of people watching her. Not people like us, and not for the same reasons. Protecting her, he said.

So all we did was take notes.

I didn't see the big deal about this girl. She didn't do anything unusual. She had just graduated from some fancy university in Denver and was living at home with some family before leaving for Kansas for more college.

We stayed there for two days, but then on the second night Adam woke me up in the hotel room and said we were leaving. He was stuffing my clothes into a bag and talking in a rush. Almost like he was in a panic.

On the jet ride home, I heard him talking to McKay on the phone. Telling him that there was a whole team of Company surveillance on Sasha Cherlin and we needed to get the fuck away from that shit.

He never explained that to me and I didn't ask. I was tired that night and slept the whole trip, even after we landed and were driving back to Old Home.

And then, once I was home, I didn't care anymore. By the time I was thirteen I didn't care about anything but Nate. He was my whole world. And it was summer so he didn't have to go to school every day. We loved the summers most of all. That's when we had the most fun out in the woods.

Donovan was there when I got home, but he debriefed me quick. He didn't record it. And he didn't ask me about why Adam had to come save me from that man who wanted to slit my throat in San Francisco. He just listened as I gave my report and said, "Mm-hm. Mm-hm. Mm-hm." And then he, Adam, and McKay locked themselves up inside Adam's office and I went out to play. Even though it was barely dawn.

Nate didn't care what time I came to his house. I would climb this big old cypress tree and get up on his roof, and then shimmy my way through his little attic window and wake him up.

His grandfather was sick, sick by this time. So I probably could've walked through the front door and gone up the steps like a normal person and no one would've said boo about it. But nothing about Nate and me was normal so I didn't bother pretending that it was.

Thirteen was a banner year for me and Nate. We weren't at the kissing stage. Yet. But we were making our way there. Slowly but surely, we were growing up and getting ready to do grown-up things.

Our favorite thing to do that summer I was thirteen was to take his little fishing boat up the river and go into the little town to eat ice cream and laugh. We even had a couple friends there. And I told stories about us. Because of course, they didn't know who we were. Nate's school was on the other side of the river, and I didn't go to regular school. So we could tell these kids anything we wanted.

I did all the talking because Nate is only good for telling stories about facts. And these kids would roll their eyes at him when he started rambling on about the birds of the swamp or the moss on the trees.

But I liked that about those kids. Especially the girls my age. I liked that they saw Nate as some backwater nobody with a weird fascination with nature. Because that meant he would stay mine and he would never look at those girls who lived in that town the way he looked at me.

This was the summer we started to hold hands. And every time he reached for me and his fingers laced with mine, I would get a chill through my whole body. The good kind of chill. Not the kind I would get on a job that was going wrong.

And I was doing jobs nearly every week that summer. The Company was up to lots of things that year and they called Adam and me out all the time to clean things up. That was how Donovan and I decided to describe killing. Clean-up jobs.

I got a lot better at things that summer too. I didn't mess up as much. And sometimes—most times, actually—Adam didn't need to save me anymore. He just sent me off to do my thing and waited for me to come back.

But there was this one time in Miami the next year, when I ran into a problem called Nicholas Tate.

Both Adam and Donovan knew Nicholas Tate. They had known him for years, I guess. Because they were all Untouchable Company kids and apparently that was a small group of people.

I was teamed up with another girl like me. Her name was Wendy and I liked her a whole lot. I had never met another me. I had been told that Sasha was another me, but she was old and I didn't work with her.

This girl was the same age as me. She had blonde hair and blue eyes just like me. And an attitude that never ended. I was fourteen at this point and the jobs I was doing were getting more and more serious. So meeting a girl who was my age, and like me, and to be able to work with her… that was special.

Wendy was wild. She reminded me of myself when I first came to Old Home and ran away to live in the woods. And her and I together… wow. We were a pretty good team. She knew what she was doing, and by this time, so did I. So we did quite a few jobs together that year. She was always with a man called Chek. And her job with him was mostly to watch his back when he met up with another man called Johnny. And Adam and me were also sent to watch this Johnny person too. But we were not to clean him up. We were just supposed to make sure that this meeting between Chek and Johnny went off without complications. And they did. And I learned, over time, that they were both part of another branch of the Company called the Way. Because there had been that incident in Santa Barbara eight years ago that had rearranged the Company into other, smaller, sub organizations to stay under the radar.

I had a run-in with that Johnny the next summer and this is when I first saw Nicholas Tate in the flesh. Until then he was just this… *figure*. This… *bad person* I was not to go near. But that summer I was sent in to steal a biological sample from this island down in the Caribbean. It was a pretty important job and McKay spent weeks going over the details of what I needed to do because this was in a lab and required me to wear a special suit and use special equipment to handle the sample. It was very important that I used the suit and equipment properly and contained the sample because it was dangerous. And if that sample somehow got inside me, I would die a nasty death.

McKay was very worried about this job and tried to talk Adam out of it. But Adam would not relent. One night, just before we left Old Home, I heard him tell McKay that this was the endgame. And if I didn't go in and grab this sample, everything we had done would be pointless.

Of course, the job went a little awry. It was probably above my pay grade if I'm being honest. But I did my best. I ran into that Johnny guy just as I was stealing my sample and getting ready to dart out of the facility. They took me prisoner and then I had to tell them a few truths to get out of it or I knew that Adam and McKay would show up—maybe even Wendy too. And then things would get real messy.

But back to Nicholas Tate. Adam and I were in a parking garage where he put the car. We were driving to some town up north where the jet was waiting, and then, just as we reached the car Adam got a phone call. He looked at the screen, then at me. And told me to, 'Stay right here, Indie. I'll be back in a minute."

So I stayed. And that's when I saw a man on the other end of the parking garage level. And I was thinking. Who is this man? How do I know his name? Because that was the first time I had ever seen Nick Tate and his name was immediately in my head. Like one minute it wasn't there. And then it was.

Nick Tate.

I looked over my shoulder, trying to see if Adam saw him too, but he was just disappearing into a stairwell. For privacy, maybe. And when I looked back, Nick was walking towards me.

I wasn't sure if I should run, or scream, or get ready to fight him. But it didn't matter. He stopped about half way and just looked at me.

Then… then I couldn't move. And my head was spinning.

And then I blinked my eyes and he was gone.

Just… poof. Gone.

And before I could make sense of that—before I could ask myself if I had just made him up or if he just decided to walk away—Adam was back. Telling me to, "Get in the car, Indie. We've got to go."

I had a hard time making sense of that afternoon. The whole way up to the airfield where Adam and I were catching a plane I wanted to ask Adam about Nick. Tell him what I thought I saw.

But there was another voice inside my head during that ride. One that told me to, *Hush. Be still and quiet. Say nothing.*

So that's what I did.

I said nothing.

After that job was over Donovan said he was proud of me. I think that was the first time he ever said that. He told me, "You made an executive decision, Indie. And it was the right thing to do." Because I had not only talked Johnny into letting me go without giving up any information about Adam, McKay, or Donovan, I had brought the sample back too.

And I didn't die.

So I did the whole thing right. I put the suit on right, I got the sample off the island and contained properly, and I got away as clean as one could expect after being caught and held prisoner on a superyacht for nearly twenty-four hours.

I felt good about that. I felt like… I was on my way. Things were going really well with the jobs and I was definitely very good at them by this time.

But the very best thing about my life back then was Nate.

Even though I wasn't allowed to tell Nate what I was doing when Adam and I left, I was allowed to tell him approximately how long I would be gone.

There was a lot of discussion about this right about the time I was turning fourteen. Adam didn't want me to say anything to Nate. Adam didn't like Nate. McKay didn't like

Nate either, but I was starting to get the feeling that Adam kinda hated Nate.

But McKay said, "She has to tell him something. Whether you like it or not, they're close friends. You don't wanna see him lurking in the woods when she's gone, just waiting for her to come back. And that kid will be a problem if she keeps too many secrets from him."

Adam countered with, "That kid is nobody. And his grandfather is on death's door."

Then they saw me spying on them and Adam pushed his office door closed and I didn't hear anything else after that. But that was OK. Because I was picturing Nate lurking in the woods around Old Home, just waiting for me to come back.

He probably did do that and McKay just didn't see him. Nathan St. James had more up his sleeve than even I knew about. He was some kind of superhero out in those woods. Nothing could touch him.

So I had already decided, before I went to do that job on that island, that I was gonna have my very first kiss with Nathan St. James when I got back.

He didn't know it yet. It was a secret plan. But I didn't think he'd mind. I knew because he was my boy next door. And I had already read that paperback book too many times to count so this was just how things were supposed to be.

Nate and I were fate.

I made a whole plan for how I was gonna entice Nathan St. James to kiss me. Of course, I could've just kissed him all on my own, but that's not how the story went in the book.

In the book the boy did all the preparing. He planned the whole thing from top to bottom and beginning to end. And by the time that kiss happened, the girl in the story had been swept right off her feet from all the romance.

So I planted ideas in Nate's head.

My birthday is in May, and on the night I turned fourteen Nate took me by the hand out into the woods. We were careful not to trip over any snakes as we made our way over to the river and down on the sandy part that always showed up when the water was a little low. It was spring, and the water was really low that year, but we didn't care because that just meant in the summer there would be a lot of beach to wander on.

But he took me by the hand. And he didn't have any plans to kiss me back then. He just said, "There's a full moon tonight, Indie. Do you wanna go look at it with me down by the river?"

I never said no to Nathan. Ever. I was up for everything. So we went moon-watching that night. And there were fireflies out. Tons of them. And I made a big deal about those fireflies. I let him know that I loved the way they lit up the night and I told him that I wished the night was thick with them. So thick that they would light up the woods and make magic.

That was the first hint about how I wanted my first kiss to go down.

The next hint was a few weeks later. Nate had asked me to go up to the river town with him to grab some supplies for his grandfather. And while we were in the drug store we got ice cream, like we always did. Only this time I said, "I wish I could eat an ice cream cone at night in the woods with you. Wouldn't that just be so refreshing, Nate?"

He agreed. But there was no way to take ice cream cones home on the boat. It took almost an hour to motor back down the river to our little beach where he hid his boat in the trees. And even then, we'd have to walk a good way on to get to our familiar woods where we liked to hang out.

But this was just an idea for planting, not an idea for doing that day.

Adam always had supermarket ice cream in our freezer because he liked to eat it at night too. On the porch or out under the pavilion, though. And in a bowl. Not out in the woods in a waffle cone. But I didn't want to eat Adam's grocery store ice cream in the woods out of a bowl. I wanted to eat drug store ice cream from a waffle cone.

The next hint I dropped was about the mosquitoes.

Now, these little critters were just a way of life in the swamp. We had mosquito netting hanging down over a pavilion on the Old Home grounds. This was in the fancy garden between the house and the duck lake. This pavilion was McKay's favorite place. And even though it was hot and sticky in the summers, more often than not—and weather permitting—this is where you could find McKay when he was not training me, or building things, or talking to Adam about plans.

McKay built the pavilion that first summer I came to live with them. In fact, he was in the middle of the project when I arrived. And by the time my life as a runaway in the woods was over, he was almost done with it.

It was like an outdoor living room and it was the shape of a fat, stubby L. The short length of the L was meant as an outdoor kitchen and dining area and the long end was meant for comfortable conversation or watching football in the fall.

There was a large outdoor fireplace that had a big ol' flat screen TV over it, and neither of those were there when I first came. It took another year for him to collect enough stones to build the fireplace. So he and I built it together the following summer.

But that fireplace made up the interior corner of the L. I wanted him to put it on the exterior corner of the L because it was gonna block my view of the lake. But McKay said, "People who come down here want to look at the lake, not that ramble of forest behind us. So what is the point of building this beautiful fireplace only to put it behind us and never look at it?"

It made sense.

But that first summer, once I was done runnin' away, McKay let me help him finish the pavilion off. By this I mean decorate. McKay can make anything with his hands. Anything. So I looked through a bunch of country magazines and found some porch swings for him to make. One was your traditional swing you find on a porch, but the other was more like a bed. It was a long rectangular platform that you could lie down on and it felt like a tire swing.

And once he hung that from the ceiling in his pavilion that was my spot. Two or three pushes from McKay while I was lying on that swing and I would fall asleep like a baby.

Anyway, my point is that McKay would hang mosquito netting around the perimeter of the pavilion in the summer and put out lots of citronella candles to keep the bugs away. And we would eat dinner out there in the evenings. Sometimes Adam ate with us, but not all the time. It was a special place just for McKay and me.

So I hinted to Nate that it would be nice if the fort we had made in the woods a few summers ago had some netting to keep those mosquitoes out.

And that was my plan. That's how I wanted my first kiss with Nathan St. James to happen. In the woods, thick with fireflies, eating ice cream cones, in our fort, safe from mosquitoes.

I didn't say anything else after that. Not about my dream, anyway. But the night before I left for that island job Nate and I took a walk like we always did before I had to leave town. By this time, we held hands a lot. Not in front of McKay or Adam, but whenever we were in the woods, or down by the river, or out on the north side of the duck lake looking at birds and mossy trees.

So we were out taking our nightly walk, holding hands, just being happy. And I said, "Nathan. I'm gonna be gone one week this time. It's a big thing I have to do. And it's dangerous. And I would like for us to do something special when I get back."

He paused our walk in the woods and said, "What kind of thing would you like to do, Indie?" And I always appreciated that he never asked about the jobs. Was always just satisfied that I told him when I would be back.

I replied, "I would like to do something childishly grown up, Nathan."

That's it. That's all I said.

I had done my part and the rest was up to him.

But we had a date now. A real date. And we both knew it.

One week from that night I would come home and Nathan St. James would have something special planned for me.

What it was, I didn't know for sure.

But I hoped it was a kiss.

My very first kiss.

He was leaning up against a tree when I got home. I didn't see him right away. I went inside, feeling giddy because the job went well. I came home alive, at least. And with the sample. Adam took it, and then as soon as I got out of the truck, he left to go drop it off somewhere.

Donovan was there, of course. To debrief me with one of our recorded conversations. And that took a while. I didn't see Nate until after dinner with McKay, which we ate indoors that night. He was stressed out about the job because it didn't *really* go off without a hitch. I had been caught, and held prisoner, and questioned, and then left floating in the middle of the Caribbean Sea in one of those round life rafts and had to jump into the ocean and swim to Adam's boat once he finally found me. So all that worried McKay. But I had talked my way out of my sticky situation, and Adam had picked me up, and we'd come home, so I was fine. But McKay was broody like that when the jobs 'got complicated'.

So it was hours and hours after I got home that I looked out the window and saw Nathan St. James leaning up against that tree. Grinning like some fool boy who was about to kiss his girl for the very first time.

He was wearing faded jeans that were tattered in the thighs and knees because he wore them so much. Nice tatters though. Tatters that made him look tough and showed his skin just enough to make me want to see more. And he was wearing a white ribbed tank top that hugged his stomach and chest muscles and showed off his upper arms and strong shoulders.

His hair was too long that summer. It touched his shoulders and then curled up just a teeny bit. And it hung in his eyes just enough for him to hide behind it a little and look mischievous and cute.

He was nearly fifteen now. Almost as tall as McKay. And he had the beginnings of a shadow on his face. Ever since that spring, the girls in the river town had started flirting with him. Batting their long lashes and looking at him over their shoulders as they passed us by.

But he never looked at them. He only ever looked at me.

When he saw me in the window that night he whistled. Not a regular whistle. Or a wolf whistle. But a bird whistle. The high-pitched chirp-song of the tree swallow that flowed out from his lips like easy water going down the river.

My stomach did a flip and even though I had promised Adam that I would not wear my white church dresses into the woods years and years ago, I put one of them on anyway. A short, cotton one I had slightly outgrown the year before so that the hem of it hit me high above my knees. The straps were thin and soft. The bodice had ruching and was tight, so my breasts—which had started growing bigger just that year—were prominent. And it hugged my waist before flowing out just a little over my hips.

I went outside and took Nate's hand and I let him lead me into the woods. He kept stealing looks at me, grinning in that way that made his dimples peek out in his cheeks.

It was dark. There was no moon that night. And he was not taking me to the fort we built when we were younger. He took me over to the duck lake, but not so that McKay could see us if he was looking through the cutaway trees. We went off a little ways, to a part of the woods we didn't spend a lot of time in before because it was thick with underbrush and overgrown trees.

At least together we didn't spend a lot of time out here. But it was becoming very clear that Nathan St. James was living a double, hidden life behind my back. Because there was a path I wasn't aware of.

"Take your shoes off," he said.

"I thought you hated when I walk barefoot through the woods."

"I made a deal with the snakes tonight. They won't be bothering us."

Which I thought was cute. Because I had made that same deal with the water snakes when I first arrived at Old Home.

So I did take off my shoes and the dirt had been raked so that it was soft, and deep, and cool between my toes.

The air in this part of the woods was cool as well. Not sticky and humid like it was by the water.

Soon we were in the middle of a clearing. Everything was dark and felt like a secret. Then he turned and said, "Close your eyes, Indie."

I thought for sure this was it. He was gonna kiss me. So I smiled and closed my eyes. He wrapped a handkerchief around my head and covered my eyes so I could not peek.

My stomach flipped and fluttered as he did this. He was standing behind me and I could feel his soft jeans brushing up against the back of my knees.

"Now, don't you move," he cautioned me.

"I won't." I practically giggled.

And then he walked away.

I almost looked. It took every bit of self-control that McKay had taught me over the years not to peek.

But he called out to me every few seconds to let me know he was still there. Doing things. I could hear him doing things. Nathan St. James can walk softly in a forest. Like a deer. So quiet you could not hear him or know he was coming until he was upon you.

But he didn't walk soft. He made noise so I would know I wasn't alone.

Not that I was scared of the woods. I wasn't. And he knew this.

He just wanted me to understand that he was there.

I was patient.

Then he said, "Take off the blindfold, Indie."

I drew in a very deep breath and let it out before I took off the blindfold. Because I knew he had done something special. Just for me.

And when I slipped that blindfold down my face and let it hang around my neck, I could not even understand the beauty all around me. It was just that gorgeous.

Nathan St. James had turned the darkness into something lovely and sweet.

There was a treehouse cradled deep in the body of an old, thick pecan tree. But when I looked closer, I could see that it was really three trees, all wound up together and leaning off in different directions.

I knew these trees. Had been by here once or twice in our wanderings. But that treehouse had not been there.

It was just a platform with no walls. But it didn't need walls because there was a canopy frame over top of it, and hanging from that canopy frame were long curtains of mosquito netting.

And the reason I could see all this was because there was light up there. Flickering, soft, gold light.

"Come on," Nate whispered, and he took my hand again. "Let's go up. There's more."

I think I held my breath as we climbed up to the platform. And then I let it all out in a rush when he held up the netting so I could crawl under it.

Inside our little house were dozens and dozens of mason jars filled with fireflies.

I gasped. And then laughed. And looked at him with so much love in my heart, I thought I might split in half.

"What did you do?"

"I made you a home," he said, and his Louisiana accent drawled those words out just the way I liked them. So smooth. "Something childishly grown-up."

I crawled across the platform and onto an old braided rug I knew came from the floor of his bedroom. And turned to face him.

He crawled up after me. Stalked across that floor on all fours with his blue eyes locked on mine. Until his hands were planted on either side of my shoulders and I could feel his stomach pressing and easing up along mine as he breathed.

He was grinning like a boy who was about to kiss his girl for the very first time.

We were so close. Just an inch or two apart when he stopped and just stared at me. And I stared back. His face was lit up with firefly glow, flickering shadows that softened him and made him deliciously hard in the same moment.

"I have one more thing for you," he said.

I took another long breath, and let it out real slow. Because I knew he was gonna kiss me.

But he didn't.

He backed up a little and reached over underneath a thick pile of the mosquito netting, and opened a cooler.

I giggled.

Because inside that cooler, tucked between millions of ice cubes, was a gallon of ice cream from the drug store. And he had waffle cones too. I leaned back on my hands, my stomach a mess of gorgeous misery from the anticipation of what was coming. I watched him scoop out the ice cream and fill up the cone and hand it to me. And when he did that again, to make himself a cone too, I memorized the muscles in his arms, and the curl of his blond hair along the top of his shoulders, and the way he kept stealing looks at me with those eyes that were the color of almonds in the shade.

Then he said, "Come on over here, Indie."

And we scooted over to the edge of the platform and dangled our legs. The netting tickled my thighs as we gazed though it and watched the night as we licked our cones.

We talked. I told him about how I was in the ocean this time yesterday, sitting in a life raft.

He didn't ask one question about that. Just smiled at me and told me how this time last night he was hanging the netting and bringing the rug up from his bedroom.

I forgot all about the kiss. I was that lost in him.

We licked our cones and laughed and joked. He sighed a lot. And so did I.

And right when I wasn't expecting it, after our cones were all gone and we were settled and happy, he leaned over, looked at me as his fingertips brushed along the side of my cheek, and he said, "Close your eyes now, Indie. I would like to kiss you. And I want you to remember it in your mind's eye when I do that."

So I closed my eyes and almost lost my head in the two or three seconds it took for his mouth to touch mine.

At first it was a soft kiss. His lips were gentle and easy to kiss back. And then his mouth opened, and mine opened with it, and his tongue was cool and he tasted like mint chocolate chip.

We kissed for a long time. Just like that. Sitting side by side, with our bodies turned inward. One of his hands on my face and the other playing with my hair. My hands on his shoulder, drawing in his heat, and on his thigh. Poking my fingertip through the tattered hole in his jeans so I could feel his hidden skin.

Finally, we pulled back and smiled at each other.

And my life was perfect.

We stayed up there for hours just talking about things. What we would do tomorrow, and the next day. How we would spend the summer coming up here each night before bed. How he loved me and I loved him back.

And then McKay started calling my name from the house and we knew the night was over. Nathan said, "Now we have to let them go."

And at first, I didn't understand. But he picked a jar of fireflies and unscrewed the lid. Some of them were clinging to it and they flew off. But still stuck inside the netting. So they were fluttering and flittering around my head the way my stomach was fluttering and flittering when I climbed up here with Nate behind me, pressing his chest into my legs so I would know he would catch me if I fell.

We set them all free like that.

And then he lifted the netting on one side and we climbed down and sat in the dirt to watch them fly off.

But they didn't fly far. They stayed close. And they lit up the forest all around us.

And that's how we ended the most magical night of my life.

McKay didn't say anything when I got home. He was sitting on the top step of the porch drinking a green bottle of beer.

Nate walked me all the way up to the bottom step and said, "Good night, Indie," and then he turned and walked home.

I smiled at McKay as I pulled the screen door open. He was glaring at Nate's back as he disappeared into the woods.

But he didn't say a word.

The next morning, I got my period.

I woke up feeling sick and crampy and then saw the blood when I went to the bathroom. I knocked on McKay's door, because Donovan had left to go back home the night before and Adam was still out on his delivery errand for the biological sample.

Not that I would've gone to either of them over McKay in a situation such as this.

McKay was not in his room so I went downstairs and found him in the kitchen.

I knew what a period was but there was nothing in this house to take care of my new problem. So I had to say, "McKay. Can you take me to town to buy some tampons?"

He was squinting at the newspaper when I said this and when he looked up, he had an expression on his face like I was speaking some foreign language he didn't understand.

"What?"

"I got my period. I need to go to town. Can you take me?" I asked it softly. My mood was still perfect and calm from the night before. Not even my monthly curse could change that.

He hesitated for a moment. Not because he was gonna say no. There was no chance of that happening. Probably just to consider all the new things he would have to think about in regards to me, from this day on.

And then he said, "I'll get my keys."

In the drug store—this was not the same drug store as the river town, a different one that was closer to the mansion—McKay folded his arms across his chest and frowned at me in the feminine products aisle as I tried to make sense of all my options. The pharmacist, who was a woman in her forties, came out from behind the counter and helped me. She must've taken pity on McKay's confused uneasiness because she grinned at him a lot. But maybe that was just because McKay was handsome.

When we got home, he left me alone for a little while as I figured everything out, and then, when I finally emerged from the upstairs bathroom that was reserved for me, he said, "Indie, we need to talk."

But he didn't want to talk in the kitchen. He took me outside to the pavilion with the mosquito netting and told me to take a seat on the bed swing. So I did. And he sat in the porch swing, and he talked. He talked so damn long he had to light the citronella candles.

He told me about love. And sex. And babies. And birth control. And how I needed to make sure Nate didn't talk me into anything I didn't want to do. And how yes was yes, and no was no, and maybe was also no. He said that part a lot. And that I could come to him with any sort of problem, no matter how personal it was.

He squirmed the entire time. And I already knew all this stuff. I have the goddamned internet on my phone, for fuck's sake.

But I let him go on like that for hours. I watched him struggle. I thought it was damn cute the way he forced himself to be responsible for me and my new womanhood. And when that night was over and I tucked myself into bed, I loved him more than I had the day before.

Two weeks later he took me to the orthodontist and I came home with braces on my teeth.

And a part of me found that funny. And another part of me kinda knew that it was McKay trying to keep me a little girl just a little bit longer. Even though I knew that wasn't really the reason I was getting braces. This appointment had been on his calendar for three months.

But that's how I stole a deadly infectious disease wearing a hazmat suit, got caught, was taken prisoner, then let go and left adrift on a life raft in the middle of the Caribbean Sea, had my first kiss with my first love, became a woman, and stayed a kid all in the same two-week period.

No pun intended.

CHAPTER ELEVEN

MIND CONTROL IN CHILDREN: A CASE STUDY OF COMPANY ASSASSINS

INTERVIEW WITH INDIE, AGE 15.5

SESSION #87

DONOVAN: OK, Indie. Calm down and tell it to me again. How did you meet this girl?

INDIE: I told you. She came to me. She would meet Nate and I in the river town where we go to pick up supplies for his grandfather and eat ice cream.

How long has this been going on?

I dunno. Years. We've been going there for years.

And this girl? She met you there every time?

No. She was new last summer. Just popped up out of nowhere.

She's a town kid?

No. I told you, Donovan. She's like me. Only… from somewhere else.

I need you to start at the beginning and tell me everything. Do not leave one single thing out. Do you understand?

…

Indie!

I hear you. I'm just trying to sort out where the story starts, for fuck's sake!

Don't swear at me.

…

OK. So last summer Nate and I were in town getting supplies and ice cream—

How did you get there? Did you drive?

No. We take the boat. And don't interrupt me.

…

OK. Like I said. Last summer Nate and I were in town getting supplies and ice cream and this girl was hanging out at a table and chairs near the ice cream parlor area. She was licking a cone. I think it was butter pecan but it could've been—

Indie.

You said tell you *everything.*

Unless the flavor of the ice cream is important to the story, leave that out.

Fine. She was just sitting there eating her ice cream while Nate and I were choosing our flavors. She was kinda messy. By that I mean her hair was wild and tangled. Like she'd been walking through the woods for too long and forgot who she was.

What did she look like?

I'm gettin' there. She had blonde hair, like me. And blue eyes like me too. But she's only twelve. And people were kinda side-eyeing her. Probably wonderin' who the hell she belonged to. But it's the swamp, and people come out of it at the weirdest times, and no townie people want to get involved with some random swamp child who turns up out of nowhere because you never knew who their daddy is. But I could not stop lookin' at her. Because she was so obviously not of this world.

What do you mean?

She was a Company kid, Donovan. Even I could see that. Hell, even Nate noticed something was wrong with her. She looked like me, and she was young, and alone, and acting like this was no big deal. She wasn't looking for her mama, and while she did have a fearful look on her face, it wasn't the scaredy-cat fear you see in kids. It was the kind of mean fear you see in… *men.*

Did she approach you first? Did she try anything?

No. Nate and I sat down at our regular table to eat our cones in the air conditioning. And I took my chair, and he took his chair, and I was facing her. So she and I were looking at each other. And then she licked her cone and winked at me. Then she got up, threw it in the trash, and walked outside.

What did you do?

Well. I knew this was a big deal. And I didn't want Nate involved. So I hesitated a little. And I ate my ice cream like normal. And Nate ate his—Donovan. You said tell you everything. If you want me to skip to the important parts, just say the word. But don't give me that *look* when I tell you everything!

. . .

So I tell Nate, "You go do your shopping. I need to talk to that girl."

Just like that? You told him you needed to talk to some random swamp child? And he—what? Said, "OK. Meet up with you later?"

He's not as stupid as you guys think, Donovan. He might not know what we do, but he knows it's not normal. And when I need him to butt out and let me take care of things, I give him a look.

A look?

That tells him I'm working now and he has to butt out.

And he's fine with that?

I would not call it *fine*. But he doesn't make a big deal.

OK. So you go outside. What did she tell you?

I was ready for her. If she was coming for me, I was ready for her. And she was years younger, so I wasn't worried when I followed her down the block and into an alley. She was lookin' over her shoulder as she walked, making sure I was following. So we get in the alley and she stops. And I walk up to her and say, "I really hope no one sent you here to kill me because I am not an easy girl to kill."

What did she say?

She said, "He came for me when I was on a job in Mobile. And I knew about you from my handlers. So when I saw him I knew they were dead and he was coming for me next. So I ran off and found my way to you. I've been watching you for weeks now. I'm not here to kill you, Indie, but I have to tell you that he is coming for you just like he came for me."

Who?

That's what I said. And she said, "Nicholas Tate."

Jesus Christ. Why the fuck didn't you say anything last summer?

Because I knew Adam would not let her stay.

Oh. My. God. Tell me this girl has not been *staying* with us?

Not exactly.

Indie.

She stayed with Nate. His grandfather is so sick now, he needed the help anyway. So she helped him.

...

Donovan?

...

Donovan? Do you want to hear the rest?

Skip ahead to what happened today.

OK. So today we were in town. Angelica—that's her name—Angelica was in the drug store getting Grandfather's medication. Nate and I were in the hardware store because Nate needed some nails and glue to fix the carpet that was coming up in his living room, and when we came out, she was gone.

Gone where?

That's what we said. So we went looking for her and found signs of a struggle in the alley where I first talked to her. Then we saw a trail going into the woods, and we followed that too. That's when we saw them. They were screaming at each other down by the river. Angelica was bleeding from her nose and her mouth. I think he hit her in the face. But she hit him back because he was leaning to the side, clutching his ribs. Like maybe she got in a good kick or two. His lip was swollen and he was wiping a little bit of blood off it. So we missed the first part of the fight. But I knew she was putting up a good one. I started going in. I figured two of us against one of him? Those odds weren't bad. But Nate grabbed me by the arm and put a hand over my mouth and dragged me away. And then that

Nicholas guy, he tackled Angelica, and knocked her out with one punch. He threw her into a boat and sped away. I was so mad at Nate. So angry that he didn't let me help her. But I didn't want to hurt him so I couldn't fight back. But I heard something, Donovan. And it scared me.

What? What did you hear?

He said Adam.

Tate did?

Yes. He was ticking off names to this girl while they were fighting. Telling her he knew everything. And he said… Jack or Jacks—something like that. And Chek, and Adam. I heard it. So he knows about us. He knows, Donovan. He knows about Wendy, and me, and Angelica. Do you think he got Wendy too? Do you think he'll come back for me?

…

Donovan?

I'm thinking.

OK. But… Should I go and get Adam now?

Yes. Go get Adam.

SESSION #87 cont.

Close the door, Adam. And where's McKay?

He took Indie outside.

Nicholas Tate jumped a girl upriver and took her.

What?

She was Company.

Wait. What the fuck are you talking about?

Indie just told me that she and Nate have been hiding a Company kid—a goddamned twelve-year-old Company assassin called Angelica—in Nate's house, since last fucking summer.

…

Did you hear me?

…

Adam!

I fucking heard you. I just… don't understand what you just said.

He came for her, or maybe Indie, I'm not quite clear on that. And he got this Angelica girl. You ever heard of her?

No. But how the fuck is Nicholas Tate in goddamned Louisiana? He's supposed to be down in Honduras running drugs.

Well… I don't know what you want me to say about that. Indie said this girl came to her and Nate last summer talking about how she was on the run from Nicholas Tate. They hid her in Nate's house, and today, while they were upriver in some town getting supplies,

Tate came, knocked the girl out, shoved her into a boat, and took her away.

...

He said your name.

What?

You heard me. He said your fucking name. Indie told me three names. Jack, and your dude Chek, and then he said Adam. This was your plan, remember? Nicholas and Harper Tate. James Fenici. Sasha Cherlin. This was your fucking plan and the whole thing is in play and you never told me a goddamned thing about this. What the *fuck* is going on?

I haven't talked to Sasha in ten years, Donovan. This is not my plan.

Well, this has Sasha's name written all over it. She and Nick are a team like McKay and Indie are a team. And he said your name, Adam.

I haven't talked to Nick since we were kids. You know that.

I don't know shit right now. We had a deal, remember? We were gonna do this together. *Our* way. And this is not our way and it is most decidedly not together.

I'm not a part of this. I swear to fucking God, I'm not.

When Nicholas Tate comes to steal a Company kid and says the name Adam... what can I do but assume?

...

Nothing to say about that?

It wasn't me. Remember? Remember that time you told me there was another Adam in play? It must be him. Not me.

Hmm. Or… there was never another Adam and it was always you.

Donovan. Believe me—

I don't know what to believe right now. I feel a huge disconnect with the team. I'm away at school and you three are here doing who the fuck knows what. I don't know what else to tell you, Adam. I don't even know what we're doing anymore. I don't know why we're doing it, or what we're getting out of it. And Indie… she needs help. You and I both know—have known for a long fucking time now—that I'm not going to be able to keep her sane.

Donovan. Listen to me. You're all she's had. I get it. You're feeling responsible—

Fuck you, Adam. You're responsible for this shit show. Not me.

You're the one who told me to buy her.

You're the one who's been running her for the past four years. Not me. I'm just a way to ease your guilty conscious.

I don't even know what you're going on about. You wanted this, Donovan. For your stupid research paper.

Go get McKay. I'm done with you for now.

SESSION #87 cont.

DONOVAN: Where the fuck have you been?

MCKAY: Why are you taping this?

Because this is an Indie debrief.

Exactly. Indie's debrief. Turn it off.

. . .

Turn it off, Donovan. Or I walk out.

SESSION #87 NOTES – PRIVATE

I think it's time to stop. I'm not even sure why I started this shit.

I'm not certified, I'm not equipped, and I have a really bad feeling that this girl's mind has been fucked with by someone who knows a helluva lot more than I do.

And if this is Carter… well, he certainly had better teachers than I did.

Who am I kidding? No one taught me shit. I've been following a training manual twenty years out of date and making this shit up as I go.

It needs to stop.

CHAPTER TWELVE

adam

NINE YEARS AGO

There is a really big part of me that wants to stay out of it. All of it. But this was my plan. I bought Indie with this endgame in mind.

And Nicholas Tate has been part of the plan since the beginning.

But Nick Tate and I don't seem to be on the same page anymore.

The drive from Old Home to Daphne, Alabama takes about two hours and I spend every minute of that drive thinking about what I need to say and how it needs to be said.

Nick Tate's story is as long and twisted up as that snake that wanted to squeeze Indie back on the island. The son of the Admiral, one of the Company Untouchables—maybe even the *most* untouchable, until he wasn't, that is—Nick didn't grow up like most people. Not like McKay, not like Donovan. Not even like me.

Most of his life was spent as an invisible. He was born on a superyacht. No birth certificate. No formal schooling. But trust me on this, no one underestimates his intelligence or his skills.

The last time I saw Nick we were plotting the death of our fathers.

That turned out fairly well for me.

But in order to save James Fenici during the Santa Barbara incident—another Untouchable, sociopathic Company assassin, in love with Nick's twin sister, Harper—he ended up the prisoner of a Central American drug lord.

That's where he's been for the past ten years.

Or… not.

Since apparently he was here in Louisiana this morning and now we have a meeting in Daphne, Alabama.

Just as McKay was walking into the office to talk with Donovan the gate buzzed. I got in my truck, drove down there, and met a messenger who handed me a thick yellow envelope.

I tipped the girl, she left, and I found a burner phone inside when I opened it up.

One number in the contacts.

I pressed send and Nick picked up. "It's been a long time, Adam."

I noted three things about his voice.

One. It was deep. Ten years ago, we were still kids. Both of us just eighteen years old. We are no longer kids.

Two. He had a slight Spanish accent. And by Spanish accent I mean he sounded like a fuckin' gangbanger.

And three… he was very calm.

Six words tell me a whole lot about what Nick Tate has been up to for the past ten years. Maybe I didn't grow up on a superyacht, but he and I were cut from the same cloth.

"What the fuck did you do this morning?"

"I hear you *bought* one of them?"

"If you mean Indie, then yes. I did. And I do not fucking appreciate you showing up like this morning and scaring the fuck out of her."

"Was she scared?"

"What do you want?"

He paused. Sighed. "There's another plan in play. Right now, in fact. Everyone's here."

"Here? Where?"

"It's a metaphor, Adam. All the players are back, but Sasha is the star of this show. You're gonna sit this one out."

"I don't know anything about this. I helped her out ten years ago and I haven't seen her since."

"I know. This is her moment. We don't need you."

"So why are you here fucking up my good thing?"

He laughed, just a little, on the other end of the phone. "Good thing? You have one of those *psycho assassins* living in your fucking mansion, Adam. Did you know she was hiding that girl I caught this morning?"

I didn't. But I didn't want to admit that, either. Indie was decidedly off script. And when your little psycho assassin went off script and Nick Tate showed up from the dead to fill you in on it, things were a little more serious than simply… *off script.*

They were off the rails.

"So you got what you came for? We're good?"

"*Half* of what I came for."

My stomach roiled when I realized what that meant. He came for Indie too. Just didn't get her yet. "She's mine, Nick."

"No." He paused. And I imagined him shaking his head. "No. She's not yours. She is the Company's. And before you tell me how much you paid for her, I already know. I know everything, Adam. She is not yours. She is *mine.* I run that program. She came from *my* training center."

"And so… what? What the fuck are you doing? Taking them all back?"

"You could say that." There was a long silence on the line after that.

"Why are you calling me?" I finally said.

"I'm texting you an address. You have two hours and fifteen minutes to get there. Then I just… move on without you."

And the call dropped.

Two hours and seven minutes later I'm parking the truck on the side of the road. There are three people on the Gator Boardwalk in Daphne, Alabama. None of them are Nick Tate. Just a man, a woman pushing a stroller, and a small child.

I head that direction and find my way to the part of the boardwalk that goes under the northbound lanes of AL-42 traffic and there he is. It's windy and cool today. High fifties, maybe. Heavily overcast and a little bit of drizzle in the air. He's wearing a black hoodie with the hood over his head, but I know it's him.

He side-eyes me as I approach and I stop for a moment, taken aback.

"Nick?" I whisper it. And the traffic above us on the bridge is so loud, I can barely hear it myself, so I know he doesn't hear it. That's probably why we're meeting under this bridge. Just in case anyone is listening. Or if I came wired, I guess.

Nick turns to face me full on and I find myself holding my breath. There is a nasty, thick scar down the side of one cheek and his neck is ringed with tattoos.

Chains.

"Nice to see you again, Adam."

I can't talk. I don't know how to reconcile this guy in front of me with the golden surfer kid I last saw ten years ago. They are not the same person. Not even close. And for a moment I just stare at him, unable to believe my own eyes.

"What… what happened to you, Nick?"

He lifts his head up a little in a sort of nod, then says, "Come down here so we can talk."

I hesitate. Because I'm suddenly unsure if I even want to get that close to him. The whole drive over here to Alabama I was pretty confident that I could handle Nick Tate. But all that confidence is withering fast as I process just how little I know him these days. A lot has happened in the ten years since he was taken down to Central America.

But I'm here. There is no way out but forward. So I close the distance between us in fifteen steps. He leans his forearms on the top rail of the fence that overlooks the water and I do the same. There are no gators down there that I can see. But Nick is silent and studies the water anyway.

I wait as long as I can, but I'm anxious and I need to make sense of whatever the fuck it is he's doing. For all I know he's put some kind of team together and he got me down here, two hours away from Indie, so he could send them in and take her out.

McKay too.

But I force myself to remain calm. "Well… what can I do for you?"

He draws in a breath. "I'm taking it down for good."

"We tried that already. I don't even know the exact number of Company upper circle who died that night in Santa Barbara, but it was over two hundred. And we're still here. And I'm still working. So that's fine. If you want to do it again, I won't get in your way. But you leave my girl out of it. You got the other one, the one I didn't know about. But you can't have Indie. And if you came here to tell me something different, we're gonna settle this before you leave."

He shoots me a crooked smile. "Big, tough words from you today, Adam."

"And why the fuck are you telling people I'm working with you?"

He frowns. "What the hell are you talking about?"

"I've been hearing my name come up with yours and I don't like it. I helped you out that *one* time. And you know damn well we haven't been in contact since."

"Oh. *Adam.* No. Not you. Some other dude. He's in the FBI. Doesn't even know he's Company. Yet. But he's part of my plan."

"What plan?"

"Don't worry about that part. I don't need your help this time. I have it all covered. But…" He pauses. Stares at me with hard, cold, brown eyes. "I can't leave these girls behind."

I shake my head. Not understanding. "What… I don't get it. Where are you going? Where are you taking them?"

But then it hits me.

He's not going anywhere except down with this fucking Company ship.

"You're killing them." It's not even a question. "You're taking some kind of last stand and you're making them go down with you."

"They're all fucked anyway, Adam. You and I both know that. The only reason you're still alive is because your father backed you out of the program when you were twelve."

I'm not sure if he's trying to say I would've never cut it as a Company assassin or if he's hinting that he'd have already killed me by now if my father had put me through the same early training Nick had.

Doesn't really matter though. I only have one thing left to say to him and then I'm leaving. "It's not Indie's fault, Nick. It's not your fault. It's not my fault. She didn't have a choice. I didn't have a choice. You didn't have a choice. This is just the life we got stuck with. So if you think killing little girls is the only way you can find the absolution you are so obviously looking for? Well, fuck you. Just… fuck you, Nick. There is no absolution for you. Your father made sure of that."

"And your father made sure you got out."

"I didn't ask him to do that. And Indie didn't ask me to save her, either. But he did. And I did. And I'm not gonna let you come in and rip her world apart just so you can feel better about yourself when you land in hell."

"Is that where you think I'm headed?"

I almost laugh. "Are we done here?"

"I don't know, Adam. Are we?"

"Stay the fuck away from my kid. You hear me? She's not like us. She's definitely not like you."

He flips his hood down to reveal an almost completely shaved head. It makes him look even more dangerous and diabolical than he did with it up. And I can't lie. My fuckin' heart skips a beat. Adrenaline shoots through my body and my muscles are tense and ready if he decides this is where we part ways on bad terms.

This cannot be the boy I knew. It simply *can't* be him.

But it is. I can see him underneath the tattoos and scars. He's… *in there*. Somewhere.

"She's not different. They all say that, Adam. Every one of them says it. And they might even all believe it. But it's not true. She's *not* different. Not from me. Not from you. Not from McKay. Not from any of us. And if you keep her—"

"*If* I keep her?" I scoff. "Motherfucker, she's *mine*. Forever."

"If you keep her, there will be a price to pay. And when that day comes…" He shakes his head. "I'm gonna be down in hell, laughing at you."

I stare at him, defiant now. My heart isn't skipping because he scares me. It's thumping hard because if he comes at me, I will kill him right here. Hand-to-hand combat style—in full view of that little family on the other part of the Gator Boardwalk bridge—and not give a single fuck about it.

Nick assesses me. Probably asking himself how even of a fight it is these days. Wondering how low I've been lying these past ten years. Wondering if I got lazy and decided to let McKay do all my fighting for me.

But it hasn't been McKay taking Indie on those jobs. And he probably knows that.

Still. His father made sure he was the most dangerous kid to ever come out of the Zero program and the past ten years down in Central America certainly haven't softened him up any.

Finally, he grins and puts up both hands in an 'I surrender' gesture. "Hey. You do you, bro. If you say you've got her under control?" He shrugs. "Who am I to say different?"

I work my jaw, still tense. Say nothing.

"We good then?"

"We're good," I whisper. "As long as you stay the fuck out of Louisiana."

He grins at me. A crooked, messy grin that says more than words ever will. "Don't worry about that. I'm on my way to Colorado right after I leave here. Got people to see, places to go, shit to do." Then he extends his hand towards me.

I look at it for a second. Then let out a long breath and take it.

He quickly turns it into some drug lord secret handshake that I'm clueless about. But we end it with a bump. And then he flips his hood back over his head, turns away, and walks off.

"Hey," I call after him. "Did you kill her?"

He turns around, hands in his hoodie pockets, and walks backwards. "Who?"

"That girl you got this morning?"

"Not yet," he says, still walking backwards.

"It's not her fault, Nick. Indie has me, and McKay, and Donovan. We're gonna take care of her. I promise. We won't let this happen to her. And you don't have to kill that girl either. It's not her fault."

I don't know why I say that. But Indie has changed me. I don't see her as the psycho kid inside that snake cage back on the auction island anymore.

I see her the way she is now. Happy. Pretty well-adjusted. Just another teenage girl.

He stops walking and shakes his head at me. "What do you think I should do? Just… find a couple of cool-headed ex-Company assassins and drop her off for foster care?"

I shrug with my hands. "It's not a bad idea, dude. She didn't ask for this. Don't take her down with you."

He smiles. Shoots me with his finger. And then turns back around and continues walking.

I watch him until he's up over the ridge and out of sight. Then I take out my phone and call Indie.

"What's up?" she says.

And I can breathe normally again.

"Hello? Adam? What the fuck?"

My heart stops skipping.

"Are you OK? Do you need help? What's going on?"

The fear ebbs back.

"No. I'm here. Just checking on you. What are you doing?"

"What? I'm over at Nate's house. We're watching a movie."

"Watching a movie, huh? That better be all you're doing with *Nate*."

"Shut up. Where are you?"

"I'll be home in a couple hours. But I just want to say that… your friend isn't dead. He took her, but…"

"Oh, thank God. I like her. She was cool. And I felt so bad."

So bad, you're watching a movie right now like it was nothing?

I want to say that. But don't. Because then I might have to admit that Nick was right. She's not OK. She will never be OK. She was bred to be a sociopath just like me. Just like Donovan.

And yeah… just like Nick.

"Well, have some… good, *clean teen* fun. And don't be late for dinner. You know McKay hates that."

"Oh, my God. Whatever. See you then."

And she drops me.

I'm smiling, pretty satisfied with how this meeting turned out, when I realize something.

Nick. He said… McKay. He said, *She's not different. Not from me. Not from you. Not from McKay. Not from any of us.*

But that's not true. We aren't all the same. McKay isn't like us. He will *never* be like us.

There's a two-hour drive home. And I should be thinking about Nick Tate and what the fuck he's up to with the Company.

But that's not what I'm thinking about.

Nick can do whatever he wants and he can think whatever he wants. I don't really give a fuck. We barely work for the Company these days anyway. The odd clean-up job here and there is like a vacation compared to what the other teams do. And they can't touch me. They know that. The whole fucking arrangement since I bought Indie has been one long win-win as far as I'm concerned. If that Shadow of Secrets calling himself Nick Tate wants to take some people out with him, go for it, dude.

Just leave me out of it.

I'm done with that shit.

No. What I'm thinking about is Nathan St. James. Because he and Indie are getting pretty fucking tight. And I get it. He's the boy next door. Indie has this tattered-up romance novel about some teenager falling for the boy next door. I don't even know where she got that thing. Maybe on one of her clandestine trips upriver for supplies? Which reminds me—I maybe need to put some kind of tracker on her. We didn't even know she was going upriver and apparently she's been doing that for years.

But she's got boyfriends on her mind. And while it could be worse—she could've fallen for the local high-school football jock in the nearest town—I'm not ready for her to start dating.

But then I wonder… maybe she's been dating that kid this whole time and I didn't know it? Because I'm dumb. I'm a twenty-eight-year-old dumbass man who has no clue what teenage girls think about and I let McKay handle all that shit. And she's been hanging out with Nathan St. James since she was ten. So… like… have they been kissing and shit?

I get this weird, sick feeling in my stomach when I think about that. I don't wanna think about it. But she is fifteen. And back when I was fifteen, I was fucking around with all kinds of girls. Who were also *fifteen.*

No. I don't like where this Nate thing is headed. Not one bit.

Indie has a job to do. And I probably got a little too comfortable with Nate because he's just been a fixture around Old Home for so long, I started assuming he was one of us.

Which he sort of is. His father was, at least. He was a lot older than me growing up so I didn't pay much attention to him. And I was busy being me. In fact, I don't even know what happened to that guy. I don't even know where Nate came from. Just… one day he was there.

He wasn't a baby. And there was never a mother over there. Just the grandfather and then the kid. He was about four, maybe, when he showed up. Five at the oldest.

And it occurs to me that I should look into this shit. It occurs to me that I should've looked into this shit a long-ass time ago.

When I get home McKay's truck is gone. I was gonna talk to him first since he's the one who pays the most attention to

Indie on the day to day. But I look across the lake and then the next thing I know I'm heading down the path that leads to the little brick carriage house.

I even sneak a little. Like I'm spying. And when I started down the path I didn't intend on spying. I just figured it was time I had a little chat with Grandpa St. James. Make sure we're all on the same page here as far as my… Indie… goes.

Which then has me wondering what I should call her when I talk to the old fart.

She's not my little sister. And she's not my daughter.

So yeah. This is probably why I let McKay do this shit. There is no word for what Indie is to me.

Except the actual description of what Indie is to me. Which is my little bought-and-paid-for psycho assassin kid.

But I can't really say that.

So I stop just off to the left side of the house to think about this for a moment.

Hello, Mr. Grandpa St. James. I'm here to have a talk with you about your grandson's intentions with my…? My what?

Friend? Not really.

Ward? That sounds very Charles Dickens.

Minor dependent?

I go with that and continue towards the house. It's as good as anything. But I'm just coming up to the front when I hear giggling.

And you know what? It's not the kind of giggling you do when you're watching a funny movie.

It's soft giggling. And then a word. "Stop." Just one giggly word. "Stop it." And again.

And that rational voice inside me is screaming, *Go home. Talk to her later. You do not want to know what's happening in there.*

Which is very good advice. And I should listen to myself.

But I don't. I walk to the window and peek in.

Indie and Nate on the couch. Heads together. Lips, if not touching, just about to. His hand squirming its way up her shirt.

She giggles again. "Stop it! I told you. Not until later!"

"Not until later?" I echo.

And then I realize the window is open and they just heard me.

"Adam!" Indie squeals and she's up on her feet so fast, I almost think I was seeing things.

But no. Her shirt is pulled crooked, one bare shoulder exposed.

"What the fuck is going on here?" My voice is low and growly and threatening.

"Oh, fuck," Nate says. "I'm sorry. We were just messing around."

I stare at him. No. *Glare at him* through the window. And then the next thing I know I'm inside, grabbing him by the fucking shirt. Pushing him up against the wall. Knocking shit over as he struggles to get away. Indie is tugging on my arm, and then a picture falls off the wall, and somehow Indie is on the floor. Looking up at me. Screaming. "He was teasing me! That's all! It was a tease!"

I hear it. I get it. I do. But I can't bring myself to take my fucking fingers off this kid's throat.

He's choking now, his hands gripping mine. But he's a fifteen-year-old kid and I'm a twenty-eight-year-old asshole. So there's no hope for him at all.

And then there's a blinding flash of light in front of my eyes and ringing in my ears as something very hard and solid hits the side of my head.

I wake up with a piercing headache and McKay bent over me, shaking me by the shoulders.

"He's coming around."

That's McKay.

"Oh, thank God. Adam? Oh, my God. Adam? Are you OK?"

That's Indie.

I blink a few times, trying to focus my eyes, and then McKay is pulling me up to a sitting position.

My head *throbs*. I reach for it and find a hard crust of blood matted into my hair.

My head swivels to the side and I barely make out… Nathan. Little coward. Standing in the far corner. Arms crossed over his chest. A red ring of fingerprints still bright around his neck. And he has the fucking nerve to scowl at me.

"You," I croak.

"Easy, killer." McKay pulls me to my feet. "You took a hard hit. And it wasn't him."

"I'm so sorry, Adam." Indie is all up in my face. Eyes darting back and forth, searching mine. "I didn't think I hit you that hard. But you were gonna choke him out! And I told you, he was teasing me! That's it! That's all it was!"

But that wasn't all it was. My head is pretty foggy right now but I saw what I saw. His fucking hand up her shirt. His lips on her mouth.

I direct my glare at McKay. "You're supposed to be watching her. Do you have any idea what she's doing over here?"

"I'm not doing anything! We were watching a movie and you came in—"

"I saw you, Indie. Kissing him."

"Oh! Kissing him! Call the fucking FBI. Two teenagers were kissing!" She turns to McKay. "Do you believe this shit?"

"Indie." And McKay *growls* her name. "Go home."

"No! No! I'm not leaving you two here with him! So you can what, choke him to death this time? You didn't see him, McKay! He was an animal! He was practically foaming at the fucking mouth!"

And in this moment McKay looks at Indie like… well, let's just say the last I saw this look on McKay's face, he was in the middle of killing someone. "Go. The fuck. Home."

Indie stomps her foot and folds her arms across her chest. "I'm not going home. I'm staying right here until this is settled."

I touch my head again and this time my fingertips walk up the baseball-sized lump to find the gash in the middle. It fucking hurts. And then I look around and find the weapon. A silver candlestick on the floor. Dried blood on the top edge.

McKay looks down at it too. Then up at me. "She hit you."

"No shit."

"I had to!" Indie is still hysterical. "You morphed into a violent freak!"

McKay's fingers come up to my head and he touches the wound. "The bleeding has stopped but you definitely need stitches and…" He trails off, but he's just staring at my head.

I glance down at my white thermal shirt and find one whole side of it crimson with blood.

McKay looks at Nate. "Get him some fucking ice, will ya?"

"How long was I out?"

"A long time." McKay sighs, then looks over at Nate in the kitchen, then back at me. "What the fuck happened?"

"I told you what happened!"

McKay points to Indie. "Shut your fucking mouth. You hear me? Because if you say one more fucking word, I will bend you over my goddamned knee and spank you like a fucking child."

"I'd like to see you try." She is defiant till the end. I will give her that.

Nate comes back from the kitchen and hands McKay a dishtowel filled with ice. McKay hands it to me, and I take it, gingerly pressing it up against my head. Then I look at Nate. "Where the fuck is your grandfather?"

He points to the bedroom.

I squint my eyes in confusion. "He's here?"

Indie positions herself in front of me so I can't see Nate. "He's sick, OK? He's been bedridden for months now. And you would know that if you knew anything about me at all!"

I look at McKay. "Did you know this?"

He nods. "I knew."

"And you let her come over here to… *watch movies*?"

"Oh, my God!"

"Shut up, Indie!" McKay and I say it at the same time.

Then McKay turns to me. "Look. I get it. We need to sort this out. But I think we should just take you into the emergency room and make sure you're OK. She hit you fucking hard, Adam. You most certainly have a concussion. You were out for almost thirty minutes. I was about to call a goddamned ambulance."

I point my finger at Nate. "This isn't over."

And then I walk out—mostly by myself, but actually with a lot of help from McKay. Indie follows. And somehow, they get me back over to my own property and into McKay's truck.

I have emergency surgery to relieve swelling on my brain, spend two days in an induced coma, then spend another ten in a hospital in New Orleans under observation as a slew of random nurses and doctors come in and out of my room telling me how lucky I am to be alive after falling off that roof.

So it's actually two months later when McKay, Donovan, and I pick this conversation back up.

Indie has been grounded since the 'incident' at Nate's house. I know she feels pretty bad about what happened because McKay tells me she hasn't complained once about being locked up in the house.

And she's nice to me.

I'm not saying she's been mean to me all these years, but I am not her favorite… *guardian.*

Funny how there's a legit word for a person who takes care of a random kid who is not related to them, but no good word for what that kid is to said guardian.

Ward?

No. Dependent. That was the word I decided on. But maybe protégé is more accurate?

My memory is still a little bit fucked since the 'incident'. But I'm mostly fine. McKay shaved my head the day I came home from the hospital so I didn't have that huge patch of baldness where they cut me open after Indie… you know.

I don't like to think about it.

Haven't worked since that day. But turns out it doesn't even matter. Nick Tate was fucking serious. The Company is… well. I'm not sure such a massive global organization can just be *erased,* but the whole thing kind of just… fell apart.

I haven't gotten all the details yet since it went down while I was in that induced coma. But McKay told me what he knew. And Donovan knew a little more because the auction island was raided by law enforcement in the Bahamas and the CIA. And his grandfather, Gerald, killed himself during the final standoff and Donovan was notified of that by the estate lawyers.

But other than that? Fuck if I know what happened to the Company.

Fuck if I care.

Good for Nick. I hope he and his people are happy. I have a more immediate problem to think about.

Indie.

Right now, McKay, Donovan, and I are in the TV room in the back of the house, just off the kitchen. Actually, I'm sitting on the couch that faces the wall of windows that look out onto the backyard. Donovan is sitting at the kitchen bar talking to McKay as McKay makes us tomato sandwiches.

I glance up at McKay. He's smiling and laughing at some story Donovan is telling him about one of his girlfriends at Duke. He's in his second year of lab rotations for some kind of clinical neuroscience PhD.

But, with the exception of a few weekend trips back to North Carolina for some exams and meetings about his research, Donovan has taken the semester off and has been here with us since the 'incident'.

Indie has a session with him twice a day now.

I don't like to think about it. And actually, I'm not even that worried about Indie. She's been the model—ward? Dependent? Protégée?—since I came home from the hospital.

No. My immediate problem right now is Nathan St. James.

Every time I'm out walking in the gardens and see that stupid little brick house, I want to blow it up with that fuck of a kid inside.

Today is the first day that Indie has been allowed to have him over since I caught him trying to shove his hand up her shirt two months ago. This was McKay's idea and Donovan concurred that it was a good one, so I didn't even bother fighting them on the matter.

So right now, as I look out the long wall of windows, I can see them sitting on lounge chairs, under a huge umbrella, in front of the pool. Talking. Laughing. Eating tomato sandwiches that McKay made for them before he started making ours. It's not warm enough to swim, and it's drizzling a little, but the pool is heated so they could if they wanted.

Indie is wearing cut-off denim shorts and a faded red hoodie with thick, fancy, white letters that say *Flower Power* across the front. She has her long blonde hair pulled up in a ponytail and large, dark sunglasses obscure her eyes. Her knees are pulled up and she twirls a purple and yellow pansy in her fingers as she talks, shooting Nathan shy glances every few seconds.

Nathan is wearing jeans, white t-shirt, and a red-and-brown checked flannel that reminds me of old, dried blood. He doesn't have sunglasses on, so I stare at his eyes as they laugh at Indie's jokes, narrowing down and crinkling at the corners.

I think I hate that kid.

McKay is suddenly in my face, setting a sandwich on a plate down on the side table next to the couch. Donovan takes a seat next to me, his sandwich in his hand, already half eaten. McKay sits in the chair across from me and obscures my view of Indie and the fuckwad boy next door. He props his ankle on his leg and points to Donovan. "Go ahead. Tell him what you told me."

I look at Donovan, wondering what this is gonna be about. Already weary of the conversation that hasn't started yet.

He looks back at me for a moment, like he's not exactly sure who I am anymore. "The Company is gone, man. I'm talking these people have disappeared into the woodwork completely."

I hate that look. Anyone who has ever been in a serious accident understands this look. Anyone who was ever been… *reduced* knows this look. It's a look that says, *Are you* sure *you're OK? Are you super, one-hundred-percent positive you're OK?*

And they're only lookin' at you like this because they know damn well you're not anything close to OK. I take a deep breath because I know Donovan is just concerned about me. "So?"

McKay leans back into his chair. "So we don't have any jobs."

"So?" I ask again.

Donovan takes over. "Well, we *could* have jobs. If we wanted to go freelance."

"What do you care?" I ask him. "You've got a job in LA."

"You have to do something with Indie, Adam. You can't just lock her up here and expect things to turn out OK. She needs focus. And I've got a shit ton of contacts who still need things… taken care of."

I squint my eyes at Donovan, wondering what he's *not* saying. "Clean-up?"

Donovan shrugs. "Among other things."

"What other things? Stealing? Killing?"

"All of the above."

I look at McKay. "Is this what you want to do now? Just… go out on our own?"

"What else is there to do? I mean, we could retire, I guess. But dude, I'm twenty-seven years old. I'm not ready to retire. And unlike our nerd friend here, I haven't been preparing for a life outside the Company. We have to do something. And what is Indie gonna do? Go to high school? Get a fucking college degree in assassination?"

Donovan laughs and I scowl at him. "It's not funny, Donovan. It's a real fucking question."

Was Nick Tate some kind of soothsayer? Some kind of psychic? I'm not sure. All I know is that he was right. Indie is not OK. Indie will *never* be OK. And even if McKay and I wanted to… I dunno. Go out and get jobs. Or do nothing. She doesn't have that option. She has no purpose aside from what she was bred and trained to do. And when I bought her, I knew what that meant. It meant from that day forward, until she dies, she is my responsibility. I have to be there for her whether I want to or not.

Because she is unfit to live in society. We don't talk about it much, but we all know. She is Nick. She is James Fenici.

She is not Sasha Cherlin.

So it's either be there with her. Every day, all the time. And put her first. Or… kill her. Put her down, as we say in the Company. And I'm not even close to being ready to do that.

"Which is why I'm bringing up the option to go freelance."

"With you as our… what? Coordinator?"

Donovan does one of those open-palm shrugs, huge shit-eating grin on his face that says, *Aw, shucks. What else can we do*? You know the look. He's a fucking snake-oil salesman right now. "There are a lot of people like us, Adam. Lots of teams who have nothing to do now. They need guidance. We could… *provide* that guidance."

"Or," I counter, "we could quietly slip away into obscurity and hope Indie…" I know it's never going to happen, but I say it anyway. "*Adjusts.*"

"McKay just said he doesn't want to do that. And you and I both know Indie goes with McKay if he leaves. She's not staying here with you."

I glare at McKay but he's already got his hands up in surrender. "I'm not going anywhere. And neither is Indie. She's happy here, Adam."

"Of course she is. She's got her little boyfriend next door."

Hmm. I didn't mean for that to come out so… *venomous.* But it does. And everyone hears it. I backtrack a little. "What do you propose, Donovan? Spell it out for me."

So he starts talking.

And a few years later I was the leader of the most ruthless private army to walk this Earth since the Ten Thousand brought terror and fear to Ancient Greece.

But I'm getting ahead of myself…

CHAPTER THIRTEEN

mckay

PRESENT DAY

Adam is not here. That becomes very clear once we enter the house and find it utterly silent. There are white sheets covering everything. I'm talking tables and chairs—even the paintings on the walls.

Indie looks around like she's never been here before, fingertips gently trailing across a white sheet covering the foyer side table. She pauses on the edge of something hidden beneath the sheet.

I know what it is. I remember every detail about this house. I've memorized every squeaky floorboard. I know which chair to sit in if you want some morning sun. I know there are four doors in this house that swell up in the summer so you can't close them without a good hard shove. I know which windows gather condensation in the winter. I know where Indie likes to throw her jacket when she comes in out of the rain. I know where Adam sits when he wants to think and I know where Donovan likes to write in his notebook.

And right now, Indie's fingertips are tracing the outline of the little stone dish where we all used to drop our car keys when we came inside.

She pulls a sheet off a large portrait of the four of us hanging in the hallway leading to the kitchen and TV room in the back of the house. She pauses at the painting, frowning and squinting at our faces.

Adam commissioned it. We took a photo first, then had it digitally painted. He hired some photographer friend of Misha's from New Orleans to come up for a photoshoot in the gardens between the house and the lake. We have tons of framed photos from that shoot hanging in the house, but this one was our favorite.

We were all in the pavilion and it was night. It was summer, hot and sticky. Indie was wearing an off-white dress with cotton lace. Cotton because she complained that regular lace was too itchy. Adam had this dress made for her. Hired a fucking seamstress and everything. She had a flower crown on her head made of buttercups and columbines that Adam had made special by a florist in Baton Rouge. Her hair was very blonde that summer and her skin was tanned bronze from long days sitting out at the pool, her childish afternoons of swamping long over by this time. She was a little over sixteen, I think.

Adam was wearing a full-on summer suit. Tan coat and slacks. Off-white shirt. Light blue tie that set off his eyes. His hair was too long and, like Indie's, very blond. He wasn't very happy when I shaved his head after the brain surgery so he let it grow for almost a full year before he cut it again.

I was wearing faded blue jeans and a white button-down. No tie. Sleeves casually pushed up my forearms. My hair was cropped short to help alleviate the summer heat and I had stubble on my jaw that was probably two days too long.

And Donovan was wearing gray slacks and a light blue shirt. No coat, but he had a gray tie on. His dark hair was styled, and his look was more sophisticated than Adam's, even though he was underdressed.

We were all piled on top of the bed swing I built for Indie. It still hangs from the long dark beams under the pavilion's pitched roof. I saw it out of the corner of my eye when we pulled up. Though the comfy pillows and blankets aren't there anymore.

I was in the middle, sitting a little farther back on the swing with Adam on my right and Donovan on my left.

Indie was sitting in front of me, between my legs. Leaning against Adam's shoulder with her hands in her lap. My arms were around her in a protective embrace and I had both of her hands in mine. Donovan has one arm draped casually around my shoulder and the other one was holding onto the chain that supported the swing.

We looked like a family.

And we were, I guess. Kind of.

Indie had strung white fairy lights around the perimeter of the pavilion and there were dozens of candles of various heights surrounding us so that our faces were lit up with the glow of flames. And we didn't notice them at the time, but there were fireflies in the background. We only saw that when the proofs came back. And this was the only one they showed up in, so it was our favorite.

We looked magical. Like everything was right in the world.

And it was. The Company was gone. We were working, but only on our own jobs now. And we were happy that summer. We were.

But it didn't stay that way for long.

"I remember this."

Indie's statement draws me out of the past and back into the present.

There is no glow of fireflies now. No romantic lights or flickering candles. The whole house is gray with the late winter dawn.

The switch in light from the walk to the house from the car throws me for a moment. Like a spell. But it's not magic. It's just the rising sun.

Indie is too pale. Donovan is standing in the living room off to my left—hands in his pockets, shoulders much broader than I remember them being—looking out the window, so I can't see his face.

But I know what he's looking at.

Or, rather, what he's *not* looking at.

The little brick house that used to be across the lake, but isn't anymore.

"What did Adam say, Donovan?" I ask.

Donovan doesn't turn around when he answers me. "He said he'd be here."

Indie huffs. "Well, he's not."

"Are you hungry, Indie?" I ask her.

"Maybe a little." Then she turns to the long, curved staircase that goes up to the second level. The spindles are white and the steps and risers are dark wood, like all the floors in the house, except for the kitchen and TV room, which have slate floors.

She stares up, squinting a little, like she's remembering something she forgot.

I turn back to find Donovan. Make sure he's seeing this. I mean, that was the point of coming here, right? Make her remember?

But he's not paying attention.

"Hey, Donovan. You wanna like… join us?"

He turns, but slowly, hands still in his pockets. And it takes his eyes a few seconds too long to meet mine. "What?"

I nod my head at Indie, who has started climbing the stairs.

"Oh. Sure. You go with her. I'll find us something to eat."

Indie is almost at the top now, looking at all the other photos that hang in the upstairs hallway.

"Call Adam," I say. "I'll keep an eye on her."

He nods. And I follow Indie upstairs.

She's peeking into Adam's bedroom. He had the largest one on the front side of the house that faces the driveway and the south gardens.

I stand next to her and take in his room. Everything is covered in white sheets but I don't need to remove them to know what's underneath—a large four-poster bed in the middle with nightstands on either side. Two chairs make an intimate seating area off to the left, and a massive armoire made of dark wood balances the whole thing out on the right.

Where does Adam live? Why don't I know this?

I suddenly feel like he's hiding things from me. Which, to be honest, I should've figured out four years ago when he disappeared. But I had so many other things on my mind after Indie took off that day.

Indie moves on to the next room, which is Donovan's. Smaller than Adam's, but still large. Same kind of furniture. Four-poster bed, armoire instead of a dresser. All the furnishings up here are antiques and are probably as old as the house, which is over a hundred years old. Only the stuff downstairs is new.

Then she looks across the hall at my room. It's not as small as hers is, but smaller than both Donovan's and Adam's and the four-poster bed and armoire make it feel crowded.

Indie loses interest quickly and heads down the hallway to her own room. She doesn't pause at the entrance like she did for the others, but goes right in and by the time I catch up with her she's sitting on her double bed with the painted iron frame. Her eyes are downcast and her fingertips gently caress the quilt that kept her warm for all the years when she slept up here.

She absently kicks off one boot, then the other. Wiggles her bare toes. Which are painted, I notice. Dark pink.

And for some reason that bothers me. Indie with painted toes. It makes her four-year absence so… real. Like… did she have a pedicure? Did she paint them herself? Where would she do something like that?

I tried to track her that first year. I felt obligated. I mean, I did turn her into this… bloodthirsty sociopath, right? The least I could do was keep an eye on her and make sure she didn't lose her mind and start offing people. But she literally disappeared. No trace. By this time Adam, Donovan, and I had been running ex-Company teams for several years. We had connections. Not anything as intricate as what we had before the Company fell, but it was enough to get intel and keep teams alive.

Even with all that, Indie was gone. I found some security cam footage of her truck right after she left. Had a decent, if spotty, track record of her as she made her way east towards Mobile. But after that… nothing. That was under two hours.

Two hours.

That's all it took for her to wipe herself off the map.

It was a weird time for me. I was so fucking confused. I kept playing what happened back in my head over and over again. Donovan left right after Indie, claiming he couldn't be a part of this. So it was just me that night.

Just me. All alone in this house.

I've been alone here before. Every time Adam and Indie went on a job I stayed behind.

But this wasn't that kind of alone.

This was… loneliness.

Adam wasn't picking up his phone. I called him constantly through that night, but he never picked up once. Finally, I had left so many messages his voicemail was full and I gave up. I went up to my bedroom and fell asleep, confident Adam would call me with some kind of update.

He sent a text.

A fuckin' text that said, "It's over."

Just thinking about that fills me with hot anger right now.

How do you send a text like that?

I called him back that same day. He didn't answer. I texted. He didn't answer. So I busied myself tracking Indie on the various security cams.

I figured, *OK. Everybody needs a moment. We just need to get our heads on straight and figure this out.* And then they'd all be back.

No one came back.

Well, I guess that's not true. Obviously, someone covered the furniture in white sheets and shut the house up.

But everyone moved on so I moved on too. Went to my machine shop. Turned the upstairs into a livable apartment. Started making some art pieces. Mostly outdoor sculptures. Opened up a fucking Etsy shop.

Which makes me chuckle a little, that's how stupid it sounds. I was a thirty-two-year-old retired child-assassin trainer selling metal art on Etsy.

But I like my fucking Etsy shop. It calms me. Gives me purpose. And I sell a shit ton of art on there.

Once Indie left there was nothing. I had nothing. She was my everything. I probably could've been happy if Adam had come home. Probably could've stayed in the business if he was there.

But he disappeared too.

He'd moved on. The things that happened that day could not be fixed.

We were all… *broken.*

Indie gets up from the bed and walks over to her closet. She has a real closet, unlike the other rooms. I expect it to be empty, or maybe hold all her old clothes, smelly and moth-eaten. But inside her closet are dozens of pieces neatly hanging from the rail in clear plastic garment bags.

She takes one out and turns to hold it up at me. "What's all this?"

"I dunno."

"Should I open it?"

"Why not? It's your closet. Must belong to you."

She furrows her brows and frowns, but doesn't say anything as she takes the garment bag over to the bed and lays it down. You can tell the quality of a thing by the sound the zipper makes when you open it. And this one has a nice, deep, ripping sound that conjures up images of Italian leather purses and handmade luggage.

"Huh."

"What is it?" I walk over to the bed and look down as she eases the hanger out of the top of the bag and takes the dress out.

"I never bought this."

"I guess Adam did."

She turns to look at me. "Why would he do that?"

I shrug again. "Maybe he was hoping you'd come home one day."

She stares at me for a long moment. "Maybe." Her gaze wanders over to the open closet door, and for a second I think she's going to go unpack everything. Check it all out. But she drops the dress back on the bed and turns to the window.

This is when my heart skips two or three beats.

But before I can stop her, she's walking over to it and looking out over the duck lake.

I wait in the middle of the room, holding my breath. Because the little brick house that used to be visible from her window isn't there anymore.

She glances down at the windowsill and picks up an old rifle scope, then puts it up to her eye and once again looks across the lake.

"Indie?"

"What?"

"Are you hungry?"

And just as those words come out of my mouth, Donovan calls up the stairs. "Hey! There's no fucking food here. Like… none, dude. I'm gonna go hit up the store. You guys want to come?"

I'm about to say yes when Indie answers for me. "No. We'll stay here."

"OK. You want anything special, Indie? Sweet tea? Or lemonade?"

"Beer?"

Donovan and I both laugh. And for a short moment I feel like maybe this is all gonna turn out OK. He's gonna go to the store and come back with beer. And we'll all go outside and sit under the pavilion and drink it like that day four years ago never happened.

"Beer it is." And then I hear Donovan's footsteps across the hardwood floors. A few seconds later comes the sound of the front door closing.

But Indie is still fucking peering through that scope across the lake.

She lowers the scope and turns to me, smiling.

"What?" I whisper it.

"I love this place. God, I love this place. Why did we ever move, McKay? Like… OK. I remember that the Company went under or whatever." She waves a hand in the air, dismissing that thought. "But we had work after that. And it was pretty good, right?"

I nod at her, unable to say anything. Because it *was* good.

Until it wasn't.

"You wanna…" I sigh. "I dunno. Go watch TV or something? Take a walk?"

Her smile slowly broadens and she takes a few slow steps towards me until almost all the distance between us has been erased. She reaches for me. Takes hold of each side of my open leather jacket and tugs me the final step towards her.

Into her.

"No. I do not want to watch TV or go for a walk. I want to be here with you."

Then she leans up on her tiptoes and pulls me down to her at the same time.

And we kiss.

And this time the kiss is nothing like the last time. It's not tentative and hesitant.

She opens her mouth and I respond by doing the same. And then the tip of her tongue slides across the tip of mine and there is nowhere in this world I'd rather be than right here with her. There is nothing I want more than to kiss her forever. Steal all the breath inside her, and replace it with mine. Fill her up and make her whole again.

That's what I tell myself when I spin her around and walk her backwards towards the bed. The back of her knees bump against the mattress and then she reaches down, grabs the dress and the garment bag, and shoves them on the floor.

She's still got a hold of my jacket and she pulls me down with her when she sits and then leans back on the bed.

I brace both hands on the mattress on either side of her head and press my chest into her breasts.

Then her fingertips are once again fumbling with my belt, and the button on my jeans, and then my zipper. And when her cool palm wraps around my quickly hardening cock and squeezes it, I almost pull away.

Almost.

Because even though almost everything about this is wrong, and has been wrong since that very first day she came here to live with us at Old Home, it suddenly feels… maybe not *right,* but certainly inevitable.

I know who she really wants, and it's *not me.* It's not Donovan, either. And it's certainly not Adam.

It's Nathan St. James.

But he's not here and I just don't care anymore.

I want her.

I have always wanted her and that's the only thing that matters.

Our kiss continues. But I want us both naked. Now. So I nip her lip and stand back up, shrugging off my jacket and letting it drop to the floor at my feet.

She sits up too, squirming to get her arms out of her jacket, and then she's tugging on her sweats as I kick off my boots and lift my t-shirt over my head. I let it fall to the floor on top of the jacket and just stand there as her eyes practically caress me as she studies the hard muscles of my stomach.

I reach for the hem of her t-shirt—"Let me help you with this"—and then lift it up over her head. She has no bra on now. No panties either. She is quickly naked and all I want to do is look at her body. Her firm, round breasts and tightly peaked nipples. Her small waist and the wide curve of her hips. The way she bites her lip when she's thinking hard or very nervous.

She bites it now, conscious of my staring eyes.

Do I make her nervous?

Even if I do, I'm not gonna stop.

I was never allowed to look at her like this. From the day she first walked through this door until the day she walked out, everything about Indie Anna Accorsi was forbidden.

She tried a few times. Once she turned eighteen everything changed around here. And every once in a while she'd find me alone in the house and she'd sit in my lap and hug me. Try to force me to make a move.

But I didn't.

I wouldn't.

See, here's the problem with my love for Indie.

She's not just mine. She's ours. And if I messed around with her, Adam would mess around with her too. Oh, I know what he'd say if he was here and this was a real conversation. He'd say nah, it wasn't like that.

But it *was* like that. It was like that for all of us. Even self-righteous Donovan wanted her that way. He just knew he was last in line because he wasn't around enough.

So Adam can pretend that he wouldn't be jealous if Indie and I became a thing, but he would've. And then… I don't know. I don't know how that works.

It doesn't, I guess. And that's why I always ignored Indie's hints.

But I can't ignore it anymore. If she had not left that day, if Adam hadn't left that day, if Donovan hadn't left that day, if I had not been the only one to stay—we'd have already figured this out.

But they did leave. So this is where it all starts, I guess.

This is the next beginning.

Indie reaches for my jeans again, parting the fabric over my lower stomach, pulling open the zipper and tugging them down just over my hips until my cock springs out, fully erect and throbbing.

Her firm squeeze makes me close my eyes, and when I open them, she's dropped to her knees in front of me.

"Sit on the bed."

It comes out of her mouth like a command.

I don't have to be told twice. I have been dreaming about her lips wrapping around my cock for four long years. I turn and sit as she scoots out of the way and repositions herself in front of me again. She tugs my jeans down my legs the rest of the way, pulls them off completely, and shoves them aside as she opens up my legs and fits her hot little body between my knees. Her palms caress the top of my thighs as she gazes up into my eyes and for a moment I wonder if she's thinking about… *him*.

She smiles at me.

And I know she's not. She doesn't even remember him. Not really. She looked out the window across the room with a fucking scope and didn't see a goddamned thing.

Nothing to see. Not anymore. But that's beside the point.

The point is… she's here with me now. Just me.

I lean my hands back on the bed to get a better view of her as she lowers her head and opens her mouth and then…

"Oh, fuck." I moan it. Because her wet tongue slides up and down my shaft as she holds my cock gently in her palm. Then she squeezes it and slides her lips over the top of my head and bobs down until they seal around the upper part of my shaft.

I hold my breath. That's how good that feels. And I know we just had sex last night, but it feels like it's been several lifetimes since I've felt this good.

She begins sucking me off in earnest, taking me deep and holding me inside her for long moments of pure bliss. My fingers are tangled in her hair, gripping and twisting it all up. Urging her to keep going. She sucks on my head and pushes me into her throat and there is nothing I want more than to just come all over her fucking face.

But not yet. Not this time. Maybe next time.

I still want to be careful with her. She might be a sociopathic killer but she needs gentle guidance right now.

So I stand up. My cock falls out of her mouth and her eyes go wide as she looks up to meet my gaze.

"Please. Do not tell me no, McKay. I will—"

"Shut up, Indie. And lie on the bed."

Sometimes that gentle guidance needs a firm hand.

She stands up with a smirk on her face, confident that I won't be stopping before we really get started, and then crawls across her mattress and lies down flat.

I crawl over her legs and then knee them open. She obeys, bending her knees to maneuver around my legs, and then raises them up so her wet pussy is in full view when I look down.

My hands rest on the top of her knees and I push her legs back as I ease my cock up to her opening. She bites her lip again. Like the anticipation is killing her. And then she lets out a long rush of air as I enter her and push myself deep inside her pussy.

I lean forward and rest my hands on the mattress on either side of her head. Kiss her mouth. I want to kiss her mouth forever. Never let her take another breath that isn't shared between us.

And then I fuck her. I fuck her with hard, penetrating thrusts. I fuck her until she begins to moan and wail. And then I fuck her soft, gently moving my hips as I whisper things into her mouth. Things like, "I fucking love you, Indie." And, "You will never walk out on me again." And, "You're mine. And the only people I will ever share you with again are Donovan and Adam."

Because even though I know it's wrong, it's already something we've *done.*

And she giggles at that last part. Like she's forgotten everything that's happened so completely, the thought of being shared between me, and Donovan, and Adam is actually something good.

When she's close, when her body tenses and her back begins to arch, I come inside her. We climax in the very same moment. And I do not give one fuck that there's no condom and I have no idea whatsoever if she's on birth control.

She is mine.

And when Adam and Donovan get home, she will be *ours.*

Again.

Indie Anna Accorsi has always been *ours.*

It's just the only fair way to do things.

Adam bought her, after all. Donovan kept her mostly sane. And I loved her. I loved her enough for all of us.

So do I mind? Do I care that I will never be allowed to possess her completely?

No.

I can share with them. But I can't, and won't, share with Nathan St. James. None of us will.

She is ours. Not his.

And if there's one thing we came to terms with after what happened that day four years ago, it's that Nathan had to go.

In the months after Adam's brain surgery and the fall of the Company we learned to deal with our new situation. Which was mostly good, but it came with cons too.

Adam was recovering in a downstairs bedroom because he had some trouble with physical coordination when he got home from the hospital. He was in physical therapy four days a week for almost three months. And then he started doing a lot of martial arts with me in the side yard where I trained Indie.

Adam was always a tough fucker. And a little brain surgery wasn't gonna keep him down. He didn't have any real lasting side effects of that incident, other than a few personality changes. But honestly, he was just a little quieter after he came home. Maybe he was just keeping more things bottled up instead of saying whatever the fuck he wanted, whenever the fuck he wanted to. But I maybe liked new Adam more than old Adam, if I'm being honest.

The jobs though, those were a little bit more stressful than Adam's recovery. Obviously, we weren't working in that time frame. We all needed a break. Indie, to forgive herself for practically killing Adam with a candlestick. Me, because I was the one who trained her to do that shit. Adam, for barging in on Indie and pushing her into a corner where she felt she needed to respond. And Donovan, for not predicting this loyalty switch in a situation where all things were supposed to be equal.

But I'm not sure Donovan could've known that Indie would have conflicting loyalties when it came to Nathan St. James. Sure, they were friends. But… were all things equal?

Anyway. Donovan was home almost the entire time, with just occasional trips back to Duke when he needed to make an appearance. But after a few months of that Donovan showed up one day and said he'd been accepted into some residency program at UCLA for plastic surgery. He quit his medical scientist program and moved west that summer. In fact, he's spent almost the entire four years that Indie went missing in two residency programs and just got his board certification last summer.

And when I stop to think about just how long that dude has been in school—the entire fourteen-year period since Adam bought Indie—his brain kinda freaks me out.

But my point is—not everything about the Company falling was good for us.

For one, there was no one to call if you got yourself into a sticky situation. No one to swoop in and bail you out. So we had to turn down a lot of jobs that involved high-level officials. That was the major difference in the before and after. The new jobs were very low-key. Stealthy kind of things. And a lot of them involved Indie going off on her own.

Because, while we could no longer just assassinate senators and shit like that, we could still use them effectively. If the person who hired us had enough money, that is. We just squeezed them in other ways.

Mostly by using their kids.

This is how Indie attended three separate prep schools filled with the offspring of CEOs, and congressmen, and movie stars.

Indie was the least affected by this change. She wasn't even really aware that there was a change. She just figured she was older now. More competent. And we were giving her more freedom.

Which we were, but not because we wanted to.

Every time we had to send her away Adam was quietly stressed. Because he used to go with her and now it was me. He's a tough dude. And in a fight between us I'm still not sure he couldn't kick my ass even after the brain injury. But we all decided he was going to stay home and I was going to go when the jobs started up again.

Not that I did much more than get an apartment and live in a nearby town while Indie was stealthily doing her boarding school jobs. At least I was close if she needed me.

But you can only get away with that kind of job a few times if there's no Company around to cover your ass and after three, we were done.

Adam didn't sit on his ass while Indie and I were off squeezing important people using their kids. He amassed a whole crew of former Company assassins he knew from back in the day and pretty much started a private army. And those guys were not as disciplined as we were. At all. It was kind of a free-for-all two years after the Company fell.

Lots of them ended up with hits on their heads. Just way too unstable to keep alive. Even more got killed, or killed themselves, or ended up in prison when the full effect of no Company support finally hit them.

No shadow government to bail you out this time, my friend. So sorry. Please accept this compensation package for keeping your fucking trap shut and pleading guilty before trial.

Or… *Bang, you're dead.* For opening said mouth during your trial, or getting caught in the first place, or botching the job altogether.

There was a lot of that last kind of clean-up. These dumbasses actually figured they were free after the Company went under.

They weren't.

They had bosses. And Adam was one of them. Not the only one, not by far. He didn't step in and take over. No one did. That was the problem. All this infrastructure the Company built was suddenly flapping in the wind. And every former Company wannabe was trying to get his or her share.

The really important thing that happened after the Company fell and Adam recovered was the realization that Nathan St. James wasn't going anywhere.

Indie was in love.

I will say this about Adam back in those days. He was a good fucking sport about all that Nathan shit. He never said a fucking word to Indie about Nate again.

But I did. Fuck her. She was not in charge of shit. She was sixteen years old and under my thumb for the duration. Because Donovan was obviously moving on to more lucrative opportunities in plastic surgery. (Insert eyeroll. Why that dude felt the need to work so hard when he had so much money was beyond me.)

And Adam had the good sense to let Indie do her thing.

I would catch him though. Standing in the formal dining room looking out the window at that little brick house across the duck lake. And I have known this asshole since we were kids. I could practically read his mind.

He wanted to kill Nathan St. James with a burning passion.

He hated that kid hard.

Nate, to me? Eh. Whatever. Indie just *thought* she was in love back then. And she made a lot of mistakes with that guy. A lot of mistakes. But that's what young people do, right? Anyone with a teenage daughter will tell you that the harder you fight them, the more they resist. So I went a little easy on her during that year and a half when she was doing the boarding school shit and the other, bigger, clean-up jobs in between.

Probably too easy.

And then… people started dying. Lots of people started dying. All former Company in one way or the other. The news was calling it a secret epidemic. Some sinister shadow organization had gotten to the world's rich and powerful and… poisoned them? Maybe. No one was really sure.

All we knew was that everyone left over from the upper circle from the Company days started dropping like flies.

Everyone but us and a few others, that is.

But I don't want to think about that shit right now.

Indie is lying in my arms in her childhood bedroom and I am happy for the first time in four years.

That's what I want to think about.

She's mine.

All mine until Donovan and Adam get home.

Then, after we sort out Adam, *then* we can think about what really happened in the past and try to come to terms with it.

Try to move forward.

Try to see how this is all gonna work out.

CHAPTER FOURTEEN

Indie

Things changed between Adam and I after the incident. He was never the most talkative of the guys. Always preferring his own company, even when we were all together in the same room. Adam is just one of those contemplative thinkers.

But not in the same way as McKay.

McKay is thoughtful and introspective.

Adam is creepily quiet and calculating.

Yeah. That's how they're different. When McKay is thinking he's wondering about things such as why that man stopped his horse in the woods on a snowy evening.

That's a poem by Robert Frost. I didn't know that until I went to boarding school and we had to study that poem. And I had never actually caught McKay reading that poem—though there was a book of poems by Robert Frost in the Old Home library. But the minute we started discussing it in literature class I knew that if McKay had ever read this poem, he would've pondered all these same questions.

I, for the record, do not think that man was contemplating suicide in the snowy woods on his way home. I think he was just taking a moment to admire the beauty of where he was that night.

My teacher said I was wrong. That the imagery and word choices were set up in such a way that everything pointed to an ending, i.e. death.

But I just didn't care. I wasn't gonna agree. And Robert Frost denied it anyway. Maybe he was lying? Maybe he just wanted people to keep thinking about his pretty words and not feed them easy answers? That's possible. But in my mind, it's as simple as this:

You do not *kill yourself.*

What is the point of that? Someone else is always coming round the bend trying to do that for you. You don't make it easy for them.

And I knew McKay would agree.

Here's what I think about that poem—once it's written it doesn't really matter why that man wrote it. It only matters how I interpret it. And I choose to see things my way.

Anyway, Adam wasn't contemplating poems when he was thinking.

He was plotting.

I'm not saying that's a bad thing. Because it was Adam's plots and plans that made us such a successful team. Especially after the Company fell and we had no more support. So I'm just saying he was different than McKay in this regard and that's why he was the boss.

But after the candlestick incident he started making me uneasy.

Sometimes he would look at me funny. Not like I was amusing. When I was smaller, I could see those thoughts in his mind at times. He liked me. I know he liked me. I could just tell by the way he took care of me on the jobs. He didn't say, "I love you, Indie." Ever. But I knew he loved me.

After he came home from the hospital, I wasn't so sure anymore.

I would catch him staring out the dining room window. And while there are a lot of very pretty things to look at through each and every one of Old Home's windows—the lake, the gardens, the pavilion, the woods, and from some of them you could see the river—that's not what he was looking at through the dining room window.

He was looking at Nathan's house.

I knew he blamed Nate for what happened to him that day. Even though I was the one who struck him in the head with the candlestick and sent him into surgery and then months of physical therapy and recovery, he did not blame me.

That much I knew.

He blamed Nate. And from that day on he hated him.

But Adam never went over there again. He kept his distance from Nate and me. Even after things calmed down and McKay lifted my grounding and let Nate come over to visit. McKay said I was not allowed to go over to Nate's house anymore, but that Nate could come here. And that was fine with me. We weren't trying to be sneaky. We just wanted to be together.

Anyway. Adam was quiet after he came home from the hospital. He was a little wobbly with his walk and even though no one mentioned it, he slurred his words a little for a few weeks. But that passed and pretty soon his hair grew out and mostly covered the large scar down the side of his head. And we all moved on.

Moving on meant jobs. And we had lots of jobs at this point.

Adam was very busy planning and plotting and organizing the leftovers. That's what we called them. All the other assassin teams that were left adrift after the Company fell.

We didn't have any meetings at Old Home for obvious reasons. We didn't generally mix business life with personal life. So Adam had a warehouse in Baton Rouge and another one in New Orleans where he met with the leftovers and sent them on missions.

But the objective of leftover life was modified from Company life. We were soldiers for hire now. And no one gave us orders. Some of the teams still killed people. There was always a market for that. We called those clean-up missions. But sometimes teams kidnapped kids—this was often in foreign countries after a disgruntled parent would run off and take the child with them. We'd go get them back. We called those recovery missions.

Or we would steal things. High-ticket items like paintings and jewels. We called those thieving missions.

Or sometimes they were just boring intelligence-gathering jobs. And then we'd take pictures and compile a dossier and hand it over to whoever paid for it. We just called that reconnaissance.

And then, of course, I did those three stints in boarding school. I had to make one girl look like she committed suicide—that was, ironically, during the time of that Robert Frost poem. And then the second time I had to kidnap a girl. Or at least lead her to the team who was gonna kidnap her. I'm pretty sure she was held for ransom and let go. And the last one got a little messy at the end because Adam lied about it.

There were a lot of jobs. That is my real point. And there was a lot of money too. And by this time, I had my own bank account in the Cayman Islands that came with a debit card. So I bought myself a car the winter before I turned seventeen.

Donovan was busy with his plastic surgery stuff at UCLA so he only dropped by about once a month, if that. Not after every job like he used to. But we talked on the phone a lot. And he recorded those conversations too. He was still taking notes as well. I could hear the scratching of his pen on the other end of the line.

But Donovan wasn't there when I bought my car. McKay was. He took me into New Orleans to get it because I ordered it online. It was actually a truck, because we lived on a dirt road in the middle of a swampy forest and that was only practical. But I wanted it the way I wanted it, so I got a custom order.

That summer I turned seventeen Adam was obsessed with the gardens. Now, we had always had nice gardens around Old Home. I don't think I explained this properly in any of my previous journal entries, but they were beautiful. Many evergreen hedges, and pea-pebbled pathways, and regular flower plantings, and even a few fountains. Some summers they looked better than others because gardeners were always hard to keep since we lived so far away from everything.

But that summer I turned seventeen Adam took care of the gardens all by himself. And I took notice of this because he had never done that before.

By this time, we were talking again. Adam and I were never the best of friends. He was more like a… not a father, but that kind of figure. He was someone I took orders from. And not the same way I took orders from McKay. If McKay said, "Indie, you may not go to the movies with Nate tonight," I would say, "Please, please, please!" with wide eyes and praying hands, and McKay would often give in.

Adam wasn't in charge of my movie dates. Adam was in charge of my *life*. And I did not bother begging him for anything because he just never relented. He made up his mind and his mind was made up. That was that. I either obeyed or I didn't and paid the consequences.

I learned pretty early that disobeying Adam was not gonna get me far. He was much easier to be around when you just did what you were told.

So my relationship with Adam, from the time I was ten until just after my seventeenth year, was mostly just following orders and going to church with him.

He was a stickler for that Sunday trip to fucking church.

But things started to change the summer I turned seventeen and saw him on his knees with hands in the dirt in our gardens.

At first, I just watched him from one of the windows. He had lots of deliveries from a nursery in a town about thirty miles away. They would pull up in their truck and Adam would stand there and point as they unloaded them. He would tell them exactly where to put each pot. But he didn't ask them to help plant them. He did that part himself.

We had a small backhoe in the garden shed—which was really more of a building than a shed—and every other kind of garden equipment you can imagine. That's where Nate and I got those chainsaws to clear trees back when we were eleven. And every morning in the early summer that year I turned seventeen, Adam was up with the sun digging holes and planting things.

I watched him do this for five days. McKay was busy with a few of the teams Adam told him to run, so he was in and out during this time. And Nate was busy with school things. And his grandfather, who was very, *very* ill at this point.

And I was alone.

Just Adam and me.

So on day six of this planting stuff I went outside in jeans and mud boots and asked Adam if I could help. It was like six in the morning, but it was already hot. So Adam took off his baseball hat, wiped his brow with the back of his hand, pointed to a row of potted evergreen shrubs, and said, "You can do those, Indie. Just put them in the holes and cover them with a nice mound of dirt and three inches of mulch. Then, when we're done, you can water them."

I nodded and did that. It took me all day.

They were not much to look at when all this took place and I said so when I was done. But Adam just smiled and leaned on a shovel. Then he said, "Don't worry, Indie. This coming winter they will have pretty purple flowers with a scent you will die for. And next fall they will have bright red berries and the thrushes will come from miles around to feed on them. They will stay through the winter and the next spring we will have small, cup-like nests on all the trees and they will be heavy with blue-green, brown-speckled eggs."

He was smiling when he said all this. Like talking about the berries and the birds was a fond memory he was conjuring up from long-ago days. He sounded a lot like Nate back when we were kids and my heart made room for Adam that day.

I think… I might even have fallen a little in love with him.

Because that was a new side to Adam that I had not seen before. I had never once imagined Adam as a boy growing up here at Old Home the way I did. I had no idea he was a swamp kid, like me.

But how could he not be?

He has no brothers and sisters. There was probably no one here but him when he was small. No mother. None of us had mothers. And the more I thought about it, the more I could picture Adam being Nate when he was small. Just a boy, all alone in the woods next to the duck lake and the river. Fishing from a little boat. Making fires on the beach and catching fireflies in jars to light up forts in the night.

I started wondering if he had a girl like me when he was young.

I even asked him once, late that summer when McKay was gone and we were taking advantage of the pavilion without him. Adam was watching college football on the TV over the fireplace and I was lazing around on my bed swing. And I said, "Did you have a best friend when you were a kid, Adam?"

He didn't look at me right away, just kept watching the football game. We had barbecued that afternoon. Hot dogs. I was still full from eating three.

But eventually his eyes found mine. "What do you mean? Like... McKay?"

"No. Did you have a girl like me when you were growing up here at Old Home? Or were you all alone?"

It came out sadder than I meant it to. Because I didn't want to imagine Adam all alone. It made my heart hurt.

"I didn't have a girl like you. Not until you came along. You're one of a kind, Indie."

I chuckled. Because I knew he was saying it to *make me* chuckle. But there was a stab of pain in my chest when he said that.

"I'm sorry, you know. For hitting you that day. I didn't mean to hurt you."

His eyes went sad then. And I wanted to take it back. But I didn't take it back. I couldn't take it back. I had been wanting to tell him that since he woke up on Nate's living room floor covered in blood.

Finally, he sighed. "It's just who you are, Indie."

His reply hurt me more than it soothed me. Because… was that girl who hit him in the head with a candlestick who I was?

I gave him a brain injury. He almost died. And sure, by this time I had killed my share of people on different jobs. I had hurt more than that too. But I never wanted to hurt Adam. If McKay had not insisted on taking him to the emergency room, he *would've* died, or at the very least gone unconscious and never woken up again. His brain was swelling up and cutting off his oxygen flow. And even though he recovered, and by this time he was mostly back to normal physically, he had to have therapy for months afterward. And learn to say a few words all over again because his mouth didn't quite work right.

I *did that* to him. And I was very, *very* sorry.

But the truth was… I didn't actually *remember* doing it. I didn't know how that candlestick got in my hand. I didn't know how it struck Adam on the side of the head. I didn't remember any of it. And that scared me. Really bad. And I wanted to tell this to Adam but I didn't want him to worry about me or think I was losing it. Because I had heard Donovan talking to McKay and Adam over the years. He was always worried that one day I would 'lose it' and that's why he'd been coming to talk to me since I was a little girl. So I didn't lose it. So I could hold everything together in a tight, tight ball and never go insane.

But I didn't know how to say that. I should've started with this train of thought instead of 'I'm sorry'. Because now it felt like the conversation was over.

So I got up from my swing, walked over to Adam, and sat in his lap. And I hugged him. And then I was just… more sad than afraid. Because I had hugged McKay millions of times by this point in my life. And Donovan, a couple dozen, at least.

But I had never, ever, not once, hugged Adam. Or thanked him for saving me from that snake. Or giving me this home. Or making sure I was taken care of by McKay. For saving my life in the early days of those jobs. Or anything else that he'd done for me since I first became his more than seven years ago.

It took him almost a full minute to relax and put his arms around me, and hug me back. But when he did, something changed between us.

We both felt it.

And then his head turned and he kissed me on the cheek and pulled my face into his neck and whispered so softly, I could barely hear his words, "I love you, Indie. No matter what you do, I'm on your side, kid. Always and forever."

I stayed in his lap. Enjoying this new closeness between us. But then he slapped my leg and said, "Get up. I gotta go inside. Got some work to do before I go to sleep."

And I got up, and sat back down on my swing, and watched him walk away.

But that's how I came to be the one to plant an entire circle of daphne shrubs around the central garden that had the biggest fountain in the middle.

It's one of my fondest memories growing up.

Nate spoiled it a little the next day when he was over and we were walking through the garden. He was scowling at them as I pointed them out and told him how much I had enjoyed working with Adam in the gardens that summer. And this made me mad because I loved those shrubs. Everything about them reminded me of Adam.

They didn't have berries this year because we planted them when they were dormant. So I had to tell Nate about the berries and how this time next year they would be beautiful shrubs. But Nate told me they were poisonous and even though some birds, like thrushes, *could* eat them, nothing else would. Because they would die. And he said I should rip them all up and plant something else.

Of course, I was not going to rip up these shrubs. These shrubs belonged to Adam and me. They brought us closer together and I liked Adam when he was working in the garden.

I liked him a lot.

Everything between us had changed that summer after I turned seventeen. I finally felt like all four of us—me, McKay, Donovan, and Adam—we were all really together for the first time since I came to live with them.

And some of what Nate said came off as jealousy because Adam and I spent every day planting things, and watering things, and pruning and picking things. We talked about birds, and life in the swampy forest, and how different our garden would look in just a year or two.

We spent a lot of time together while McKay was off running jobs and Donovan was learning plastic surgery.

And if I was with Adam, I could not be with Nate.

Those two were never going to see eye to eye.

Two days after Nate told me to rip up that garden Adam told me he was sending me to another boarding school. I would start the fall semester at an elite school three hours away by plane and I was leaving the next morning.

This was the third time I was being sent to interfere with some important person's daughter.

At least… that was what I thought at the time.

Later I would learn the real reason.

I left my bedroom in the middle of the night by way of the window, and the roof, and the tree, and walked down the path Nate and I had created between our two houses six years ago. Lots of things had grown back by this time, and the boughs of the trees that lined the path made a canopy of leaves in the summer. So it was almost like a tunnel.

Nate was outside waiting for me. I had not been to his house for over a year now. I had played by the rules and kept my word. But when I called Nate and told him that I was leaving the next day and I would be gone all semester, he begged me to come over.

He was very sad that night. His grandfather had been bedridden for years by this time. And no one had expected him to even live this long. But now he was truly not doing well and we all knew that death was knocking on his door with intent. It's a sad thing to wait for someone to die. And Nate was the kind of boy who felt things deeply.

So I decided to disobey and sneak out.

We walked out into the woods to that old treehouse where he first kissed me when I was fourteen. Three years we'd been dating. Three whole years and we'd not done anything other than kiss and that one time he tried to feel me up.

But that night before I left for school, Nate had the treehouse all rigged up like that night he first kissed me. With fresh mosquito netting and jars filled with fireflies.

I knew what he wanted. And I wanted it too. I was ready. Seventeen and ready. Nate was going to turn eighteen in just a couple months and while on the one hand I felt like our childhood was slipping away from us, I just couldn't wait to see what the rest of my life had in store for me.

Because I pictured myself with Nathan St. James forever. I could not imagine a time when he was not there for me. I wanted him to be my first. He *was* my first. In almost every way.

He held my hand as we walked through the woods towards our treehouse. And we kept trading shy looks at each other. I was smiling wide and feeling jittery in my stomach. He didn't say much and neither did I.

But by this time in our friendship, we didn't need words.

I climbed up the ladder to the treehouse this night the same way I did that other night. With him right behind me. I wasn't wearing a dress. I had grown out of those a while back. So I couldn't feel his chest bumping up the back of my bare knees like the time when he first kissed me. But I could feel his heat. And our shared desire too.

I crawled across the platform and turned over to watch him do the same. And he crawled right up my body with no hesitation at all, his hands planted on either side of my head as he leaned down and kissed me on the mouth.

I was hungry for him. And when he pressed his hard, muscled body down on top of mine, I could feel his hunger for me against my stomach.

I reached for him. Unsure, really, what to do next. Of course, I knew how to do it theoretically. But not precisely. So I was out of my element and for the first time in many years I needed his guidance.

He went slow. First, he lifted my t-shirt up and cupped my breast with the palm of his hand, kissing me the whole time so I didn't feel obligated to say anything. Then he took my hand and placed it over the hard bump in his pants. My fingertips squeezed a little and the length of it made me think of the snakes of long ago. Both the one that wanted to eat me that night and the ones I made that deal with in the swamp when I came live here.

It took a while to get all our clothes off, but there was no real hurry. We had all night in the woods to figure it out. But soon enough we were both naked. He had brought up a comforter from his bedroom and that was what we were lying on. It was soft and old and smelled like Nathan.

Then he turned me over and straddled me, his cock sliding between my legs like a tease. He kissed the back of my neck and nipped my earlobe, and then, without saying another word, he reached down, took a hold of his cock, and pressed it between my legs until it bumped up against that tender spot that my fingers had been drawn to in the middle of the night for several years now.

I gasped when he penetrated me. I hadn't imagined sex happening like this, with me on my stomach and him on top of my back, but that made everything better, I thought. I couldn't see him. But I knew it was him.

He started whispering things to me that made me breathe heavy and fast. Things I'd never been told before. Things like, "I want to be inside you, Indie," and, "I want to fuck you hard."

I don't know where he found these words, but they were doing strange things to my body. I wanted him inside me. I wanted him to fuck me, hard or otherwise.

It was painful. I'm not gonna lie. But it felt good too. All of it felt good. The weight of his body on top of me. The way he sat up once he was in, and lifted my hips up and grabbed them. Hard. Gripped them tight as he thrust into me.

And then he grabbed my arms and lifted me up so we were both on our knees and he was fucking me from behind.

It wasn't what I thought it would be.

It was better. So much better.

And then he pushed me down onto the blanket and pulled out. A few seconds later something hot streamed across my back. And he asked me, "Did you get off, Indie?"

I wasn't really sure what that meant, but I had an idea. I said, "I don't know."

And he laughed. "You'd know, if you did. Turn over. I'll show you."

So I turned over and he lifted my legs up and put his mouth on that sweet spot and licked me until I knew for sure.

We stayed up in the treehouse until dawn. Then we put our clothes back on and he walked me back to the edge of the gardens and kissed me goodbye.

"I'll see you at winter break," I told him.

And he said, "I'll be here."

CHAPTER FIFTEEN

SESSION #WHO-GIVES-A-FUCK-I-LOST-COUNT-A-LONG-TIME-AGO

INDIE: I am not having this conversation with you!

DONOVAN: Sit your fucking ass down and shut your mouth.

Fine. I'll shut my mouth. That's exactly what I want to do.

What the hell was that all about?

Ask Adam. He's the one who just freaked out and almost killed Nate! *Again*! He's lucky I didn't—

You didn't *what*?

I didn't mean it like that.

Then what did you mean?

I'm just saying! Adam can't just fly off the handle every time Nate pisses him off! He's my boyfriend, Donovan! And you guys don't get any say in that!

OK. Let's take a breath and start over. You came home from break and then what happened?

You know—

I just walked in the fucking door, Indie. It was a long flight, OK? Help me out here. I have no fucking clue what's happening.

OK. Fine. There was no job.

What do you mean?

The school? It wasn't a job, Donovan. He actually sent me away to fucking school!

OK.

You knew, didn't you?

I didn't. I swear. I thought it was a job.

So did I. But he never sent me details. Just told me to lie low, pay attention in class, and join at least two clubs.

Hmm. Did you join clubs?

What does that have to do with anything?

I'm just curious. Which clubs did you join?

Fuckin'… debate and the school newspaper.

Good choices.

That's not why we're here. Who cares about the stupid clubs?

I'm just catching up, OK. So how was school?

How was school? How the fuck do you think school was?

Did you like it?

I was pretending to be someone I wasn't. So no. I didn't like it. And now I learn that it was all fake. Adam sent me to boarding school to keep me away from Nathan.

Did you ask him why he did that?

I don't care why! It's not his decision to make!

Well, it kinda is. He's your—

He's my… *what*? He's nothing. He's not even my legal guardian!

Jesus, Indie. You are fuckin' moody today. Do you want to go to your room and think about things and I'll come back later?

Ha! Oh, that's almost funny. Newsflash, Donovan. The days of sending me to my room are over. I'm seventeen—

Exactly. You're *seventeen.*

—and I'm not a kid anymore. You guys aren't in charge of me! I'm in charge of me. And I don't want to go to school!

You do realize that sounds pretty childish, right? I mean, every kid goes through a phase where they don't want to go to school.

I'm going to choke you if you keep patronizing me like that.

Good word, by the way. I like that one. Patronize. I've never heard you say that one before. Is it new?

Fuck you.

Look—

No. You look! It's not funny. Stop laughing at me.

I'm not. I'm just kinda enjoying this a little.

Asshole.

I mean… I've missed you, Indie. I've missed this. Adam called me last summer and he was talking about you.

What about me?

Just… you know. How you were growing up and what comes next.

It's not his decision. It's my decision.

I know. He knows. But he wanted to talk about it with me so we could be ready. You know? For that day when you walked out and never came back.

What? Wait… *What*? I'm not walking out. And even if I did leave, I would come back, Donovan. I'm not walking out. I just want a boyfriend.

And that boyfriend has to be Nate?

Who else would it be?

Well, that's kind of my point. You don't know anyone else your own age except Nate. And now, those girls you just spent a semester with. Did you like any of them?

I guess. They were OK. But I wasn't Indie with them. I was this girl named Jane. I mean… *Jane*? Come on. I'm not a Jane! I'm an Indie!

Did you lose your accent?

What accent?

Your Louisiana accent.

I never had an accent.

You so did.

Did not.

OK. But… do you think you're talking differently?

Can we get back to the point?

Yes. Good idea. OK. So what are your plans?

For what?

The future, Indie. Do you see yourself going to college?

Ha! Haha!

Then what are you going to do?

Um… exactly what I have been doing.

So you're going to just be a criminal your whole life? Is that what you're saying?

Look who's talking.

I'm a doctor. I have a job. And a life.

Do you have a girlfriend?

Several, actually.

Well… I didn't know that.

You don't know anything about me,.

So it seems.

But that's beside the point. We're not here to talk about me. We're here to talk about you. And what was happening in the living room when I walked in the house.

Adam was gonna choke Nathan to death, that's what was happening.

But why? What did he do?

How do you know *he* did something? Maybe *Adam* did something?

Indie. You're making me tired.

I'm just saying!

What. The fuck. Happened?

. . .

Indie?

I think you should just… talk to McKay.

Why?

Because I told him everything already and he didn't freak out. It's not a big deal.

But you're here. In front of me. Why can't you just tell me?

It's just not a big deal. OK? Things just… happen. Sometimes. Accidents, you know, and—

Oh. My God. No. Tell me this is not—

It was an accident! I swear! And I didn't even know for sure until last week!

You're pregnant, aren't you.

We only did it once and he didn't even come inside me. He came on my—

Oh, my God. Nope. Nuh-uh. I don't want to hear this. This interview is over.

SESSION NOTES:

These notes will be informal since this wasn't a regular interview. More of a fact-finding mission. Indie and I did talk more after I turned the recorder off. She didn't want to go back out and face Adam, but she did want me to check on Nathan. So she waited in the office while I went out and made sure Adam and McKay didn't kill that little fuck.

Unfortunately, they did not.

So when I came back in, I told Indie he was fine. Which was a slight exaggeration because it was clear that Adam took a hit to the face, and that means that Nathan took at least one punch, if not more. And there was no way to find out how much damage Adam did. Also, McKay was missing. So he might be over there killing the asshole as I record this.

Indie is up in her room and Adam is sitting on the porch, making sure she does not sneak out. She admitted that's how she met up with Nathan the night before she left for school.

I feel bad for Adam. I really do. He's doing his best. Indie has not been the easiest child to raise. I might've painted the earlier sessions in a slightly optimistic and positive slant.

She has been… difficult. And while she is mostly settled now, and reasonable, every once in a while, she does something reckless and harmful. To other people, but also to herself.

I've been reluctant to go into detail about those incidents because they all happened after the Company went down and I figured this was no longer a professional study, but more of a private one meant to help her and not be a guidance document for future generations of Company kids.

I think what I'm trying to say is... we maybe all forgot who and what she really is. And now she is most definitely pregnant. She showed us her little pee stick she managed to buy a few days ago while she was still at school. And actually, she had six of them. Apparently, she didn't want to believe she was pregnant, which leads me to conclude this actually was an accident. But... Company kid gets pregnant and has another Company kid—that was the one thing Adam and I were trying to avoid back on that day when he bought Indie. I will spell it out for you—she was not meant to be a concubine and have good little Company babies.

And now Adam is telling me that Nathan is probably Company too. Never trained, obviously. But it's not the nurture I'm worried about here, it's the nature. His genetics with her genetics equals Company kid.

I want to fucking drink myself into unconsciousness right now.

Bottom line: Nathan St. James is a problem. We can deal with the baby, but he's a whole other matter. Because it's clear from the incoherent babbling I got out of Adam before I came back in here to write notes that Adam thinks that kid is up to something.

I will find out more later, but right now Indie has priority.

SESSION NOTES: (cont.)

OK. McKay didn't go kill Nathan. He went into town to buy another pregnancy test. He needed to see it in real time, I guess. And... yup. She's pregnant. From what she told me, that happened the night before she left for school, so my handy-dandy doctor training tells me she's about fourteen weeks along.

She will not be getting an abortion. This was the only thing the four of us agreed on during our little emergency family meeting.

Adam sat in the dining room with his head down on the table, while the rest of us sat in the living room. But we could see him from where we were sitting and let me tell you, it wasn't a pretty sight. He's taking it hard. Very hard. Even McKay is handling this better than Adam. And if I had to make a prediction about which of us would freak out most should Indie ever come home pregnant, I'd have picked McKay every day of the week.

But he's had the most practice with Indie's bouts of insubordination. And OK, maybe calling a baby insubordination is a little bit callous, but… this was not in the plan. So it is what it is.

McKay is dealing.

Adam is not. I think he really was coming up with ways to kill Nathan St. James without Indie finding out. But there is no way. There is no way to get rid of that kid without one of us getting the blame.

SESSION NOTES (cont.)

New development. Nate's grandfather died the day after Christmas.

Indie wanted to go to the funeral.

Fucking wonderful. That's how that went.

Just to clarify, that was irony. It sucked. Because Adam made us all go with her.

Once a team, always a team.

SESSION NOTES (cont.)

Indie ran away. Well, not exactly. She went to Nates and then she called me and said she wasn't coming home.

Adam is going to kill Nathan St. James with his bare hands.

McKay now thinks we should poison him.

I'm… on the fence. But leaning towards bare hands.

SESSION NOTES (cont.)

Nathan St. James has been arrested for statutory rape.

CHAPTER SIXTEEN

6.5 YEARS AGO

Let's just be clear. That little fuck had it coming.

I can't exactly pinpoint the reason why I hated Nathan from the first moment I realized he was helping Indie when she was living in the woods those first few weeks after I bought her, but I don't really need a reason.

He helped her. I should've thanked him for that. He fed her. Made sure she wasn't tripping over the snakes or swimming with the gators. If he had not been there, who knows what she would've done. Maybe gone into the marsh and never come out. Not because something bit her or ate her. Not because she starved or died after drinking dirty river water.

She could've just kept walking and taken her chances. She'd have been caught by someone eventually. But with no birth certificate or parents she'd have ended up in foster care and by the age of seventeen Indie Anna Accorsi would've been a statistic, or a drug addict, or some deadbeat criminal.

And I do get the irony. I made her a criminal too. But we're not deadbeat criminals. She has been trained, and she is safe, and I did everything I could to make sure she grew up understanding *limits*.

So I owe him.

I do. And I get that.

But I do not like him, and I do not trust him, and that boy is eighteen and my girl is seventeen, so… that little fucker had it coming.

Of course, the charge did not stick. Nathan St. James is already home. And now the fucking town of Pearl Springs, Louisiana has taken an interest in us. I do have a birth certificate for her, and papers from the Bahamas saying I am her legal guardian, and she has a US passport. On the surface, everything is in order. But things are not in order. The documents are bogus and if they take a good look at our paper trail for Indie lots of red flags will start popping up.

She is allowed to have dual citizenship in the Bahamas until she is twenty-one if she was born abroad. Both her passports say she was born to a Bahamian father and an American mother in the US Virgin Islands. Thus, she is a legal citizen of both countries. Whether that is true or not, I have no idea. But all the papers I use to prove legal authority over her here in the US come from the Bahamian courts.

Which is fine, as long as no one looks too closely. And so far, no one has.

But Indie, pissed off as she is, has filed a request for emancipation in the town of Pearl Springs. She is, right at this moment, outside screaming at McKay that the minute that order is granted she and Nathan are getting married.

I'm sitting at the dining room table with my arms crossed and my legs kicked out in front of me, listening to Donovan, sitting across from me, go on and on about how this is just a threat. She's not serious. She will come around. McKay will handle things. And I should just leave her alone.

I almost laugh. Because I wasn't even the one who went into the fucking Pearl Spring Police Department and filed a complaint against Nathan St. James.

Donovan was.

I glare at him now. "You do realize that the town of Pearl Springs will be all up in our business over this shit?"

"It's nothing we can't handle."

"How, exactly, will we *handle this*, Donovan? Are we going to kill them? Are we going to blow that whole town up? Wipe it off the map and pretend it was never there? There is no more Company. That town was never Company. Never has been, never will be now. I don't know a single goddamned person on the city council. They are not gonna ignore us. They might not be able to take her away or charge us with anything, but they will find us… *interesting*. They will take notice. This is not gonna blow over. Some teenage girl who they have no record of—never attended public school, never took part in anything but church *three towns over*"—I'm so fucking pissed right now—"doesn't have any friends except for this boy she got pregnant by. And lives with two men, both of whom are over thirty and neither of whom are related to her. You don't think that's gonna draw some attention? What the fuck, Donovan? What the actual fuck were you thinking?"

"I just thought—"

"And she thinks *I did this*." I cut him off because my question was rhetorical and I'm not really interested in his fucking psychobabble right now. "She is seventeen and a half, OK? In six months, she could leave and never come back."

He sighs. Rubs the side of his temple with the palm of his hand. "Maybe that's not a bad idea."

I stand up. My chair goes flying backwards. And I pound my hands on the table as I lean over and stare him in the eyes. "What the fuck did you just say?"

"Maybe… it's time for her to go off and find her own way?"

"Her own way doing *what*, Donovan? Is she going to college? Is she gonna… waitress down in New Orleans? What exactly will she be doing as she's finding her own way?"

He, of course, has no answer.

"She's going to *kill people*, Donovan. That's what she's gonna do."

"You don't know that."

"She's gonna lose her fucking mind, and get bored, and start doing jobs on her own. And then one day that job will go bad and her instincts will kick in and that's it. It's over. She will revert back to who and what she really is and this world will not be a better place because of it."

He grinds his teeth for a few moments. Stares past me while he thinks. And then his eyes finally meet mine. "Maybe she should come live with me?"

"With you?" I laugh. Very loud. "With *you*?"

"At least I can help her."

"Help her do what?"

"Deal, Adam. That's why I'm here, remember. I keep her sane."

"You don't keep her sane! I keep her sane. McKay keeps her sane. You just come and go like this girl is your hobby. You're busy living in LA working eighty hours a week on this plastic surgery dream. You're not even qualified to treat her mind. You never were."

He huffs and leans back in his chair. "I'm more qualified than you. And you seemed fine with it for the past seven years."

"Because we were a team. Because we were under Company protection. Because I had no other *choice*, Donovan."

"And what choices do you have now?"

I point at him. "Fuck you. She is not leaving. She is not marrying that boy. She will have this baby here and we will take care of it."

Donovan has the nerve to smirk at me. "And how do you think Nathan St. James is gonna feel about that?"

"I don't give one flying fuck what Nathan St. James *feels*."

"Is that so?"

I whirl around and find Indie standing in the archway between the front hall and the dining room with her arms crossed.

"Yeah. That's so."

McKay is standing behind her, shaking his head. Warning me to shut up. But I don't feel like shutting up. I have things to *say*. We are gonna have a come-to-Jesus moment with this girl. Right here. Right now.

"Listen to me, Indie Anna. And listen good. You're a good kid. A really good kid. But the only reason you turned out this way was because we had you on a tight leash."

"A leash?"

"It's a figure of speech, and you know that. No one put a fucking leash on you, Indie. We've given you everything you've ever needed. We made sure you didn't have to worry about anything—"

"You turned me into a killer."

"No, baby. You were *born* a killer. We"—I point to me, and McKay and Donovan—"we keep you in line. Without us—"

"Without you *what*?" She is in a very mean mood right now. So when I don't answer her, she keeps going. "I'm gonna tell you how this will go down, OK? Because the moment you walked into that police station and filed that complaint against Nathan, I chose a side. And I chose his side."

I could tell her it wasn't me, it was Donovan. But she *wants* it to be me. She can deal with me betraying her like that. But Donovan? I don't think she could handle that. She trusts him most. She might even love him best, I'm not sure. It's a close one between Donovan and McKay. The only thing I do know for sure is that I am not her favorite. And if I betray her, she will get over it. Hell, she probably expects me to betray her.

So instead I say, "What does that mean, Indie? You're taking his side?"

"It means I'm moving out for good, Adam."

"To where?"

"To Nathan's house. His grandfather is dead. He's all alone over there. It will give me some space."

I ponder this. It could be worse. A lot worse. She could say they're getting an apartment in town. Or fuck, they're moving to New Orleans. That would be a disaster.

"McKay has already agreed."

I look at McKay. He just shrugs at me with his hands.

Then I look at Donovan, who is nodding his head. "I'm all for this, Indie. I think it will be good for you too." Then Donovan looks at me. "And she'll be just right across the lake. Hell, that house used to be part of this property. It's… it's… this is good. Trust me." He looks back at Indie. "But you still need to meet with me."

"Why?" Because for some reason, I'm angrier about Donovan's offer to take Indie to LA than I am about Indie's announcement that she's moving in with that punk, Nathan. "Why you, Donovan? You're not even here."

"Because she has to talk to someone. And what are you gonna do? Huh? Where else are you gonna take her for therapy? You just gonna waltz into some counselor's office and say, 'Hey, my kid here was brainwashed by some psychotic secret organization when she was little and we need someone who can talk her down off the ledge when she gets the urge to *kill people*?'"

"OK." Indie huffs and throws up her arms. "That's enough. Here is my final decision. I am moving out. Today. I will withdraw the emancipation request so we don't get too much scrutiny in the local courts. But I'm not meeting with you anymore, Donovan. I'm fine." She directs her gaze to me. "I'm grateful for everything you guys have done, but I don't need therapy anymore. I'm over it. I'm over the jobs. I'm over the killing, I'm over the Company. They've been gone now for two and half years. It's done, you guys. We're rich, we're still alive, and we're done. I want to marry Nathan St. James, have his baby, and be a mother. You can stop worrying about me now. You did a good job and I will never be able to repay you or tell you how much I appreciate you. I love you. All three of you."

Her eyes dart to mine when she says that. And I know she loves me. She just doesn't tell me much. So she wants me to hear this.

"I'll be right across the lake. It's barely moving out. And I'll probably be over here every day anyway, because Nate still has one more semester of high school."

High school. The fucking dumbass is still in high school.

I want to kill that kid with my bare hands. I want to wrap my hands around his throat and look him in the eyes while I choke the life out of him.

The only thing keeping me from doing that is… she would hate me. Forever. There would be no way to take that back once it's done. And I'm not talking about Nathan's life. I'm talking about Indie's rage.

I shrug and sigh. Because her mind is made up and I have long since learned to pick and choose my battles with Indie. "Fine. You can move over to the carriage house with Nathan. But Indie, I'm begging you. Do not marry that boy. If you love him now you will love him in three or four years. There is no real reason to get married other than to… to prove that you can walk away from us whenever you want. I know you can walk away. You have been able to walk away since the day I brought you home. You don't have to prove anything anymore."

She stays quiet, biting her lip a little as she looks at McKay and then Donovan.

"You don't have to choose, Indie. That's what I'm really saying. You can have him and us. It's all fine."

She lets out a long breath. A huge sigh of relief. And that might just be the best outcome I could've hoped for. She doesn't *want* to walk away. She wants to keep us. A*ll* of us.

And as long as we accept that, she will stay.

"I can live with that."

Now it's McKay's turn to sigh. And I realize he is against this marriage idea as well.

Well, of course he is. She belongs to him more than anyone. He was the one who took care of her on the day to day. He took her to the doctor when she was sick. He made her meals every day. Called her home from the woods every night. Paid for those braces that straightened her teeth. Hell, he even went to parents' night when she was in those schools.

But the more I think about all this shit, the more enraged I become.

Because Indie is mine.

Mine.

McKay helps her move out too. He boxes up her room and drives it over to the carriage house in his truck.

It's well after midnight when the lights from his truck pass through the dark front room of the house.

I'm waiting for him in the TV room off the kitchen when he walks in. Our eyes meet as he crosses the room and sits down next to me on the couch, sinking back in the cushions with a sigh.

"I hate that fucking kid."

I can't stop the laugh that comes out with my words. "Me too, dude. Me too."

"And Donovan is pissing me off."

"Tell me about it."

"Do you know he wanted to take her to LA?"

"He mentioned it."

"Fuck him. He doesn't get to walk in here after all these years and tell us he knows what she needs."

"No shit."

"And Nathan St. James. I mean… I guess he's OK. But for some reason, I hate that little fuck."

"He ain't so little no more."

"No shit. Did you know he was on the football team?"

"Get out of here. That pissant puke?"

"He told me. Showed me his varsity jacket too. He's even got a football scholarship to Ole Miss for next fall."

"What?"

"Yeah. The offer came in the mail last week. He thinks Indie and the baby are gonna move to fucking Oxford with him next summer."

I am… stunned. "Do you think she'll go?"

"I dunno. Not if she's smart."

"Well… better a Rebel than a Gator, I guess." We both laugh. "But seriously. That's like a five-hour drive, McKay. She can't move to Ole Miss."

"I know."

"She's not OK. She will never be OK. They fucked her head up so good before she came to us, there's no telling what could happen if we weren't around to keep her in line. She doesn't even understand it, ya know? Because she blacks out when it happens and then we… well, we just bring her out of it and pretend it didn't happen. Seven times Donovan had to fly in and do an emergency brain un-fuck."

"Preaching to the choir, brother. But what are we gonna do? She's got her own money. And a truck. And in six months she'll be eighteen and we'll have no more say in anything."

"Should we tell her? We could tell her. Try to make her understand."

"She won't believe us. I mean what are we gonna say? 'Hey, Indie. I know you want to move out with your little baby daddy and be a normal grown-up like everyone else. But you can't. Because you have a hidden evil killer lurking deep inside you. Except you don't know about it because we've been keeping it secret for all these years so you don't go insane.' She would flip out and call us a bunch of liars."

"We have the tapes."

"Shit. That's a fucking can of worms all its own. Why the hell you and Donovan felt the need to record all that shit, I'll never understand. If anyone found them, we'd be heading for the fucking electric chair."

"No one's gonna find them. I've got them hidden."

"Hidden where?"

"Here in the house."

"Are you shitting me? Dude. If the FBI ever got wind of us—and let's be clear, that black ops division that protected us all those years, they are not on our side anymore—if they ever got wind of us, they'd come tear this whole place down to find evidence."

"They're safe. Trust me."

"You should burn those tapes. Like… tonight."

"I did burn the tapes. The interviews are all in my safe on a hard drive now and it's encrypted with a self-destruct firewall. I paid this hotshot kid genius from Oxford to do it for me and that dude. Trust me. He knows how to hide shit on a hard drive."

"Some asshole kid from Ole Miss?"

I laugh. "No, you dipshit. Like the real Oxford. In the UK. He's ex-Company. Or he would've been if it hadn't gone down. Now he's just a hacker with a pedigree, I guess. But I knew his older sister. I'm not worried about the tapes."

"And Donovan's copies?"

"I assume he took the same precautions. He *is* a genius, right?"

McKay does one of those head-shaking eyerolls. "Well… anyway. If she heard the shit that came out of her mouth during those post-blackout interviews, she'd lose her mind forever. We cannot play those tapes for her. And that's the only proof we have that we're not assholes."

I think about this for a moment. Because he's right. The only proof of what and who Indie Anna Accorsi really is can't be used to change her mind. It will only make things worse.

McKay thinks for a while too because we're both quiet. But then he gets up and looks down at me. "So what should we do? Just wait it out and see if she wants to stay here with us when Nathan goes off to college? Because that doesn't sound… *proactive* enough for my tastes."

"Nah. Mine either. But leave it to me. I got a plan."

He narrows his eyes at me. "What plan?"

"Just… let me handle it."

I spend the next several weeks doing a lot of thinking and a lot of spying. The thinking part… well, I feel bad for that. But not the spying part.

Because I start thinking back to that day of the auction and how different life would be if I walked away with no one.

Just… left. Empty-handed. Came back here, did whatever. And then the Company would fall five years later and I'd be free.

No little girl to worry about.

I mean, the fact is—Indie Anna Accorsi upended my entire fucking life. I haven't really been looking for a girlfriend, but there's no fucking chance of having one now. Not since Indie came along. How the fuck do I explain her? And I get it. If I could tell someone normal about this, they'd say, "Just call her your sister."

But I don't want to call her my sister. That's the point. She's *not* my sister. I don't think of her as my sister. Or my kid.

She is Indie. She is my girl.

People can take that any way they want. It's just the truth.

She's *mine*. In every sense of the word. And she will be with me, in one way or the other, forever.

But she comes with a price. And that price has been high. Most of her fuck-ups came early in the training and the Company was still around back then. Everything got handled. One phone call and whatever mistake Indie made was erased. And everyone who got in the way of that erasure was taken out too.

But after the Company fell things got decidedly more complicated.

I guess it was fine for some, but not for us. I know people wanted the Company gone. Hell, I wanted them gone too and I played my part in their demise. But life is a lot more complicated without them than it ever was when they were in control of shit.

The whole world changed afterward. I'm talking… governments changed. New world leaders were suddenly elected. People who had no idea the Company even existed saw this and it made them uneasy. They didn't know why they were uneasy, but it was the fall of the Company that caused these things.

Several stock markets crashed. Not in the US, but lots of other places. I mean, turn on the news any night of the week and it's nothing but chaos. The whole planet is filled with crisis after crisis. And even in countries that have traditionally been stable, things are going off the rails quickly. Those that were traditionally unstable just got worse.

And I get it. People want to feel in control. They don't want some secret cabal running shit behind their backs. But sometimes the devil you know is better than the one you don't.

Just thinking this shit makes me feel like one of the bad guys. And I swore up and down, the whole time I was growing up, that I would not be one of the bad guys. But am I any better now, without the Company, than I was before?

I'm not talking about money or prosperity. I have too much of both to be worried about that. I'm talking about that high road I thought I was on. That moral compass I thought I was holding.

But I am doing exactly the same thing I was before the Company fell. Only now I'm exposed. There is no one covering for me.

Sane people would say, "Well, just stop doing that shit, Adam. Stop taking those jobs. Stop killing people. Stop all of it."

But I *own* a Company killer. What am I gonna do with her? What will happen to Indie if there are no more jobs? Let me spell it out for you. In a way, she's like a heroin addict. She needs it. She needs that life. So if I stop the jobs, if I force her to conform to societal norms, how long before she crashes and burns? And who will she take down with her?

If it was just me, I could probably live with that.

Hell, I could probably even live with her taking down Donovan.

But not McKay.

So these are my choices:

Protect her and give her jobs to do that keep her in check.

Or kill her.

That's it. Those are my options.

There is no other way this plays out. It's either work with who she is and mitigate it, or put her out of her misery and move on.

Because Indie Anna Accorsi is… *insane.*

So I'm in the middle of mitigating when I see Nathan St. James exit the diner in Pearl Springs and walk across the street to the parking lot where his black Ford truck is parked.

I'm in the back seat of said truck. Waiting for him.

I've been watching Nate for several weeks now. I had a hunch about this kid. He's not a bad guy. Not like me.

But he's not a good one either.

Definitely not good enough for my Indie.

It's not late. But it's midwinter and it's dark as fuck out tonight. So Nathan gets in his truck and doesn't see the shadow sitting directly behind him. Not until he goes to turn left off First Street and checks his mirror.

His foot slams down on the brake as I grab him by the hoodie with one hand and yank hard until he starts choking. Then I hold up the gun so he can see it. "Keep driving and this whole thing is gonna turn out OK, Nate. Do something stupid, and you won't have to worry about it. Because you'll be dead." I watch him in the rear-view mirror as he opens his mouth to speak, but I cut him off. "Whatever it is you're gonna say, it's not gonna change things. And I'm not interested in having a conversation with you, Nathan. I'm here to deliver a message and go on my way. If you hear my message and heed my message, you'll go on your way too. If you choose to ignore it, well… then things are gonna get dicey. Nod if you understand me."

He nods.

"Good. Head towards the highway like you're going home. And by the time we get there all this will be behind us."

Nate and I have a chat. And that chat includes little details about his life that I'm one hundred percent sure Indie has no clue about. All these years I pegged Nate as just the boy next door. Some pussy kid who got lucky when my girl came to live in the big house across the lake.

But then I heard he was playing ball. And he was good enough to get himself a full-ride scholarship to Ole Miss. Which, OK, I get it. Ole Miss isn't Harvard by any stretch. But it's no joke, either. So I started wondering what else I didn't know about our friend *Nate.*

I needed some specifics.

Which led me to specifically finding out about that hot cheerleader he's dating from high school. The one he just had dinner with.

Specifically… he banged her in the front seat of this very truck just two hours ago.

Specifically… Nathan St. James has a thing for rough sex.

Because he had his hands around her throat, squeezing her windpipe, the whole time they were fucking. And if I find out he choked Indie when he got her pregnant, I will cut off his cock, shove it into his mouth, and let him experience sexual asphyxiation for himself.

Not that I'm real worried about anyone hurting Indie like that. She can most definitely take care of herself. I just want to set some ground rules for my buddy *Nate.*

And then, just as we turn down the dirt road that leads to Old Home and the little driveway to the carriage house, I tell him what we're gonna do about this little problem.

So when I walk past the duck lake towards my house, and Nathan St. James is safely tucked away inside his with *my girl*, Indie, who is none the wiser about our conversation, I feel a little bit of satisfaction.

Not a lot.

But enough.

For now.

CHAPTER SEVENTEEN

mckay

PRESENT DAY

I wake up to the sound of Donovan and Indie talking downstairs. They aren't sharing secrets or anything. Just some normal conversation. And I figure they're putting groceries away, because I can hear the tell-tale crinkling of plastic bags and the refrigerator door being repeatedly opened and closed.

I don't really want to get up. I feel like I could sleep for months and still not be ready to get up and face what's coming. But I do. I get myself together and wander into the hallway, still half listening to Donovan and Indie. Though things have gone quiet down there now.

I peek over the railing that overlooks the foyer and arched entrance to the front rooms. Someone—Indie or Donovan—has pulled a bunch of the white sheets off the furniture and has piled them in a heap just in front of the dining room.

Adam not being here should feel weird. It's his fucking house. But so much about that dude has been weird since Indie disappeared, I think I've become immune to it. We've talked a few times. Mostly texted. But I have not seen him since that day everything went down.

I don't know that I fully expected Indie to come back. I mean, I had always hoped. But there was a big part of me that figured she'd get herself killed somehow. Who knows how? Any number of ways, I guess. Or that she'd just… forget about us. All of us. Because Indie is very good at forgetting. She's very good at losing track of things.

Herself, mostly. But lots of other things too.

But here we are on the verge of something.

And it could go a lot of different ways. I guess we won't know that until Adam shows up and we get Indie to remember what happened and explain what she was thinking that day. Why she did what she did.

There are two ways to get downstairs from the second floor. The front stairs, which I am standing in front of. And the back stairs that lead directly into the kitchen. And for a second I'm not sure which route to take. I could throw those sheets in the laundry if I go down the front. But I could sneak up on Donovan and Indie in the kitchen if I take the back ones.

I choose the front ones, fairly certain I don't want to sneak up on them.

So I go down, pick up the sheets, and I'm heading towards the laundry room on the other side of the front room, trying to mind my own business, when I hear them.

Do I get jealous? Doesn't everyone? So… yeah. I do. But this is something I need to come to terms with. I have fucked her twice now. Twice in the span of less than one full day.

But that doesn't mean she's mine.

She is *not* fully mine. Or Donovan's. Or Adam's.

She is ours and that's just how it is. We can deal, or choose not to, but there is no way around that fact.

Still. I know what they're doing in the kitchen.

At least I think I do. But then I hear them whispering. I place the sheets on the stairs and wander down the hallway to the back of the house where the kitchen is. Trying to be quiet so I can catch a few words.

Because while I would be happy to give them their privacy if they were fooling around, secrets are something else altogether. I don't actually like secrets. I've been living with them my whole life and they are a burden I could do without.

I stop and press my back against the wall just before the archway opens up into the combined family kitchen area. Straining to hear them. Because while I like Donovan, I've never fully trusted him. All those tapes. I told Adam they were a bad idea but Donovan wanted them for some paper he was writing back in the day. And even if Adam put all of his on some super-secret hard drive, Donovan didn't. I know that because he brought them with him. A whole fucking bag filled up with Indie's thoughts.

I hear Indie say, "They're gonna find out, Donovan."

"It's fine," Donovan whispers back. "I can handle them."

I should get really suspicious about this line of conversation between Indie and Donovan, but I figure it's about them. Something to do with their relationship. And I'm not sure that's any of my business.

I wait there for a little bit longer. Hoping—and not hoping—I will hear more. But then they really are fooling around because I can hear kissing.

I go back the way I came. Pick up my sheets, take them into the laundry room, and shove them into one of two commercial washers. Then I go back upstairs, put on my boots, and jacket, and come back downstairs making noise.

It's juvenile. But fuck it.

I don't care. I slam the door on the way out too.

But the last place I want to be is outside. Because that's where everything happened that day. And everywhere I look there's a bad memory waiting for me.

It's raining again. Not hard, but a healthy drizzle. So I head to the pavilion. My one spot on this vast acreage of marshy woods that is all mine.

Of course, I have not been out here in four years and it looks it. Leaves everywhere. All the cushions, and pillows, and blankets that made this place feel homey and comfortable are gone now. There used to be mosquito netting around the perimeter in the summer. And in the winter, I would hang thick, canvas curtains all the way around to keep the wind out.

I don't much like the hot, sticky summers but Louisiana winters are perfect. Adam and I used to watch football out here all fall. Then basketball all winter. And when Indie was still small and young, we'd have movie night with her. That was fun. And we'd all pile on top of that giant swing I made and just have a little bit of fun. Try and forget who and what we were.

It was good. It really was. Even when Donovan was here. I mean, that guy was mostly just a downer. But it wasn't his fault he was only here after a job and most times Indie wasn't herself.

I head towards the garden shed because if those cushions and curtains are still here, that's where they'll be. It's not a shed. Shed is just an easy word to describe it. It's a pretty big building. Probably started its life as a barn a hundred years ago. It's been renovated though. Concrete floor now. Nice drain in the middle so we could hose off the floor when it got too dirty. And it's got a huge door, which is metal and rolls up like a garage door these days, but probably started out as some real nice wood back in the day.

Adam packed everything up real neat after we abandoned this place. Well, hired someone to do it, I guess. White sheets on all the furniture the way you see it done in movies. Which is so Adam. He's so fuckin' proper. So fuckin' orderly. So fuckin' conscientious. So fuckin'… *Southern.*

My point is that all the outdoor cushions are inside those special bags you buy for such cushions when you want to put them away and keep them nice over the winter.

But then I realize they are all piled up inside something and my heart seizes up. Like a fist just reached into my chest and gave it a squeeze.

I walk over to the crib and trace my fingertips down the dusty white wood of the headboard. Indie picked this crib out. She wanted this crib for her little girl so bad I could see the longing in her eyes when she, and Adam, and I were walking through that baby store when Indie was six months pregnant.

She wanted everything to be perfect. All the beautiful things were on her mind back then. Everything was pretty.

Magnolia Accorsi was born the second week of June, nearly bald, and with yellow skin because she was jaundiced. But next to her mother, she was the most perfect thing I had ever seen. And I would just like to state for the record, I did not vote for Magnolia. I mean, Jesus Christ. I couldn't decide if the name was pretentious, or Bohemian, or just plain Southern. I wanted to name her something very simple. Like Ella. Or Amy. Or, if I was gonna go a little crazy, maybe Katherine with a K.

But that baby girl didn't have a chance in hell of ever being simple. And now that I think about it, the name makes sense. Indie and her flowers.

I made everyone call her Maggie, though. Or Mags. I would say, "Hey, Mags. How you doin' today, sweetie?" And she would turn her head towards me and smile. And sometimes giggle. And you know what? All those years I missed of Indie's childhood just faded away when Mags did that. Those missing years didn't matter anymore because little Mags was the spitting image of her mother.

It was like I got a second chance.

Indie did not move to Ole Miss with Nathan because Nathan broke up with her just a few weeks after Maggie was born, stating that she and the baby belonged at home, not in some second-rate family dorm room. And he deserved a chance to figure out who he was while away at college.

Indie was heartbroken, of course. But we were there. All three of us because Donovan was making an effort to be home most weekends.

And then Nathan went away to Ole Miss and didn't bother us again for two whole years.

But when he finally did work up the nerve to bother us again—he did it in a *very* big way.

"What are you doing?"

I startle and turn to see Indie standing in the doorway, immediately positioning myself between her and the crib. There's a tractor in the way too. And lots of equipment and boxes. So I'm pretty sure she can't see the crib.

I don't want her to remember like this. I don't want those memories to hit her in the chest like a fucking fist when Adam isn't even here yet.

So I say, "Hey, Indie," like none of this is a big deal. "Will you go into the house and get some blankets? I'm gonna hook the TV up, and hang the curtains, and put all the cushions out. We can eat dinner out here tonight and watch a movie like old times. That would be nice, right?"

Indie smiles for a moment, maybe picturing this idea in her head and deciding she likes it. "Yeah, OK. I'll be right back." She turns, but then she stops and looks over her shoulder at me.

"What?" I ask, afraid maybe she did see the crib.

"You know… you're always welcome to join us."

I huff a little, because I know what she's talking about, but I say, "What?" again. Like I don't understand.

She rolls her eyes and turns away. Starts walking back towards the house. But then she calls over her shoulder. "You know what I'm talking about, McKay. I'm not playing games with you."

I do a little salute to her back. *Yes, ma'am. I do. Just… not in the mood to have that conversation right now, thank you.*

Adam talked about this once. Just once. Just before Indie's twentieth birthday.

Look, I'm not stupid. I know what Adam wants from me. From us. Well, maybe not Donovan. But definitely me and definitely Indie.

There has always been this bond between Adam and me. Sometimes it was like brothers. Other times it was like friends. But every now and then, when we were teenagers, mostly. I would catch him watching me. And when I did this he would not avert his eyes. He would not play it off. He would just stare.

So this time, right before Indie's twentieth birthday, he came up to me outside. I was fishing on the river. Or… pretending to. Just thinking mostly. Because that was right about the time Indie started to unravel.

Adam took a seat in the sand next to me. Bent his knees up and rested his forearms on them. His hair was a little too long still from the shaved-head incident. He just didn't wear it the same after that. So he was looking at me from under some hair that had fallen over his eyes.

And he said, "We could…"

He paused then. I remember that pause. Because for some reason I knew what he was gonna say. I just fuckin' knew. So I was holding my breath. Because I didn't want to talk about it. I wasn't sure what to say, or how I felt, or anything.

But he didn't catch that. Or maybe he did, and decided to ignore it. Because after he was done pausing, he said, "We could just all be together, McKay. You. Me. Indie. I think it would make her happy. Maybe even… change her a little. And it would solve a lot of problems."

I looked at him. Turned my head, but nothing else. And just looked at him.

He sighed pretty heavily and went back to staring at the water and we were silent for a little while.

He got up to leave. Just figured he was gonna let his offer hang there, I guess. And I decided I actually did have something to say about that.

"I don't think it'll work."

He was on his feet now. So he was staring down at me. "Which part?"

"Any of it."

"Why not, McKay?"

"Because we don't even know that's what she wants."

"I'm not really asking about her, McKay. I'm asking about you."

Which I knew. Obviously. I'd know this man since I was nine. "I don't know if that's what I want, either."

"Me? Or her?"

And then there was nothing else to say but the truth. "You."

"Oh." That's all he said. Just that and he walked back home. Left me there to fish.

And you know, if he was asking me again today, I might have other opinions about it. A four-year separation will do that to people.

I turn back to the crib and start picking up the bags of outdoor cushions and throwing them over the tractor towards the open door.

But her offer lingers in my head as I work. It rattles around in there like an echo. *You're always welcome to join us.*

Is that how it ends? The three of us sharing her like that?

It's not like we haven't done that before.

Just the one time. But I know she and Donovan had a little affair a few months before the very bad day when everything changed. Donovan was always the one I figured she'd go to because they are only five years apart. He had just turned twenty-five and she was nineteen when I first caught them together.

They were in the laundry room and I watched the whole thing. They knew I was there. Indie did, at least. But it was almost like… she wanted me to watch. She was trying hard that year to entice me into something more than friendship.

And I'd be lying if I said I didn't want it. I did. I wanted to rip her fucking clothes off and fuck her into next week.

It just felt so… wrong.

That's why she was with Donovan that day in the laundry room. That's why she wanted me to see it. And even back then—even when she was sitting on top of the washing machine with her jeans pulled down her legs and her knees bent and hiked up to her chest so Donovan could gain access—even then I stayed.

If I thought I could walk away and leave her with Donovan and Adam, I would.

But I can't.

There is no girl in my future not called Indie Anna Accorsi.

I'm throwing cushion bag number twelve when Donovan appears in the doorway and catches it. "What the hell are you doing?"

"What's it look like? I'm gonna fix up the pavilion. Why don't you make yourself useful and start to get all those cushions out?"

"Did she see that?"

I look at the crib, then back at Donovan. "If she did, didn't mean anything to her. She didn't say a word."

"Well, this is risky, McKay. We have a plan. And I, for one, would like to stick to that plan."

I'm on my last bag of cushion, so I don't toss it, just carry it over to Donovan and stand in front of him. "What aren't you telling me?"

"What do you—"

"Don't fuck with me, Donovan. You're hiding something. I can tell. So what is it?"

He hikes a thumb over his shoulder, motioning to the house. "Is this about what happened back in the kitchen?"

"No. It's not. It's something else and you know it. So don't try to change the subject. What the fuck are you hiding?"

He sighs. I'm really not in the mood to discuss the intricacies of how Indie fits into our adult lives, so this was mainly a diversion away from that subject. But they were whispering in the kitchen. I can't let that go.

"OK. But you can't be mad at me."

"Mad about what?"

Donovan looks over my shoulder. Maybe at the crib. Maybe at the tractor. Then his eyes find mine. "She came to see me."

"Who?"

"Indie."

"When?"

He lets out yet another long breath. Shoves his hands in the pockets of his slacks. "Twice, actually."

"And you didn't tell us?" I'm… kind of stunned about this revelation.

"The first time was about two years ago. She stayed the weekend with me. And I was gonna call you guys on Monday, but when I woke up, she was gone." His eyes go soft, like they're pleading with me to understand. "I was gonna call you. I swear. But then she wasn't there and I felt like… like maybe you didn't need to know. I get it, McKay. I understand how you feel, but I have feelings too. And I love her just as much as you do. I looked for her, but…" He takes his hands out of his pockets and shrugs with them.

"And the second time?"

"The second time she just… she was just… *watching* me."

"What do you mean?"

"Outside my apartment. I saw her on the street from the front window. It was raining and—"

I laugh. It's always raining. The air outside the shed is a mist of drizzle right now. Calm, but with the threat of more to come.

"—by the time I got downstairs, she was gone. And then… I started thinking I made it up. So I didn't call that time, either."

"When was that?"

"About a month ago."

"Hmm. She was watching me too. For ten days, she said. What do you think it means?"

"I dunno, McKay." He looks over his shoulder at the house. Indie is coming down the porch stairs holding a bundle of blankets in her hands. He looks back at me. "I think she remembers. Some things, at least. But maybe not the things we want her to, ya know? So we need to be careful."

"You don't need to tell me that."

"I just left another message for Adam. He didn't respond."

"No surprise there. She wants to kill him. Did she tell you that? She came back because she thinks he took Nathan and did something with him and now she wants revenge."

"Yeah. She told me. She says she wants us to help her. She's just mixed up, McKay. She's not gonna kill him."

"You don't know that."

"I started talking her through it. She understands. Or at least she's starting to." Donovan turns and calls out to Indie, because she's close now. "We're having movie night? I can't wait." And then he picks up a handful of cushions and walks off to start putting the pavilion back together.

I watch them as they meet up under the protection of the high-pitched pavilion roof, smiling and joking like there's nothing to see here. Then I turn back to the shed and walk behind the tractor as I take out my phone, bring up Adam's contact, hesitate for a moment, then press call.

It rings four times, then the voicemail picks up. "You got me. Leave a message." I hang up at the beep and decide to text him instead.

When are you getting here?

I stare at my phone for a few moments, watching as it says 'delivered'. But it doesn't say 'read'. I haven't talked to Adam in a while. So that might be his phone settings. But then again… maybe he just didn't read it.

And he doesn't answer back. So. Whatever.

I make several trips over to the pavilion and drop off bags of cushions while Donovan and Indie unpack them and start placing them in their appropriate places on the outdoor furniture. And pretty soon the pavilion is starting to feel like home again.

The next time I look at my watch it's after three and I'm starting to get hungry.

Cooking was always part of my job here. I was the one who made Indie's meals when she was growing up. But when I start hanging the curtains around the pavilion Donovan offers to make dinner tonight. Indie thinks that's a good idea and wants to help. So they go inside and leave me to finish up.

I'm just threading the last pole through the curtain grommets when my phone dings in my pocket.

I almost fall off the fuckin' ladder. Because the notification chime tells me it's Adam.

I fish my phone from my pocket and stare at the screen.

His text says: *Is it safe?*

What do you mean?

You know what I mean.

I think about this for a moment, not really sure how to answer.

Adam must get antsy because he texts me again. *Does she remember, McKay?*

No. She doesn't remember.

Then I can't come.

I press call, because I need to have a conversation with this dude and I don't want to waste time typing.

He picks up on the first ring this time. "What?"

"You have to come. We can't do any of this without you, Adam."

He sighs. And I can just picture him running his fingers through his hair in frustration. "What are you guys doing right now?"

"I'm putting the pavilion back together and Indie and Donovan are starting dinner. Where are you? Are you close? Far? Can you make it for dinner?"

"I don't know. Let me think. I'll get back to you soon."

The call drops and I just stare at the screen for a moment, conflicted. I want to call him back and set him straight. But there's no way to justify Indie's behavior over the past few years. I didn't tell him that Indie came back to me asking to help her hunt him down, but he has to know she blames him for whatever is going on up in her head.

She *always* blames him.

If she had seen Adam yesterday, she would've… well. I mean, I have to be honest with myself here. She probably *would've* killed him. She would've tried, at least.

Can Indie kill us? I mean, you know. Hand to hand type shit. Anyone can pull a trigger, I guess. But if it came down to some kind of fist fight. Some kind of mixed martial arts type shit… would she win?

Yeah. She would.

Not because she's better at it than we are, but because I would not be able to finish her. I would pull my punches I would let her win, or, at the very least, I would let her walk away.

And somehow I don't think I'd get that kind of reciprocal consideration from Indie. Because if she was going to kill us, it would not be *her* doing it.

Today though? Would she kill Adam tonight if he decides to show up? I just don't know. I have no fuckin' clue what's running through that girl's head.

Sex. Obviously.

Which I can't pretend I don't enjoy.

It would be a sick thing to admit I have loved Indie this way since I first laid eyes on her when she was ten. It's wrong.

On every level. And it's not even true. I mean, I did love her immediately, but I wasn't thinking of her sexually until well after she was eighteen.

Still. It's fucked up. We all know it's fucked up.

And part of the reason she lost her mind was because of us.

And what we all did on her twentieth birthday was the trigger. That was the day when Nathan came home from school and saw us. All of us. Together. Right over there. On that swing I made Indie when she was just a little girl.

That act of passion shattered our lives into tiny little pieces.

And after that day was over… we knew there was no way to ever put it back together.

CHAPTER EIGHTEEN

Maggie was the most perfect baby alive. So small and sweet. And she smelled like… like a spring rain on a sunny day.

The pregnancy was hard. I'm not gonna lie. After the whole truth was out and I moved in with Nathan, everything seemed OK. Like this was all gonna work out just fine. Living over at Nate's wasn't much different as far as I could tell. Only my view now was of Old Home and not the brown-brick house. His grandfather had passed a few weeks earlier, but his grandfather had been sick for as long as I could remember. So that wasn't much different, either.

To be honest, the real difference was McKay. Because he wasn't there to make dinner for me. Which sounds ridiculous, but I did not know how to cook. And Nathan kinda expected to be fed.

Which was also weird, because Nate was the one who did all the cooking too.

I don't know. Something changed between us after I moved in. I didn't read a lot of romance books, just that one about the boy next door. But I figured it couldn't hurt to find a few more to study. I just needed some pointers about this romance thing, that was all.

But all the romance novels for sale in the river town were old and out of date. People were still using telephones in them, for fuck's sake. So I'm not sure I did myself any favors by reading those for tips.

Nathan liked to go into New Orleans for dinner or shopping. But this was weird for me. Don't get me wrong. I've been all over the fuckin' world. I'm no stranger to cities. But always on a job, never really just for fun.

When I was younger McKay took me to the zoo once. It was fine. But it reminded me of the island where Adam bought me. And that made me think of snakes and there were enough snakes in my backyard, thank you. I didn't need the zoo to remind me of that.

And he took me to the Space Center in Huntsville once. We stayed for a few days. I liked that more than the zoo. At least there were no cages.

And then we did have plans to go to Disney World for my twelfth birthday, but something came up and we didn't go. Then the next year, when McKay brought it up again, I said I felt too old to see Disney World for the first time. He tried to change my mind. Said it was for all ages. He even sweetened the pot and said he would make Donovan and Adam come with us, but I still said no.

But other than that, we didn't get out much. I enjoyed the river trips Nathan and I took up to the river town. And the ice cream, of course. But I didn't like the town where he went to school very much. I always felt like people looked at me weird.

And of course, all of Nathan's friends lived there and he played football for his school. So those first few months we were living together as a couple, he always wanted to go there and meet up with his friends on the weekends. So I ended up just staying home with McKay and Adam when he did that.

We weren't having sex, either. Not that I cared. Our relationship wasn't about sex. But we used to kiss a lot. And hold hands. We didn't do that anymore after I moved in, either.

And then, by the time Maggie was born, I was ready to go home to my own bed in my own room. The little brown-brick house was fine, I guess. But it was small, and old, and to be honest, it smelled a little bit like Nate's dead grandfather.

I don't know. I could not get that smell out of my nose. McKay told me that smells get funny when you're pregnant. But it was the same after Maggie was born.

So I just moved home.

A few weeks later Nathan broke up with me.

Or maybe that's not quite the right word. Was he really my boyfriend? No. We were friends. Friends who used to like to kiss and hold hands and who had sex exactly one time, but other than that... even my old raggedy romance books told me that was not a boyfriend.

And that hurt. And it hurt even more when he said he didn't want the baby and me to go to college with him. Because he said, "You don't fit in, Indie. You live in another world from the rest of us."

Which I could not exactly argue about. Because I did live in another world. But it wasn't my fault that I was Company. Even though, by this time, there was no Company. That made very little sense to me. There was no more Company, but I was still Company. There was no way to *not* be Company.

It hardly seemed fair.

But back to Magnolia. Maggie. Mags. She was my new world. And she was not Company. She would never be Company. That gave me hope. And being with her—and seeing McKay and Adam dote all over her, and Donovan would come, and then he would dote on her too—that made things a little better.

For a little while.

The holidays were fun that year. Very fun. McKay always went out of his way to make sure we had nice holidays. He cooked Thanksgiving dinner and Adam and I would bake frozen pies. We tried to make them from scratch one year, but everyone agreed that the frozen ones came out better. So that's what we did from then on.

And most years it was nice enough to eat Thanksgiving dinner outside under the pavilion. Adam would make a fire in the fireplace and watch football, and Donovan was usually there. He and I would play cards. And McKay would make us all clean up the dishes afterward because he was the cook. But he helped anyway. So all four of us would be in the kitchen washing and drying dishes and putting things away.

And then the house would go dark and we'd all hang out on the couch and watch TV. Usually an old horror film.

But Maggie's first Thanksgiving was even better. I decided to cook instead of McKay. I figured it was time to learn some domestic things. McKay couldn't always be there to take care of me. Besides, he had carved out a place in the garden for a playset for Maggie. He was working on that the first year. And let me tell you, it was something else. A big square of garden and hedges were ripped up to make room. McKay built another pavilion over it with a big ol' skylight so future Maggie could play outside in the rain if she wanted, but still have a big patch of sun when it was nice out. And the play set was no ordinary play set. It was almost like a treehouse. There were two slides, and a swing set with a baby swing and three regular swings. It even had a little kid climbing wall and a rope bridge.

I swear. Those hands of McKay's could make anything.

Nathan St. James didn't even come home for Thanksgiving that first year.

I thought, OK. His grandfather was dead. And winter break was coming up and that was a long one, so for sure he'd be home for Maggie's first Christmas.

But he didn't come.

And there was this missing piece inside me after that. Like… he was never there. Like I had lost something and I was desperate to find it again.

I tried to put it out of my mind. I did some odd jobs on the side. Kept busy.

But it really messed with my head.

McKay and Adam liked Christmas. They were like little boys. We didn't buy each other a lot of presents, but we always had presents. McKay always made me something. He made me a dollhouse that first year. I was maybe a little old for it since I was ten and half. But I liked it anyway. And played with it for a few years, at least. He made Adam a knife. A fucking *knife*. Like forged that thing in flames out in a special fire stove thing behind the shed. And it was a nice one too.

He made Maggie a rocking horse for her first Christmas. She was six months old by that time. She could sit on it and rock a little if we held her.

It was special. And I was happy. But I really did expect Nathan to come home and see us. And he didn't.

After the holidays were over, I told Adam I wanted to go back to work. He said no, of course. That I had a job and that job was called being a mother. But it wasn't enough for me. It should've been. I realize that. It just wasn't.

But I didn't pester him about it because once Adam makes up his mind his mind is made up. It's always been that way.

But I had a mind of my own as well.

I had my truck. I could go into any town I wanted to shop or whatever. I did that sometimes. I'd put Maggie in her seat and we'd drive all over the place while McKay and Adam were off doing things I used to do, but was no longer allowed to.

And that was when I first saw Angelica again. I was nearly twenty at the time. Maggie was getting big and was about to turn two that summer. She was making good use of that play set McKay had built her. And everyone was home during Easter weekend.

Everyone but Nathan, that is.

I slipped out of the house when Maggie was napping and McKay and Adam were watching TV, and I was walking in the woods like I used to and there she was.

Just… there she was. One minute nothing. Then, poof. Angelica was in the woods with me. Like she came out of nowhere.

And she started telling me all about these jobs she was doing. I was stunned, to say the least. Because I had thought that Nick had killed her years before. But then I tapped my head and remembered… oh, that was right. Nick didn't kill her. Adam said something about her going to live with someone like him. Someone who could raise her and take care of her until she was old enough to do it herself.

She said, "Indie. Come here. I have a job for you." And then she whispered all the details into my ear.

And I smiled.

It was like I had just woken up from a long dream.

Like I was back.

Right before she left, she put her finger to her lips and whispered, "Shhhh. Don't tell no one, Indie."

So I didn't.

PART THREE
through the gate

And here we are. The point of no return. You opened your eyes when you opened the door. And even though you haven't passed through yet, it's inevitable now.

You know what's behind you. It's all very familiar and safe. But people who feel safe often get giddy with stupidity.

They forget why those walls were built in the first place. They forget why the gate was locked. They forget what's waiting for them on the other side.

And they don't care anymore. They can't stand one more second of safety. They need new. They need different. They need anything else but *same*.

Something has to give.

CHAPTER NINETEEN

INTERVIEW WITH INDIE – age 19.9

SESSION #178

DONOVAN: OK, Indie. What the actual fuck? You've been missing for two weeks and—

INDIE: I already told you. I don't want to talk about it.

I know you don't want to talk about it. You've made that very clear. But I have been equally as clear that we will not leave this room until you tell me where you've been and what you've been doing.

...

I'm not fucking around, Indie. I will lock you in this room until you talk.

I'll find a way out.

I will drug you. And then no, sweetie. You will not find a way out. I will keep you here for as long as I need to.

Because you cannot go missing for two weeks with no explanation.

I'm a grown-up, Donovan. I can do whatever the fuck I want.

You have a child, Indie. If you walk away from her, that's called abandonment. And we won't put up with it.

Is that a threat?

Yeah. That's a fuckin' threat all right. I have serious concerns about your mental state and your ability to take care of Maggie right now.

I'm her mother, Donovan. You're no one to her. None of you guys can stop me from picking her up, walking away, and taking her with me.

Wanna bet? You wanna try us, Indie? Because we've already agreed that you will not leave this house with Maggie. That is one hundred percent truth. And we're no one to her? Really? I heard her calling Adam 'Daddy' last week. That's no one?

Adam isn't her daddy. Nathan is.

And Nathan is not here, so—

OK. Let's start there. Why isn't Nathan here, Donovan?

I couldn't really tell you for sure. He was too young to be a father? He wanted to play football instead? He wanted to fuck girls in college and have a good time?

That's not why and you know it. You can say all those nasty things to try to hurt me, or shock me, or whatever. But that's not why he left and never came back. We both know one of you did something.

What did we do? Because I know for a fact, I didn't do anything. I can count the number of times I've talked to Nathan St. James on one hand. And all of those conversations happened before you were fifteen. So, no. I didn't do anything to keep Nathan away from you. He's just a boy who walked away as far as I'm concerned.

Well. I'm happy to hear you weren't involved. But aside from the fact that one of you got him arrested—

He was quickly released.

—he also called me once, you know. And he told me different.

When?

A few weeks after Maggie's first Christmas.

Is that right?

Yup.

What did he say?

He said… "I hope you're happy." But it wasn't sarcasm. It was real. He *hoped* I was happy.

Is that it?

No. That's not it. He also said… he said he was sorry.

Sorry for what?

For cheating on me. And before you let that smug smile creep up your whole face, that's not why he left, either. He didn't leave me and Maggie for another girl. Or college. Or anything like that.

Then why did he leave?

Because he said he made a mistake. And once that was pointed out to him, he knew he could never be there for me the way you guys could. That's how I know one of you said something to him.

Why didn't you say anything? Why didn't you come tell us he called and told you those things?

Because I didn't want to believe it. I didn't want to admit that…

Admit what, Indie?

That you guys didn't really love me. That you were all just… *afraid* of me. That's all. That's the only reason you come, right, Donovan? To keep me sane? I have heard Adam say that so many times, I lost count. "You need to come right now, Donovan. She's done something." "You need to set her straight, Donovan. She said something." What did I do? Huh? What did I do that was so bad, Donovan? What did I say that scared you guys? Three grown-ass men? Two of whom kill people for a fuckin' living? How did I scare you? Can you tell me that, at least? Because I don't understand what is so wrong with me. What do I do that scares you so bad? Do I stalk into your rooms in the middle of the night with a knife? Tell me.

There are a lot of question marks in that statement.

Only one counts. Why do I scare you?

First of all, McKay doesn't really kill people for a living, so he'd probably appreciate it if you didn't go around spreading that particular rumor.

Oh. Excuse me. He only *trains* killers. Got it. Big difference.

And you're wrong, you know. We're not afraid *of* you, Indie. We're afraid *for* you.

What does that even *mean*?

It means that you disappear for two weeks with no word and then come back refusing to talk about it.

So? It's my life, right?

You have a child. You can't just—

Exactly. My. Child. Not yours. Not Adam's. Not McKay's. She's *mine*.

Who did you think was taking care of her while you were gone on this trip, Indie?

You know who.

Adam and McKay?

Of course.

And what if they weren't home when you decided to walk out? Then who?

That didn't happen. They were home. I knew they were home.

OK. Let's go back to that night. Walk me through your decision to leave. Can you do that?

...

Indie, I'm not judging you. I'm really not. You're a good mother. You're a very sweet girl.

But? There's a but in there, right?

But... you do have to admit your life is far from normal. And you have done things—

Things you guys made me do!

I understand that. It's about the things you do, but also the way you react after you do these things.

Because I'm mad at you right now? Because Adam took Maggie and I don't know where she is?

You know where she is. He took her to the fuckin' zoo.

Oh, God. The zoo. That's perfect. Take her to the fuckin' zoo. Maybe he'll put her in a cage and wrap a snake around her too.

Uh... OK. Let's talk about that for a moment. Why would Adam do something like that to Maggie? He

wasn't the one who put you in that cage, Indie. He didn't wrap that snake around you. He saved you.

Did he? Do I look saved?

He brought you here. He gave you McKay and me.

To keep me sane.

So what? Does it matter why we're here? We *are* here, right? We never left.

You left.

I did not. You knew where I was. You knew what I was doing. And any time you asked me to come see you, I did.

It's not the same.

Well… I can't take that back, Indie. The Company told me to become a doctor and—

PSYOPS!

I know that. I was there. But that's not what I am now. You know that. You know I walked away from it as soon as the Company went down.

And you could've come home after that and you didn't. You went to LA.

For my residency. Indie, it's not fair. OK? I don't live for you. None of us do. I have a life of my own.

Well… so do I. That's what I was doing for those two weeks. I was living my own life.

It's different.

No, it's not. You get to be you and I get to be me. And Adam gets to be Adam and McKay—

It's not the same and you know it. You know how I know it?

I'd love to hear your theory.

Look here. Do you see what's in this bag?

Tapes. So what?

Your tapes, Indie. I have recorded one hundred and seventy-eight sessions with you, including this one right now. This is why it's different. And you can play dumb all you want, but somewhere, deep in that head of yours, you know it's different. This is just you being pissed off and making me work for the answers, that's all. You feel in control when you fight me. You feel in control when I have to drag the answers out of you.

…

My point earlier was this. It's not that we're unhappy with your job performance, Indie—

Oh, my God. Really? My *job* performance?

—it's the way you react after the job is over.

I don't understand? How do I react?

You don't react. That's why we worry.

What should I do? Cry and be depressed? How should I act after I do a job?

It's not really how you react after most of the jobs. Just… some of them. Like this one.

What?

This job you were on.

I wasn't on a job.

You were, Indie. You know you were. Right now, you're just lying to me and I don't like it.

So… I'm crazy because when I come back from certain jobs I don't react right?

Well, that's part of it.

Tell me the other part, Donovan. Because I'm tired.

You don't remember them, Indie. That's what I'm trying to say. You don't remember them. And I have a feeling you don't remember these past two weeks either. And that's why you're acting like this. You don't want me to know that. But we already know. We've practically had this same conversation half a dozen times before. And you don't remember it. That's why I tape them.

…

Do you believe me?

Maybe you could play those tapes for me?

No. I don't think that's a good idea.

Then… then maybe you're just lying.

Do you remember where you were for the past two weeks?

…

You can't just shake your head, Indie. This is an audio recording. And I don't want to narrate like this is a court transcript. I want to hear you say it.

Fine. Then yes. Some of it.

Some of it?

Most of it.

Tell me… who were you with?

Why do I have to be with someone?

Indie. You're making me very fuckin' tired. I'm not messing around. I am very fuckin' tired right now. All I need is a few very simple sentences of where you were, what you did, and who else was there. Then we can all eat dinner and relax.

You mean pretend none of this happened? I thought that was part of my problem?

There's a difference between keeping secrets and pretending it never happened.

I'm sick of secrets.

So stop keeping them.

All of them?

Don't start with me. You know which secrets I'm referring to.

You're gonna be mad.

OK. I might be. But what do you think will happen if I'm mad? Do you think I will hurt you?

Of course not.

Do you think I will hate you?

I don't think so.

Do you think I will help you, Indie? Do you think Adam, and McKay and I will protect you, no matter what you tell us?

Yes. I know that.

Then why are you afraid of us? That's the better question here. Not why are we afraid of you, because we're not. Why are you afraid of us?

Don't be stupid. I'm not afraid of you guys. I just…

You just don't remember, do you?

I already told you, I remember some of it.

Tell me those parts. And we can go from there.

…

You can sigh all you want. And did you hear that? I think Adam and Maggie are home. Don't you want to see her? You can give her a bath. You can take a bath together. You always did love bubble baths. Come on. Tell me the rest. You know this has to happen. Why did you leave?

Because I… I got offered a job.

What job?

You know. The regular kind.

You went to kill someone?

Maybe.

Who, Indie? I need to know who.

No one you'd know. It was no one important.

Then why did they need to die?

Because they were bad people.

How do you know they were bad?

Because she told me.

Who, Indie? Who told you to kill the bad people?

...

We're there now, sweetie. You're already there. One more word and we're done here. OK? Just tell me who it was.

Angelica.

Who?

You know. That little Company girl that Nick Tate came and… abducted back when I was fifteen.

You're… sure? It was Angelica?

Yes. Why?

Because Angelica lives very far away from here, Indie. Like… on the other side of the fuckin' planet somewhere. No one even knows where that girl lives. Maybe three people in the whole world, tops. And none of them live in this house.

So? I did jobs in lots of faraway places. And no one knows where I live either. Except you guys.

Indie… Angelica is *retired.*

Well… I think that would be news to her.

So you're telling me that Angelica Fenici is *working*? That she came to you and gave you a job? And that's where you've been for the past two weeks? With Angelica?

Yup. Can I go take a bath with Mags now?

…

Donovan?

What?

Are we done? Can I go take a bubble bath now?

Sure, Indie. Yes. I think that sounds like a good idea. Send Adam in, will you?

ADAM!!!! DONOVAN WANTS TO TALK TO YOU!

I could've done that.

Good night, Donovan.

Good night, Indie.

…

ADAM: What's up? What did she say?

She's lost her fuckin' mind. At least… that's the best-case scenario here. Because if what she just told me is true, then we have a very big problem.

SESSION NOTES - PRIVATE

I don't think I can do this anymore. I know I've said it before, but this time I mean it. I can't go through this again.

This is the eighth time.

Eight times Indie has gone off script.

Eight times we had to backtrack her every move and figure out what she did.

Eight times we told ourselves it was a one-off.

Eight motherfucking times we played her favorite game. The one called Let's-Pretend-*That*-Didn't-Happen.

Eight. Goddamned. Times. I've written a session note just like this.

And that, right there? That's the definition of insanity.

I try and remember why I took this job. Why, exactly, I talked Adam into buying this girl. And I swear to God. I know I did this. I remember those words that came out of my mouth back on that island. I have the motherfucking session tapes, and notes, and private thoughts from Indie's first year and I have read them so many times I could recite them from memory.

But for the life of me, I cannot come to terms with what *the fuck* I was thinking.

Carter is dead.

Dead. Dead. Dead. Like everyone else. He is *dead.*

He's not out there running little girls like Indie.

He's not out playing Company.

He's gone.

That was my father's final job before Adam and I helped Nick, and Sasha, and James kill two hundred people in Santa Barbara.

But I was young, I guess. So fuckin' sure of myself. My brain, and my money, and my Untouchable status.

I can't *do this* anymore.

CHAPTER TWENTY

adam

FOUR YEARS AGO

Indie has to be lying about Angelica. I don't know the girl, but I know who she's with. Just before the Company totally fell apart, while I was still in the hospital, I got a letter from the Shadow of Secrets himself. He was thanking me for being one of the 'good guys'. Which made me pause and ponder the meaning of 'good' for a while. But then, when I read on, he told me he thought about our little talk down in Daphne, Alabama and decided to let Angelica live. She was with his sister, Harper, and James Fenici.

I didn't think much about it back then. I mean, I was on to the dude. It was only a suspicion, but in my world a good hunch is just about the same thing as the truth.

I knew things no one else did. Even Donovan didn't know as much about what was really going on as I did.

But here's the only thing that matters now.

There is no fucking way in hell that James Fenici let his girl, Angelica, go back to work. It's also highly improbable that Angelica took off the way Indie did. James Fenici would hunt her down, take her home, and tie her up until she came back to her senses.

But I get the feeling that Angelica is a lot better-adjusted than Indie and thus has never lost her senses.

This doesn't make me feel any better though. Because that Nick shadow was right when he warned me that Indie will never be normal. She will always have that secret side that makes her dangerous. And here we are. Not even twenty years old and she's delusional.

Regardless, I have to find out about Angelica. This situation is serious and there is no more room for hunches.

It takes almost a week to hunt down James and leave enough messages with various mutual acquaintances for him to notice me. And then another week before I see that dude—just as scary as I remember him from back in the day—leaning against a brick building and watching me with piercing green eyes from the corner of Royal and St. Phillip in New Orleans as I make my way over towards Misha's little bar.

I stop short and just look at him, trying to decide if I should back away or keep going and have the conversation I asked for.

A horn honks and I realize I'm standing in the middle of the street. So I continue crossing St Phillip just as he pushes off the wall and meets me at the curb.

He points to Misha's bar, just a few storefronts up. "Let's have a drink, Adam."

I don't say anything. Just follow him. This meeting is no accident, obviously. If you mention James Fenici's name enough times to the right people, he will appear like a conjuring at the least convenient time.

I was going to Misha's anyway, but I wasn't planning on introducing her to the most infamous Company assassin to ever walk this earth.

He opens the door for me and a small bell jingles above our heads as we enter. It's early afternoon, but inside it's dim, and the shadows play against the walls.

I flash two fingers to Misha, who is behind the bar and watching me curiously, then point to a table in the back. James follows me, and for a moment we nearly fight over the chair that faces the door.

I put my hands up and back off, taking the chair with the next-best view.

James leans his forearms on the table, hands together, his green eyes smiling along with his mouth. He stares at me for a moment as Misha appears with two glasses of whiskey. James glances up at her, says, "Thanks, Misha," and then downs it in one gulp and says, "No more for me, thanks."

I catch Misha raising one eyebrow at me. But I send her a look that says, *Don't ask*. And she takes the hint and leaves without a word.

"Would you consider her a good friend? An acquaintance? Or just a booty call?"

I glance at Misha, who has returned to her spot behind the bar, but with her back to us now. "Good friend, I guess."

"You might want to rethink that."

"Oh?" I look at him, not sure what to make of that statement.

"She sold you out once."

"Once? When?"

"More than once. Few years back. Before everything went down."

"Well, I'm still here. Must not have been too serious."

"That's how she bought this bar, you know."

"Did you come here to warn me about Misha? Or because I spoke your name to the right people?"

"Both, I guess. I've been waiting for you to get rid of her. Thought I'd speed that up a little. Seeing as how you're starting to settle in here."

Is he… has he been watching me? I'm *not* afraid of James. He's old now. Early forties, at least. I'm in my prime. And I don't know what he's been doing for the past five years since the Company fell, but I've been busy running shit. Some might even refer to what I've put together as a mini-Company—minus all the political connections because pretty much all those people are dead now. And James Fenici might even be one of those people who see things that way. I might not be off-the-rails insane like he is, but I can do damage if I have to.

Still. The thought of him keeping track of me is… unsettling.

"I wasn't really in the market for some personal advice, James—"

"What kind of market are you in, then?"

"I have a question for you about Angelica."

And that. That right there. That look in his eyes. Yeah. My stomach clenches up. Because there is something deeply wrong with this man and he might be able to hide it most of the time, but just uttering Angelica's name brings up the animal lurking beneath the surface.

His eyes are narrowed down into very thin slits. "What about her?"

"Let me just explain that the reason I'm asking is because Indie has told me some things and she brought up Angelica's name. That's it. That's the only reason I'm asking. OK?"

"So ask."

"Is she working?"

His eyes open wide again. "Angelica?" He laughs. "No, brother. And she's not for hire, either."

Both of my hands go up in defense. "I'm not looking to hire her. It's just… Indie. She's… she said that Angelica came to her with a job. She said they're working together."

James leans back in his seat. His whole posture changes, becomes more relaxed. "She's mistaken. Angelica lives at home still. She just turned eighteen a few weeks ago and she might have big dreams about all the possibilities her new adult status might bring, but…" He chuckles a little. "Yeah. That's not gonna happen. She's about as normal a girl can be after spending her childhood being trained by the Company."

I let out a long breath. "OK."

James nods. "That it?"

"Yeah. That's it."

"You having some kind of trouble with Indie I should be aware of?"

"Nothing we can't handle."

"Well, excuse me for saying so, but you don't seem too sure about that, Adam."

"We have a system and it's been working… *OK.* So far. But she took off for two weeks and we didn't know where she was. Then she fed me this story about Angelica and I just… I already knew it was bullshit but I had to hear it from you. You understand, right?"

"Believe me, I get it. Not a single fucking day goes by that I'm not looking at Angelica with a critical eye. Is she being aggressive? Did she just look at that person funny? I have to know where she is every minute of the day or I go insane. And if she disappeared for two weeks…" He shakes his head. "No. I would not deal with that very well. Did you try to trace her?"

"She's… good at what she does."

"I can imagine. No clue, then?"

I shake my head. "But we have Donovan, you know. He's been treating her this whole time. I don't know if Angelica had a trigger word—"

"Fuck, no."

"—but Indie does. Did. Maybe still does." James just stares at me and I get nervous again. Not for me. But for Indie. Because he could… he could decide Indie has to go. He could decide she needs to be put down. He could decide this little family we've made over the past ten years is now over. "Donovan was training in PSYOPS… before. Ya know? And he's good. He's got it under control."

James folds his arms across his chest, clearly not convinced.

I stand up, my drink untouched, needing this meeting to be over. "Thanks. I appreciate you coming all this way to talk to me. I need to get going now."

He nods, but doesn't get up or say anything.

So I turn and start walking.

But then he calls out, "Don't forget about my first warning, Adam. That was not a suggestion. It was a command."

I stop. And for a second I don't understand what he's talking about. But then I catch Misha's eye across the room and remember.

Get rid of her.

James Fenici just told me to get rid of Misha.

"And listen," he calls again. This time I look at him over my shoulder. "It's a hard lesson to learn, but not everyone's worth saving, Adam."

I nod my head and then keep walking. Straight out of the bar. Right back to my truck. And then I drive all the way home trying to figure out how I'm gonna tell McKay that Indie is *sick*.

CHAPTER TWENTY-ONE

mckay

After Adam's call I go inside to check up on Donovan and Indie. See how dinner's coming. Let them know we can eat outside if they want.

They're both in the kitchen. Donovan must've bought beer when he went to the grocery store because they are both holding green bottles in their hands. Indie is sitting on the kitchen island facing Donovan, who is leaning against the counter next to the stove.

Both of them are laughing when I walk in.

Indie sets her beer down, hops off the counter, and comes over to me, slipping her arms right around my waist as she leans into my chest.

I watch Donovan for a reaction. He meets my gaze and shrugs.

I grip Indie's shoulders and push her back a little. "What was that for?"

"Just... you." She glances at Donovan. "Both of you." She looks back at me. "But I've hugged him already so it was your turn."

Hugged him. Sure. "Is dinner ready?"

Donovan opens a cupboard, grabs four plates, and sets them down on the counter. "Just waiting on you. You wanna set the table, Indie?"

"My old job is still mine, I see." But then she must count the plates because she lifts one of them up. "Are we expecting Adam?"

I say, "No," just as Donovan says, "Maybe."

"Which is it?"

I shake my head. "No. He texted me. He can't make it."

Indie makes a little pout face, something I have not seen her do in many years. "Well, that sucks."

"I thought you wanted to kill him?"

"What? That's crazy, McKay. What the hell is wrong with you?"

Donovan and I both glance at each other, eyebrows raised.

He breaks the silence first. "Go on, Indie. Set the table. We'll bring out the food."

"You guys just want to talk about me, don't you?"

I ignore her and open the silverware drawer, grab enough for three people, and then close it with my hip and hand it all to Indie. "There you go."

She smirks at me. "I can take a hint." She leaves. I wait a second, then follow her to the front door and peek out to make sure she's going to the pavilion.

Donovan is already behind me. "What did he say?"

"He said he's not coming until she remembers what really happened that day."

"How's that gonna be helpful? We need him here when she remembers."

"He knows that. He just doesn't care."

I turn to look at Donovan. He's running his fingers through his dark hair. "Well, fuck. Now what?"

"I guess… I guess we lead her through it, Donovan. Have a session with her."

"Hypnosis? Or just a regular one?"

I shrug. Because this isn't my area. "Whatever you think is best."

He lets out a long breath. And for a moment I get this sick feeling in my gut that he's gonna refuse. That Donovan

Couture has had just about enough of this little distraction called Indie, and he's gonna wipe his hands and walk away.

I'm ready if he tries. I'm ready to block him. Talk sense into him.

But I don't have to.

He nods. Sighs again. "OK. Then hypnosis. But we should eat first. Give me time to think about how to best handle this because it's been a long time, McKay. I would never have called myself a PSYOPS expert, but it's been a long time since I had to think about it."

I am relieved and out of words so I say nothing. Just go back to the kitchen and start piling spaghetti into a large bowl while Donovan transfers marinara sauce and meatballs into another bowl.

He grabs some serving spoons, I grab the bread, and then we go outside.

And the minute I step into the pavilion it feels like the old days. Back before we knew she was sick. Back before that afternoon of her twentieth birthday when what we had was good, and innocent, and right.

But that's wrong too.

Because nothing about this has ever been right.

We set everything on the table and eat.

But I'm not even here with them.

I'm back there.

On that day.

The day everything changed and nothing was ever the same again.

Indie was wearing a yellow party dress with a short fluffy skirt made of tulle or whatever you call that shit. That see-through gauzy fabric that always reminded me of ballerina outfits.

It was strapless and the bodice had little crystals woven into the lace around her breasts. Adam had it made for her. He always bought her a dress on her birthday.

This one was a little risqué for my tastes, but she was twenty. And a mother.

Twenty fucking years old. Finally. It felt like a milestone. Ten years we'd been taking care of this girl. Ten years she'd been running our lives. One decade. That's something, right?

From the moment she stepped out of Adam's truck to the moment she disappeared, everything at Old Home revolved around Indie Anna Accorsi.

I'm not gonna lie and say it was all good, because it wasn't.

And I'm not gonna pretend any of it was easy, because it wasn't.

But I would absolutely do it all again.

Nathan St. James came back into our lives that morning. He was home, I guess. Because one minute we were planning our day in the kitchen after breakfast and Maggie was dancing around like a little spinning top, very excited about something that involved a pony, and then there was a knock on the door.

All of us turned to peer towards the front of the house with curious looks. Who the hell was at our door?

We all went into the hallway, but Adam went ahead of us towards the foyer.

We could see him. The front door was open, so there was only a screen.

Nathan St. James. In the motherfucking flesh.

And then something really weird happened. Maggie said, "Nathan." It was a distorted version of his name. Said the way only a small child could say it.

And the whole fucking place went quiet.

And then it went… *unquiet.*

Adam said, "What the fuck?"

And Donovan said, "Have you been talking to him this whole time?"

And I didn't say shit. Because I could not find the right words.

Indie ignored all of that and just smiled. "Hello, Nathan. Come on in."

Nathan had enough sense to *not* come in. Adam was standing at the door, blocking it.

But I had finally found my words. "Indie. Why is he here?" I said it in the calmest voice I could manage. But my heart was beating fast and furious. It was a jackhammer inside my chest. Fluttering and pounding so fast I couldn't count the beats if I wanted to.

Indie looked at me like I was an idiot. "He's her *father*, McKay. I told him he could see her today. He's gonna bring her back tonight for cupcakes."

"Yay!" Maggie was clapping her hands, jumping up and down like a little crazy person.

Donovan, and Adam, and I looked at each other like… *Did you know about this*?

And clearly, none of us had.

Indie gently nudged Adam out of the way of the door and opened it up. "Come in. I'll get her dressed. Be right back."

Then she picked Maggie up and took her upstairs.

Adam shot me one more look, then he and Donovan followed her up, leaving me alone with that little fucker from across the lake.

Did we have a say in this decision? I wasn't sure. But I *was sure* that Indie didn't seem to think we did, or she would not have pretended this wasn't happening until it actually happened.

Nathan St. James was now a huge twenty-one-year-old man. I'm talking that boy must've been in the gym all day, every day for the past two years. That's how big he was.

I was not small, either. Never have been. And I was certainly not afraid of throwing down with the fuckhead next door. But not while Maggie was here. And if Adam had wanted to get rid of Nathan with a fight, he would not have been upstairs trying to talk Indie out of… whatever the fuck this was.

Nathan and I both heard every word of what was happening up there.

Adam was saying, "What the hell? What the hell, Indie?"

Donovan was saying, "Are you out of your mind?"

Indie was saying, "Jesus Christ. It's one day. Calm down."

Maggie was saying, "I want to ride pony!"

Meanwhile, Nathan and I were just staring each other down like he was a Hatfield and I was a McCoy, which was not that far off the mark.

Finally, Nathan broke the ice. "Hey, McKay. How's life been for ya?"

I morphed into some polite Southerner I did not even recognize. Because I replied, "Just fine, thank you. How about yourself?"

"Can't complain much. But I hurt my knee in football last year and lost my scholarship. So I'm gonna sell the old place to cover tuition. That's why I'm coming home this summer for break. I have to spruce it up a little before I put it on the market. The electrical is a big ol' mess. I turned on the heater this morning, just to see if it was still working, and the damn thing caught fire."

Again, I was out of sorts. Because I replied, "If you need any help with that, you let me know. I'm a fairly good electrician."

He nodded his head at me. "Thanks. I'll keep that in mind."

But then I snapped out of it. "Where are you taking Maggie? Across the lake? To that fire trap?"

Nathan just… chuckled at me. "No. We're going to the zoo in New Orleans. I can't remember the last time I went to the zoo."

Which spurred another pertinent comment from me. "When was the last time you saw Indie?"

He hesitated a little. I have often wondered if Nathan St. James understood who the girl next door really was. And it was during this short hesitation when I realized—he did. "She's been coming to see me."

"When?"

"The whole time, McKay. She would just show up at my dorm in Oxford out of the blue after Christmas that first year. And then I got a house with some of my football buddies and she'd show up there too. Even though I never told her I moved. I never asked her to come. But… McKay. You gotta know, I did love her. I'm sorry things… well, I'm sorry. That's all. And I love Magnolia too—"

"Maggie," I corrected him.

"Maggie. And then Indie started bringing her up to see me."

"She did?"

"She did."

"When?"

"I dunno. Every few months, I guess. Over the past year or so. And I knew I was gonna be back this summer to get the house ready for sale so… I took a chance and asked if I could spend a day with my daughter."

"This day?"

"Today. That's right."

"It's Indie's birthday today."

"I know. But she said this was the only day she could do it."

Then it started to make a little bit of sense. Indie thought that because it was her birthday, none of us would make a fuss about this. But the sounds that were coming from upstairs said otherwise. Adam and Donovan were still having their say.

Suddenly nothing about this day was right. My head was fuckin' foggy and Nathan's words started to echo. But I managed to say, "The zoo, huh? Does Indie know you're taking Maggie to the zoo?"

"Yes, sir. It was her idea."

And that just didn't make *any* sense to me. Because I knew for a fact that Indie hated the zoo. And she had just let us know that a few weeks prior, after she disappeared and came back, when Adam took Maggie to the zoo.

But there was no more time to question Nathan because everyone came bounding down the stairs. First Indie, holding Maggie in her arms, and then Adam and Donovan trailing behind her.

I looked Indie dead in the eyes and the room started to spin. "Are you sure about this?"

"Why wouldn't I be sure? I told him he could have her for a day. He's excited about it, McKay. And so is Maggie. He's her father. He should know her."

Donovan, Adam, and I all looked at each other like we just popped into some alternate realty by mistake. That was how much sense this made. And that was how I felt too. Like this wasn't really happening. Like I was back in my bed, stuck in a dream.

But then Indie turned to Nathan. "Can you just give us a minute? I'll bring her out to your truck."

Nathan nodded his head at her, then me, and then left. Skipping down the porch steps like he didn't give one fuck that his visit was causing all this trouble.

Adam slammed the front door. Not the screen door. The real front door. So it slammed good and hard. Then he turned to Indie with angry eyes. "What the fuck, Indie?"

"She's been up there to Oxford to see him, Adam." My words coming out a little bit slurred. "And she took Maggie. To *see* him."

Indie set Maggie down and crossed her arms, defiant. "She's *my* daughter."

"And you belong to me." Adam was seething. Maggie was already heading for the door.

"OK. Let's just all calm down."

But Adam turned to Donovan and his stupid rational words and pointed his finger in his face. "I will not calm down. We have no clue what kind of man Nathan St. James is these days. He's been missing for two years. Maggie doesn't even know him."

Maggie was twisting the door handle, trying to open it. "I want to zoo. I want to ride pony."

Which spurred me into favorite-uncle mode. "There are no ponies at the zoo, Mags. If you want to ride a pony, I'll get you a pony. You can keep it here and ride it all over the woods."

"McKay, are you on drugs?" Indie was incredulous. "What is wrong with you? We're not getting a pony just so you can stop Nathan from seeing his daughter."

I pointed my finger at her. "What is wrong with you?" But she was right. Because I knew there *was* something wrong with me.

"Indie." Donovan was interrupting. "Did you go up to Oxford to see Nathan when you went missing?"

"I'll be right back. You guys are making a huge deal out of nothing and ruining my plans for today." And then Indie scooped up Maggie, opened the door, and walked out. Taking her daughter over to Nathan's truck.

Adam looked at me, confused. "What plans?"

I just shrugged.

We all went into the front room and peeked through the closed curtains at what was happening out in our driveway. Indie was still holding Maggie as Nathan messed with a car seat in the back cab of his truck.

I looked at Donovan. There were two of him. "Where did he get a car seat?"

Donovan didn't answer.

And then Indie handed Maggie—*our* Maggie—over to Nathan so he could buckle her in the seat.

Adam stepped away from the curtain and started pacing the room, raking his fingers through his hair. He kept saying, "What the fuck is she doing? Why is she doing this? Something is wrong. Something is very wrong here."

Donovan stepped back as well. But I could not take my eyes off Nathan and Maggie.

I felt sick. There was this feeling in my gut. This gross feeling that I had missed something here. Things were happening and I couldn't make sense of them.

Donovan was talking. "Just… remain calm. We'll figure it out."

And then Indie was whooshing through the door with a big, bright smile on her face and both hands in the air like she was surrendering. "Just listen to me, you guys. God. You're all a bunch of stupid men. I planned this so we could all have a day together. Just us. Like the old days. Remember them? How much fun we had? I've been stuck in this house for two years. I'm twenty. My childhood is over. And I want to have a day with you! All of you!"

Donovan was not buying one bit of this. "So let me get this straight. To celebrate the fact that you're no longer a teenager, you just handed your child off to a stranger?"

But he was swaying back and forth a little as he talked. Or maybe that was me?

"He's not a stranger, Donovan. Stop being stupid. He's her father."

Adam was shaking his head. "*We* are her fathers."

Indie laughed. "You're jealous." She looked at all of us in turn. "That's what this is about. Nathan St. James is the gentlest person I know."

Adam snorted. "Oh, for fuck's sake. You are the worst judge of character—"

"Fuck you, Adam!" She was all up in his face, pointing her finger. "You're ruining my birthday!"

I stepped between them and looked at Adam. I had to place my hands on his shoulders to steady myself. "He's gone now. It's done. So… just… let's try to have a nice day."

I looked over at Donovan and he was nodding. "It's done, Adam." But then he looked at Indie. "What time is he bringing her home?" His voice was what I like to call 'doctor professional'. Better known as emotionally detached. But his words were somehow… wrong.

"They'll be back at four."

All three of us looked at the grandfather clock in the hallway. I thought it said ten forty-five. But I wasn't sure.

Adam said, "Five hours and fifteen minutes. He better not be late or I will hunt him down—"

"He won't be late. He's meeting a contractor over at the cottage at four thirty."

This seemed to pacify everyone. At least, momentarily.

Indie took advantage of the momentary calm and walked up to Adam and slipped her arms around his middle. She gazed up into his eyes with a look I'd never seen on her face before.

Donovan and I traded glances. I thought this was a new look for him too.

"Don't you get it?" Indie was asking Adam. Then she looked at me. And then Donovan. "I wanted to spend some time alone with you guys. All of you. That's how I want to say goodbye to my teens."

Then she did something I had never seen before. Ever. She leaned up on her tiptoes and kissed Adam right on the mouth.

This was not a goodnight kiss like she would give me. It was… it was open-mouthed and filed with tongue.

It was fuckin' hot.

And then… then Adam kissed her back.

He put both hands on her cheeks and kissed her like she was the love of his life. He kissed her like he was about to rip her clothes off and fuck her up against the front door.

He kissed her like Donovan and I weren't even *there.*

And that's the day I knew… Indie wasn't the only one with secrets.

We all had them, didn't we?

Indie Anna Accorsi had played a starring role in our fantasies since she was ten years old, but up until now they'd all been dress rehearsals.

That day of her twentieth birthday?

That was opening night.

CHAPTER TWENTY-TWO

Indie

If I had to choose between them, I would die. There is just no way I could only choose one.

I need them all.

I don't even care if that's selfish. I want them all.

And if I thought I could have Nathan St. James, then I would. I would have him too. I would keep all four of them because they are each different, and unique, and give me something I can't get from anyone else.

Every single way they fill me up has been written in this journal. So if it's not clear by now, there is nothing left to be said. There are simply no words to describe my need.

But I am afraid that you will see this and you won't understand. And I don't care if you are Nathan, or McKay, or Adam, or Donovan. I need you to understand.

How many other ways are there to describe Nathan St. James? He is my boy next door. He is my best friend. He is the firefly-catcher, and the treehouse-builder, and the swamp-charmer.

Oh, I know what Adam would say. "He was running around on you back in high school." *Yes, Adam. He told me all about what he did. He told me that you caught him. He told me what you said to him. And I get it. If Nathan loved me best, he would be more careful with my heart. He'd be like McKay.*

McKay is so very, *very* careful with me. McKay is my *soul.* He is my trainer. He is the dinner-maker, and the hair-washer, and the nightmare-chaser.

But McKay will never admit he has always loved me. That I am his first, and only, one true love.

So I have Donovan. Donovan is careful too. He is my mind-reader. My note-taker. He is the light in the dark, he is the filler of holes, he is the voice in my head that keeps me calm during my stormy nights of insanity.

But he's part-time. We all know it. He will never take me with him to LA and I wouldn't want to go. This is my home. Right here. This is where I belong.

And that's where Adam comes in. Adam. My owner. My knight. My protector. He is my partner in crime. The fixer of mistakes, the leader of us all, the untouchable one.

He is like a mean old dog who will bite anyone who gets too close.

Everyone but me.

He lets me get close.

But will he share?

Will any of them share?

Only if I make them.

So this is how I made them…

I kissed Adam in the hallway. Nathan St. James wasn't even down the driveway yet with our daughter when I rose up on my tiptoes and put my mouth right on Adam's. When he placed his hands on my face and leaned into it.

McKay was just two feet away. Shifting his feet, and his gaze, and wondering if he should make me stop. But what would that mean?

He didn't know. Or he did, and couldn't admit it.

I was looking right at Donovan when I kissed Adam. He would be the easiest to turn because he was the least invested in what happened tomorrow.

But would he come back for more?

I didn't know.

I didn't have any idea why they were still here with me.

When I pulled away from Adam his eyes were closed. And they didn't open right away. It was like he was still there. Still lingering in the moment when our lips touched.

When his eyes finally did open, I could see myself in them. A distorted shadow of a girl. Something black and not altogether whole. She scared me. She still scares me. Every time I see myself in a window, or a mirror, or a drinking glass, I am afraid of the monster looking back.

But his gaze held me captive. Forced me to see the girl I've been trying to outrun my whole life.

I went still. And then I made another executive decision. Just like that time Johnny Boston captured me and held me prisoner on that yacht.

I let that girl in.

Or maybe I should say… I let her *out*.

It was time.

McKay broke the silence when he said, "What the fuck was that?"

Adam brought the back of his hand up to his mouth and made a fist. He held it there against his lips like he was coming to terms with something. And he would not look away from me. So I kept looking at that shadow girl reflected in his eyes. I could not unsee her now.

Donovan let out a long sigh. I figured this was the moment when Donovan walked out for good. Cut his losses and said goodbye. Or maybe just left without saying anything. Because he is smart. And he knows about the lovely darkness hiding inside me. He sees my gorgeous misery.

But he didn't move. Just stayed right where he was.

Adam looked away first and broke the spell the shadow girl had over me. At least for a moment.

"Adam?" McKay was still asking his question.

But Adam just looked at me, then at McKay, and said, "I don't know."

Then someone said, "You know," and I realized it was me saying that. Or some part of me, at least. And she kept talking. "You all know. We all know what's going on here. Why do we have to keep pretending? Why can't we just… accept it? And be who we are?"

"What are you… *talking* about?" Donovan was confused. I understood that. He was not a cold man. Not really. He was fun, and he smiled, and he helped me through lots of things. But he was like me in a lot of ways.

Detached and far away.

Then McKay walked across the foyer, opened up the door, and walked out.

I panicked. Because McKay was not the one who was supposed to walk out.

Donovan was. I could deal with Donovan. I could lure him back with the promise of secrets.

But I never had control of McKay like that.

I looked at Adam and said, "Stop him. You have to stop him."

Adam looked at the door, which McKay didn't even bother to slam behind him, and then back at me. "What am I supposed to tell him, Indie? What exactly do you see happening here?"

I looked at Donovan for help. But he was shaking his head at me.

So I looked back to Adam and said, "I don't care what you tell him, Adam. Just make him stay. Don't let him walk away. This will not work without him."

Donovan walked across the foyer and grabbed me by the arm. He jerked it, angrily. "What the fuck are you talking about?"

But I was still looking at Adam.

Still seeing that dark shadow of a girl in his eyes.

And I said the only thing left to say. "It's the only way to save me from myself."

CHAPTER TWENTY-THREE

donovan

PRESENT DAY

It's an awkward dinner of spaghetti and meatballs, garlic bread, and wine. We've had this same meal, minus the wine, in Indie's case, dozens of times in the past. Maybe even hundreds. McKay used to make it a lot because back when Indie was small, she was a very picky eater. McKay worked hard on expanding her palate because he would eat anything. Food was an adventure in his mind. So he was always trying introduce new vegetables, or some kind of fish, or whatever at dinner time. And dinner, like church, was a constant in Indie's life. She had to be home every night at seven o'clock to eat with McKay—and sometimes Adam and I, if we were around— or she would be in a lot of trouble.

But Indie was a simple girl when it came to food and didn't like much. McKay finally gave in and just started making her favorites. And spaghetti and meatballs was one of the few things I did actually learn to make because we ate it so often.

On the surface everything around us almost seems the same. It didn't take long to make the pavilion go back in time. A few cushions, and pillows, and blankets and it's almost like we never left.

But then again… all you have to do is look across the lake and see the missing carriage house and that illusion fades quickly.

I do my best with small talk, filling them in on the partnership I'm about to buy into back in LA. Indie asks a few questions about my specialty—assuming, as most people do, that I'm heading for a career in breast implants, puffy lips, and face lifts.

But that was never the plan.

Facial reconstruction is where my skills lie. I have spent a fair amount of time repairing cleft palates in Mexico over the years. I have been on my own ten-year plan since I first saw Indie back on the island. Not that she'd know. Or Adam, or McKay for that matter.

But that's only because they never asked.

I have never been part of the team in the eyes of Adam and McKay. It has always been the two of them against the world. Indie is the go-between. She's not really Adam's little assassin. She's not really McKay's little obsession.

She is their reason to stay together.

So why am I here?

I lost track of that answer a while back now, but it started as a long, convoluted maze of rambling—possibly delusional—thoughts about my brother, Carter.

Twins. Identical twins.

Every Untouchable child has an identical twin. Every single one.

We always have doubles. That's what makes us so untouchable. This secret project was called the Negative Program.

But there is only one reason to keep two copies of the same thing.

One is a backup. It's just that simple.

Adam had a double once. He just doesn't remember his brother because he died at birth.

That's the real reason McKay went to live with Adam when he was a kid. Mr. Boucher wasn't buying Adam a playmate, he was buying himself a back-up copy.

I know this because my family wasn't really running a sex slave auction for little girls on the island. That was just an excuse to hide what's really happening behind the scenes. The Couture Family had been running the Negative Program since its inception.

James Fenici has a twin. His name is Vincent.

Nick Tate had a twin too. But her name is Harper. That got a little messy for obvious reasons.

Adam had a twin, and he died.

I had a twin and his name was Carter.

Of course, most of them die early—before thirty, for sure. James Fenici, Adam, and myself are the only exceptions to that rule. But often in their teens. They take a hit, or they go insane, or they are killed when they show sociopathic tendencies too early.

Carter and I were ten when they separated us.

Right after the Santa Barbara massacre.

It was too early.

They should have known better.

They should've learned from their mistake with James and Vincent.

I didn't really join this little team to keep Indie sane. Oh, that was part of it. Because I needed her. I needed the secrets locked inside her head. I *did* like her. In fact, I liked her immediately. Indie was a cool child. She was tough, and smart, and she had this *very* special memory that would lock things up in deep dark places and hold them tight like a vault until someone came along with the key, opened her up, and asked just the right questions, in just the right way, so they could spill out.

He did that to her. Carter. He did that. I know he did. I would recognize his handiwork anywhere because we learned how to do it together. We trained in PSYOPS together as children. And Carter was much better at it than I was.

But they took him from me. The stole him from me.

And for a while I thought he was dead. One of us had to die, right? Eventually?

But then Indie came along and I started to poke around in her mind. This was how I spent my time on the island. Those girls were like little quizzes for me. Little tests.

I would be their friend. Their ally. I would bring them special treats. Little cakes and sweet juices. I would let them cry, and whine about how unfair life is, and complain about anything they wanted. I would listen and then I would lie to them as I picked apart their minds for practice and told them it was all going to be OK.

Until Indie came along and I found that secret place inside her head. And I recognized it for what it was.

Carter's work.

That's why I needed Adam to buy her. That's why I joined his team.

But I did not have the key to unlock that vault inside Indie's head. She never told me a single fuckin' secret. I figured that out fairly early. By the time she was fourteen for sure. I knew there was no way I'd get the information I was looking for and then the Company fell and Carter never made contact with me, so… I dunno.

I just let it go, I guess. Moved on. Accepted the inevitable truth that my brother really was gone.

I had not seen a single sign that he didn't die the night my grandfather lost his mind and ripped us apart—but even if he was alive, our work together was over.

The Negative Program was over.

Everyone in my family was a doctor, every boy for as long back as the Founding, was a doctor. Every single one of us followed the same path.

PSYOPS

But it wasn't *just* PSYOPS.

It was surgery too. Mind and body. That's the goal for the genius boys bred into the Couture family.

Carter and I are identical in every way. Right down to the wiring in our genius brains. We started manipulating people before we could talk. And we had this kind of "twin language" with our hands, and our eyes, and our body movements.

We were fluent in three languages by the time we were five. We learned how to control subjects under the PSYOPS drugs by the time we were seven. He took over his first mind when he was eight and a half. He did this like it was his God-given gift. Like his only purpose on this planet was to fuck up the minds of others.

He scared people the way Indie scares people. And my grandfather decided to end it after Santa Barbara.

He blamed Carter for that mess. I'm not even sure why. We were ten, for fuck's sake. If Carter was in on it, he didn't tell me.

Maybe that's why I'm still alive?

But Carter and I… we were never meant to be two separate people. We were always supposed to be one.

My grandfather made a mistake taking my brother from me.

Huge. Mistake.

And he paid for it with his life.

I have kept current on the advancing technologies in psychiatric therapy. Much more so over the past two years than the three prior to that. And I would like to try something with Indie tonight.

I know Adam is not coming back here until he's sure things are safe and the quickest way to get there is to figure out where Indie's been and what she knows.

I would like to be very clear. I never lied to her. Not once. Not ever.

But I haven't been completely forthcoming with any of them. And when it comes to Indie, I have taken great care to hide things.

Not about me. I don't care if they find out what I'm up to. That was always the plan.

But I have hidden things from Indie about herself.

And tonight I will pull back the cloak she's been wearing and set her free.

McKay is initially resistant. He doesn't speak when I present my offer, but I know him well enough to hear what he's not saying.

If McKay had his way, he'd never let Indie know the truth. If he had his way, he'd keep her ten forever. I know it. I can see it in his eyes.

He didn't want to do what we did on Indie's twentieth birthday. He was the one who walked out. Not me. Not Adam. Him.

But he didn't get far. There is no way McKay would walk away from Indie. Not ever. Even if Adam hadn't chased him out the door after Indie made it clear what she wanted from us that day, he would not have left. He might've gotten in his truck. Maybe even started the engine. But he would not have left.

But things have changed now. Indie was the one who left and McKay had no say in it. He will do anything to keep her now.

Anything.

So when I make my offer and he's silently resistant, I know that from McKay, that's implied agreement.

INTERVIEW WITH INDIE - AGE 24

SESSION #191

DONOVAN: OK, Indie. You know the drill. Tell me what we're doing.

INDIE: Oh, for fuck's sake, Donovan. We all know what we're doing.

MCKAY: We need to hear it from you, Indie.

McKay, you're not supposed to say anything. Indie, say it out loud or we can't get started.

Fine. We're doing hypnosis so you guys can help me remember what I've been doing and where I've been for the past four years.

OK. Tell me the last thing you remember from your twentieth—

I… I just don't think this is a good idea.

McKay, you are to keep quiet. Or you will have to leave.

I just—

It's fine, McKay. I need to know this stuff. It's time. I can't go on like this. And I know why Adam isn't here.

Why do you think he's not here, Indie?

Because he's afraid of me.

Is that the only reason?

You guys—

McKay! Shut up! … Go on, Indie. Are there any other reasons why Adam would not want to see you right now?

I mean… I'm sure he's maybe… upset with me.

Why would he be upset?

Because I disappointed him.

Can you think of any specifics? What exactly did you do that disappointed him?

I dunno. But he's like that. He's not like you, McKay. You never walk out. Adam does. And so do you, Donovan.

OK, we're getting off track here. So let's focus on the main reason we're doing this. I'm going to hypnotize you now, Indie. And then I'm gonna ask careful questions. If at any time I feel like you should not continue, I will pull you out of it. I will take care of you, do you understand?

And I'm here too.

McKay, if I have to tell you one more time—

I'm just saying. She knows I won't let anything harm her. No matter what she finds inside her head.

Fine. Do you understand, Indie?

Yes. I do. And thank you, McKay.

You're welcome, Indie.

OK, try to relax now. Let your whole body go heavy... let your mind become dark and blank. Take deep breaths with me. In and out. Slowly. Yes. And I'm going to count backwards from ten.

....

Ten. You are in the swamp, Indie. You are ten years old. Muddy, and tired, and hungry. But you're happy because Nathan St. James is cooking you fish on the beach.

...

Nine. You are eleven years old, Indie. You are out in the back learning to defend yourself with McKay. He is hard on you, but you don't mind. Because he's gonna make sure you're a tough little girl who can handle herself.

...

Eight. You are twelve and on a job with Adam. Something goes wrong. But that's OK. Because Adam is there to protect you. You come home and you are just fine.

. . .

Seven. You are thirteen and you're getting better at this. You can fight now. And every once in a while, you can pull one over on McKay and take him down.

. . . .

Six. You are fourteen and you just got home from a very dangerous job. You could've died if you made a wrong move. But you didn't make a wrong move. You did everything right.

. . .

Five. You are fifteen and the Company has fallen. But they didn't get you. You were with us.

. . .

Four. You are sixteen. You and Nathan are closer now. More than just friends. He holds your hand in the woods and you like that. He makes you feel special. All your jobs are much easier now. You do them well and you make your own money.

. . .

Three. You are seventeen. Your jobs take you far away sometimes. And you might even leave for weeks or months. But you always succeed and when you get home,

we are always here for you. You bought yourself a truck and have more freedom because we trust you.

...

Two. You are eighteen. Maggie is born. The birth was hard for you. It took fourteen hours but when it was over, you forgot all the bad things and only thought about the good. You are very happy, even though Nathan went away to college, because you still have us.

...

One. You are nineteen and Maggie is one. You are happy and so is your daughter. Adam can't put her down and McKay is constantly shopping for educational toys on the internet.

...

OK. Indie. We're here. Your twentieth birthday. You were keeping some secrets that day. Secrets about Nathan. Do you remember who Nathan is?

Why are we here again?

You know why we're here, Indie.

No. But why *this* birthday? I don't want to—

Indie. This is where all your problems started. We have to go back and see it more clearly. So you can deal with it and—

No, it's not. They didn't start here. They started back when I was fifteen. When Angelica left me.

. . .

Uh… I know I'm not supposed to say anything, but—

It's OK now. She's under. But be quick.

Is this going the way you thought?

Not exactly.

I know we just started, but what the hell happened at fifteen that we missed?

Let's just keep going, McKay. This might be important. Indie, can you still hear me?

Yes.

Good. What problems did you have after Angelica left you?

Well… when she left, he didn't.

Shh. McKay. Let me do this. Indie. Who didn't leave? Are you referring to me, and McKay, and Adam?

No. The other one.

What other one?

The big one. With the dark hair and dark eyes.

. . .

Does he have a name, Indie?

Mmm-hmm.

What is his name?

Carter.

. . .

I don't know a Carter, Indie. Can you tell me who Carter is?

He's Angelica's… Adam.

McKay. Let me do this. Indie… Carter… he… runs her? He's Angelica's handler?

Mmm-hmmm. He brought her to me.

What the fuck is she talking about?

Shhh. McKay. Please. Why would Cart—why would this guy bring Angelica to you, Indie? Tell me. Why?

Because he knew Nick Tate was after her. And he was hoping Nick would take me instead.

What the actual fuck, Donovan!

McKay. If you interrupt me one more time, I swear to God, I will throw you out. Do you understand? She's trying to tell us. Let. Her. *Talk.* Indie. You're breathing very hard right now. Can you take deep breaths for me?

I'm not supposed to tell anyone. It hurts.

What hurts, Indie?

My head hurts. Like… someone is squeezing it.

…

OK. I'm gonna bring you out—

The hell you are! Indie. Did this man tell you something? Did he… did he give you a secret?

McKay!

Shut the fuck up, Donovan. Someone got to her. Nine fucking years ago! And you didn't even know! One hundred and ninety times you've done this and you didn't even know! Indie. What did this man tell you?

Secrets.

Did he give you a word? Did he tell you a word, Indie? A word that would… make you do things?

My head hurts.

That's enough, McKay. I'm gonna bring you out—

Indie. Did you ever see this man again?

Yes. He came all the time.

When?

He came that day. Just a voice. Just a voice on the phone.

I'm gonna count to ten now, Indie. And when I get to ten, you will be awake and you will not remember—

Fuck you, Donovan! Indie—

One.

Indie. What was the word? Tell us the fucking word!

Two.

I can't tell you. He'll know.

Three.

He's not gonna know, Indie. I promise.

Four.

Stop counting, Donovan!

Five.

He called me to tell me happy birthday. And that it was going to be a wonderful day. That I would have all the love I could ever want if I just did as I was told.

Six.

What did he tell you to do?

Seven.

He said I needed to hand Maggie over to Nathan. And then—

Eight.

Donovan! Shut the fuck up!

—and then he would take over.

Nine.

Take over what? Indie? Take over what*?*

Me.

Ten.

CHAPTER TWENTY-FOUR

adam

PRESENT DAY

She baked cupcakes.

I know that's a stupid place to start with all the other things that happened that day. But I've thought about her twentieth birthday for four years, trying to force it to make sense, and it all goes back to the cupcakes.

Indie didn't cook. She might've tried a few times when she was living with Nathan those few months before Maggie was born, and she did try to cook Thanksgiving once after Maggie was born, but she was no cook. McKay took her feeding seriously. He did almost all the cooking. And Indie was too busy playing in the swamp to take much notice of what he was doing or how he did it.

And as far as I could remember, never once did she *bake.*

But she put the dress on early too. A birthday dress.

It was a gift I had been giving her since she turned eleven. I think it was maybe McKay's idea, at first. But it became my thing over the years.

He and I were still trying to understand this girl and how best to raise her up to be able to do the things the Company was asking her to do, but also the things we'd want her to do, if we ever did manage to take the Company down.

And yes. She was my weapon. But I didn't want to hurt her. I wanted her to be as well-adjusted as she could. Live a nice, almost-normal life in between jobs.

It was hard. I'm not gonna lie. It was very hard. McKay had brothers, but he was the youngest. Population control was something the Company took seriously so the how the McKay family got three boys, I never did understand. Nor did I ask. Probably should've. But it didn't matter in the end. McKay's whole family was killed when the Company fell. Gun dealers were one of the first targets. Supply chain and all that. But that wasn't the only reason they were first on the list.

Anyway. Back to the dress and the cupcakes…

Everything about that day was weird from the start. Indie's birthday was a big deal for us, as well as her. Ten was young by anyone's standards. A ten-year-old wasn't much use in our line of work. A smart, capable twelve-year-old like Sasha Cherlin—that was something else entirely. But Indie was no Sasha. She would never be Sasha. Sasha's father took very good care of her from day one. I wouldn't go so far to call that man one of the good guys, because he went along just like everyone else and Sasha was dragged into this fucked-up life by his actions, but he did his best and his best was damn good.

Indie, on the other hand, didn't have that kind of upbringing until she came to live with us. And the first year was mostly us trying to calm her down. Tame her into something that resembled a child. So we did holidays right and by the time her eleventh birthday rolled around she was making good progress.

McKay was planning a party. He wanted something special because we couldn't do anything big. She didn't go to school so her only friend was Nathan.

Back then we were much more tolerant of Nathan. He was a very good influence on her in those days.

We came up with this idea that her birthday would be a garden party in the pavilion, which had quickly become her favorite place once McKay was done building it. She would lie on that swing all summer long in the evenings after dinner.

I hired a seamstress to make Indie a special dress for her birthday. And every year we would dress up and have a nice dinner outside. Then we would go down to the lake and float candle boats across the water and send paper lanterns up into the sky.

It was quite magical, even for a cynic like me.

Her twentieth birthday would mark the tenth time we had this little celebration and I'm sure she was excited about it. Maggie was there and she had a special dress too. One made from the same fabric as Indie's.

But this was a nighttime thing. We didn't do it in the morning. And Indie never baked anything for her birthday. McKay always bought a cake from a bakery a few towns over. I can't recall a single time we had cupcakes.

So I should've known.

Everything we did for Indie was based on consistency. That was why she had to be home for dinner every night. That was why she had to go to church every Sunday. That was why she had a bedtime and a ritual to go with it.

Same was good. She did well with same. She needed a routine. We made her wake up at the same time every day, even on the weekends. We made her do her lessons at the same time every day. This was how we kept her in check and maintained control.

And everything about her twentieth birthday was… different.

She woke up earlier than usual. And I don't know why I woke up. Maybe it was the sweet smell of baking cake that drew me up from sleep, or maybe it was Maggie's laugh drifting up the stairs.

I threw the covers off and got out of bed, not even bothering to put a shirt on. When I opened my door, I saw

Donovan sleeping in his room. I don't know why that guy doesn't close his bedroom door when he sleeps, but he doesn't. It's weird, I think. To sleep with your bedroom door open. But whatever.

I rapped on his door. "Get up. Indie's already downstairs." And then I went down the hallway to McKay's room. His door was closed, but not locked. So I opened it up and paused for a moment.

He was sprawled out diagonally across the mattress with the covers all twisted up in his legs. Face buried in his pillow, hands underneath.

"Get up, McKay. Indie's downstairs cooking or something. She's trying to start this day without us."

He moaned and rolled over. And I waited. Because he wasn't wearing a shirt either and for a dude, McKay was kinda nice to look at. I have been wishing for that man's abs for as long as I could remember. He had like a… twenty-four pack. And that fucking asshole didn't hit the weights half as hard as I did.

But he made me smile. McKay kept everyone happy around here. Not just Indie.

He cracked one eye and looked at me, his face all lopsided from the effort. "What?"

"Get up. She's downstairs doing something in the kitchen. Can't you smell it?"

He made a big production of sniffing, then turned back over. "I'll be there in a minute."

I was just about to head downstairs when I noticed Indie's room. She had the smallest bedroom on the second floor. There were lots of other bedrooms in the house. Two on the west side on the first floor. We didn't really use that wing. And then another one up on the third-floor attic. We didn't use that space, either. So when Maggie was born she just moved into Indie's room. We put the crib along the longest wall where there was no window. And she had just recently grown out of that so now she had one of those little toddler beds. I didn't even know that was a thing until a couple months ago when McKay and Indie came home with it.

She was into Disney princesses back then. So she had princess shit everywhere. Sheets, and pillow cases, and a quilt I had made for her specially by the dressmaker seamstress last Christmas.

But that was when I realized that Indie's dress wasn't hanging on her closet door like it should be. That's where I always put it. Every year I had this dress made. And I would hide it from her until the night before her birthday when I was sure she was asleep. And then I would creep in and hang it up on her closet door so she would see it first thing when she woke up.

The hanger was there, but the dress was not.

So the smell of cake was my first clue, but that empty hanger was the second.

Because she put the dress on before breakfast and that was not how this day was done. This day was done with McKay waking Donovan and me up first, and then Indie, who was a late sleeper.

She even fed Maggie something different that day. Cereal from a box.

McKay did not buy cereal from a box when he went grocery shopping. Cereal to him meant oatmeal. Which we didn't eat often because... oatmeal.

But when I went downstairs and walked into the kitchen there was a box of Cocoa Puffs on the kitchen counter. It looked so out of place I stopped at the island to just stare at it for a moment.

Then I looked at Maggie. She was sitting in her high chair, one hand rolling Cocoa Puffs around on the tray like they were toys, and the other busily grabbing handfuls of the soggy chocolate balls from a bowl and stuffing them in her mouth.

I did say something. "What the hell is this?" Or maybe, "Why is she eating that crap?" And I noticed that Indie was wearing the dress, but I was so distracted by Maggie's bowl of cereal that I didn't have a chance to comment on it.

Then McKay was there, shirtless and his sweatpant shorts showing off the fucking cut muscles of his waist. And he just breezed right past me, picked that bowl up off the high-chair tray, and plopped it in the sink.

I looked at Maggie to see how she was gonna take this new development. Her lips were gettin' pouty like she was gearing up for a wail. But McKay snatched a spatula out of the canister we kept the kitchen utensils in and pointed it at her. "I don't want no lip from you, missy. You're having pancakes."

I guess Maggie decided that was an offer she could live with, because she didn't cry.

Then Donovan was there, scowling at everyone. "What the hell is going on here?"

He was shirtless too. And he was a good eight years younger than me, so yeah. He had the body of a twenty-five-year-old. But that dumbass wore real pajama pants to bed and these were light, light blue with tiny pinstripes. And his hair was all standing up on his head, so he was hard to take seriously in the morning and no one bothered to answer.

He took a seat on an island barstool right next to Maggie and started making faces at her.

Indie was watching us with a smile on her face as she frosted cupcakes with a butter knife. I told you she wasn't a baker. They were pink and had something mixed into the frosting. Little bits of dark red things.

I asked her the same question though. "What the hell are you doing, Indie?"

"You can see with your own eyes that I am baking." She stopped her frosting and beamed a smile at me.

And I remember thinking, *Well, at least she had the good sense to wear an apron so the damn thousand-dollar dress I had made specially for her didn't get ruined.*

But then I said, "Why are you baking?"

McKay was already gathering up ingredients for pancakes, so he wasn't paying attention. Donovan was busy talking to Mags.

"Because Maggie wanted cupcakes and dewberries for breakfast, so we went out and picked some berries and I made cupcakes."

"Dewberries?" I was confused. Did we have dewberries on this property? I didn't think so. But it had been twenty years since I went wandering around anything but the gardens.

But that's when McKay paused his kitchen duties, finally realizing that things were… *off.* "We're not eating cupcakes for breakfast. And your birthday cake is sitting in the freaking fridge. I picked it up yesterday afternoon."

"Cupcakes. Pancakes. I'm not sure there's much difference, McKay. Besides, I wasn't gonna let her eat them. They're for later." Then she set her butter knife down, wiped her hands on her apron, and panned a hand at a tray of champagne glasses and a pitcher of what looked like orange juice. But the open bottle of champagne nearby told me it was not just orange juice. "We're having mimosas, too."

So then I was thinking. *OK. We have Indie up early. We have cupcakes. We have boxed cereal. We have the dress. And we have mimosas.*

We didn't let Indie drink. Ever. It was a rule.

All this was settin' off little alarms in my head. But I couldn't place my finger on why. It was all unusual, but there was nothing *bad* about any of it. Still, my stomach had that feeling it gets when a job is about to go wrong.

Donovan finally joined the conversation. "We don't drink champagne for breakfast."

Indie aimed a smile at him now. "We do today. I am no longer a teenager and I want to celebrate."

"You're not old enough to drink yet, either." That was McKay, who was only half paying attention again because he was plopping pancake batter onto a skillet.

"Jesus Christ. You are all a bunch of old men. Don't ruin my birthday before it even gets started. Have a freaking drink."

She started pouring up mimosas and handing them out. McKay paused his cooking, took a glass, and smiled at Indie like she was the light of his life.

And she was. I knew that. We all knew that. McKay loved Indie so fiercely hard it made my heart ache for him.

Then we all had a glass and Indie lifted hers up. "To the first day of my twenties." She paused to huff out a laugh. "You know, I never really thought I'd make it this far." She looked at each of us in turn, her face a little more serious now. "I would not be here without you guys. So… thank you."

And that… *that* we could drink to. So we did. We drank, and McKay gave Maggie the first batch of pancakes. And he cooked some more. And Indie refilled our glasses and we drank those too. Donovan was teasing Mags, trying to steal pancakes off her plate. And I just… watched them as all this happened.

Really and truly thankful that I bought Indie at that auction ten years ago.

We had a little family here and it was good. Everything was good.

Until Nathan St. James showed up at the door.

That was when things really got weird. And I'm not specifically talking about Nathan. So. Whatever. Regardless of what Indie thought, I was not jealous of that kid. Not ever. I didn't like him. And I didn't think he was good enough for Indie. Especially after I caught him with that cheerleader from high school. But it wasn't him.

It was *her.*

She was the weird thing that day, not Nathan.

She kissed me.

And I did kiss her back. I could lie and say I didn't want to, or I wanted to take it back after it happened, but I did want to kiss her and I didn't want to take it back.

I wanted to do it all again.

Because the God's honest truth was… I loved her. I had always loved her. From the first moment I saw her in that snake-wrapped cage, I loved her.

And by this time, her twentieth birthday, I *wanted* her.

The only thing standing in my way was McKay.

So when he walked out after Nathan left and Indie kissed me like I was the only man in her life, I followed him. I wasn't even thinking about Indie in that moment. I know what I said over the years.

I paid for her.

I paid for everything, come to think of it.

She is mine.

But I knew, one hundred percent *knew*, that Indie was not mine.

She was ours.

And if I had her, he would have her too.

That's not McKay's style. At all. Believe me, I have tried. If the way I feel about Indie is love, then the way I feel about McKay is… obsession.

But he's even more traditional than I am. Donovan was always more progressive, and I wasn't sure Donovan mattered, really. He was here, he was there, he was all over the place when it came to Indie.

But McKay. He was different. If he walked out, everything would fall apart. This house of cards we'd been building with Indie for the past ten years would cease to exist.

That was always what I loved about our life. That it was something shared. I knew better than most that having everything in life except people you love to share it with was no way to live. And when I bought Indie, I made a promise to myself. Two, actually. One, that she was not coming home with me to be my plaything like the other girls who were bought on that island. Two, that McKay was my first priority, no matter what. He was my best friend. And when he said he would do this with me, when he agreed to be on my team… I agreed to be on his.

We were a package deal. Whatever happened, we were in this together.

Some might say, *Well, if you would choose McKay over Indie, then maybe you don't really love her.*

But I would disagree. I wasn't choosing McKay over Indie.

I was choosing us.

All of us.

Outside McKay was angry. I didn't blame him. But Indie was twenty now. And I told him that. I told him she could make up her own mind. We raised her as well as we could. We gave her everything she needed. She had a childhood, and she had Nathan as she was growing. We hadn't forced her to love us. And if McKay wanted to walk away there was nothing I could do to stop him. But if he did, I would walk away too.

That was the deal.

I would go with him and not stay with Indie. Either we did this together, or not at all.

So if he walked away, I walked away. And Indie would be left with Donovan.

And that probably would've been fine. Donovan could take care of her as well as either of us. But I knew McKay would not walk away if I went with him and left her behind.

It was emotional blackmail. I get it. But I didn't care. It worked.

McKay stayed.

And we went back inside to find Indie and Donovan sitting on the couch in the TV room. Her back was to us because she was sitting in his lap, straddling his thighs, and Donovan's hands were caressing her ass. Lifting up that flirty skirt of her dress to reveal the skin of her hips.

I recall thinking… *What the fuck is happening right now?* I knew this was not in the plan. A kiss in the hallway, OK. That was the first step. I figured we'd be taking steps. Maybe even baby steps. So I was shocked to find Indie and Donovan like this. And I think McKay was too. Because we looked at each other with the same furrowed brows.

I was about to say something when my head started spinning.

Not in a bad way, either. But a soft spin. My body relaxed a little. My muscles went slack. I was looking McKay in the eyes when this change inside me was taking place.

He laughed. Like… *laughed.* Loudly. And said, "I feel drunk."

That was when I remembered we drank all that champagne. And that feeling in my gut—that signal I get when the job is about to go sideways—it just floated away.

And that was when everything changed for the second time that day. But it would not be the last.

Indie and Donovan paused their kiss. And they both looked over her shoulder. Donovan looked a little confused, like he was feeling the effects of the morning mimosas too. But Indie was smiling at me. Or maybe McKay. It was hard to tell because we were standing shoulder to shoulder and her eyes were wandering between us. Almost as if they were unfocused.

And then she was up on her feet, erasing the distance between us.

And the next thing I knew… we were kissing.

All three of us.

It was the most exciting moment of my life.

Her hand was grabbing my cock. And when I looked down at it, her other hand was grabbing McKay's.

And the next thing I knew she was leading us both over to the couch. I sat down on Donovan's right and McKay sat on Donovan's left. And Indie got back in Donovan's lap and whispered, "This is my present. This is all I want today. Just to be with you."

But she meant us.

All of us.

Because she was not Donovan's, or McKay's, or mine.

She was ours.

Finally.

That's what I remember thinking. *Finally.*

Because even though I would not admit it until that very moment, this was what I really wanted when I bought her at that auction. And every single moment between the island and her twentieth birthday was just… a lie.

One long, fat, delusional lie.

After that I don't really know what happened. I know I was hard. I know her mouth was on my cock. Several times. I know I was inside her. We were all inside her.

Donovan was first. She was clawing at his shoulders when she sat down in his lap. Her head fell back a little, her eyes rolling back in her head. McKay was unzipping her dress. Pulling the bodice down to her waist so his hands could cup and squeeze her breasts.

She was kissing him. And I remember watching. Like I was just an observer, outside of things. Just floating there above them. But then her hand was reaching in my pants to squeeze my cock. She was pumping it up and down. Slowly. Confidently. And I had this fleeting thought, this sick tightening in my stomach. Wondering… where did she learn to do this?

But then I remembered that McKay said she had been seeing Nathan up at college. So I guessed she learned all this stuff from Nathan. It bothered me. And it still bothers me now.

I remember her riding me. I remember being buried deep, deep inside her. My hands were on her hips, urging her on, and she was writhing in my lap. Then I looked up and Donovan was behind her, fisting his cock as he eased forward. He gripped her ass with one hand and held his dick stiff and the next thing I knew he was sliding inside her. I could feel him inside her.

My head rolled to the side and I caught McKay's half-mast eyes. He was leaning back into the couch cushions, jerking off as he watched.

I don't even know if he fucked her that day. I could not say, even if my life depended on it. The whole thing was a blur because she drugged us.

She put something in those drinks.

I knew it. But I didn't care.

There are flashes of memory after that. But that's all they are. Just flashes. It was her birthday and we were doing birthday things.

I think.

We ended up outside in the pavilion. All four of us stretched out on that bed swing Indie loved so much. I remember the swaying of it. All of us. Swaying like babies in a cradle.

I can't recall another single moment of such pure happiness. Not before, not since. It was perfect. Warm and sunny. Just the right amount of cooling breeze passing over our hot, sweaty bodies. Pink cupcakes on the table next to bottles of champagne. And the paper lanterns and floating candles were ready for us to light them up with fire and set them free to float up into the sky and across the lake. Carrying our dreams and desires to the gods of the Louisiana woods.

The birds were singing, and in the background, there was this low thrumming hum. And I realized that the cicadas were back. After thirteen years of living underground getting ready to emerge and breed, they were back like a secret hiding just out of sight.

I was stuck in some dream state thinking about those cicadas, thinking Indie wasn't even living here the last time they came. I wanted to tell her all about them. All the little things I had learned about them growing up because I knew she would understand the demon bugs living under our feet.

I loved Indie for many reasons but I mostly loved her because she understood this place. She knew it was the garden of good and evil. Just like that garden I plucked her out of ten years ago.

She had learned the way of the woods.

She had made deals with the snakes and the gators.

She knew better than to pass through the gates without caution.

And then I remember Nathan St. James looking down at our naked bodies. His mouth was moving but I couldn't make sense of what he was saying. His words weren't coming out right.

All I knew was… first he wasn't there—and then he was.

And that was when *everything* changed.

And not one bit of it could ever be taken back.

I have been reliving that day for four years.

Wondering about all the ways it went wrong when I should've been celebrating all the ways it went *right.*

CHAPTER TWENTY-FIVE

PRESENT DAY

For some indeterminable amount of time everything is silent.

Indie is lying on the couch, eyes still closed. Donovan is leaning over her, the word *ten* still echoing in our heads.

I'm holding my breath, waiting for something to happen. I'm not sure what. But my world was just rocked to the core and for some reason I feel like this needs to be acknowledged with a natural disaster of epic proportions, or a fucking troop of trumpeters, or something.

"Indie!" I finally exhale with that one word. I grab her shoulder and shake her, then look up at Donovan. "What the fuck! What the fuck, dude! She was gonna tell us the trigger word!"

"She *can't* tell us the fuckin' trigger word, McKay. It doesn't work like that. She told us what she could. Forcing her to say more under hypnosis is unethical."

"Fuck you and your ethics! Someone got to her! Someone triggered—" I grab my head. I want to pull my hair out. "That's what happened on her birthday four years ago. That was the trigger!"

"She drugged us. She came on to us and made us…"

"What? Made us… *what*?"

"None of that would've happened if we weren't drugged. Don't you get it? He sent her to kill us that day!"

"No shit, asshole!"

"And he's been working her for nine years, McKay. You don't think he built in some kind of self-destruct mechanism?"

I pause for a moment. Thinking. Trying to come up with the answer to this new problem.

"Her mind is messy right now. We can't just go poking around looking for answers and not expect there to be consequences."

Indie moans on the couch. Then her eyes fly open and she sits straight up like a puppeteer is pulling her strings. "What. The fuck!"

"Indie!" I kneel down next to her, my hand on her shoulder. "Are you OK?"

Donovan is right beside me. "Do you remember any of that?"

Indie looks at him, then at me, her eyes wide and her mouth open. "What did I say?"

Donovan stands back up and sighs. "We were talking about your birthday, Indie. Your twentieth birthday. Do you remember what you told us?"

She squints a little, then lifts her head up to him. "Maybe?"

"What do you remember? Tell us, Indie. Tell us what you remember."

She closes her eyes and swings her legs over the side of the couch, her fingers grasping for my shoulders like she needs to steady herself. "I'm not sure."

Donovan sits down next to her. "Try harder. Just… take a deep breath and let your mind go blank. Then think back to what we were talking about. I led you into it with a timeline. And when we got to your twentieth birthday, you stopped me and went back to when you were fifteen. Can you tell us—"

"OK. Hold on." I put a hand up to stop Donovan. "We need to know that, but first… I need to know if you remember what happened on your twentieth birthday, Indie. I need Adam here for this and he can't come home until you remember what happened that day."

She opens her eyes to look at me. "Why can't he come home?"

"Don't you remember? Yesterday you wanted to kill him, Indie. He doesn't trust you."

She starts shaking her head. "No. I didn't say that. Did I say that? Why would I say that? Oh, my God. My head hurts so bad."

Donovan stands back up. "OK. That's enough. You need to rest for a little bit, Indie."

"Rest?" I can't believe he just said that. "No. We're so fucking close, Donovan! We can't stop—"

"She's tired, McKay." Donovan's voice is low and serious. "And her head hurts. We need to let her relax." He turns to Indie. "It's a lot to process, Indie. I just want you to close your eyes and try to sleep."

"I don't know if I can."

"Just try, OK? If you wake up in a few hours, we can try again. And there's always tomorrow."

"But he thinks—"

Donovan cuts her off. "It doesn't matter what Adam thinks. You're here now. You're home. And you're with us. We're gonna figure it out. OK?"

He pauses to let her agree but it takes her more than a few seconds to even manage a half-hearted nod.

"OK. Good. McKay and I will be right out in the kitchen. If you need anything, just come find us."

"OK." Indie's voice is small and for a moment she sounds like little Indie again. The little girl I knew before we turned her into… *this*.

Donovan grabs me by the arm and turns me towards the door. I leave the office and walk down the hallway into the kitchen. Sit on a bar stool and prop my elbows on the granite island so I can hold my head in my hands.

It's pounding too. Like it was that day everything happened.

Then I have this sudden, irrational fear that someone got to me too.

No. That's not even possible. I was never one of the kids like Indie.

But Adam could've been. I say 'could've been' and not 'might be' because I know he's not like Indie. If the Company got inside your head, you don't make it to thirty-seven without knowing that. They trigger them young. And if these kids don't have people like Adam on their side, they get used up and thrown away by the time they're twenty.

Ironic then. Isn't it? That we thought we did everything right for our girl and on her twentieth birthday all that hard work was gone in an instant.

"Well." Donovan sighs.

"Yeah. At least now we know where it all went wrong, I guess."

"It's not gonna help us much though."

"Do you…" God I don't even want to ask this question. "Do you think that Indie's been with this Carter guy for the past four years?"

Donovan doesn't answer right away and that gives my stomach plenty of time to roil with the thought of someone controlling her like that.

"I don't know, McKay. But the most important thing is that she's here with us now. And we need to make sure she doesn't leave."

"How do we do that? I mean… if she wants to leave…" I don't finish. Just let the obvious hang there in the moment.

When I look up at Donovan, he's chewing his thumbnail, his lips forming a deep frown as he thinks. "We need to tell her."

"No." I shake my head. "No. She doesn't even remember Maggie, Donovan. How are we gonna tell her? And she looked right over at the empty space across the lake where Nathan St. James used to live and didn't even comment that the fucking house isn't there anymore!"

"I don't even know what happened to that fucking house, McKay."

"I bought the land. After… you know. And then I had the house razed."

"What?" Donovan looks at me. And for a moment I think… he's gonna figure it out. That genius brain of his is gonna put two and two together and come up with the square root of something I barely understand.

And then he'll know the truth. He'll know what else I did four years ago.

But he just lets out a long breath. "That was a good idea. I don't think I would've thought of it. So… you? You handled all the… *details* after?"

I nod. Hesitantly.

"OK. Well… that's good to know. But Indie can't move forward until she remembers what happened that day. She needs to know, McKay. We've come this far. Just… we have to fuckin fix this."

"She will lose her mind all over again. I think we should just concentrate on where she's been and who this Carter guy is. He's the threat, not her. Forget the fuckin' past. It's over now."

"And how do you suppose we do that? Hmm? We can't put her under again. I know this Carter guy, McKay. He's very good at his job. He went off the rails fifteen years ago and now that the Company is gone, there is no way to reel him in."

"You *know* him?"

The response I get from Donovan is something in between a nod and a shake of his head.

"How do you know him? From where? Who is he? What is he? Is he PSYOPS? Is he a Zero?"

Donovan sighs. "Both, I think. Or maybe neither. I'm not sure it matters. What matters is... what matters is that he took her mind, McKay. He's got it. And there's no real way for us to get it back without his permission."

I stew in that for a while, thinking. There has to be a way. I never thought I'd wish that the Company was still around. The whole time they were in charge all we wanted was out. But if they were here Adam or Donovan could go to... *someone*. Ask for a favor. Get a face to go with that name. And then we could hunt him down and end this shit for good.

"Hold up," I say, because I just had a thought. "How did Indie get to my house?"

"That's... rhetorical, I assume?"

"I mean, she got to my house somehow. And this Carter guy wasn't a part of that."

Donovan pauses. It's a long pause too. "For all we know he sent her to you. He knew you'd call me and then we'd bring her here. He could be out there in the woods somewhere just waiting for us to leave her alone for a moment so he can trigger her again. Finish what he started. He was after *us*, right?"

"Was he? Do we really know that?"

"Well... she did *drug* us, McKay. I can only assume she did that with the explicit intention of finishing the job. And if Nathan hadn't come and interfered, I'm sure we'd be dead right now."

"I think she got away. And that means she got to my house somehow. And she had to be staying somewhere. I mean, she told me she was watching me for ten days. She came alone, Donovan."

I get up from my stool, grab my jacket, and head down the hallway, grabbing my keys from the little dish on the table by the front door.

Donovan follows me. "Where are you going?"

"Home. I'm gonna go see if I can figure this out. We need answers and if you're not gonna put her under again, we're not gonna find them here."

The drive back to my shop takes almost two hours. I pull into the driveway and the familiar sound of gravel under the tires of my truck is soothing for some reason. After I turn the truck off, I just sit there for a while, looking at the front of the shop in the dark. It's starting to rain again. Figures. It's always fucking raining when shit goes wrong.

I have a little shed at the end of the driveway, just off to the right of my shop. That would've been my first guess about where she was staying if I didn't have it locked up so tight. It's where I keep my motorcycle and this neighborhood doesn't have the lowest crime statistics.

I get out, shove my hands into my jacket pocket, and shrug my shoulders up like this might defend me from the thick drizzle. Then I turn and look down the driveway and start walking out of instinct.

She would be somewhere close, but not here.

I'm only walking for a few minutes when I see it.

Her truck. Black, like Adam's. But it's old now. And it looks like it's been through hell. I circle it first, warily glancing around to see if anyone's watching me. It's nearly nine at night, but this neighborhood is mostly industrial. So people come here for work, then go somewhere else at night. So there's no one that I can see.

There's a dent in the passenger door and her tailgate is being held up with a bungee cord. But it's not locked. I slide into the driver's side and close the door, even though the dome light overhead doesn't work or is set to the off position.

There are clothes on the passenger seat. A pair of jeans and another flannel—holes in the wrists for her thumbs. That makes me smile. And there's a dried-up magnolia flower hanging from her rearview mirror.

I start searching. I'm unsure of what I'll find, but I need to go through every inch of this truck. Every piece of garbage is a clue.

A receipt from McDonalds. She paid cash with a fifty-dollar bill. So she's not broke.

Mud on the floormats. Which could mean she's been in the woods. But then again, there's lots of gravel driveways around here.

Lots of spare change. One of the coins is a British pound. I close my eyes and feel sad about that for a moment. Because however she got to the UK, and whatever she was doing there, none of it was good.

What I don't find is any ID. No passport, either.

And after I climb into the back cab and don't find anything more useful, I'm just about to give up when I get an idea.

I lean forward and pull down the hidden arm rest between the seats.

Then I hold my breath for nearly an entire minute because I can't believe my own eyes.

I find a journal.

I just stare at it because I want the answers to be in there so bad and once I open it up and look, I'll know either way if they are.

Indie was always writing in journals. Donovan made her do that. He wanted her to have a place to put her thoughts where she knew they were safe.

I pick it up and stuff it under my jacket, get out of the truck, jog back to my place, and go inside. I don't even bother going upstairs, even though the shop is frigid. I just turn on a light, sit down at my little work table, open it up and start reading...

3/3
Keep Out.

These are my thoughts.
This is my mind.
And YOU do not belong here.

I get it baby girl. I really do. But I'm sorry, sweets. I do belong here.

So I turn the page and keep going.

Nathan St. James was the boy next door…

CHAPTER TWENTY-SIX

donovan

PRESENT DAY

I sit in the kitchen for a long while after McKay leaves, just leaning my forearms on the island with my head in my hands. Thinking, thinking, *thinking.*

Trying to force the past twenty years make sense.

I made promises to Indie when she was ten.

I promised her Adam and McKay. I promised her a home. I promised her I'd be there. That we would all be there and she would never be alone again.

But I was a *kid.* Am I really still responsible for a promise I made when I was fifteen years old?

Haven't I done my best? Didn't I come when they called? Didn't I *fix* her?

A little, at least?

I want to believe that my influence helped her. It *had* to have helped.

But if I take a good long look at how this whole thing has played out, I would have to admit that Indie was never fixable.

She was someone's *plan.*

I was not the chosen one, Carter was. Our father made this clear the year we turned eight. I was the copy. I was the disposable twin. I was the backup.

Carter was the only one who mattered.

Until he didn't.

Until he started to scare people.

Until he needed to be *dealt* with.

Did Carter do this to Indie? Did he escape and then come back for revenge? Is this some elaborate plan to get even with me for taking his place when it should've been the other way around?

Or was Indie his girl from the very beginning?

She never said his name when I questioned her. She never said, *Carter did this to me*. But I have always suspected. I could feel him in there. In her mind. It was like he left fingerprints.

PSYOPS was done with Indie by the time she arrived on the island. Not as in her mind control was complete. But as in she was not a suitable candidate the way they had hoped. She was rebellious and tough and those were always necessary traits when you train up a Company child to kill people. But she was also… *wrong*. There was something wrong with her. Everything they did to her—she wasn't ever scared. And it wasn't a ploy, either. She just doesn't understand fear the way most people do.

She doesn't feel things the way most people do.

My grandfather didn't think she'd sell at the auction. But not only did she sell, she was the highest-priced girl that whole night. People were calling in proxy bids from all over the globe to bid on Indie Anna Accorsi. What all those other men were planning on doing with her, I didn't know. Nor did I care.

But I should've cared.

That should've been my first clue that everything about this girl—from her appearance, to her attitude, to the secrets she was keeping in that little vault inside her mind—they all pointed to *Carter*.

Because I see it so clearly now. I see what happened that night we were pulled apart wasn't the end of Carter Couture.

It was the beginning.

And everyone who bid on Indie that night knew it before I did.

I truly did think I could save her.

But I see my mistake now.

I understand what it takes to save a Company killer like Indie.

It takes more than I ever gave her.

I look up and find the clock, realize several hours have gone by since McKay left and decide to go check on Indie and see if she needs anything.

It's the least I can do after failing her so miserably.

I didn't close the door to the office when I left her in there. But it's closed now.

My heart actually skips. A hard, thump inside my chest. Then nothing. Like I am dead. Then another hard thump.

I open the door and switch on the light.

"Indie?"

She's gone.

Holy fucking shit. She's gone.

I walk around the house, calling her name—"Indie!"—throwing open doors and peeking into all the rooms.

Nothing.

She is gone.

I go outside and call her, the way McKay used to call her when she was small. "Indie! Indie Anna Accorsi! You come home right now!"

Nothing.

She's gone.

I go back in, pacing the hallway, then look up the stairs. Take them three at a time. Practically run down the hallway to her room. Throw open the door and flick on the light.

Empty.

I whirl around, open McKay's door.

Empty.

I go to Adam's door and find it already open. But dark inside.

When I flick on the light she's there.

In his bed. Sleeping with her face pressed into his pillow and under his covers like this is where she belongs.

I lean against the wall and close my eyes, trying to get my heart to slow down. I try not to imagine all the ways this could've turned out differently. Then force myself to stop and just be thankful that this time, this one time, everything is OK.

I turn the light off, walk across the hall to my bedroom, and position a chair so I can see into Adam's room.

Then I grab the bag I brought with me from California and I pull out the ancient tape player.

I grab tapes at random. Does it really matter which one I listen to?

At first, I think it does. But after I'm done listening to the seventh one, I realize something.

They all say the same thing.

They are all Indie, in her own words and her own voice, begging me for just one thing.

The truth.

Every single time she asks me to tell her some truth.

And every single time—while I do not lie—I hide that truth from her.

I sit there in the dark and ask myself the same question over and over again.

How?

How the fuck do I live with myself?

I can't do it anymore. I know she's fragile. I know I was the one saying we should not tell her too much all these years.

But I can't do it anymore.

So I grab one tape.

Just one.

It's the only one that matters. I put it inside the little machine. And then I take it down to her room and place it on her pillow.

Then I close the door and go back to my room.

And I wait.

A little while later I hear the familiar sound of truck tires on the driveway outside.

McKay is back.

A long breath comes out of me and I feel like I've been holding it in since he left. And when the front door opens and closes, I get up, walk to the top of the stairs, and look down so I can force him to hear me. He *has* to hear me.

It's time to give her the truth.

But it's not McKay looking back up at me from the bottom of the stairs.

CHAPTER TWENTY-SEVEN

adam

PRESENT DAY

I want to believe that people are good. I want to cling hard to the idea that trust, and loyalty, and love are all that matter. I want to have faith in the life we created with Indie and the way we raised and supported her.

I want her to be strong, and resilient, and safe.

And if you had asked me the day after her twentieth birthday if I still believed all that stuff, I would've said yes.

Hell, if you had asked me a month later or even a year later, I'd still have said yes.

But four years?

My convictions are wavering.

It's not even that I'm afraid I don't know her anymore. It's this sudden fear that I never did. That we got her all wrong.

The best-case scenario being we simply misunderstood her. We missed something. Some critical hidden component that, once applied to her treatment, will patch things up well enough for her to keep going. For us to stand by her.

But it's the worst-case scenario that scares me.

What if… what if this is just *who she is*?

What if, no matter how well we nurture her, she is just bad?

I've heard it go both ways.

Evil people are born.

Evil people are made.

I need someone to offer up a definitive answer in this regard. I need some fucking assurance that what happened was a one-time thing.

But not even James Fenici could give me that piece of mind. The last thing he said to me when we parted ways four years ago was… *It's a hard lesson to learn, but not everyone's worth saving.*

I get that. Probably better than most. But how do you know? Where is that line? The one that tells you when it's time to give up and move on?

This is what I think about the whole drive up to Old Home. Because I have to know. I can't give up on Indie unless I know for sure she's gone and there's no way to save her.

I made a promise to myself that day back on the island. I promised to protect her. To never let that snake get that close again. And I'm not really talking about snakes. We lived in the middle of the fucking swamp with so many snakes all around us, we were practically trippin' over them.

None of this ever had anything to do with the snakes.

It was about the *garden.*

And the gate.

And the ignorance we cultivated inside those walls.

Her ignorance. Her secrets.

And mine too.

And finally, one day, it all caught up with us and we were squeezed, and crushed, and eaten when her veil of ignorance was lifted and her secret snakes finally came crawling out of the walls be built around her.

But that's just it. Her secrets. Her ignorance. Her snakes.

I can't let her go out there alone. I can't let her face that evil by herself.

What kind of man kicks a little girl out of the Garden of Eden?

Am I that man?

Obviously, I have decided I am not. But I pause at the gate of Old Home just the same. To think it through one last time. To thoroughly understand the consequences of this action. Because once I see her again… it's over. I will stand by her side no matter what comes next.

And that might be my downfall.

That might be the end of all of us.

I don't know why I do it, because there's no one but me on this dirt road tonight, but I signal before I turn into the driveway of Old Home.

I guess I just want my decision to return to be definitive. Even if I'm the only one who ever knows it.

McKay's truck isn't in the driveway and the house is mostly dark when I pull up in front. But there's a light on somewhere. Upstairs. Maybe the hallway or Donovan's room. And probably the kitchen too.

I turn my truck off and get out, closing the door softly behind me like I don't want to be heard.

Then I take a deep breath and walk up the porch steps. Open the front door, close it. And look up the stairs.

Donovan is standing there, like he was waiting for me.

Then I see a shadow behind him. Creeping along the hallway.

I want to reach for my gun, but I don't have it.

If I had it, I might use it. And no matter what, that would not be how this night ended. So I didn't bring it.

Donovan turns before I can say anything. Sees Indie walking up behind him.

Her eyes search his for a moment. Then she looks down to find mine.

There is an eternity of silence as I wait to see what she'll do.

Will she kill him with a candlestick? Will she shoot him? And me? Did she already kill McKay and that's why he's not here?

How? How will she end this journey we've been on together for the last fourteen years?

But she doesn't strike Donovan. She doesn't pull out a gun and shoot me in the chest.

She starts to cry.

She begins to sob.

Donovan is reaching for her as I take the stairs three at a time. I crush against her, pushing her into the wall so I can wrap my arms around her, and press my body against her, and hold her captive.

So she cannot escape.

So no matter what, she will never get away from me again.

I love this girl. I have loved her from the very first moment I saw her wrapped up in hungry snake. And that's when I realize… that sick fuck Gerald was right. I didn't see it that night on the island. I saw the sickness inside everyone but myself that night.

She is special to me and it all started that night I freed her from that cage.

I will die for this girl. Whatever it takes to save her, I will do it.

Her knees buckle, but I hold her up. And Donovan backs off, hitting the wall and sliding down it like he can't stay on his feet one more second.

"Shhhh," I tell Indie. "Shhhh. It's OK now. I promise. You'll be OK."

She's shaking her head no. She might be small. She might be young. She might be missing huge chunks of her memory.

But she is not stupid.

There is no such thing as OK in her future.

There is no way to take back what happened on her birthday.

But I lie to her. I hold her and lie to her just the same. I don't even care that I know it's a lie. I will not give up hope.

I have one little secret in my back pocket that could help her. It won't take away all the pain, but it won't sting as much afterward, either.

I just need her to meet me half way. That's all I need. That's all I expect.

I back off a little and take her face in my hands. Lift her chin up so she has to see me when I tell my lies. "Listen to me. OK? Just listen to me for a moment. We can fix this, Indie. We put those walls back up, lock that fuckin' gate, and keep all the snakes out for good."

She's still shaking her head no. "We can't fix it. We can't ever fix it." Her eyes are filled with water, all glassy and red. I want to force her to stop talking. I want to force her to see it my way. But I can't.

Everything is out of my control now.

"I made a deal with the snakes." She sobs out the words. "But I never made a deal with the flowers, Adam. I forgot all about the fuckin' *flowers*."

Relief floods through me. She remembers. I don't know how much, but it's enough to set things right for a moment. I hold her face firmly and say, "Darlin'. You didn't have to. Because I made that deal myself."

Then I kiss her.

I kiss her on the mouth the same way she kissed me that day, right downstairs in the foyer. I kiss her like she's mine. Like she's ours. Like she is the only thing in the world that matters.

Donovan is on his feet, his arms around both of us. Then the front door slams and we all come apart like a fluff of dandelion seeds in a gusty wind.

McKay is there at the bottom of the stairs, holding up some book, sopping wet and out of breath as he tries to get words out. "*Ours*. She's still ours and this proves it."

He's not wrong.

But he's not exactly right, either.

I want him to be right. But this is all very complicated and messy. And what Indie needs right now is… simple. There is only one way to make it simple.

So I say, "No, McKay."

"What do you mean?" He's bounding up the stairs. "I'm telling you, she's written it all down in here. It's all fixable."

Donovan guffaws and McKay, Indie, and I look at him as he leans against the wall. "Are you fucking *insane*?" But he's looking specifically at McKay. "We can't fix this shit! People are dead, McKay! *Dead*!"

"Who's dead?"

I turn to look at Indie, my heart sinking into my stomach. "I thought you remembered?"

Donovan is shaking his head. "She doesn't. And this is all so much fucking worse than you even know, Adam. Tell him, McKay. Tell him what she told us."

CHAPTER TWENTY-EIGHT

mckay

PRESENT DAY

Tell him what she told us.

Well… that's easier said than done. I glance at Indie. I want nothing more in this fucking world than to take her into my room, put her in my bed, and keep her there forever.

But I can't. We are here to deal with the situation.

"Indie. Can you please go to your room and let me talk with Donovan and Adam for a moment?"

She presses her lips together, rolling them inward a little as she squints at me. "Who's dead?"

"We're gonna go over all that," I say. "But first, I need to talk to Adam and Donovan. I know you don't have to follow my orders, but this isn't an order. It's just a request. Ten minutes, Indie. Can you just give us ten minutes? Please?"

She looks at Donovan. Then Adam. Then back at me.

"We gave you four years," I add. "Four years, baby. You can find ten minutes for us. I know you can."

She looks at Donovan. "Where will you guys be?"

"In here." He points to his bedroom. "We'll be right here. I promise."

"And then you'll tell me what's going on? You'll fill in all the blanks I have?"

We all trade uneasy glances.

Indie points to her journal, the one I'm still holding in my hand. "Are the answers in there, McKay?"

I shake my head. Not the ones she's looking for. "We're gonna tell you what we know. But I need to talk to them first. It's very important that we do this right."

"Something bad happened, didn't it?" Her eyes are very sad right now. And for a moment I think… she's gonna remember all on her own and then we won't have to tell her the truth. But that's the easy way out. And nothing is easy when it comes to Indie Anna Accorsi. Because the sadness in her eyes fades as I watch. They just go… empty. The way they were last night in the bathtub. "OK. I guess I can give you ten minutes."

She turns away and walks to her door, looks back at us one last time, then opens it, and disappears inside.

Donovan is pushing Adam and me into his bedroom. He looks down the hallway real fast, then closes the door. Not all the way. He leaves it open a crack. And then he begins to whisper. "OK, listen to me, Adam. And don't interrupt. Someone got to her when she was fifteen—"

"What?"

"For fuck's sake, Adam. You're as bad as Indie. I said don't interrupt me. It's a long story and we have it all recorded so you can hear all the details, but someone got to her. Someone has been triggering her all these years. We think she might have been with him since she disappeared."

"That's not true." I have to interrupt. Because I read her journal and they didn't. I hold it up. "I found this in her truck. It was parked near my shop. I read the whole fucking thing and she never once mentions being with someone else. It's just all about us."

Donovan shoots me a look. "Well, where was she?"

"It doesn't really say that, either. But it's all her memories, Donovan. Everything about us, and Nathan—"

"Jesus. Fucking Christ." Adam turns away and grabs his head. Then he spins back. "How many other fuckin' people have read that?"

"I don't know. But that's not the point. The point is… she's still ours. Even if whoever has been triggering her is still inside her head, she wants to be with us. Listen to me." I open up the journal to the page I dog-eared and read it out loud. "'If I had to choose between them, I would die. There is just no way I could only choose one. I need them all. I don't even care if that's selfish. I want them all.' She was talking about us and Nathan."

Donovan huffs. "Well, that doesn't fucking help!"

"Specifically *us*, Donovan. She understands she can't have Nathan."

"Well, I really hope so. Because he's…" Adam pauses to lower his voice. "He's fucking *dead*."

"Right." I sigh.

Donovan snatches the journal out of my hand and turns to the beginning. Then he points to something at the top of the page and holds it up. "Did you see this? What does this mean?"

I squint my eyes at his pointing finger and find the marks on the page.

It says… 3/3.

Adam looks at me. "Three out of three, McKay. Three fuckin' journals. Did you find any more?"

"No." I shake my head and close my eyes. "No. Just this one."

"None of this matters, you guys. What matters is that she's ready for the truth. The truth is the only thing that matters. What happens between us, you, her, whatever—that's secondary. We need to spell this shit out for her right the hell now. We need to explain that someone has been triggering her and then I need to take her back to LA and put her under the care of—"

"Fuck you!" Adam yells it. "Fuck you, Donovan! You are not—"

"—a friend of mine who specializes in—"

"—taking her back to LA with you! She belongs here!"

"—mind-unfucking!"

"What the hell are you talking about?" I'm still fairly calm, but only because I don't think Indie would go with him. "Mind-unfucking? Really, Donovan?"

"It's a thing in LA. Trust me. There's so many fucked-up people in LA this is something they do."

"Well, I feel better now. How about you, McKay?"

I point at Adam. "You disappeared. No one's seen you in four years either. I'm not sure you get a say in this."

"So you think she should go to LA?"

"I'm not saying that either. I'm saying if anyone knows what's best for Indie, it's me."

"You!" Donovan is incredulous. "You're the one who's been telling her everything's fine all these years. You're the one who's been playing house with her."

"You're the one who spent a night with her two years ago and didn't bother to tell us about it."

"What?" Oh, Adam is more than incredulous.

"Maybe if you had called us, we could've fixed this two years ago! But no. You wanted to fuck her first. And by the time you were done, she was gone."

"What the fuck is happening right now?"

"He fucked her, Adam. That's what's happening. He fucked her downstairs in the kitchen earlier too."

"You fucked her last night, McKay!"

"She's mine."

"She's not *yours*." Adam is angry. "Everyone just shut the fuck up! I'm making this decision. She is mine! And I want her right here in Old Home. All of this can be fixed if—"

"Dead people cannot be *fixed*, Adam!" Donovan is waving his arms in the air. "She needs professional help. We tried,

OK? We tried and we failed. Why can't you two just face that fact? We fucking *failed*!"

And I have to be honest here. All that talk and all those thoughts about how she is ours? Yeah. No. It's never going to work. Because suddenly we all have very different opinions about what's best for her.

Adam takes a deep breath and when he talks again, his words are low and soft. "We didn't fail. We just didn't have all the information, that's all. I agree we should tell her the truth. Slowly. Carefully. And then…" Adam looks at me. "And then we let her choose. And if what it says in that book is true, that she loves us all the same, then… fine. We deal with it then. But if she wants to stay here with me, then that's her decision. If she wants to be with you, McKay, that's her decision."

"And if she wants to go to LA with me?"

Adam looks at Donovan. "Fine. If that's her choice, I'll deal with it."

We're all silent after that.

But then we hear a noise. Someone is talking down the hallway. Donovan opens his bedroom door all the way and we listen.

But it makes no sense.

Because that voice… that voice is *Donovan's.*

And it's coming from Indie's bedroom.

"Fuck," Donovan says. And then he's rushing down the hallway.

CHAPTER TWENTY-NINE

PRESENT DAY

I feel like a little girl again.

They make me feel like a little girl again.

And maybe yesterday I would've put up more of a fight about being sent to my room, but today… I don't know. Everything is fuzzy. And I feel like it's been fuzzy for so long, I can't remember not feeling this way.

But that's not true. In the early days everything was so clear.

Nathan was my best friend. McKay was my teacher. Adam was my protector. And Donovan was my sanity.

It was so easy back then. So simple.

And now it's all so complicated.

All the ways they each completed me are now so mixed together, I can't think straight anymore.

I walk over to my window and look out. It's dark, so I can't see anything. But I still know—like I just *feel*—that something is missing out there.

What is it?

Why won't they tell me?

I walk back over to my bed and sit down, stare at the bathtub, then smile because that tub just… God. It just holds all my favorite memories of McKay. How he'd make a bubble bath for me at night and wash my hair and comb it out. How good that felt. And how easy it was to be with McKay.

How simple.

Donovan is messy. And so is Adam.

Donovan is always trying to peek inside my head. He wants all my secrets. And Adam? Adam just… well, I don't really know what Adam wants. Compliance, maybe? Submission? I'm not sure.

But McKay. McKay just wants *me*. He's not looking for what's hidden beneath all my layers and he's not trying to use me as a weapon. I think McKay just wants to take care of me. But not by force.

Like when he used to cook my dinners. He always made something I didn't like, but he didn't make me eat it. He just asked me to try it.

"Just give it a try, Indie. One bite. And if you hate it, spit it out and I'll never serve it again."

Most of the time I did spit it out. But not always. I really thought I hated sweet potatoes. I refused to eat them for three Thanksgivings. But then one year I took a bite and they were good.

I liked mangoes too. I put up a big fight over mangoes. Which was stupid. But I liked them in the end.

That's the best thing about McKay. He never wanted more from me than I was willing to give. He was patient. He was just… there. Every time.

And maybe he didn't save my life the way Adam did. And maybe he didn't save my mind the way Donovan did.

But he saved my *soul.*

Which is ironic, since Adam was the one who made me go to church.

McKay saved my soul.

I'm not sure why I feel that way. I just know it to be true.

I flop back on my bed. I can hear them arguing down the hallway. Not all of it. But Adam is yelling, as usual. And

Donovan is being self-righteous, as usual. McKay doesn't say much, but when I do hear his voice, it's low and calm. That's just his way.

I reach over to grab one of the quilted pillows to put under my head, but my hand bumps into something hard.

I sit up and look at the tape player. "What the fuck is this?"

I hold it in my hands, wondering where it came from. Who put it here? Then I pop the button to open it, take out the cassette tape, and read the writing on the label.

INTERVIEW WITH INDIE
AGE 20.0
SESSION #190

I think I die when the meaning of those handwritten words sinks in. I think my heart stops and I float out of my body like a ghost.

This was the very bad day.

This was the day I lost it.

This was the day I…

I put it back in the machine and press play.

Donovan's voice fills the room. Then mine.

He is panicked.

And I am crying.

CHAPTER THIRTY

PRESENT DAY

I throw open the door, cross the room, and rip the tape player out of her hands.

I press a button and my voice stops talking.

Indie just looks up at me like…

"I know I put it there." I'm desperate to explain as Adam and McKay come in behind me. "But…"

Indie holds out her hand, palm up, and says, calm as can be, "I want to hear it, Donovan. Give it back."

I turn around and look at Adam. He's glowering at me. But his words come out slow, and smooth, and *mean*. "What the actual fuck, Donovan? You gave her that tape?"

"I was… I thought…"

"It's *my* mind, Donovan. And now it's time for you to give it back."

I turn to McKay. "McKay…"

"Give it to her. She needs to know the truth."

And that just pisses me off. Because I have been wanting to tell her the truth about who and what she is for years. And now I look like the one who was keeping those secrets. "Fuck it." I throw the player onto the bed. "Fuck it then. Listen to it."

I walk out of the room, go back into my room, grab the bag filled with tapes I brought with me, and then take it back to Indie's room and toss it onto the bed. "Listen to them all, Indie. Be my guest. I have nothing to hide anymore."

I walk over to the bath tub and take a seat on the edge. Lean over to put my head in my hands. "I did my best. I swear to God, I did."

But I don't even think they hear me. Because Indie has already resumed the tape.

OK. OK. OK. OK. OK. Listen to me, Indie. *Listen* to me.

Oh, my God. What did I do? What just happened? Where is Maggie?

I'm gonna put you under—

Holy fuck! Holy! *Fuck*!

I'm gonna count backwards from—

Where is she? Where *is* she?

Ten. You're… everything's… great. Ten.

Maggie!

Nine. You're calm. You're breathing easy!

Oh, my fucking God! What did I do?

Eight… fuck this shit.

What are you doing?

Hold still.

What are you doing? Donovan!

Hold still!

Ow! What the fuck!

Just calm down, OK? Just calm down.

You just stuck me in the neck with a needle!

It's for your own good. It will calm you down. I can't put you under if—

I don't need to go under! I want to see my daughter! Where the fuck is my daughter?

Adam's taking her to the hospital.

Hospital! Oh, my God. Oh, my God! I killed her. Did I kill her?

Listen to me. You need to calm down, OK? You didn't kill her. She…

What? What did she…

…

…

Indie? Can you hear me?

Mmmm.

Good.

…

Good. OK. Let me think for a moment. There's a lot to unpack here and I need to think. So just… don't move.

…

All right. I think I know where to start. When you woke up this morning, Indie, what did you do?

I got Maggie from her bed.

OK. Then you made breakfast. But you were serving mimosas this morning. Do you remember that?

Mmm.

What did you put in the drinks, Indie?

Orange juice.

What else?

Champagne. That's how you make a mimosa.

What *else*, Indie?

Nothing else.

That's not true and you fucking know it! You drugged us! I know this because I just gave everyone a fucking dose of Narcan and suddenly we could all think again. *What did you put in the drinks*!?

I… nothing. I didn't do it.

There was something else in there. I can tell. I still feel weird. Something that wasn't an opioid. What was it?

…

Fuck. Fuck! Fuck! Fuck!

Where's Nathan? Wasn't Nathan here?

Oh, my God. Indie… I need you to remember, sweetie. I really do. I need you to remember what just happened because I can't. I really can't. I don't want to do this anymore. This is way above my paygrade. I'm not equipped. Someone else needs to—

He saw us.

Yes! Yes. OK. He saw us, Indie. We were… Fucking A, man. Why me? Let's just—

The tape stops and I look up to see Adam holding the player in his hands. "What?"

"Above your fucking *paygrade*?"

"What do you want me to say? I didn't know what to do! I was twenty-fucking-five years old. I was still drugged! I didn't finish my PSYOPS training. You *know* this. I kept telling you she needed someone else!"

"Just…" We all look at Indie. "Keep going. Press play, Adam. I need to hear the rest."

—go back to that moment when Nathan appeared.

He was mad.

He was so fuckin' mad.

He was yelling at us. Screaming at us. I got up and… I couldn't see Maggie. I was looking for her. And then I saw her in the garden.

Yeah. She was in the garden.

But she wasn't in her playground. She was by the shrubs near the big fountain. I started to go over there, but Nathan pulled me back and… I fell down.

Yeah. I was… we were all naked, you know. And I was trying to figure out what happened. So I was going towards the house when Nathan took a swing at me.

Yeah, he hit you hard. And then… then he and Adam were fighting. And then McKay was trying to pull them apart. But he was falling down.

You drugged us, Indie! Why did you drug us?

And then I heard Maggie crying. God. She was crying so hard, Donovan. Remember? Did you hear it?

I heard.

I ran over there. I tried to run over there. But Nathan caught me. He was shaking me and yelling at me. But Adam was there. He was fighting with him again. And I got to Maggie and I saw… Oh, God. She ate the berries! She ate the fucking berries! Why are there berries on that fucking bush? It's only May!

I don't know. I don't fucking know.

She was screaming! Her mouth was all red. It's my fault! It's my fault! I picked those berries that morning and put them in the cupcake frosting. I told her they were delicious! I told her that, Donovan! Why the fuck did I put those poisonous berries in the goddamned frosting?!

Adam has her at hospital. He's taking care of it, Indie. It's gonna be… It's gonna be OK.

Then Nathan was there. Screaming at me. He said… he said… "This is all your fault, Indie. You planted those bushes and I told you! I fuckin' told you they were poisonous!" And it is! It's my fault!

It's not your fault, Indie.

It is! It is, it is, it is! And then…

What? What happened next?

No.

Tell me, Indie. I need you to tell me.

I… I hit him. I hit Nathan in the head with my foot. It was a spinning kick. I didn't mean to… I heard something crack. Oh, my God. Where is Nathan? I broke his neck! I broke his neck! I saw him fall and his head tilted to the side and—

Don't worry about Nathan. McKay is taking care of it, OK? It's gonna be fine. Don't worry about Nathan. This is all *his* fault.

I killed him! Oh, my God. I killed Nathan. And Maggie is dead! Ow!

I need you to sleep now, Indie. I just gave you more sedative. But I'm gonna tell you something right now, OK? I'm gonna say something very important and I want you to listen to me very carefully. Can you do that?

Mmm.

OK. Good. … OK. Listen to me. You're not going to remember this. At all. You're going to forget everything and—

The tape stops. Adam is still holding the player in his hands.

"What the actual motherfucking *fuck*, Donovan!"

I look up at Adam. But there is nothing left to say. They heard her. They know what I did. And they have to know *why* I did it. Both Nathan and Maggie *died* that day and… "Adam. She lost…"

But I can't even say it out loud. Maybe I didn't like Nathan. Hell. OK. Whatever. I can admit the truth now. There's no point in denying it anymore. We all hated his fucking guts.

We were gonna… I dunno. Bribe him to just disappear, maybe?

Some threats if that didn't work?

But no one was *really* gonna *kill him.*

"I'm sorry, man. But she was not going to come back from that. It was the only way I could—"

"Fuck you, Donovan." We all turn to Indie. Her face is covered in tears. "Fuck you. You're not in charge of what I get to know. You're not allowed to erase me like that! You erased my daughter! You erased my boy next door!" She stands up and crosses the room to the window. Then she spins around. "Where the fuck is his house?" She looks at Adam. Then McKay. And then me. Because of course. I always knew she would blame me. I was the one in charge of her mind. "You erased his *house*?"

I look at McKay, willing him to take over. But he has his back turned to us, one hand pressed up against the wall near the door, leaning into it like he's about to collapse.

"I think you need to leave, Donovan."

"No. I'm not—"

"Leave! Donovan! Now!"

"Indie, listen to me—"

"Donovan. Get the fuck out."

I turn to Adam, shaking my head. "No."

"Just... Donovan. Don't make this hard, dude. You need to go. Right now. We'll figure this out and—"

"You need to go too, Adam."

"What?"

Well... I didn't see that coming.

"Both of you. Just... go. I need to be alone."

McKay finally turns back around to face us. He's scrubbing both his hands down his face. I wait for him to talk sense into her. To make her change her mind. To... *fix* this!

But he simply nods. "OK, Indie. We'll go."

"Not you, McKay. Jesus. You're the only one who tells me the truth. You're the only one I can trust. Just... *them.*"

McKay—who ten minutes ago I would have bet a million dollars would be gloating over this new development—shakes his head and frowns. "No." He looks at me, then Adam. "We all go. Or we all stay. That's how this works. You don't get to pick and choose which of us is allowed to love you, Indie. We do things for you that maybe feel wrong. But we do them because they feel right to us in the moment. We're just… doing our best. So if they go, then I go too. If you want to end this today, then that's how this ends."

There are many long moments of total silence. Then Indie sniffs loudly and drags the back of her hand across her face, wiping away the tears that are already dry.

Is she sad? I can't tell.

Like… that is so fucked up. *She* is *so* fucked up.

And *we* did that to her.

"Fuck this." Adam turns away and walks out, his boots stomping all the way down the stairs, the front door slamming behind him. A few moments later we hear his truck. Then the fading sound of tires on gravel as he leaves.

McKay huffs and shakes his head, then looks at Indie. "That's great. That's just goddamned great. You know we're on your side. And if you don't, Indie, then… you know what? *Fuck you.*"

Her face is stoic again. Just blank.

I stand up and turn to McKay. Shrug with my hands. "I gave her that tape because I *wanted* the truth to come out. So… there you go, dude. She's all yours. I'll be downstairs if you need me. Because I'm *not* walking out."

I couldn't even if I wanted to.

Because after all these years. After all that poking and prodding inside her mind. After all the desperate hope, and all the disappointing dead ends, and all the ways in which I failed her, and Adam, and McKay, and myself, and yeah, Carter too.

Just when I finally admit that he's gone and move on—today, of all days, she gives me the gift of a clue.

And that clue might as well be a little piece of paper that says, *Carter was here.*

There is no way I'm walking out now.

CHAPTER THIRTY-ONE

mckay

PRESENT DAY

Donovan slams the bedroom door behind him when he leaves, his feet stomping on the stairs on his way down just like Adam's did.

He's angry. I don't blame him. None of this is really his fault. Hell, none of this is really anyone's fault.

It's just… fuck if I know what it is.

Indie is standing in the middle of the room staring at the bedroom door.

"I want to hear the tapes, McKay. All of them. Right now. I need to know why this is happening to me. I need it to all make sense."

"OK." I scrub my face with my hands. Feeling very alone, and tired, and sad all of a sudden. "OK. We can do that. Which one do you want to listen to first?"

"Does it matter?"

"I don't know, Indie. I really don't know. I never listened to them. Not after the first few. It always bothered me."

She turns to me. "Why?"

"Because… you're always someone different with Donovan. And Adam, too."

"What do you mean?"

What do I mean? How can I explain it? "You were just… defiant with them. And you were complaint with me."

Her shoulders relax a little but her frown deepens. "Because I loved you best."

"You didn't. You didn't, Indie. You just…"

"I just loved you *best*, McKay."

There are equal parts of me that both want to believe that and reject it in the same breath. "Indie. I need you to hear something right now."

"The tapes?"

"No. Yes. No. We're gonna listen to them. But I need you to know this before we start. You don't belong to me. You don't belong to anyone. But if you stay with me, you stay with Adam and Donovan too."

Her shoulders go tense again.

"I thought that was what you wanted? That's what you told us on your twentieth birthday. That's what you wrote in that journal. If I had to choose just one of them, I would die. Remember that?"

She nods.

"So we are gonna listen to those tapes but you are not going to judge them. You hear me? Donovan's right. We did the best we could."

We lock eyes and stare at each other. And maybe, for the first time ever, I see the girl who really lives inside that head of hers.

The scared little girl. The one that knows she's not whole. I want to tell her that it's OK. That's she's other things. She's brave, for one. And smart. And beautiful, and funny, and if she could just face the monster we've kept locked inside her head for the past fourteen years, there will be something good on the other side.

But I don't say it. Because I'm not sure I believe it myself.

Indie rallies and takes a deep breath. "OK."

"Where do you want to start.

"From the beginning, I guess."

I agree and walk over to the bag. Donovan is one neat motherfucker. The tapes are in little soft-sided, mini-cassette-tape storage bags, arranged according to year. I never understood why Donovan used a cassette recorder when these things are practically obsolete. But the answer hits me, in this very moment, that this might've just been the way he was trained. Twenty years ago, it wasn't so unusual to use such a device.

And then another revelation hits me too.

Twenty years ago might be the last time he had an actual, *real lesson* in PSYOPS.

I rub my hand down my face and swallow down fourteen years of regret.

What. *The fuck*. Have we done to this girl?

I know it's not all our fault. It's pretty clear that we picked Indie up in the middle of something. Someone, probably someone called Carter, got to her first.

And she sure as hell didn't come with an instruction manual, so whatever. I put the first tape into the recorder and press play.

Indie paces the floor as her own little girl voice fills the room. She stops and looks at me. Smiles at me.

It's a fun tape, I guess. She was busting Donovan's balls pretty hard that first time.

But they don't stay fun for long.

The first time Indie Anna Accorsi disappeared and came back with blood on her clothes and no memory of what she did or where she was, she was twelve years old.

Indie faces the door and presses her head against it as she listens to Donovan's questions. Her own, hesitant, answers. Which are not answers. She never remembered anything, no matter how hard Donovan tried to coax it out of her.

The next one she's normal again. Lots of them are totally normal. She is a happy girl content to talk about frogs, and Nathan, and the things they get up to in the swamp.

But she disappeared eight times before her twentieth birthday. Eight times she left us and returned with no memory of where she went, or what she did. So we have to get through seven more reality checks.

Even though most of the tapes are no longer than ten minutes, there are a lot of them and it takes a *long* time. By the time we're finally at the last one before that very bad birthday, she's huddled in the corner of her bedroom, hugging herself the way Donovan taught her, sobbing quietly.

I want to go to her. Hold her and tell her it's all gonna be OK.

But I'm not sure it is.

When that tape is over, there's nothing left but the one we played first. "Do you want to hear the last one again, Indie?"

She wipes a hand across her face. Sniffs loudly. And then turns her body so she can see me.

She is a beautiful fuckin' mess.

She is a pretty little nightmare.

A gorgeous piece of misery and cloak of lovely darkness.

But she is *my* mess. She is *my* nightmare. She is *my* misery and *my* darkness.

So I smile at her.

She sniffs again. "Why are you smiling at me, Core McKay? There is nothing to smile about."

That makes me smile even wider. She never calls me Core. "Because I love you, Indie Anna Accorsi. I don't care what you've done, I still love you. And you're not the only mess in this house. We're all a mess. We're all hiding darkness inside us. We're all filled with regrets, and shame, and we were all born into the same fucking nightmare. But you know what?"

"What?"

"We're still here, Indie. We made it this far. And if we can make it this far, we can keep going."

She presses her face into her knees and shakes her head. "I remember him now."

"Who?" I answer too fast. Too eager. And she looks up at me, startled. "I mean… well, Indie. It's not gonna change anything. But… if you tell me, I will help you, baby. I will do anything to make it better. Who do you remember? Carter? Is that who?"

She nods. "I lied to you."

"It's OK, Indie. We all lie sometimes."

I cringe as soon as the words are out of my mouth. Because that's the truth right there. We all lie sometimes? That's almost funny. Lies… lies are what *we do.* We were all lying to her tonight. Only Donovan has a clear conscious right now. He's the only one who came clean.

"What did you lie about, Indie?

She looks down at her hands in her lap and plays with a piece of string from her t-shirt. She doesn't say anything, just shakes her head.

"It's OK. You can tell me. I won't judge you. I'm not leaving. No matter what you say, I'm here. I'm staying."

"That man, Carter?"

"What about him?"

"He wasn't Angelica's handler. He was mine."

I let out a long breath of air. I knew this. We all knew this. But hearing her say it makes it real.

"Were you with him? These past four years?"

She looks up at me and squints her eyes. Like she can't quite remember. But then she nods. "Most of the time. But I got away. He's gonna know I came home."

"Do you think, Indie… do you think he sent you here? Do you think that's why you got away?"

She shakes her head. "No. There was a fight, McKay. And I won."

"Did you kill him?"

"No. But I tried to." Her eyes begin to beg at me. "I *wanted* to. But I couldn't. It was like… there was something inside me. Something that wouldn't let me finish it."

"That's just programming, Indie. He put that there."

"Can you take it away, McKay?"

"No. But… maybe Donovan can."

She's quiet for a long time after that. Hugging herself around her knees. Just a little bundle of a girl wrapped up in shadows and fear in the corner of her childhood bedroom. "What really happened that day, McKay?" She lifts her eyes up to meet mine from across the room. "To Nathan and… Maggie."

I picture all the stupid things she could do once this last bit of truth is told. Kill herself. Kill me. Kill all of us. Disappear. Start killing other people. Go insane. Go back to Carter, whoever the fuck that asshole is. Take your pick, none of it is good.

Forgetting was good for her. And us.

That was the best thing for her and we all know it. Adam can blame Donovan all he wants, but he has to know, that was the best thing for her. Donovan had no idea she'd take off that night and never come back.

I'd like to think I can recall every detail of that night. But it's not true. The drugs. They were strong. And even after Donovan dosed us with the Narcan, I didn't feel completely normal.

Nathan wasn't dead when Adam left and Donovan took Indie inside.

But by the time I got done with him—he was.

I walk over to the tub and turn it on.

"What are you doing?"

I ignore her. Just grab a dusty bottle of cheap bubbles from the floor and dump in ten times more than I need.

"McKay—"

"You wanna take a bath with me?"

"What?"

I drop my jacket on the floor and then lift my shirt over my head. "You heard me."

My eyes find hers and she frowns at me. "Why?"

"Because I've wanted to take a bubble bath with you for… hell. I can't really admit how long. It's kinda sick, Indie. So please don't make me say it out loud."

She's quiet as I kick off my boots and take off my jeans. And then I'm standing there naked as she stares into my eyes.

"It's up to you. Everything has always been up to you. I hope you know that. We didn't make you do anything, Indie. We always gave you a choice. Maybe that choice was hard to find at times, but it was always there. So I'm getting in the tub now. And I'm gonna forget about what just happened for a little bit. And what happened four years ago too. Because if I don't, I will lose my shit. I know I'm supposed to be strong for you. I know I'm here to be your rock. But I can't do it right now. I can't face that day, I don't want to think about it. I can't feel that sadness again. That defeat. That realization that no matter how hard I try, I cannot control things. I'm wrung out, child. I'm just… used up and wrung out and I would like to take a fuckin' minute to just… forget. Because I never had that luxury and I need it, Indie. That's all. I just need it."

These might be the truest words I've ever spoken to her. This might be the most honest moment in my life. Because I have done things, and I am still keeping secrets from her, and… I'm just fuckin' tired. That's all. I'm just fuckin' tired.

I turn away from her and get in the tub. Embarrassed to admit how good this feels.

Have I ever taken a bath before? Maybe. Back when I was a kid. But I don't think about being a kid anymore, either. I had to wipe it all away after the Company fell. So I'm sure as hell not gonna go there now.

I just close my eyes and sigh as the water fills up around me.

A few moments later I hear floorboards squeaking and peek open one eye to find Indie undressing. It's quick. She's only wearing those same sweats and t-shirt I gave her yesterday.

And Jesus fucking Christ. All this shit happened in one fucking day. Fourteen years of memories packed into a single fucking day.

It makes my head spin.

Why am I still sane?

Or am I? Maybe we're all crazy?

I hold Indie's hand to steady her as she gets in the tub. Then she turns around and sits down. Leaning back into my chest.

I wrap my arms around her, close my eyes, and sigh.

"Adam's not gone."

I open one eye, then close it just as fast. Too much effort. "How do you know?"

"I just know."

"I know too. So listen to me. We're doing this. But then we're gonna get into bed and sleep. And that's it."

"What do you mean?"

"I mean… the four of us have to figure this out. Figure *us* out. We can't just keep having sex. You're not mine, you're ours."

She's quiet for a minute.

"Do you understand why?"

She nods her head.

"Tell me."

She exhales and takes a moment. I give her that moment because like that little girl she was when she came to us, this relationship we have sure as shit didn't come with an instruction manual.

"Because we're friends."

I smile. That was not the answer I would've given, but it's a good one. "We *are* friends, Indie. It's a very strong bond. And we can't go messing it up just for sex."

"It's not just sex, McKay."

"I know. I know it's not. And that's why we need to unravel things slowly. Because if we go too fast, we'll start tying more knots."

She seems content with that answer because we're both silent for a long time after that.

I think about Nathan. I feel like I've been thinking about that kid my whole life at this point. And there's nothing I can do to change the way it turned out. What happened, happened. And I have to live with it.

So I take my own advice and start to forget…

Indie falls asleep first, and even though I'm determined to stay awake—leftover paternal responsibilities, maybe?—I can't help it. I drift off.

When I wake up the water is going tepid. So I get up, help her out, dry her off, then myself. And then we put night clothes on.

She finds a t-shirt and shorts in her dresser drawer. Old clothes this time. From before. And I find a pair of sweats in my room.

Then I go back to her room, climb into bed next to her, wrap my arms around her middle, tug her back up to my chest, and close my eyes. So ready for this day to be over.

"You didn't wash my hair."

I open one eye. "What?"

"You didn't wash my hair. Or comb it out. So I just want you to know, that bath didn't count."

I hug her a little tighter and then drift into a dream where all this happened, and nothing is different. The bad, and the good. The laughs and the tears. The things we did right and all of the mistakes.

They come to me in dream, after dream, after dream.

And still, I hear myself insist…

I would do it all again.

When I wake in the morning I feel like I'm having déjà vu because I can hear Indie and Donovan talking down in the kitchen. I swing my legs out of bed, then wonder how she got out of my arms without waking me up.

God, I'm getting too old for this shit.

Anyway, the conversation downstairs doesn't sound heated or confrontational. So I give myself a break for the security lapse.

When I wander into the kitchen Donovan is still wearing yesterday's clothes. Motherfucker really did stay downstairs all night. He's sitting on a barstool at the kitchen island and Indie is sitting on the counter, searching through a cupboard.

I walk over to her, grab her by the waist, and swing her off the counter. "What the hell are you doing?"

"Oh, good. You're up. We're hungry."

And for a second… I swear to God, it's ten years earlier. She is fourteen. The Company hasn't fallen. Indie never got pregnant. I am making breakfast. Donovan is probably gonna leave a little later to go back to school. Adam will come downstairs any minute now and say something to make us groan.

Everything is perfect.

But of course, this girl standing in front of me isn't fourteen and while things *might* get better, they will never be that good again.

I do realize it's fucked up to want the Company back. But after nearly ten years without them… I just can't talk myself into it anymore.

Things did not get better. Nothing got better. The world is still filled with evil people, it's just a whole new set of evil people we have no authority over.

When I think about the Company these days all I feel is… powerless.

"So… pancakes?"

I glance at Donovan, decide he's taking this new day well, and scratch my neck as I nod. "Sure. I'll make us some pancakes."

If there was some fly-on-the-wall person watching us, they'd peg us all sociopaths. Who has a night like we did and then wakes in the morning talking about pancakes?

We do. That's who.

Because we've been playing the game of Let's-Pretend-*That*-Didn't-Happen for so long now, it's just business as usual.

I'm just starting to whisk up some batter when the familiar sound of truck tires on the gravel driveway leak in from outside.

All three of us stop what we're doing to look down the hallway at the front door.

"Adam." Indie darts down the hallway. "I knew he'd be back."

Donovan sighs. Which makes me sigh.

We are all so tired. Donovan and I drag ourselves after Indie and it feels a lot like Christmas Day, when Indie would get up early. Very early. And force us all down here to open presents.

Of course, we were excited for Christmas. And of course, we're glad Adam came to his senses. But it's early. Or maybe too late? And we're just… exhausted.

But when we step out onto the porch we see Indie there. Stock still. Hand over her mouth. Staring at Adam's truck.

And when I stare at the truck, I see why.

Because looking back at us from the driver's side is Adam. But looking back at us from the passenger side…

Donovan takes a step forward. "What… the fuck?" Then he's going down the porch steps.

I walk up next to Indie, stunned.

Because in the passenger side is… Maggie.

But it's not possible. She *died.* Adam *told us* she died in the hospital from liver failure after eating those daphne berries. It took three days I remember that so clearly. Three days of waiting to see what happened to our precious little girl. Three days of agony. By the time Adam's text came in, both Indie and Donovan had been gone for two days. Indie by way of bedroom window. Donovan just called a fuckin' car to take him to the airstrip where he kept his stupid jet.

But it's her.

It's Maggie. I would recognize her in a crowd of a thousand.

So obviously, Adam is a damn liar.

Adam is talking to her inside the truck. He's pointing at us. I put an arm around Indie and pull her into me.

She struggles for a moment, but then relents. "I don't understand what's happening. Is that—"

The little blonde girl—spittin' fucking image of her mother—gets out of the truck and starts walking towards Donovan.

Adam meets Maggie on the other side of the truck and takes her hand. Maggie is nearly six now. She smiles up at Adam. The two of them walk up to the bottom of the porch. I stare at him, but he doesn't meet my gaze. He looks at Indie.

"I told you last night I made a deal with those flowers. And I am a lot of things, Indie Anna Accorsi, but I am not a liar."

"You told me she was *dead*," I say, contradicting him.

"I never said that, McKay. I sent you a text."

"That text said she was dead, Adam."

"No, McKay. That text said 'it's over.' And I meant it. It was over. Maggie spent three days in the hospital and then I took her home with me."

"What home?" I'm angry and it's not easy to hide. "Because you sure as hell didn't bring her *here*."

"My house in Baton Rouge."

I suck in a deep breath. Still holding tight to Indie.

"You had no right." I'm so fuckin' pissed.

Donovan walks over to Maggie and bends down. "Hey there, Mags. Do you remember me? I'm Donovan."

But Adam and I are still having a conversation and Indie is too shocked to move out of my embrace.

"I had every right, McKay. She tried to *kill* us."

"Adam." Donovan stands back up. "We're not gonna have this conversation in front of Maggie."

Adam is still looking at me. "Maggie already knows. I told her everything on the way over here."

He told her everything. A six-year-old girl. I want to grab him by the neck and shake some sense into this man. Because I see what he's doing. I know what he's done.

Indie made a choice last night and she chose me. And Adam has been keeping Maggie secret all this time. Secret from *me*, not Indie.

Me.

Because he knew if Indie came back and blamed him, he has this little surprise in his pocket to get back in her good graces.

Never mind that I already talked sense into her. Never mind that I already smoothed it over. Never mind that *I had his back from day one.*

And maybe that makes me sound callous. I am happy she's alive. I'm… fucking *thrilled* that she's alive. But this feels a whole like we just started a new game of Let's-Pretend-*That*-Didn't-Happen.

"Maggie?" Indie finally speaks and pulls me out of my heated thoughts. "Is that really you?"

Maggie looks up at Adam and he nods. "Go ahead. You know who she is."

Maggie leaps. Like a fuckin' gazelle. And two seconds later she is huggin' her mama. Indie is crying. Hard. Like… I have never seen Indie cry like this before. And pretty soon my eyes are tearing up too.

Even Donovan is crying. Hell, even Adam is crying.

When we lock eyes again my anger subsides a little.

He is not a bad man. He can't help who he is any more than the rest of us.

We are just… *liars.*

"I just needed to keep her safe, McKay. We all stretch the truth for the same reason, don't we?"

His Southern accent, which is almost always *mostly* hidden—like it's a secret that confirms who he really is underneath—comes pouring out of his mouth with his words.

"We lie to keep each other safe, right? Even you do it, McKay. Even you had to make choices that day, remember? That's all this was about. Nothing else. Just that." Adam swipes a tear off his cheek. And then he narrows his eyes at me. "You understand, right?"

And then I get it.

Because I do understand.

And he knows *why* I understand.

We *are* playing a brand-new game.

And that game isn't called Let's-Pretend-*That*-Didn't-Happen.

It's called I-Know-What-You-Did-To-Nathan-St.-James.

CHAPTER THIRTY-TWO

You have this image of people.

They are strong, and loyal, and truthful, and protective. They say things like… *Write it down*, and *Eat your vegetables*, and *Do it just like I tell you.*

They are tall, and handsome, and smart.

They give you a home, and your own bedroom, and a swamp filled with fireflies, and a duck lake with a boy on the other side whose mere presence convinces you that this is all gonna be OK.

And you believe it.

Because you are small, and young, and scared, and lonely.

You write it down, you eat those vegetables, and you do it just like they say.

But then one day you realize you're not so small, or young, or scared, or lonely. You realize you're bigger, and older, and braver, and surrounded. And you see them for what they really are.

Just people.

Just men.

Just humans who make it up as they go, like the rest of us.

They are liars, and cheaters, and killers.

They are sick, and twisted, and ruthless.

They are afraid, lonely, and scared, just like the rest of us.

But they are yours.

They are mine now.
They are all *mine.*

I did drug them. And that was all me. I wanted what I wanted and I wanted *them.* I will not apologize for that.

But they are mine now.

They are all *mine.*

So I keep that secret to myself.

But picking those berries with my daughter. Telling her they were delicious. Mixing them up in the frosting.

None of that was my idea.

It was *his.*

I failed. None of the people he wanted to kill that day died.

I don't feel bad about that because it wasn't my failure.

It was *his.*

EPILOGUE

adam

THREE MONTHS LATER

I've been lucky. I'm not too proud to admit that. The fucking stars aligned for me many times over the years.

I was born into the Company.

Into a family of Untouchables.

I was given Core McKay as a gift.

I was withdrawn from the Zero Program and the Negative Program and given a second and third chance.

I have a trust fund, ten mansions, fifteen warehouses, and eight-hundred leftovers doing my bidding.

I have three partners and a little girl.

I have everything.

And *he knows* I have everything. So of course, he's gonna try and take it from me.

But I'm only gonna say this once, Carter Couture.

It's *mine*. And you can't have it. Not one fuckin' bit of it.

The day Indie drugged us and we all had sex was just one more fortuitous event in a long line of good fortune as far as I can tell.

Yeah. Shit went wrong that day. Pretty much everything went wrong that day. But Maggie and me? Everything about that went right as far as I'm concerned.

I didn't mean to make McKay and Donovan think she was dead. It's just… Indie tried to *kill* us. What was I supposed to do? What choice did I have?

I knew all about Carter Couture. I knew all about their little Negative Program they ran on that island. I knew Indie was fucked from the first moment I saw her and I knew Donovan was in on it.

I knew he was looking for Carter.

I knew McKay was my double. Oh, I know what people think about that. How could McKay be your Negative, Adam? He's not your twin. But come on, people. Keep up, OK? Why do you think Donovan wanted to go into plastic surgery? I mean… fake tits? Plump lips? Face lifts? Really? Is that the line of work Untouchable Company Boy Geniuses go into?

Please. Give the boy some credit. He never fooled me. Not for one second. When you go into PSYOPS and then you transfer into plastic surgery, there is only one reason for that.

To make *double negatives* for Company kids. To take their minds and twist them all up and then change their faces to match what's inside.

I knew that if the Company fell, McKay's family would be among the dead. They were keeping one of our secrets. My father told them why he needed McKay.

I knew my father was heading for an early grave. Hell, I helped Sasha Cherlin set it up. Who the fuck do you think got those drug lords to crash that wedding in Santa Barbara and shoot the place all to hell?

Her? Really? Twelve-year-old Sasha Cherlin? She's good, but… no. She's not *that* good.

OK. I will give Nick Tate some credit for that, I suppose.

The *real* Nick Tate, that is.

Not the Double Negative I met with down in Daphne, Alabama.

I cannot, for life of me, understand how *anyone* fell for that shit-show double. Didn't they see those tattoos for what they were? A way to hide the Double Negative scars? I mean, come on. Oldest trick in the fuckin' book, right?

Didn't they notice his voice? His accent? How could they not know?

Jesus Christ. That makes me laugh.

Nick Tate had a twin, just like the rest of us. And her name was Harper. At first glance you gotta feel sorry for the Admiral, right? All that genetic planning and plotting to make twins and what does he get for his trouble? A boy and a *girl*?

Such bad luck.

But, unlike the rest of us, Nick Tate wasn't a twin, he was a triplet.

I have to hand it to the Admiral. He knew how to play the fuckin' long game like a pro.

If he was still alive, I'd shake that man's hand.

But anyway… I'm getting *way* ahead of myself now…

When Maggie started screaming out in the garden, I almost lost my shit. I was fucking high. Couldn't even talk right. And Indie was going off on Nathan like a goddamned psycho. A sick fucking psycho. Nathan was a big dude and he was very good at martial arts by the time McKay stopped inviting him to train with Indie when he was around sixteen.

But she was crazy. She went *crazy*. And one good kick, man. Sometimes that's all it takes.

It's just… that *wasn't* all it took *this* time.

I know Donovan made it into the house. He was going for his doctor bag that he always brings with him. He kept the drugs he used for Indie's hypnosis in there. And that was where the Narcan spray was.

So I know he came running out yelling about drugs. And he dosed me with it and threw my clothes at me, yelling, "Take Maggie to the hospital, Adam! Right now!"

And my head cleared up pretty good. Not all the way because whatever Indie used on us, it was a cocktail. Not just one drug. But I could understand what was happening. I saw Maggie screaming. Just fuckin' screaming her little head off.

I didn't know it at the time, but eating those berries is like munching on chemicals. The inside of her mouth was bleeding by the time the doctors saw her in the emergency room. And those berries are deadly. She ate more than enough to die if I hadn't gotten her to the emergency room.

And then I saw Nathan on the ground. And Indie standing over him. Donovan was dosing her with the Narcan, but she wasn't on drugs. She was on… *PSYOPS*. So she wasn't responding at all.

Carter got to her. I knew it. I knew it right away. And McKay… McKay was bent down next to Nathan and then the next thing I knew I had Maggie in my arms and I was shoving her in my truck.

I don't even know how I got to the emergency room in Pearl Springs. They took us in right away and did something. But then we were in a fucking helicopter on our way to New Orleans because Pearl Springs was… well, ill-equipped.

I didn't even have a phone. Or my wallet. I didn't have shit. So that's why I didn't call McKay and Donovan and let them know what was up. I didn't plan this. I was not in my right mind that first day in the hospital.

But, later, after Maggie was stabilized and I was sure she wasn't gonna die, I went to my other family home in the French Quarter where I had documents and cash stashed. I changed clothes, bought a burner phone, and I had every intention of telling them that Maggie was fine. Well, she would be. They were still dealing with the toxins from the daphne berries, but she was responding well.

My head was clear by then. The drugs had worn off and I was running the last fourteen years back and forth in my mind. Over and over again.

That conversation with Gerald on the island. The girls in those cages. Donovan's words of caution and big plans for a research paper. The way people were bidding on her at the auction. Indie's little disappearing acts over the years. Angelica, James Fenici, and Nick Tate.

All those documents I was gifted when my trust fund matured the day I turned twenty-one. All those secrets that came with it.

The Double Negative Program. Which is not the same as the Negative Program. The Negative Program is just about twins. But, as the Admiral can attest, it doesn't always go to plan.

You *can* have a set of identical twins and one fraternal in a trio of triplets. But that's not how it shook out for the Admiral.

Lots of Untouchable families had this problem over the years. In fact, it's pretty damn hard to have a set of identical twins. You really gotta have the right bloodlines, and even then, it's a crapshoot.

The Double Negative program has been around since the nineteen forties. That's how they did it in the old days before scientists could manipulate eggs and up your chances. And even now, when that kind of interference is possible, most of the time, those twins don't happen. And if they do, they aren't identical. So you gotta help Mother Nature out a little bit. Rearrange that face. Add a scar here and a tattoo there. Make it all look legit.

And let's be clear, OK? Nick wasn't the chosen one. His twin sister *Harper* was the chosen one. Nick was just another expendable. Just like me, and James, and Donovan.

And I guess you *could* include Core McKay in our exclusive little group if you really wanted to. It's not the same, but it's close enough, I guess. His father did have three sons, after all. And he did agree to my father's plan.

That's how I knew the Shadow of Secrets calling himself Nick Tate down in Daphne, Alabama wasn't who everyone thought he was. He included McKay in our little group of Untouchables. The real Nick Tate would not make that mistake. Because the real Nick Tate does *not. Make. Mistakes.*

Or hell, maybe Real Nick had the Shadow make that mistake on purpose? Maybe he was dropping me a hint?

I didn't need that hint. And the Nick I knew as a boy wasn't known to be so accommodating.

But this Shadow Nick was so far gone—his mind and body so far away from the boy he started out as—he must've forgotten who McKay really was. I can only imagine the kind of mind fuck the real Nick did on his Shadow after Santa Barbara. The Company washed their hands of the whole Tate family after all those people died.

Nick wasn't taken *captive* that night.

He set himself *free.*

Free to be *himself.* And oh, yeah. You think Indie's scary? You think *I'm* scary? No. I was restrained. Indie was restrained. Even James Fenici was restrained once he fell for Harper Tate.

But Nick and Carter? Those boys are the *real* face of the Company killers.

Regardless, I'd have figured it out even if the Shadow didn't make that mistake, but that just hurried along my understanding of the situation.

But here's the thing I never understood about the Company. They do this to us. To me, to James, to Nick, to Donovan. They turn us into these killers, and mind-fuckers, and psychopaths. They chew us up and spit us out. And they never see us coming, do they?

They keep those doubles safe and give them a cushy life in big houses or too-long yachts. They send them to the best schools. They give them everything and make them *soft* so they are ready for their upcoming Manchurian Candidate political careers.

They do this, while all the while, they are making us expendables *hard.*

How did they not see this coming?

If my father were alive, I'd fuckin' slap him. Shake him hard by the shoulders. Scream in his face—*Why don't you see us coming?*

Anyway… I'm off track again.

I didn't know how deep this Indie betrayal went. The only thing I knew was that Carter was involved and I had to protect Maggie. So I sent that text to McKay. I was gonna just lie to him. Tell him straight up that Maggie was dead and then quietly disappear with her. But I couldn't.

I mean, I could. I have no problem lying when it suits me.

But lying straight to McKay felt like crossing a line.

I'm gonna be clear about this right now. I love Core McKay. My father didn't need to lecture me on how much I owe McKay. He's mine. Just like Indie is mine, just like Maggie is mine.

There is no future without McKay in it.

I didn't want to lie to him. But I didn't want to give him the whole truth in case Carter was tracking his phone. So I just told him it was over and tossed my burner just to be sure.

McKay doesn't need a phone to find me. We are connected. If he wanted to find me, all he had to do was look a little harder.

And he didn't.

So I didn't call him again for almost two years. By that time, Maggie and I were settled in. I wasn't going back until Carter made his next move.

I knew one day Indie would turn up. Carter is after *me*. I'm the one who ruined his life. I'm the one who fucked it all up when I helped James and Sasha take down the Company in Santa Barbara. I'm the one who took him away from Donovan.

But I am not an easy man to kill.

And if he can't kill me, well, then he'll just take my life. He'll take my power, he'll take my McKay, and my Indie, and my Maggie, and… well, I don't know about Donovan. I have no idea how he feels about Donovan these days.

When Maggie was released from the hospital, I took her to my home in Baton Rouge. It wasn't a great plan. Hell, I actually expected McKay to come looking for me. I figured… a week, tops, and he'd find us. And we'd figure shit out from there.

But McKay never came. And Donovan never came. And Indie never came. And Carter never came.

So hell, Maggie and I, we took off. There is only one way to escape the attention of Company assassins and that's by boat. Yachts have always been the Company's way of secretly getting from place to place. The ocean is deep, the world is wide, and there are plenty of places to get lost.

We got lost in many different parts of the ocean. We got lost on rivers too.

But I have eight-hundred leftovers doing my bidding. So I had twice as many eyes on McKay this whole time. I knew Indie popped back up almost two weeks ago. So Maggie and I flew home to Louisiana to wait and see.

Probably should've kept some of those eyes on Donovan as well, seeing as how Indie showed up at his place first. But it would've done us no good. She was still under Carter's control back then. That visit was probably part of his plan.

I'm playing a long game of my own. One so twisted and perfect, the Admiral would shake my hand back.

That's what really happened. And that's why I did it.

But here's the thing I don't understand. Why did McKay do what he did with Nathan?

He knows I know.

Because he shut up real fast when I brought Maggie back to Old Home and neither of us has said a word about it since.

I want to tell him, *It's gonna come back to bite you, McKay. Right in your do-gooder ass. You watch.*

But fuck it.

That's his problem now.

And besides, today is Maggie's birthday. So it's not a time to bring up secrets.

Everything is back the way it's supposed to be. Hell, better than I could've ever hoped.

Donovan stayed for two whole weeks after I brought Maggie to Old Home. Then he left, packed up his shit in LA, and came home for good.

McKay backed off Indie. Told us all that we're in a complicated relationship and we all have to consider the consequences before we go upsetting the balance.

I can't argue with that. But… the sexual tension around here… it's palpable. So some kind of arrangement needs to happen soon.

I ache for that girl.

No, that *woman*. Because that's what she is now.

But I ache for McKay too. And Donovan… whatever. I don't mind him being around. It's all pretty exciting. Things are about to get interesting.

Indie seems… fine. And while fine isn't wonderful, or amazing, or hell, even half as good as great. Fine is not bad all things considering. She and Maggie have been inseparable. I wish I could give back the years she missed but I can't. And I'm not sorry about that. If I had not kept my secret then we might all be dead.

Maggie—like me, like Indie—won't be going to regular school. I tutored her for the last three years, but it's summer now, so we can just think about tutors again in the fall.

Maybe Donovan will be her tutor? That asshole has more education than any one person should. But we'll see. Because Donovan still hasn't come clean about Carter. I need him to come clean with me about all that shit if he wants to stick around.

But the Indie problem—AKA the Carter problem—hasn't gone away. It's just on hold for now. Indie goes nowhere by herself. She doesn't even sleep by herself. We gave Maggie Indie's old room and now Indie sleeps with one of us. And we always have someone on watch.

If Carter ever shows up here, he's in for a surprise.

It took me a long fucking time to get to this place.

To get McKay thinking about what comes next between us. To get Indie calm enough to trust her. To get Donovan to think about switching his loyalties.

It was a twisted road of fucked up shit.

But you know what?

I'd do it all again.

We're in the pavilion right now getting ready to start Maggie's sixth birthday celebration. We have the lanterns and candle boats all ready for when the sun finally goes down. But we're gonna do cake and presents first.

She has a pretty new dress, just like her mama.

And McKay, Donovan, and I are all dressed up in summer suits.

Maggie is sitting on Indie's swing surrounded by presents and birthday cards. Donovan is pushing it, making her giggle and smile as he jokes around.

McKay is drinking a bottle of beer, sitting on his swing across from Maggie. Indie is sitting next to him, her head on his shoulder.

I'm in charge of taking pictures.

Yeah. It's pretty nice.

Maggie is impatient for the presents to start. "Can I open them now, Daddy?"

Yeah. She calls me Daddy. She always has and I'm not gonna tell her she can't.

As far as I'm concerned, I *am* her daddy.

"Go ahead, baby. But open the cards first."

"OK!" She picks up a big pink envelope and starts tearing it open. It takes her a minute to get the card out, and then she holds it up so she can read it.

It's a cute card with a snake wearing a ballerina tutu on the front. I look over at McKay. "That your card?"

"Nah, not mine."

"It's not mine, either." My head swivels to find Donovan's face when he says this.

I know Indie didn't get her that card. We shopped for cards together.

That feeling I get in my stomach when a job goes wrong is back.

And you know what?

I fuckin' love it.

But I can't be sure. So I say, "Hold up, baby—"

"Who is Nathan St. James?" Maggie's face is twisted up in confusion. She probably doesn't even remember Nathan.

But we do.

McKay is on his feet. But Donovan is closest. "Gimme that, Mags. Right now." He snatches the card and reads it, then passes it to me.

"Who's Nathan, Daddy? What does that mean?"

But I don't answer her. I don't say anything. I just pass the card to McKay.

Because that card says…

Nathan St. James is not your father.
I am.

Love,
Carter

I'd like to say I was surprised, but it would be a lie. So I just concentrate on hiding my smile and enjoying that feeling in my gut.

The one that says…

We're back, motherfuckers.

We're back.

Carter needed to learn that I could take from him just as easily as he could take from me.

And now he knows.

END OF BOOK
shit

Welcome to the End of Book Shit where JA Huss gets to tell you all her rambling thoughts on the book you just read.

This is the EOBS. And if you've never read one of my books and just stumbled into Creeping Beautiful out of nowhere, I'll have some tips for you at the end on how this new series ties in with most of my other books.

But for now… let's get to it.

I have written a LOT of End of Book Shits by this time. Eight years. January 2020 marks the eight-year point in this fiction writing career and I've been writing the EOBS for seven of those years. So… lot of EOBS's.

Here's what I want to talk about this in this one:

First of all, there are fourteen years of memories in this book and all of them are "relived" over the course of ONE DAY through different points of view. It's a complicated story. I'm not gonna deny it. But if you keep that one thing in mind it should all make sense. This story is ONE DAY in the life of

Adam, McKay, Donovan, Adam, and Indie. The timelines jumps all over (though it IS linear, for the most part) because I needed a way to tell you ALL THE THINGS in one book before we move forward. This story has barely started. That's the most important thing to take away from this EOBS. If you think of a superhero story arc, then this would be called "the origin story". How they all came to be in this one place, at this particular point in time, and THEN—THAT is when the story really starts.

Also, even though a lot happens in this book, not much really happens. Indie shows up on McKay's doorstep, Donovan joins them, they go home, Adam joins them, Adam leaves, Adam comes back. End of story.

Obviously there's more to it than that. This book is 110,000 words long (and that's before the EOBS which adds another 3700 words to the book). But that's the basic plot outline.

The theme of Creeping Beautiful is called "Coming Clean". Not making up for past mistakes, just OWNING them. And I think this is important in the context of the real world we live in. Because listen to me. This is important.

THERE IS NO SUCH THING AS A PERFECT PERSON.

I'm not perfect. You're not perfect. No one is perfect. Everyone fucks up. And once you realize this it's a lot easier to cut people currently in the middle of fucking up, some slack. (And, conversely, maybe they think you're the one currently in the middle of fucking up and they cut you some slack, right?)

Everyone makes mistakes. Everyone has regrets. Even if they eventually learn to accept those regrets and no longer regret them because mistakes are how you learn and become a better person, they have to accept them.

I have no problem with changing my worldview about things. This goes for everything. Every controversial issue you can think of, I've been on one side, then another, then another over the course of my life. Abortion is bad, abortion is good, abortion is sad. I think the death penalty rocks, I'm not sure it works, prison suck, we need prisons. I love zoos! I think zoos are cruel. I'm a democrat, I'm a republican, I'm an anarchist, I'm a libertarian, I'm a nothing. I like being informed, I like being ignorant. I want to be a scientist, I hate being a scientist. I want to write non-fiction, no fiction, no TV scripts, no really, fiction. I have no idea what I want to be. There is definitely a God. There is maybe a God. There is probably no God. Hell, there has to be something, let's just call it God. I want kids, I don't want kids. I want to get married, fuck marriage. I love this man, no this one, no, really, this one—you know what? I don't need a man. I believe in the happily ever after… but really you make your own future, and then no again, you really just need a team. It's all luck, it's all fake, it's all real, it's all lies.

At some point in my life I've had all these thoughts. And in the moment when I had these thoughts I was convinced.

And then I wasn't. Something happened, or I read something, or heard something, or fucked something up and I changed my mind.

It's as simple as that.

So the truth is--It's all just… learning.

You start out with nothing. Your brain is just neurons firing billions of time over the course of a day. And each time they fire, you make a connection. You learn to recognize things, you learn to feel things, you learn what you like and what you hate, who you trust and who you fear.

And as your brain takes in new experiences and new ideas, it makes a whole other set of connections and your opinions waver, or they don't. And your life becomes better or worse, because of it.

Seeing things in a new way and then changing your mind isn't weakness.

It's LEARNING.

That's the take-home message of my life.

It's all just learning.

I had a friend criticize me once. She said, "You change your mind a lot. I don't understand you. One day you say this, another day you say something completely different, and then you change your mind again."

I was like… "What's your point?

And I didn't say it to be a bitch, either. I just truly didn't understand what she was saying. Until that moment it had never even occurred to be that some people do not reevaluate their worldview on a regular basis.

I don't know what to think about that. But my answer to her, after she told me her point (which was that I was confusing her) was, "I'm allowed to change my mind. I'm allowed to form new opinions about things and throw away the bullshit I no longer need, and start over. I don't need anyone's permission to do that. There doesn't need to be some public coming-to-Jesus-moment where I fess up about my mistakes. I just get to do it and no one gets to tell me I can't."

She didn't get it. And, no surprise here, we're no longer friends.

But I learned something from that encounter. I learned that not everyone sees things MY WAY.

It's not that I expected people to see things my way. That's not what I mean. What I mean is this—and this had been scientifically PROVEN, OK? Are you ready? Here it is:

People see things differently.

FULL STOP.

It has been scientifically PROVEN that we all interpret the world in different ways. And this can be something as simple as what the color RED looks like, to something very complicated like "When does life begin."

This happens because we are all different. You've heard that before. As a trained scientist I heard it a lot in college and grad school. If you're in medicine they drill this fact home to you hard.

Every patient responds differently to drugs. Why? Because, while we are all the same species, we are not all the same. We are all different. Our genetic code, our brains, the neurons in those brains and how they make new connections—they all come with their own strengths and weaknesses. They are all unique.

WE are all unique.

And here's the other very important thing to realize—we can only ever know what WE FEEL, and WHAT WE SEE, and what WE EXPERIENCE.

We cannot EVER know what others feel, or see, or experience. Because we have not perfected the "mind meld" yet. You can't see inside someone's brain. You cannot BE them. Thus, you cannot ever understand how they see the world and how it might be the same, or different, as the way you see the world.

This is the mystery called CONSCIOUSNESS.

When I wrote Ford Aston it was kind of a joke. He was so "unfeeling" so "logical" so "distant". He gave no fucks. And I say it was a joke because I'm a lot like Ford and I was just kinda writing a person like myself.

Someone once asked me if I has Asperger's. I kid you not. I laughed at them. I was like "What the fuck? Why would you even think that? I have like a genius IQ, I live a pretty normal life, I'm… normal."

But… what is normal? I had always thought I was normal. But, there is no real "normal". So, hell, maybe I was some kind of high-functioning Asperger's person?

How would I ever know?

This is my point. I don't know. I'm not interested in knowing, BTW. I'm not gonna go get tested. If I do have some kind of Spectrum issue, I've learned how to deal with it so who cares?

I don't know. I can't know. Because "normal" to me is just that. Me.

This is why I love storytelling in the first person.

Because when I write a story in the first person I get to BE someone else.

For real.

This is like… a fucking miracle, ya know?

Think about it – writing a story is like being God. You get full control over everything that happens. So when I write first person I not only get to be someone else, I get to plan every action, every moment, every word, and every experience. All of it is under my control.

And I get to be them.

I get to see the world the way they see it. I get to feel emotions the way they feel them. I get to experience conflict, and problems, and make mistakes, and learn new things, and reevaluate my life, and try again, and make more mistakes, and learn from that too. When I write stories in first person I get to live OTHER LIVES.

And you—when you read stories in the first person you get to do that WITH ME.

This is the miracle of storytelling.

So when this person told me that I confused her because I change my mind about things all the time, I learned something.

I learned that her experience of confusion with me was just as valid as my experience of confusion with her.

All points of view are valid in the context of the person experiencing them.

I really do have a point that connects this to Creeping Beautiful and here it is:

Indie Anna Accorsi is the most unreliable narrator since Junco. I have written lots of other unreliable narrators before. James Fenici is unreliable, Sydney Channing is unreliable, even Sasha Cherlin has her own unreliable moments. In fact, when you think about it, we'll all unreliable narrators in the context of the "bigger world". Because we have blinders on called "SELF".

But Indie is an unreliable narrator in the very strict, literal sense of the word. She has memory lapses. So what she thinks happened, and what other people perceive as reality, are disconnected. I say this because going forward this will be important. Her relationship with Nathan wasn't the way she wrote it in this book.

It's a valid interpretation of her point of view of that relationship, but it's not the ONLY valid point of view.

McKay, Adam, and Donovan each have a point of view about Nathan too. And their views are just as valid as Indie's.

And like me, when asked if I had Asperger's and why I change my mind about things so much—there is always a moment when you realize—Hmm. Maybe I should take another look at how I perceive this particular thing? Maybe I am wearing blinders? Maybe there's another interpretation of this person, or event, or problem that can help me see it more clearly?

Keep that in mind as you read the other books in this series.

So back to Creeping Beautiful and coming clean. We have a quartet of impossibly imperfect people in this book. And… just a word of advice here—don't trust anything Indie said in her chapters. I'm sure she THINKS it's all real, and true… but the take-home message about Indie Anna Accorsi is that she's fucking ***damaged***.

McKay is filled with shame and guilt. And let's just get this out of the way right now. There is no life, there is no instance of reality where buying a ten-year-old girl at a slave auction is a good thing. Ever.

But… you know. In the world of the Company, I can certainly see why Adam and Donovan thought it was a good idea. At the very least, it was the best-case scenario in a very fucked-up reality.

But that doesn't make right.

But while McKay is part of this Company world, he's not an Untouchable like Donovan and Adam. He sees the world just a little bit different from them. He LOVES Indie. That might be the only true thing in this entire book. McKay loves that girl and he has loved her for as long as he's known her. Which brings a whole lot of other ethical and moral questions up that I didn't have a chance to explore yet. And if one of these four people has to be "the good guy" then I guess I vote for McKay. Because he feels this shame very deeply.

Donovan starts out at the most "evil" of the three men. His justification for wanting Indie to go home with Adam is simply that. Justification. He needs her for something. Now, I'm sure along the way he changed his mind about his original plan. People do that. I just spent several pages explaining how I do that—so I'm not gonna judge Donovan over his choices as a fifteen-year-old boy. But we see him in a very specific role in this book. Indie's… conscious. Her sanity. Her truth.

What we don't see is what Donovan is doing away from the others. We see interviews where he's the one in charge. He's the one asking questions. He's the one in control. His chapters are deceptively simple until we get towards the end and then—BAM. Donovan is not who we thought.

There's a lot more to Donovan coming. He's not bad, he's not good, he just is. And he's young, so he's still learning.

I don't begrudge anyone their learning.

Adam is the one we're supposed to hate. Adam is set up as the bad guy from chapter one. But I hope you realize he's not the bad guy. We haven't even met the bad guy yet. And if you think it's Carter, well… don't get ahead of yourself.

Adam wants to quit when he buys Indie at that auction. He sees no point in living other than he was gifted with this privileged life and he feels honest-to-God guilt over not making the most of it. So buying Indie and taking her home to McKay under the pretense of building a Company clean-up team is just a way for him to feel like he's participating in life.

But… there's this one chapter where he admits to what he's become after the brain injury and after the Company fell. It's actually not that many words. But they are powerful words.

"And a few years later I was the leader of the most ruthless private army to walk this Earth since the Ten Thousand brought terror and fear to Ancient Greece.

But I'm getting ahead of myself…"

So we get a hint at what's coming at the end.

Adam is in control of this shit show. He has always been in control.

Keep that in mind going forward.

And that leaves us with our last boy, Nathan St. James. If you're not sure what to think about him, that's good. After all, we get four very different opinions about this kid. Indie loves him. But I think we can all agree her character judgment is… not really up to par. But she paints an almost idyllic picture of her childhood and teen years with Nathan. I can't really object to that since her life was so fucked up from the beginning, if she wants to believe it was perfect—who am I to say it wasn't?

But Nate does very strange things with Indie. Most notably was the first time they had sex. If you were thinking… Uh, what the fuck, Nathan? Good. That's what you should've been thinking.

Adam was on to something when he started questioning who he was and where he came from.

"I don't even know where Nate came from. Just… one day he was there.

He wasn't a baby. And there was never a mother over there. Just the grandfather and then the kid. He was about four, maybe, when he showed up. Five at the oldest.

And it occurs to me that I should look into this shit. It occurs to me that I should've looked into this shit a long-ass time ago."

But of course he ends up in the hospital that night and looking in to Nathan slips his mind or… it's possible he didn't even remember his suspicions. It's also possible that he was afraid to get too close to Nathan after Indie almost kills him. So that revelation will have to wait.

Nate's story is far from over. So don't worry. You'll understand soon.

And then, of course, we have Indie.

If you formed an opinion about her I'd like to caution you here. Nothing about Indie is what it seems. You think you know—but her part of this story is slanted, and fragmented, and this is just the tip of the iceberg.

It's not that she's LYING. She just sees the world from her own, internal perspective and with her own "Indie Blinders" on.

Here's something else I want to say about Indie. And this ties in with how the world of Creeping Beautiful fits into the larger world of the Company, Rook and Ronin, and The Misters.

She is no Sasha.

I made this point several times in the book on purpose.

If you want to compare Indie to any of the Company girls I've written before, compare her to Sydney in Meet Me In The Dark.

Sydney is a case in the extreme. Not only was she a Company girl, she was owned by a sadistic son-of-a-bitch. Her life was a living hell.

I wrote Sydney that way on purpose. I think I even spelled this out in the EOBS for MMITD. Because up until that point the only Company Girls we knew were the "lucky" ones. Harper and Sasha are about as different from Sydney and Indie as night is from day.

Gonna go on a little tangent here for a sec. When I first published MMITD I got a LOT of weird comments from some of my early readers. Some of my closest early readers. They didn't get it. They didn't like it. And for a while there—maybe a year—I had second thoughts about writing that book. But then the reviews were so positive, and people fell for this couple with all their dark imperfections, that my own opinion about the book settled in.

But I remember writing in the EOBS that the reason we NEEDED Sydney was because there was no other way to show you, the reader, just how fucked up this Company world was. If you only ever saw Sasha and Harper, you might think, I dunno. It's not so bad.

No. It is. That's why Sydney needed a story.

I needed to put you into the mind of a "real" Company girl and let you experience that life for yourself. There was no other way. There is no other way to BE SOMEONE ELSE. To feel what they feel, to see what they see, to love, and hate, and long for the things they feel, and see, and love, and hate, and long for.

And Indie is like Sydney in that she was left behind.

Not by a man the way Sydney was, but by the Company itself.

She had Adam, and McKay, and Donovan. But they were left behind too.

This is the real reason I wanted to write this new series.

In the Company we saw the heroes.

We saw James, and Harper, and Merc and Sydney, and Rook and Ronin, and Ford and Ashleigh, and Spencer and Veronica, and Jax.

But we never saw the bad guys.

Oh hey. I guess we do have a bad guy in this story.

It's all of them.

In Creeping Beautiful we meet the villains.

And nope. We're not done with Nick Tate just yet.

If you re-read that ending several times just to make sure you got it right – **yes, you got it right**.

And… I'm done here. For now! ;) That's it for me.
If you want to know how all my other Company Books fit into this Creeping Beautiful storyline, keep reading!

Thank you for reading, thank you for reviewing, and I'll see you in the Facebook fan group, Shrike Bikes! (or in the next EOBS!)

Julie

If you want the complete Company story you should read the books in the order below. I made some notes about which characters first show up where, if you're just looking for a specific Company storyline.

Rook and Ronin Series

The entire Company beginnings start in this series. But each series is its own entry point. You can jump in and read them out of order as long as you follow the specific series reading order.

Tragic
Manic
Panic
Ford – Sasha Cherlin (age 12) and Merc first appear here
Spencer – James Fenici first appears here – Five is born

The Company - Rook & Ronin Spin-off – new entry point into the series

The Company – James and Vincent Fenici age 28, Sasha Cherlin age 13, Nick and Harper Tate age 18.

This is the **full story of the "Santa Barbara Incident"** where Adam and Donovan's fathers die.

Meet Me In The Dark – Merc, Sasha Cherlin age 21, Sydney Channing (Company Girl like Indie and Sasha)

Three, Two, One – STANDALONE BOOK – Jax Barlow first appears

Wasted Lust – Sasha Cherlin, age 24, with Jax Barlow.

Nick Tate, age 29, plays a major role and the rest of the Company characters also show back up.

First appearance of Angelica Fenici and "other Adam".

Wasted Lust takes place DURING Creeping Beautiful. Specifically when Indie is 15 years old and the "Company falls" and when Nick meets Adam in Daphne, Alabama.

The Mister Series – Rook & Ronin/Company Spin-off – new entry point into the series

Mr. Perfect
Mr. Romantic – First appearance of the Silver Society – i.e. The Company
Mr. Corporate – First appearance of "Five"
Mr. Mysterious – Spencer's daughters
Mr. Match – All the Rook & Ronin Kids come back to play.

Mr. Five (or just Five) – Ford's son and Spencer's daughter
Mr. & Mrs. – Ford and Spencer show back up with all the kids

The Bossy Brothers Series
Rook & Ronin/Company Spin-off – new entry point into the series

In to Her – STANDALONE BOOK – Logan first appears
Bossy Brothers: Jesse – First appearance of The Way – i.e. The Company
Bossy Brothers: Joey
Bossy Brothers: Johnny – Logan shows back up Indie first appears at age 14, Chek's first appearance
Bossy Bride: Jesse and Emma – Chek and Wendy mentioned
Bossy Brothers: Alonzo – Chek and Wendy mentioned

Creeping Beautiful – Rook & Ronin and Company Spin-off – new entry point into the series

The complete story of Nick Tate, James and Vincent Fenici, "Wendy", "Chek", Indie Anna Accorsi, Adam Boucher, Donovan and Carter Couture, Core McKay, and Nathan St. James.

Creeping Beautiful (book 1)
Pretty Nightmare (book 2)
Gorgeous Misery (book 3)
Lovely Darkness (book 4)

JA Huss never wanted to be a writer and she still dreams of that elusive career as an astronaut. She originally went to school to become an equine veterinarian but soon figured out they keep horrible hours and decided to go to grad school instead. That Ph.D. wasn't all it was cracked up to be (and she really sucked at the whole scientist thing), so she dropped out and got a M.S. in forensic toxicology just to get the whole thing over with as soon as possible.

After graduation she got a job with the state of Colorado as their one and only hog farm inspector and spent her days wandering the Eastern Plains shooting the shit with farmers.

After a few years of that, she got bored. And since she was a homeschool mom and actually does love science, she decided to write science textbooks and make online classes for other homeschool moms.

She wrote more than two hundred of those workbooks and was the number one publisher at the online homeschool store many times, but eventually she covered every science topic she could think of and ran out of shit to say.

So in 2012 she decided to write fiction instead. That year she released her first three books and started a career that would make her a New York Times bestseller and land her on the USA Today Bestseller's List twenty-one times in the next five years.

In May 2018 MGM Television bought the TV and film rights for five of her books in the Rook & Ronin and Company series' and in March 2019 they offered her and her writing partner, Johnathan McClain, a script deal to write a pilot for a TV show.

Her books have sold millions of copies all over the world, the audio version of her semi-autobiographical book, Eighteen, was nominated for a Voice Arts Award and an Audie Award in 2016 and 2017 respectively, her audiobook, Mr. Perfect, was nominated for a Voice Arts Award in 2017, and her audiobook, Taking Turns, was nominated for an Audie Award in 2018. In 2019 her book, Total Exposure, was nominated for a Romance Writers of America RITA Award.

Johnathan McClain is her first (and only) writing partner and even though they are worlds apart in just about every way imaginable, it works.

She lives on a ranch in Central Colorado with her family.